Dream Stone

Bantam Books

New York
Toronto
London
Sydney
Auckland

Dream Stone

Glenna McReynolds

Dedication

To Stan, always—
sharing breath and a turn of the wheel

DREAM STONE

A Bantam Book / November 1998

All rights reserved.
Copyright © 1998 by Glenna McReynolds.
Maps by Jackie Aher.

Library of Congress Cataloging-in-Publication Data

McReynolds, Glenna.
Dream stone / Glenna McReynolds.
p.   cm.
ISBN 0-553-10393-8
1. Wales—History—1063–1284—Fiction.   I. Title.
PS3563.C75D7   1998
813'.54—dc21   98-34135
                                                                CIP

Published simultaneously in the United States and Canada

Bantam Books are published by Bantam Books, a division of Bantam Doubleday
Dell Publishing Group, Inc. Its trademark, consisting of the words "Bantam
Books" and the portrayal of a rooster, is Registered in U.S. Patent and Trade-
mark Office and in other countries. Marca Registrada. Bantam Books, 1540
Broadway, New York, New York 10036.

PRINTED IN THE UNITED STATES OF AMERICA

BVG   10 9 8 7 6 5 4 3 2 1

Acknowledgments

The author's deepest thanks to Elizabeth Barrett,
a most skillful and imaginative editor; and to
Cindy Gerard, touchstone of the muse.

Author's Note

A number of Welsh names and words appear in the book, along with a few words of Irish, the common language being Celtic. Welsh is written more phonetically than English, with each consonant having only one sound. For example, *c* always has the "k" sound, as in *cake; s* is always as in *sit,* never as in *nose; f* always has a "v" sound. In addition to the single consonants, digraphs are used to represent certain Welsh sounds: *dd* is pronounced like the English "th," as in *breathe;* while *th* has the less soft sound of the English *breath; ff* has the "f" sound in the English *film; si* is pronounced like the English "sh" as in *shop;* and *ch* is always pronounced as in the German *Bach,* never as in *church.* The letter *r* is trilled in Welsh. Accents regularly follow on the next to the last syllable.

Since I used many foreign words in this book, as well as unfamiliar names for characters and places, I have included a glossary at the end of the book.

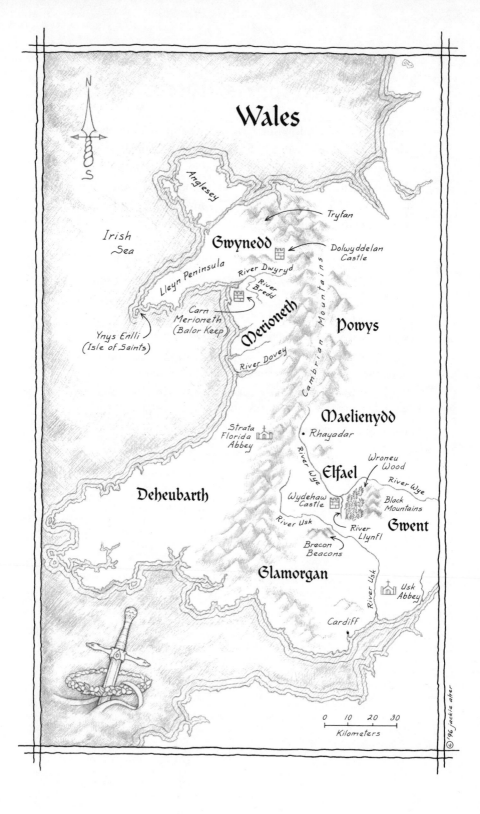

Wales

N
S

Anglesey

Irish
Sea

Gwynedd

Tryfan

Dolwyddelan
Castle

Lleyn Peninsula

River Dwyryd

River
Bredd

Carn
Merioneth
(Balor Keep)

Merioneth

Ynys Enlli
(Isle of Saints)

River Dovey

Powys

Cambrian Mountains

Maelienydd

Strata
Florida
Abbey

• Rhayadar

River Wye

Elfael

Wroneu
Wood

River Wye

Wydehaw
Castle

Black
Mountains

Deheubarth

River Usk

River
Llynfl

Gwent

Brecon
Beacons

Glamorgan

River Usk

Usk
Abbey

Cardiff

0   10   20   30
Kilometers

© '96 jackie aher

The Caverns Beneath Carn Merioneth

© '96 Jackie Aher

Carn Merioneth
(Balor Keep)

Irish Sea

Dragon's Mouth

Light caves

Cavern of the Scrying Pool

Canolbarth, the midland caves

River Bradd

Pryf Nest

Lanbardein

Damson Cliffs

Tunnels to the gates of time

Mor Sarff
(Serpent Sea)

N
S

The Deeper Caverns

Lleyn Peninsula

Irish Sea

THE RIFT

Rastaban

To Tryfan

THE MAGIA WALL

THE MAGIA WALL

Dripshank Well

Pryf Nest

Gates of Time

Lanbardein

Dragon's Mouth

Mor Sorff

Mor Sorff

THE MAGIA WALL

THE MAGIA WALL

Dangoes

Kasr-al Loop

Mindao River Slot

Ghranne Mekom (Grim Crawl)

Kryscaven Crater (entrance unknown)

The Seven Steps

Danison Shaft

Crai Force

The Painted Cavern

········ Trig's Trail

———— Rhuddlan's Trail after following Trig's

– – – Llynya & Mychael into the Dangoes

©'98 Jackie ater.

Cast of Characters

Ynys Enlli

NENNIUS—*a monk*
GRUFFUDD—*former guardsman at Balor Keep*

⧬

Carn Merioneth

MYCHAEL AB ARAWN—*heir to Carn Merioneth;
son of Rhiannon, last of the Magus Druid
Priestesses*
MADRON—*mistress of the arts of enchantment*
OWAIN—*Welshman who fought with the Quicken-
tree in the battle for Balor*
EDMEE—*daughter of Madron and Rhuddlan*

THE QUICKEN-TREE:
> RHUDDLAN—*King of the* tylwyth teg
> NAAS—*a seer*
> MOIRA—*a healer*
> AEDYTH—*a healer*

LIOSALFAR:
> TRIG—*captain*
> LLYNYA—*the aetheling*
> SHAY
> BEDWYR
> WEI
> MATH
> NIA

Pwyll
Roth

ᛞᛠ

Deep Dark

Caradoc, Wyrm-master—*former ruler of Balor Keep*

Varga of the Iron Dunes—*Sha-shakrieg lord from Deseillign*

Slott of the Thousand Skulls—*the Troll King*

Ailfinn Mapp—*Prydion Mage*

Dockalfar:

Caerlon—*a mage*
Lacknose Dock
Blackhand Dock
Frey Dock
Ratskin Dock
Redeye Dock

In a long-ago age on the edge of Deep Time, a star fell to Earth and landed not upon the great waters, but streamed a course across an island in the northern sea. Shards of the glittering orb fell like rain onto the mountains plowed up in the star's wake, and ever after, when their time came, the people of the island prized the stones of light, Dream Stones, and the great metal wrought from the star's core. In this they were not alone. Millennia passed millennia, bringing the Earth into one new age and then another before a darkling shadow came from afar, seeking the lost star.

From whence came the star and the darkness there is no record except for the star itself, which had sunk ever deeper into the rich matrix of the Earth until the surrounding rock turned the star's light inward and its heat burned a path through the Earth's mantle, opening a passage to a netherworld sea and an abyss to the core beyond.

Celestial flames, ignited by the star's fiery descent, kindled life in the dark waters of the sea, and all those brought forth by the star's fire were forever and truly called the Starlight-born. Fair of face with shining brows, they were of the union of heaven and Earth, and the Ages of Wonders were theirs to rule: the Quicken-tree, Daur, and Ebiurrane, the Kings Wood and Red-leaf, Wydden and Yr Is-ddwfn.

The descent of the darkling shadow brought the first ages to an end. The scattered tribes of the Starlight-born reunited on the ancient fortress-isle of their birth, and in the thousand thousand years that followed, they delved deep into the arts of enchantment to find surcease from the chaos manifest in the everlasting night of Dharkkum. Thus in the Dark Age the Prydion Magi came into being, and the Seven Books of Lore, and all manner of things fashioned in the cauldrons of the magi. Of these, two had the power of war. Born of a single brew in a crucible wrought from the star's great metal, a red dragon and a green roared to life and devoured the darkness, leaving naught but tattered remains of smoke and effluence. These the Prydion Magi sealed in the bowels of the Earth with crystal. The dragons they released into the great oceans of the world to churn the tides and keep the Moon coming back to the Sun so that between the two heavenly lights the shadow would ne'er fall again.

But beasts of war are ever hungry, and even as the dragons spawned their first brood on the shores of the nether sea, the magi forged a peerless sword to rule them, its edge tempered with star-wrought metal, its hilt crowned with the stones of light. A bloodspell was then cast over the people of the Earth so that forever after, those who could wield the blade would come forth in time, whenever needed.

Two such were born on the island, then known as England, in the twelfth century of the Fifth Age of Men when the threat of darkness again drew nigh: a woman-child of the Yr Isddwfn, and a man whose blood ran deep with dreams of war—Aethelings of the Starlight, bound by celestial ether.

Prologue

SEPTEMBER 1198
YNYS ENLLI, ISLE OF SAINTS
WALES

Nennius walked softly across the floor of his hermit's cell, so softly that his slippers stirred nary a grain of dust into the air. 'Twas an act of natural grace for one such as he, to step lightly upon the earth, so lightly that there were those among the other Culdee monks on the island who thought him a favored saint. A few, though, would as soon ascribe to him a more sinister designation, and in truth, 'twas to the latter group he conceded whatever wisdom was to be found on Ynys Enlli.

A single shaft of light fell through a crack in the cell door, rending the gloom and shining down upon a roughly made table and the contents thereof: books. Made of parchment and bound in oak and leather, many were copied by his own hand; some saved from their *in quaternis* states on dusty monastery shelves where they'd been left unbound and forgotten; others more outrightly stolen and secreted beneath his robes across three seas to bring them to this far edge of the world where their words had led him—back to where he'd first awakened on the shores of a cold sea, sixteen years earlier, awakened lost and consumed by madness. His years of wandering had taken him to far and distant lands, before sanity and purpose had returned. With purpose had come the search for the books. A few of the weighty tomes had been literally unearthed and pried free from the corpses of monks who had sworn to take their knowledge with them to their graves. One had been a gift, a small Psalter, given to him two years past by a hairless, disaffected brother named Helebore.

He continued past the table to the paillasse on the floor. He had missed Brother Helebore after he and the rest of the Culdees had tossed the heretical fool off the rocks into the sea. Nennius's guilt, and he'd harbored no great amount, had been assuaged, though, for the bald brother had floated, not sunk as they'd thought, and washed himself up for another year of life on the ill-fated shores of Merioneth—or so sayeth the man who lay on the paillasse.

Nennius knelt next to the straw pallet. Weary, half-crazed eyes rolled up at him from out of a weathered face nearly obscured by a shaggy beard and long, scraggly hair. Brothers William and Theo had brought the wayfarer to Nennius's cell on the southeastern shore of the island, breaking Nennius's self-imposed solitude and his peace. He did not fault them for the breach. Where else to bring a raving lunatic but to one well versed in the vagaries of unstable minds, especially when the lunatic had one's own name on his lips? *Nennius, Nennius,* the man had cried while pounding on the church door during nones.

In a rambling stream of jumbled words the man had named himself Gruffudd, a garrison guard of Balor in the Cymraeg kingdom of Merioneth on the coast of Wales, the lone survivor of a battle waged against demons in hell whilst spring blossomed on the land above. He'd spoken of a keep ruled by a boar and flashes of blue light that cut as cleanly as knives, of women who fought like banshees by their men's sides, and of a ghostly white, hairless devil priest with no eyebrows and a mouth full of rotten teeth, the Boar's leech, who had died a devil's death in the bowels of the earth, ground asunder by a creature too horrifying to recall—and Nennius had doubted not a word. Indeed, he'd felt a growing sense of excitement as the story had unwound.

"Rest, my son," he said, soothing the man's brow with a warm, damp cloth. "You are safe here."

"Safe?" A large, palsied hand scrabbled for a hold on his robes. "Helebore cursed ye. Ye must know it. Cursed and conjured and called upon Satan hisself to bind ye with the flames of everlasting damnation. He said ye tried to murder him for what he knew. 'Tis why I came, Father."

"To see if his incantations had proven fruitful?" Nennius asked, more curious than taken aback.

"No, Father. No, never," Gruffudd swore, tightening his hold. "I prayed for ye, prayed for yer salvation from his wickedness. Prayed . . . prayed for ye to save me. Helebore and his twisted faith brought naught but evil to Balor, for 'tis lost now, and not one man left alive to tell the tale except me."

"Are you so sure? If you survived, mayhaps another also found the way out of hell." He wiped the damp cloth over each of the guards-man's cheeks.

"Nay," Gruffudd said, his voice harsh. "All that fell were dragged into the sea by the demons with the lightblades. If there'd been a breath left in any of 'em, they'd a drowned afore they'd found it."

Just as well, Nennius thought.

"In the Irish Sea?" he asked, dabbing at the beads of sweat form-ing on the man's brow.

"Nay, not the wild, open ocean, but a dark one far below the land once called Balor. A doomed well it is, Father, the beach washed with blackwater waves and glowin' purplish like with the fire that burns inside the cliffs. I fear 'tis the lair of . . . of . . ." The man's voice trailed off.

"Of?" Nennius encouraged. When no answer was forthcoming, he pressed harder. "Is this the place where you saw the—" His question was cut short by Gruffudd grabbing his scapular at the neck and drag-ging his head down.

"Don't say it, Father," the guardsman warned, his breath coming short with budding panic. "Helebore called to the beast and it kill't him. I can still hear his screams." The man grew quiet, his eyes narrowing and shifting toward the door. "Aye, I can still hear him screamin' and see the beast draggin' him. It's hauntin' me, Father, stalkin' me nights. Ye must make it go away." His gaze returned to Nennius's, and his voice became tinged with desperation. "If anyone can make it go away, it's ye. Ye alone are left who knew the blackness of the leech's soul. Just ye and—and me."

"Aye," Nennius calmly agreed. "We are together, you and I. Alas, poor Brother Helebore had a black heart in search of black deeds."

"Very black deeds," Gruffudd said, then lowered his voice to a confessional whisper. "Mayhaps even blacker than ye know, Father. At the Boar's bidding, he brought a witch to Balor, a fair, lovely lass, name of Ceridwen, and she was't the ruin of us all. I thought 'twas greed, but 'twas blasphemy, pure blasphemy a'needing the witch's blood that took us into the caves time and again, may God forgive me."

"You were with Helebore when he searched the caves?" Nennius asked, giving little credence to the man's talk of a witch. Men had always found themselves in need of women, especially fair and lovely ones; and a witch, he knew, could be either this or that and seldom what was thought, depending on the whim and motive of the man in need. Many a kingdom had fallen on account of a fair face, sometimes justly so, as he well knew. And sometimes unjustly, as he knew even better.

A faint memory stirred at the edge of his consciousness, a fleeting scene of a woman striding away from him across a bleak landscape, cloak billowing, sand blowing, a flash of golden skin and even more golden hair showing between the white folds of the loosely bound turban flowing onto her shoulders. *Away from him.*

He swore silently, gritting his teeth, and turned his mind to the present. Women were a danger, especially fair and lovely ones. As for blood, 'twas a basic elixir, good for all manner of things and worthless for as many others.

Gruffudd nodded, his hold loosening on the scapular. His hand fell back to the paillasse. "I was strong once, the strongest of the Boar of Balor's men, and 'twas I who helped the leech get through the rock slides barrin' the way into the caves, but I swear I didn't know what he was lookin' for. 'Twas gold most likely, I said to myself, or silver, or gemstone, but up until the demon warriors with the blue blades came and took us so deep, we found naught but a bubblin' pool o' water in the middle of a great cavern. Helebore liked the pool well enough, but I thought to myself that he'd have to do better than that to keep his promise of riches to the Boar."

"So the master of Balor thought to get rich on Helebore's secrets," Nennius murmured, hiding a smile. Once he too had lusted after the wealth inherent in precious metals and gems.

Beads of sweat had begun to show on Gruffudd's cheeks, and Nennius carefully wiped them away.

"Rich beyond his dreams, all our dreams, that was what the leech promised, and all he gave us was death and horrors." A trembling took him, and Gruffudd turned his face aside, into the rough wool blanket covering the straw. "Ye've never seen such things, Father, such creatures as I have seen in the dark. Huge, rolling beasts wet with their own slime. S-s-s-serpents," he stuttered. "S-serpents of monstrous size, sliding and prowling through the deepest, darkest places in the earth. If they be not creatures of the Devil hisself, I know not what they'd be."

Nennius knew. His hand tightened on the damp cloth, squeezing so hard that droplets of moisture ran into the corner of the guardsman's mouth.

Pryf. The lunatic had proven to have worth beyond measure. The rolling beasts, the serpents the man spoke of, could only be *pryf,* dragon larvae.

In unconscious reflex, Gruffudd's tongue licked the wetness away. Nennius watched the small bit of liquid disappear, then glanced toward the other door in the cell, the one leading into the hill and down to the labyrinth below the island's surface. His years of searching that dark and dank maze had yielded very little other than proof that the giant worms—Gruffudd's serpents, Nennius's *pryf*—had once existed in this place, very near to this time. There was a shaft marked with the word *pryf,* but a word carved into rock was impossible to date with the tools he had at hand. He had gleaned better proof from striations in the rock where the creatures had bored their passages and left bits of dried slime on the walls, a sweet, earthy greenish black resin when solid, but easily returned to its natural state by soaking in seawater, unless 'twas too ancient. The slime he'd found had reconstituted into a lovely mess, much to his encouragement. Most telling had been the piles of fibrous material he'd found tangled and matted in a cavern nearly impossible to reach, an apse at the end of a narrow and low-ceilinged tunnel. He'd pulled the threads of one knotted bundle apart and felt their tensile strength, and he'd known what he held in his hands—the larval silk of *pryf,* spun within the last millennium by the color of it, silver but yet with a sheen of green.

For all he'd found, though, the nest beneath Ynys Enlli was an abandoned one, useless for anyone's attempt to claim immortality. Still it seemed Nennius had not been denied. Not yet. The wheels of time and life had turned and delivered upon his doorstep a bit of flotsam from the sea of humanity, dear Gruffudd, who had not only seen the mighty worms, but the scrying pool of the mists and the damson cliffs with their amethystine hues reflecting off the waves of Mor Sarff, the Serpent Sea.

'Twas there, beneath Merioneth, not Ynys Enlli, that all the pieces to man's most beguiling puzzle could be found. If the worms had made a hole, salvation was within his grasp.

Nennius shifted his gaze to the stacks of books on the table. The volumes were steeped to an unintelligible brew with arcana; 'twas both the beauty and the beastliness of them. Only long hours and diligence had led him through their strangely ciphered musings, maps, and mystic aphorisms. Only quicksilver brilliance had enabled him to piece their secrets together into the whole of man's most eternal yearning, the search for life everlasting, God's promise to the faithful.

The boundaries of time, the books had finally revealed, could be transcended through a passage that had been worked into a feverish pitch of energy by the worms. Ipso facto, the wormholes were tunnels through time. Being able to control the placement of one's self in time was the first step on the endless journey of immortality, for those so inclined. Nennius's desire was far less profane, or profound, though 'til now it had seemed no less unattainable. There were other steps to be taken in turn, and multitudes of missteps to destroy the heedless.

Helebore had never understood the last. The monk had been far too eager to make the transition. No doubt 'twas how he'd gotten himself killed—and Gruffudd had seen it all, had seen living *pryf*. Helebore had sworn the same, beneath Ynys Enlli no less, but that one had always lusted after glory with lies, claiming also to have seen the Archangel Michael and to have had a personal visitation from St. Jerome. Gruffudd, on the other hand, while possibly delusional, was far too terrified to lie.

"There is no reason for fear, my son," he said, returning his attention to the guardsman. "All creatures were put upon the earth by our Lord, and they are in His power. Did He not make Leviathan and yet tell the day of the serpent's destruction in the Book of the Prophet Isaiah?" At Gruffudd's hesitant nod, he quoted, " *'In that day the Lord with his sore and great and strong sword shall punish Leviathan the piercing serpent, that twisting sea serpent, and he shall slay the monster that is in the deep.'* Verily, your serpents do not lie outside the reach of the Lord's judgment, and you have naught to fear from Helebore's sins, for they are his alone."

"Aye, Father, I believe ye. But—but I am not so pure as to be without my own sins." Doubt lent a quaver to Gruffudd's words.

"No man is," Nennius reassured him. "But how else did you survive when so many perished, if not for the hand of God reaching out to help you in your hour of need?"

Gruffudd gave him a blank look. "I hid," he said. "Hared up the beach and slipped into one o' the headland caves, 'cept it weren't no cave a'tall, but more of a tunnel, smooth and shimmerin' with a thick layer of abalone mother o'pearl, all purplish and green."

"A tunnel?" Nennius's interest sharpened. "To where?"

"To wherever the light was comin' from, big, bright flashes of it and thunder too. 'Twas at the far end of it that I saw Helebore meet his death, his screams echoing up and down and rollin' over me, 'til I can't hardly hear anything else even now. Ye must help me, Father. Ye must."

A flush of rare exultation quickened in Nennius's veins. *Mellt a tharanau*—thunder and lightning. There was no more auspicious portent of a live wormhole, of a time weir.

"You will have sanctuary here for as long as you live. I swear this before God," he vowed, wiping Gruffudd's brow again. "But I must know more about this place that you fear. With knowledge I can protect you from it and the beasts that reside there."

And so Gruffudd told of paths and twists and turns, of the leech's chambers below the great hall of Balor, of caves that opened onto the cliff face above the Irish Sea, and of those deeper caverns where no man was safe. All the while he spoke, Nennius ministered to him with the damp cloth and soothing words.

" 'Twas a fortnight, mayhaps more, that I was't lost afore I stumbled out onto a hill that had the sun above it. 'Tweren't too far from Balor, and I thoughts to make my way back, but— Do ye have some wine, Father?" Gruffudd asked in an abrupt aside. "Me throat's awful dry, and I feel like a fever's takin' hold of me."

Indeed, the man was warm . . . *and bound to grow warmer,* Nennius thought, getting to his feet. As he passed the table, he reached out and trailed his fingers over one of the books, his prize, stolen from this very monastery. 'Twas bound in age-darkened blue leather affixed to oak boards. The leather was covered with runes worked in gold leaf, naming it as the *Prydion Cal Le.* Its final pages were a veritable farrago of heresy and alchemy penned by a man who called himself simply a bard from

Brittany, but whose reputation Nennius had run across in different parts of the world. Nemeton was his name, and his pages in the latter section of the Blue Book of the Magi (Nemeton's translation of the title) told of Druids and wild folk, and of stars far beyond this time. All fascinating enough, especially the astral references, but the true wealth of the tome lay in its earlier sections where Nemeton had translated the much older runic script into Latin, and in places, also into Welsh. 'Twas in those older leaves that Nennius had come closest to discovering the origins and the dwelling place of the *pryf*. One passage in particular had held him at Ynys Enlli for two long years, speaking as it did of an abyss that lay at the heart of a rocky isle in a northern sea—for such was the island on which he'd found the book. The passage had gone on to tell of "strange and wondrous occurrences of a terrifying nature" taking place in the abyss, thus giving the only firsthand description he'd found of a worm-hole.

And Gruffudd, dear, doomed Gruffudd, had just given him the same description with the addition of shimmering tunnels.

Nennius opened the book and watched the pages fall into their familiar, worn place. His fingers trailed down the lines of script, caressing the words written by a long-dead mage in a long-forgotten time:

Seven years past, the dragon spawn breached the mere and descended into its depths. Our fears that the swirling activities of the larvae—for such has been their wont in the mere—would disturb the crystal seals set in the earth against the scourge of the Dark Age have proven true. Yet this is not the terror, both wondrous and fell, that has brought me to these pages. Four times a Prydion Mage has descended into the abyss with the power of the ages at hand to bring the larvae out of the mere and thus secure our safety. Four times the mage has failed in the clash of battle and been lost, never to be seen again.

Today one of the lost magi returned, Navarr Kett. More dead than alive, he crawled forth from the rocky edge of the abyss amidst a cataclysm of thunder and lightning. He lies now in the Dragon's Mouth and tells a tale of a path trod through the stars to the far reaches of the cosmos, verily to the home of darkness itself. Thus Navarr Kett is the first of the Prydion Magi to transcend time and heaven and mayhaps the one to bring us to our final doom, for however we may rejoice at the miraculous deed, we must also know that the way has been opened and a path marked.

More than marked, Nennius knew. The path had been cut into

the cosmos, a sucking, whip-tailed groove snaking through the endless darkness, waiting to snare any unwary traveler.

A grimace crossed his face, and he turned away from the book with a soft curse. Kneeling by the table, he dipped a cup of water out of a bucket and returned to Gruffudd's side. He knew nothing of dragons or Dark Age scourges and could have cared less, sounding as they did of metaphorical social hysteria for the inevitable calamities of life. But he did know of time and paths through the stars, the damned unstable things. And he'd learned of worms.

Gruffudd greedily gulped the water down, spilling it into his beard and onto the paillasse.

"How did you survive underground for a fortnight, my son, without food or drink?" Nennius asked, forcing his voice to a monotonous calm and his attention back to the man.

"Oh, there was drink, Father—water." The guardsman wiped his sleeve across his mouth. "Water everywhere. Tricklin' out o' the rocks in some places and gushin' out in others, the sweetest water a man could ever hope to find. 'Tweren't drink that I was lacking, but food. There was't not much beyond a few mean bites of things skitterin' through the dark. Some of them put up a bit o' a fight, but once't ole Gruffudd got 'is chompers in 'em, they was done for."

Nennius refrained from asking what kinds of things Gruffudd had eaten. It sufficed that there was fresh water in the caves.

"Is there more that I should know?" he asked.

The guardsman shook his head. "I've told ye everything I remember and some I thought I'd forgotten. Now I'd have another cup o' water, if you please, or ale if ye hast any?"

"Ale it shall be." Nennius gave him a benevolent smile and wiped the corners of the man's mouth, his fingers closing around the cloth and squeezing, squeezing, until another drop of moisture fell on Gruffudd's lips. The guardsman licked, and Nennius slowly rose to his feet. "Rest, my son. It will not take me long to fetch your ale from the kitchen."

"Bless ye, Father." Gruffudd reached out and let his fingers graze the hem of Nennius's robe. "Yer a saint, just as I thought ye must be for Helebore to hate ye so. Sometimes he called ye names, not just the blasphemous ones, but strange names like *Corvus*. Told me 'twas Latin for raven, which I thought demned odd for a priest, but now's I's seen ye, I know where's he got it. It's yer hair, isn't it, all black like that, exceptin' for the one stripe o' white, and sproutin' like a couple o' wings off the side of yer tonsure. Aye, it's raven black a'right." The guardsman gave a distracted chuckle. "Blacker'n a new moon night or a whore's—" His mouth snapped shut, and he cast a wary gaze upward.

Nennius only smiled and made a blessing sign over the man before leaving the cell. Latin, indeed. Outside, he lifted his face to the sun. The scent of heather was on the wind, and the sound of ocean waves breaking on the island's eastern shore. He stood for a moment, silent and waiting. When the first cry came, a gasped breath of agony, he began making his way toward a small hollow of land no more than a stone's throw from the cell door. Gruffudd's cries would get louder, much louder, before they ceased for all eternity, and Nennius would as soon not have his ears overly taxed by the guardsman's death throes. There had been no help for the man's demise. Nennius could not afford to have a lunatic running around speaking of serpents and demons and Helebore, and to have his name linked to all of it. The Culdees had been strangely skittish of late—with good reason it seemed, what with worms moving in the deep—and throwing suspected heretics off cliffs was the quickest way to ease a bit of ecclesiastical skittishness.

The afternoon was growing late, a crispness in the air heralding the cool night to come. The summer just passing had been peculiarly long and warm with a fair balance between sunshine and rain, a fecund combination, as if the earth had drawn the sun's rays to it more fully than in other summers, as if the land had called only the perfect measure of moisture from out of the clouds. Now he understood why. The books had told him *pryf* were a blessing to Earth's gardens.

He smiled. Worms.

The harvest had been bountiful on Ynys Enlli and no doubt throughout Wales. 'Twould be a good year to travel, even in battle-ravaged lands. When men's bellies were full, they were far less suspicious and far more generous, whether the request was for food, or shelter, or information.

Purple heather and saffron gorse brushed against his robes as he walked the narrow path that led to a well-worn bench tucked into the hollow. A kelp-strewn beach stretched out below the windswept bower, welcoming the incoming tide, while across the sea the Lleyn Peninsula rose above the horizon. Nennius sat on the bench and let his gaze follow the dark rise of land to the south until it disappeared. A thousand emotions flooded through him, making him feel more alive than he had in years, as if he were pulling free from a long and arduous half sleep where the line between memories and dreams had grown dangerously thin, where the nightmares were of forgetfulness, not death.

He'd been so close all this time. His books had not led him astray as he'd oft feared, but had held true. A land called Merioneth was there, just beyond where he could see, nearly due east according to Gruffudd, and beneath the castle keep once called Balor lay the long-sought end of his exile, the wormhole, the tunnel through time—his chance to go home.

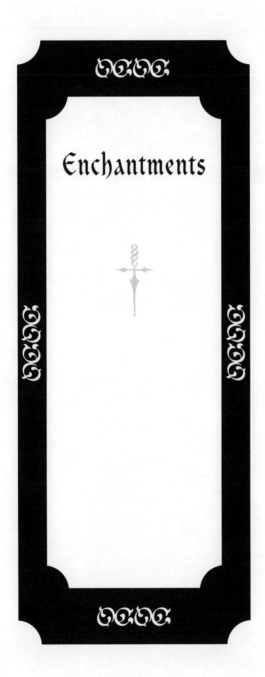

Enchantments

One treasure only the fair maid took from the dragon's trove—
the double-edged favor of the beast's untempered love.

Chapter 1

Wolves howled in the darkness. From his vantage point on Carn Merioneth's east wall, Rhuddlan of the Quicken-tree watched the fleet forms weave their paths through the moonlit forest. Swift and deadly, the shadows were hunting, coming down out of the mountains of Eryri to claim the land from the river to the sea. Wolves alone were naught to fear—but the wolves were not alone. Here and there, Rhuddlan caught sight of a more upright shape running with the animals. The man beside him nocked an arrow into his longbow.

"Hold, Trig," Rhuddlan commanded softly. He was tall and slender and wore no badge other than his bearing to proclaim his rank as king. Gray marked the pale blond of his hair and was woven into the five-strand plait on the left side of his head. A long green cloak was thrown over his shoulders.

"Ye know what they are." His captain's voice held an edge of impatience. Trig was as tall as his sovereign, but broader in girth, with a squarish face bearing the scars of a long-ago war. He, too, wore a *fif* braid streaked through with gray.

"Aye." They both knew. Men were running with the wolves. The question was, Why?

When Rhuddlan said nothing else, Trig snorted and lowered his bow. "It'll be our heads on pikes, or worse."

" 'Tis too soon to be worrying about pikes. Find your bed, if you wish. I'll wait with Naas."

Trig grumbled again. "She's been at it all night and seen naught. More 'an like, she's gone full blind on ye."

Rhuddlan let him leave with his complaint unanswered. Dawn was not far off, and if Naas was to see for him, it had best be soon, or they would have to wait the month out in hopes of another clear night with a full moon.

Behind him on the wall-walk, the old woman tended a fire of hot burning coals. She was small, a bundle of greenish gray cloak and dark gown huddled next to the flames. The brazier holding the fire had been forged of a rich alloy, giving the bronze a fey, purplish cast. The shallow rim of the pan was circled 'round with dragons in relief, all of them spouting ruby flames into billows of smoky quartz. Magic was to be done in the night. Rhuddlan but waited for the old one to pull it down out of the sky and into her cauldron.

The last wolf disappeared into the northern woods, and Rhuddlan turned toward the upper bailey of the castle. Light from the full moon slanted long, dark shadows across the grass and the scarred remains of what had once been Balor Keep. Since taking the demesne in May, he'd had his people destroying the structures built by the previous ruler, Caradoc, the Boar of Balor, and by the Boar's father, Gwrnach, except for the stone wall. That great defense he would leave for time and the old white-eyed woman by the fire to dismantle. He had need of it for now.

"Naas." He spoke her name, and the woman lifted her strange gaze. Pale irises discernible only as rims of milky luminosity were barely visible across the rising smoke. The bones beneath her age-lined skin were delicate and finely fashioned, giving her a fragile appearance. Pure deception, that was, for few had Naas's strength—and none had her singular skill with fire.

She whispered something unintelligible, then turned and added another stick to the flames. Sparks rose with the wind and cascaded by him, a thousand brilliant stars slipping through the merlons and falling to their death on the sward.

Trig was wrong. Naas was not blind, only too replete with the past to see beyond the memories of her race. Those memories ran through her veins and filled her eyes with visions of life from a long-ago world, a world she brought forth through burning heat and the light of the moon. Rhuddlan needed such knowledge if he was to keep the wolves from the wall. He needed to know what darkness threatened Merioneth, for the heralds of darkness were there, creeping into his woods and lapping at the shores of the River Bredd with black rot.

Yet 'twas not the rot in his woods or the strangely mixed wolfpack they'd seen that night that stole his sleep and put Trig on edge. Dangerous though they were, the men were yet true Men; they had not been turned. Of the danger he did fear, there had been no sightings. He'd sent scouts as far north as Finn's Road and as far south as the white horse, and none had seen sign of skraelings, the fierce and dirty beast men that were all that remained of the fell legions conjured by the Dockalfar, an ancient enemy that had once ruled the caverns below. Nor had there been any reports of disturbances in the troll fields of Inishwrath.

Nay, 'twas not wildmen and wolves he feared, but things unseen yet still felt. In the sky the tension had played itself out in thunder and lightning, *mellt a tharanau,* a summer of storms. Nearer to earth, the air held a certain heaviness, the ground a certain softness, as if the Earth herself was giving way to some greater force. Verily, one part of the Earth had given way. In spring, after the battle to reclaim Merioneth, Mychael ab Arawn had reported the breaking of a damson shaft in the caverns. The damson shafts were pure veins of crystal set into the matrix of the Earth by the mages of old. That one would crack was a grim portent, but how grim, Rhuddlan could not judge. The crystal shafts harkened back to a time long, long before his, but not beyond the reach of Naas's vision. To this end, he'd set the old woman to her fire. Five months past, he'd looked to another for answers. He had sent runners to the four directions in search of Ailfinn Mapp, last of the Prydion Magi. The wandering mage was e'er difficult to find, but that he'd had no word in nearly half a year of looking, and that not even the old men of Anglesey had seen her since the winter solstice, was another cause for worry.

Naas added another stick to the fire, and Rhuddlan looked to the sky. Dawn still lay beyond the mountains, but not for much longer. The morning stars were rising.

"Nothing lost, nothing gained. All is change. All is change," Naas muttered, drawing his attention. She reached out with a rowan branch to stir the cauldron nestled in the coals.

Rhuddlan followed the meandering path she drew in the boiling water. Steaming ribbons of vapor curled around her gnarly wand and drifted upward into the stars, streaming through smoke and sparking flames. Of asudden the old woman cackled, a dry laugh bespeaking grim satisfaction rather than delight, and a chill went through him.

"There ye are, my pretty one. There ye are," she crooned, gently stirring, stirring, stirring.

Rhuddlan saw no change in the water, only in Naas, and moved to her side. Sweat had broken out on her age-spotted brow; her eyes were wide and staring, reflecting the dance of flames in the brazier. She'd started her fire at dusk, building it piece by flaming piece to reveal her the path he'd asked her to tread, and finally, at dawn's edge, it seemed she'd taken a step.

"What do you see?"

"A woman," she said, her voice thinning to a raspy whisper. "She's weeping, she is, with blood running out of her mouth."

Blood.

Rhuddlan cursed to himself. He'd seen enough blood in his life.

So had Naas, rivers of it from out of the past, but she'd not seen blood like this. 'Twas shimmering, with a pale iridescence about it, yet she knew 'twas blood that stained the woman's yellow gown and dripped from the chunk of red, scaly flesh in her one hand. In her other hand, the woman held a knife, a steel-edged dagger from a lost age.

Rhuddlan asked her another question, but she waved him off, paying him no mind. Bothersome man. He'd asked for a vision, and by the grace of the gods she'd conjured one in her cauldron. Touch and go, it had been, touch and go the whole night long, but she'd done it, and now he could wait until it was finished.

"Aye, a vision they ask, but does they ask the price?" she grumbled under her breath, all the while stirring the small, twisted branch through the bubbling brew of water and whatnot. Days were the price, a day off her life for every minute she would look, and she knew well the passing of a minute. She counted them in heartbeats and breaths—such was the cost of looking into the past.

She knew the woman as well, not by sight, but by her presence. Naas had seen High Priestesses before in her cauldron. In truth, within the borders of Merioneth, it was a rare stew that did not have a High Priestess floating in it. This was their place, and though there were none left in the carn, they had not let it go.

"Tears and blood. Tears and blood," she murmured in a singsong cadence. 'Twas the way of the cauldron to show moments when the world had hung in the balance and lives had hung by a thread. Rarely, Naas was given a mundane glimpse into the past, but there was nothing mundane about a bloody, sobbing priestess. "What's happening here, then, hmm?"

Steam swirled across the water, and Naas stirred, each curved arc and loop of her stick marking the pool with another word of ancient script, clearing a path for the moonlight. Years peeled away within the reflection of the celestial orb, the centuries slipping through her cauldron more quickly than lightning strikes.

Ah, we've reached a little deep we have, she thought, feeling heat press into her skin from the wand and flow up into her arm. Sweat ran off her face and down between her breasts. The past was a thing of heat, always heat, and more often than not brought a little gut-churning nausea with it. Though her gaze remained steady on the water, the rest of her trembled like a wind-beaten leaf. She inhaled a fire-warmed breath, fighting the sickness, and in time the priestess lifted her arms up through the years and revealed her name. *Arianrod. Arianrod Agah.*

Aye, deep. A thousand thousand years into the past. Beyond the beginnings of the current age to the death of the last. Deep enough to burn.

Fingers singed, Naas continued stirring her chant—loop, curve, stroke; loop, curve, stroke—and felt herself sink ever deeper into the glimmering, beckoning pool of the cauldron. Welcoming water. She kept her breathing soft and deep, until Arianrod's cry welled in her throat and broke through the final barrier, near choking her with a rush of pain:

I have drunk the dragon's blood, reduced to desperation and despair. The darkling shadow has been sealed again, but at such a cost! Stept Agah is dead, his life given that we may live.

I have drunk the dragon's blood, letting it fill my mouth and descend into my body. The darkness feeds on the fire in the earth, conjuring itself in myriad deathly ways that the Prydion Magi had not foreseen. Uffern trolls arose with the smoke, and ravening wolves, and fear shadows in many forms. All were smote down by the Magia Blade wielded with the force of Stept Agah's hand, the last of the true Starlight-born.

I have drunk the dragon's blood and eaten of his flesh, and Ddrei Goch yet writhes on the shores of Mor Sarff with the pain of my taking. Half-aethelings only are left and they will not have the power to prevail over the Dark when next it comes, nor the power to wield the blade. They will need another whose beginnings even now I feel running into my veins— Savage brew searing a course beneath my skin! *My blood shall be as one with the Red Dragon's, steeped to a potent mix in my womb and sent forward through my children and my children's children until in time the fierce creature of my conjuring will be brought forth to battle in the coming age. Pray then that a half-aetheling still resides on Earth to stand by his side. Pray now that I have not damned myself for all eternity by delving into the forbidden arts of the Prydion bloodspell.* Shadana . . . shadana . . .

"Shadana . . ." Naas gasped and clutched her hand to her breast, letting the rowan wand fall. The priestess faded into the pool, her golden hair becoming a river of silver water, her eyes losing their despair and becoming the deep blue calm of the ocean, a water woman.

Naas pulled a hard breath into her lungs. *So, pretty one, you thought to drink dragon's blood and send a rare creature down to me—and for this ye died before yer time.*

The story was an old one and Naas knew it well, but she'd never seen it before this night, never seen *gwaed draig,* dragon's blood. Iridescent it was, rainbow-hued, seven colors played together in one potent elixir.

A weak smile curved her mouth. 'Twas good to know there were still surprises to be had at her age. Rainbow blood. She should have guessed as much, for the beasts had been born in a star-wrought cauldron—so the oldest stories told. She doubted them not; Naas's life was filled with old stories. They ran through her days in endless abundance, enriching some, destroying others. Arianrod's story had cost her dear. The fire was gone from beneath the brazier, the cauldron cooling in the bed of dead coals.

Aethelings, half-aethelings. She snorted. The Priestesses of Merioneth had always made much of blood and its purity, to their eventual demise. Yet 'twas the same preoccupation with blood that had led Arianrod to drink her bit from Ddrei Goch's flesh. The old beast could not have liked that.

The last remnant of the vision took flight, and thus released, Naas slumped against the parapet. A pair of strong hands caught her. An extra cloak was wrapped around her shoulders. She needed rest, only a moment's rest, then must add one more deed to the day's toll.

"Naas?"

'Twas Rhuddlan. She recognized his voice. He must be told, all of it. She just needed to catch her breath. Then she had to find the boy, that wild boy who prowled through Carn Merioneth both above and below, ramparts and caverns alike, Mychael ab Arawn. She had to find him and give him a knife.

'Twas time to call the dragons home.

A fair autumn's dawning rose along the eastern borders of Merioneth, reaching gilded tendrils across the mountains and trailing them down the hills to the cliffs standing guard over the Irish Sea. To the west the light played on the waves, limning the peaks and washing through the swells of an ebb tide, chasing the shadows of night beyond the far horizon. Yet not all the dark things that had fallen 'tween sunset and sunrise were so easily routed.

By the light of a small torch, Mychael ab Arawn made his way beneath Carn Merioneth, down narrow flights of stairs and through the black tunnels leading to the Dragon's Mouth, a cliffside cave overlooking the ocean. Time was running out. He felt it with each slip of the sun to the south, with each frosted morn. The land was changing, beginning its turn toward winter, and still he had naught to show for his months of searching.

A sudden pain doubled him over, taking him unawares, but not by surprise. Quick and clean, the flash of heat tore down the length of his left side, following the path of his scars—his ever-present reward for daring to breach the wormholes. He wrapped his arm around his middle and halted for the space of a breath, then 'twas gone. He gritted his teeth, keeping on. Such was the price of his failure, a price growing ever higher.

He made a last turn toward the west, following a well-worn track up and out to the Mouth. Light from his torch flickered along the tunnel walls that grew ever farther apart. The air was cool and damp about him, a welcome relief from the heat he'd suffered in the night. The smell of salt was strong.

He stopped where the tunnel opened onto a rock-girt shelf above the waves and held the torch high. Dragons came to light beneath the yellow flame, dragons twisting and turning in an ageless push to the sea, two mighty creatures etched into the stone. The only dragons he had yet found, and these had never been hidden from the sight of man, but indeed had been carved there as a reminder to all who would come to Carn Merioneth.

Long ago, his mother had woven her music into the ocean mists from this place, calling to the sea dragons in the deep beyond with the magic of her melodies. Long ago, he and his twin, his *gefell,* had played in the Mouth and traced the stone beasts with their small fingers—but he was a child no more, and the two women he'd loved had been lost to him. His mother, Rhiannon, was long since dead. His sister, Ceridwen, had been called to Merioneth in the spring, at the time of the Battle of Balor, to take their mother's place at the gates of time. She had done so, but only to do one deed as Rhuddlan asked. Then she had left, five months ago now, on a journey to the far north, leaving naught but a green charm and a red book for him to remember her by.

'Twas not enough.

Rhuddlan had needed Ceridwen to break the seal he'd put on the weir gate fifteen years earlier, when Carn Merioneth had first fallen to Gwrnach and his cursed son, Caradoc, the Boar of Balor. The deed had been perilous, but Ceri had broken the emerald door that had imprisoned the *pryf* in the wormhole.

Reaching out, Mychael smoothed his hand over the graven wall of the Dragon's Mouth, his fingers following the first flush of daybreak across the curves of the beasts. Rhiannon's fair songs had long since wafted away on the wind, but the remnants of another's enchantment remained in the rock to entice and confuse. Mychael had foresworn the delving of its secrets not a month past, having grown weary of laboring in vain and having realized that each breach of the wall lessened the strength of what remained. Yet here he stood again, disavowed by weakness and need, hoping against hope that this time he would find some solace in the Dragon's Mouth.

"*Quo 'Ammon' ah ethruill,*" he whispered, speaking the words of an ancient tongue that wound over and over again in near indecipherably small print through the dragon's scales—*Here lies the mark called "Ammon."*

He passed his hand over fanned wings and scalloped fins, nearing the long whiskers sprouting from the larger beast's snout. At the place where scaly lips drew back in a snarl, the stone dragon warmed to his touch as it had many times before, a spontaneous blossoming of heat coming from deep in the rock and all the stronger for having been let lie. He slowed his movement, spreading his fingers wide across the incised grooves of the dragon's teeth. For a moment he felt the promise of something more flickering on the edge of his fingertips, and his hope rose. Mayhaps at last he would see his way clear before him. In the next moment, failure crashed a resounding knell. All the warmth sank back into the stone, leaving it naught but rock, cold and lifeless to the touch.

He pulled away with a curse, girding himself against despair. 'Twas the swiving magic of the Brittany bard, Nemeton, left on the wall to mark a path; so he'd been told and learned to believe. The damn stuff lay everywhere, traces of it cropping up the length and breadth of Merioneth. But there was never enough. Never enough to tell him what he needed to know or where he should search. The bard's name promised sanctuary, but the path he'd left was impossible to follow. No mark beyond *Ammon* had shown itself, let alone whether to go forward or back.

"*Christe.*" Mychael tightened his arm around himself. He needed sanctuary and the bard's pagan magic, if not this day, then on one too quickly coming, for the truth could no longer be denied. Between the pain and the dreams that would grant him no peace, he was going mad.

He'd burned in the night, the vision that had come to him months earlier in Strata Florida Abbey returning with new and terrible force, and he'd felt with dread certainty some fiendish thing drawing near. Verily, in the worst of his delirium, it had flowed over him, silencing his screams and consuming him once more. Remembrance of the heated dream lingered still, faint images of a white light sundered by a dark flame, the scorching rip and tear of it through sinew and bone, and of the light flaring ever higher to rejoin above the swart blaze—and of a fearsome shadow advancing. Only the coming dawn had saved him.

Christe, eleison. Christ have mercy . . . *the scorching rip and tear of it through sinew and bone* . . . His sinew, his bone, all of it following the path of scars that had been blazed down his left side during his first wormhole descent, freshening them anew. The great wormhole, the weir gate, had been sealed when he'd returned to Merioneth a year past, but there had been smaller ones swirling in hidden places in the deep dark. They were all gone now. The renegade *pryf* who had made them, and the force of Time that had compelled them, had all been pulled back into the weir when the seal was broken. He'd breached the great wormhole's rim shortly thereafter, and if the lesser holes had the power to scar, the weir gate had the power of death.

Yet 'twas a lure, the flux of time, a damnable lure. The pain in the night had forced him to his knees, humbling him when humility would not suffice. If not sanctuary, he needed strength. If he would rule this land and be the master of what strove to master him, it would not be with humility as his blade.

On the headlands above, Rhuddlan of the Quicken-tree clan waited for him in the keep overlooking the sea, waited as he had the summer long for Mychael to take a vassal's place at his side. Rhuddlan waited for naught. Merioneth was Mychael's by right through his mother's line. He would be no pawn for the Elf King, who would take his heritage and hide it forever from the world of Men, from Mychael's world. Nor would he play the Druid priest for the Quicken-tree as Madron, fey witch-daughter of Nemeton, wished. He had been raised to be a monk, a Cistercian brother, and he well knew the ways of priests, well enough to realize he had been rendered unfit for holiness in any form by the changes wrought in him against his will. Transformation, sought by some to save their souls, would be the death of him, he feared.

'Twas what Madron feared too, but he dared not put himself in her hands, Nemeton's daughter or nay. For as Rhuddlan sought to turn him into a vassal, Madron thought to turn him into a priest to suit her own needs, the both of them wanting to clip the ab Arawn wings while they still could—or still thought they could. Poor sops. 'Twas far too late to stop what had begun, if there had ever been a time when it could have been stopped. He had become wild in his madness, no different than any feral creature put upon the earth by God, a being no longer subject to the laws of man, but to surges of instinct. The monks at Strata Florida would say 'twas ever thus, that wildness had always been his true nature, but they had never seen him like this. His needs had become hungers, desirous, gnawing hungers stripping away fifteen years of cloistered life and monastic rule and the layers of his sanity, denuding him down to a soul that was no pious thing.

Ddrei Goch and Ddrei Glas, the red dragon and the green, conjured the wildness in his breast that slipped ever more often into delirium. Their siren call had lured him home, crying out to him from within the maelstrom of his dire vision and the long-forgotten dreams of his childhood; home to where ancient legend said the dragons had been born of the very earth of Merioneth, yet they had not returned to be by his side. To the depths of his thrice-cursed heart he knew naught but the dragons could save him.

Unless 'twas Nemeton's elusive path into sanctuary.

Stifling another curse, he turned his face from the dawn-lit sea and stared down the dark throat of the Dragon's Mouth. Power of another sort awaited there, the power of timeless knowledge, raw and dangerous, and that yoke and those reins he would grasp with all his wild, damned heart, if he but could. 'Twas the *magia mysterium* of a religion thought to be long dead, the religion of another age. In truth, its life flowed as surely and strongly as Jesus' blood had flowed upon the cross.

Blood. That was his first curse, the bane that twisted through him like rivers of fire when the madness was upon him. He was Magus Druid by blood, his mother's blood, and the blood had begun to tell.

A movement in the far shadows of the cave caught his eye, and for an instant his pulse quickened. Then a clear voice called to him from out of the darkness.

"*Malashm.* Good morn."

No dragon this, he realized, his mouth curving in wry concession. Grim musings were unlikely to bring him what his months of searching had not, and he was filled with little but grim musings these days. Aye, and he was probably a fool indeed, looking for beasts that in truth were most likely conjured out of naught but a slip of sight and the beginnings of madness.

The speaker drew nearer, discernible only by the pale daylight glancing off silvery green cloth, but soon enough Mychael saw Shay's ready grin and the blue woad slashing diagonally across his face. No one else would bother to search him out. The rest of the Quicken-tree thought his heart too dark. He'd heard their whispers of Dockalfar, and knew they spoke of an ancient enemy that had once ruled the caverns below.

"You're up early," he said by way of greeting, easing his arm away from his side and hoping the pain would not come again.

Shay's grin broadened. "I came down to watch you brood, for no one does it better than thee." Eyes greener than a forest full of trees flashed with amusement. A five-strand *fif* braid was worked into Shay's hair on the left side of his head, a silky black plait amongst the loose strands hanging to his shoulders. In his hand, he held a small pot of woad, its wax seal broken.

"Early though you be, you're too late by half," Mychael chided him. "My morning brood is over, and I shall not partake again until eventide."

"My good luck, that," the boy said, walking out onto the cave's ledge and into the watery light reflecting up from the sea. A high wall of rock on the north side protected the natural bowl of the opening, allowing tufts of vegetation to take hold in the crevices: sea campion and thrift, scurvy grass and vetch. "There are fair tidings on the wind this morning," Shay went on, picking a leaf to chew, barely concealing his excitement. "Travelers. We could take to Riverwood and be the first to find them. Might be our last chance for a while."

Riverwood was the Quicken-tree name for the forest that spread on either side of the River Bredd along Merioneth's eastern border. The trees had previously been clear-cut from the castle walls for defense, but Rhuddlan and his clan were coaxing them back.

The mention of travelers sparked Mychael's interest. It also explained the boy's painted face. Rhuddlan commanded they all be marked thus when they ventured beyond the great wall. Much was afoot in the woods these days.

'Twas true also what Shay said about their last chance. They were to the deep dark again on the morrow, a place beyond the world of Men, though unlike the forest and mist-bound prison Rhuddlan would contrive for Merioneth. 'Twas beyond and below a mighty fault line that Moira, one of the Quicken-tree women, had told Mychael was called the Magia Wall. Time in the forest would be good preparation for the days ahead without the warmth and light from the sun, while they searched for broken damson shafts in the deep dark. Rhuddlan had shown great concern over the broken shaft Mychael had found back in the spring, and not a fortnight passed that he didn't send a troop of Liosalfar into the caverns to look for more. Mayhaps, Mychael thought, in Riverwood's cool bowers he would find some succor for the night's besetting aches. For certes, there was no better excuse for avoiding those who would bend his ear with their talk of duty.

"Have you food?" he asked before agreeing. Shay was ever hungry, having reached the age when no amount of eating seemed to suffice, and there was naught like an empty stomach to bring adventure to a quick halt.

"Enough to share," Shay assured him, patting the pouch hanging from his belt.

"Then we are to Riverwood."

Grinning, Shay tossed him the small pot of woad.

East of the Dragon's Mouth, deep in a forested glen, a heavy blanket of fog drifted over the River Bredd in the pale light of dawn. The thick stuff curled through the rushes lining the river's bank and wound its way 'round the leaves and limbs of the overhanging trees.

Llynya, sprite of the Quicken-tree clan, lay splayed in the crotch of a wych elm, resting her head on her arm, lazily dragging her hand through the vaporous mist and leaving tiny whorls in the wake of her fingertips. Below her, old Aedyth snored softly in a leafy bower tucked next to the trunk. 'Twas a homecoming of sorts that day. The healer and she had been in Deri to the south since mid-May, and though Aedyth had done her work well, Llynya knew she still had much of her strength to reclaim, much of herself to mend.

A heavy sigh escaped her, the breath of it blowing the tiny whorls to smithereens. She was not ready to face all that awaited her in Carn Merioneth, to face the changes wrought in herself these past months, but the day would see itself come whether she was ready or nay, and in truth, she dared not delay any longer. Ailfinn had been summoned, and the mage would not countenance Llynya's quest; indeed, she had the power to keep Llynya from it. For all the mage's many enchantments and calling upon of unseen forces, she was a pragmatic soul, and Llynya's needs had never weighed against Ailfinn's plans.

Her gaze fell on the runes and leaves encircling her wrist and trailing up her arm to disappear under her tunic's sleeve. The tattoo was fully healed, leaving naught but the dark blue of woad marking her skin. Aedyth had performed the ancient rite in Deri. There had been pain, but Llynya did not fear pain. Pain could be borne. That she had failed in her sworn duty could not. She had come back to right a wrong, or meet her death in the trying of it.

"And what of you, my fat little sweetings?" she asked the row of plump birds gathered on a nearby branch watching her. *"Chick-a-dee-dee-dee,* hmm? *Zzhee-chee-chee."*

She reached out her hand and tickled one soft white breast, and the bird fluffed itself into a ball of feathers. The middle one flew onto her finger, and the last hopped closer to the first to wait its turn. Llynya didn't disappoint, but gave them each a thorough going-over, rubbing their throats and the crowns of their black-capped heads.

"Pretty babes," she crooned. "Shall I tell you a story while Aedyth sleeps the morn away?"

Dark eyes watched her expectantly and not so much as a twitter or a tweet of dissent escaped the birds, all of which Llynya took for acquiescence.

And so she began, "A long time ago, in a land far and away across the waters, there lived a great Elfin King who had seven fair daughters . . ."

Mychael and Shay heard the voice at the same time. Dawn had not yet spilled into the deeper reaches of the glens, and they walked through a woodland made ethereal by night shadows and drifts of fog that grew thicker the closer they came to the river.

" 'Tis a woman," Mychael said as they both stopped.

"Mayhaps," Shay said, looking puzzled. He raised his nose into the soft breath of a dawn breeze.

For Mychael there was no mayhaps. The lilting tones could belong to naught except a woman. How could Shay doubt it? He knew the boy's hearing was as keen or keener than his own.

"Aye, I think you're right," Shay finally agreed, sounding worried. "I fear there is naught left of the child in her. It may be that I am too late."

Too late for what, Mychael didn't have a chance to ask. Nor did he have time to ask the identity of *her*. Shay disappeared before any of the words could form on his lips. He slipped into the fog as quickly as that, leaving not a trace of his passing, a common occurrence when one consorted with *tylwyth teg*, the wild folk by one name, and elves by yet another. He'd spent time with the Ebiurrane clan farther north these last few months and found them no better, except in the deep dark. Even those among the Quicken-tree who were Liosalfar warriors, the Light-elves, stuck close to one another in the deep dark.

Druids and elves. *Jesu*, but he'd thrown in with a pagan lot.

Trusting Shay to his own path, Mychael waited in the copse of hazel, listening. His hand absently touched the new and wondrous dagger on his belt. 'Twas sharp-edged steel with a dreamstone hilt, a

Quicken-tree knife, the fighting blade of a Liosalfar. It had been a gift that morn from the ancient white-eyed woman, Naas. She'd caught him and Shay as they'd crossed the bailey on their way to Riverwood, saying naught but the name *Ara* when she clapped it into his hand. That done, she'd disappeared back into the shadows of the great wall.

Dain Lavrans—the man who had saved his sister from the Boar of Balor, who had helped her open the weir gate, who had taken her away to the far north—had owned such a blade, a dagger he'd won off Rhuddlan in a fight. Mychael knew not why the old woman had given one of the rare knives to him. Shay hadn't balked at the priceless gift, but some of the other Quicken-tree might. Mychael knew Naas was a bit touched, and mayhaps it had been a mistake, an act of mild derange-ment. Mayhaps she'd thought he was someone else. The old woman *was* blind.

Already, though, the dagger seemed like a part of him, and he would not easily give it back. It felt right in his hand, the weight of it, the coolness of the crystal, and the heat of it when he held it just so. It felt like it belonged to him, as if Naas had returned something he'd lost.

The woman's voice came again, diverting him, and he set off after it. 'Twas a faerie wood through which he tracked the storyteller weaving her tale of betrayal and enchantment, a landscape rich in buckler ferns and spleenwort, primrose and pasqueflower. The smell of lavender drifted to him, while the sound of the river continually grew louder, a low rushing of water beneath the voice that led him onward through the trees.

At the edge of a clearing where the Bredd eddied around a bend, he halted by an overgrown birch, his trail come to an end. Shay was not to be seen, but the woman was there on the other side of the small meadow—if woman she was.

Stirred by the warming air, white drifts of fog washed up against a wych elm, alternately concealing and revealing the storyteller where she lay along the length of a thick branch. Wisps of the vaporous mist rolled down her body, skimming along her back, sliding over shimmery, feminine curves, and casting her in a pearly luster. Her hair, dark like Shay's, was filled with leaves and twigs, the whole of it tangled and twisted and braided in an artless, falling-down pile on her head. So fey was she, seeming only partly of this world and mostly of another, he would not have been surprised to see ephemeral wings arcing gracefully from her shoulders.

Fair maid, this, he thought. She was the beginning and end of a young man's dreams—but was she woman or river nymph?

Shay had mentioned travelers, but Mychael saw only the one, the dulcet-voiced being, conjured from mist and mayhaps his own imagination, telling her tale to a band of chickadees huddled on the branch in front of her.

". . . and 'twas then the sea grew angry and sent its waves crashing o'er the rocky crag," she was saying, dramatizing the scene by scooping a handful of fog into a sizable wave and pushing it over the branch where she lay. "The sisters clung to one another, their slippered feet bruised by the sharp stones, their hearts growing cold with despair. 'All is lost,' the eldest cried, but the youngest beseeched her sisters not to lose hope, for surely there was yet some brave soul to save them."

As he watched her, the last of Mychael's grim thoughts died, charmed to their demise by her grace. In their place came a sense of bemused wonder that grew as he moved closer. She looked to have taken a tumble from higher up in the tree with all her leaves and twigs, but other than that she appeared to be of a piece—a rare and lovely piece. He would gladly listen to her faerie lore and any other tales she might choose to tell. In truth, how often as a youth had he lain in a similar woodland place, far from prying eyes and monkish vows, and dreamed of one such as she to come and seduce him with love and a warm mouth?

Too often to suit many at Strata Florida Abbey, he thought wryly, though no dream of his had ever been answered except by his own hand. In its beginnings he'd thought that the wildness in him was lust left too long unappeased, but he'd learned differently each time its hungering edge sharpened to a cruel degree and spread beyond his loins.

And yet 'twas a sweet, seductive fancy to think one such as she could be his cure.

Nearer the elm now, he saw she wore a tunic and leggings of silvery green Quicken-tree cloth. 'Twas why her curves shimmered. Her boots were dark green with double silver rings to cinch them closed at her ankles. She was no being conjured of river mist, then, or of his too long unfulfilled yearnings. The dress confirmed her *tylwyth teg,* as elfin as the seven princesses in her story, and without doubt the reason Shay had been out in the woods that morn. He wondered that her companions had left her alone. And where was Shay? The boy's quick start should have placed him at the river long ago.

Mychael searched the clearing again, and found not the boy or a stray traveler, but something else altogether. From the curve of branch here, the twist of a stem there, he could see the Quicken-tree had been working in this part of Riverwood, no doubt at Rhuddlan's bidding. He looked closer at the plants growing near him. Delicate fronds of buckler embraced spikes of hyssop. Twiggish, leaf-laden branches of broom shrub reached into the birch and entwined themselves with the tree. All around him the woodland flora commingled and held on to one another. 'Twas a bramble, woven by the Quicken-tree to protect a place, and probably why the fair elf lingered there, feeling mayhaps overly secure. For he had found her, had he not?

His gaze returned to the wych elm. His thoughts on enchantment had turned 'round and 'round since meeting the Quicken-tree, but he had not seen any to match her.

Or had he? Thoroughly beguiled, he retraced the mist's caressing path. The leaves in her hair were green and fresh, glittering with dew. What he could see of her delicate profile between the braids and tangles was entrancing, the whole of her tugging at a memory he could not bring to the fore.

"Alas," she went on, "all the sisters but the youngest were washed into the furious sea to be drowned or dashed against the crag." Her voice swelled with the desperation of the scene; a fair mummer she. "The North Wind, rendered helpless by the dark arts of the mage, blew his icy breath down upon the last princess." And here she blew, puffing her cheeks out and turning the fog close by into a maelstrom of swirls and whirls.

"Tee-zhay-dee-dee," one of the birds blurted out.

"For certes," the storyteller replied with a sage nod, then went on. "But the mage had not bewitched all against the Elfin King. There were those of fair, kind hearts, Whistler, White-Eye, and Mast, brave chickadees, who heard the frightened cries, and daring all against the storm flew into the brunt of it to save the maids." The little birds began preening themselves to an absurd degree. "Other birds followed, swooping down to the sea, where two dozen to the princess, they plucked the hapless sisters from the waves and saved them all. And if any should doubt the tale, the whole of the valorous flight is forever engraved in the hallowed halls of Fata Morgana's palace."

At the mention of the legendary faerie enchantress, Mychael nearly crossed himself, but stopped a station or two short. In some ways he knew not what to believe anymore, and that conundrum was quickly made more complicated. Even as he lowered his hand, the dawn breeze swirled along the branch where the storyteller lay, lifting loose braids and tangled strands of hair up and away from her face and revealing the true rarity of the creature before him.

Her ears were pointed—strangely, wondrously, and sharply enough to make him wonder what she was besides Quicken-tree. None other of Rhuddlan's band had pointed ears. But if not Quicken-tree, what?

"To this very day," she told her avian audience, "elfin princesses and chickadees share a bond forged with the courage of Whistler, White-Eye, and Mast." She might have gone on to say more, except for the call of a lark interrupting.

She turned quickly at the sound, scanning the forest behind her and seeming to stare right through him. 'Twas then he recognized her. Months before, after the battle for Merioneth, he had seen her in these very woods lift the yellow off a buttercup with naught but her breath. At the time, he'd thought it a fancy of the light, but now he would beg to differ. A waiflike girl no longer, she'd well grown into the magic of the deed.

Aye, she'd changed. Sprite, she'd been called then, and a sprite she'd been, but no more. He'd thought her gone from Merioneth forever.

The lark's call came again, and she pushed herself to her feet, a supple movement seeming to require little effort. The misconception was belied when, with the same fluid grace, she revealed her strength and agility by swinging herself up to a higher branch and landing in a loose-limbed crouch. The chickadees took flight, routed by all the disturbance. The lark, he knew, was Shay, and close by the sound of him.

Llynya was the storyteller's name, he recalled, first seen on the dark shores of Mor Sarff, a girl wielding a sword with desperate fury in the heat of battle. He'd killed his first man to save her life, drawn his bow as he ran, as she faltered on the sands, and loosed his arrow with an unholy prayer that it would find its mark. The man who would have hewn her in twain had fallen, and so had the next to take up arms against her. The one after that, he'd killed to save her companion.

"Chirrr-rrr-up." Shay trilled the lark's song once more, and the sound of beating wings filled the air. Ghostly pale, a flock of doves broke through the fog, flying in from the west and making for the wych elm.

As one they settled in the tree to roost and coo about her. A smile brightened the elf-maid's face.

"Shay," she called out. "I know 'tis you who sends these fair friends my way. Ouch!" One of the turtledoves chose to nest in her hair and immediately got itself tangled in the silky strands. "Shay, you beast! Come help me!"

Mychael stood motionless, watching her as she freed the dove and moved it to a safer perch. The boy was not likely to win her heart with the bird trick, which no doubt had been his intent. A worthy incentive for the bother of finding and gathering a half-dozen turtledoves . . . or a hundred.

Shay was a romantic fool, but no more so than himself.

Cursing softly, he took a step back and looked up into the trees. Shay could not be far.

Chapter 2

Llynya resettled the dove and returned her gaze to the surrounding woods. Shay was out there, close. She knew it, just as she knew she would be hard-pressed to find him if he didn't want to be found. The fog was beginning to lift, though, which was to her advantage. Soon 'twas possible to make out the silhouettes of the birches growing along the river, of the alders and elms—and of a man standing alone in the shadows of the copse.

Startled, she went for her dagger. Closing her hand around the crystal hilt, she drew the blade partway out of its sheath. 'Twas not Shay. Had the bramble not held and let some wayfaring Welshman stumble upon them? Gods, had she grown so soft in Deri that she had lost her warrior's edge and was no longer a fit watcher in the forest, babbling to chickadees like a child while a stranger stood not ten yards distant? He had seen her. There could be no doubt. He was probably watching her even now, wondering what fool thing she would do next. She quickly looked to Aedyth and found the old woman awake, yet well concealed and alert to the danger. Thus assured, she settled herself in to watch and wait. If he passed them by, so be it. If he did not, she would lead him on a merry chase he would not soon forget. Shay must already have the man in his sights and would not have forgotten how the game was played.

The waiting did not take long. Sunlight finally reached the river, sheeting down through the forest in roseate shades of gold, and thus was the man revealed.

Llynya's hand fell to her side, the dagger forgotten as she stared in wonderment at whom the morning had delivered to her bower. Mychael ab Arawn. Ceridwen ab Arawn's twin and the Christian God's warrior, for he was the archer who had saved her life on the shores of Mor Sarff . . . *a stranger, dressed all in white, with a bright copper streak running through his golden hair, a pure flame against the glowing violet wall of the damson cliffs.*

He was looking into the trees as she had, and probably for the same reason—Shay. A swath of blue woad painted across his eyes reached from his left temple to his right and from above his eyebrows to the bridge of his nose, marking him as Liosalfar and half hiding his face in a maze of forest shadows, but he yet had the look of his sister.

Aye, he was Ceridwen's brother, and a warrior aright, tall and lean like a Quicken-tree, but he was no *tylwyth teg,* nor a mere Welshman. He was what had brought her north, not Rhuddlan's command.

Even in Deri she'd heard tales that he was half-wild, and from the looks of him, the tales were true. His hair, a tousled mélange of copper and gold, fell every which length to his shoulders yet was noticeably shorter on top where his monk's tonsure had grown. His clothes were patched and mended, his boots' leather skinned from animals. A bow was slung across his shoulder, and two knives were sheathed in his belt, one with a dreamstone hilt.

He turned, his attention brought back to her by the rising sun, and their gazes met. A frisson of warning curled down her spine even as warmth suffused her cheeks. Disconcerted, her first thought was to vanish into the woods, but her need of him stayed her flight and had her peering back at him through the elm leaves.

His was a wilder beauty than his sister's. His jaw was wider in the way of a man's, his eyebrows less finely drawn, each feature cut to a stronger, fiercer edge—and none more fierce than his eyes. Of a paler, grayer hue than Ceridwen's fair blue, they were piercing and yet translucent, baring part of his being to those with a knack for seeing it. Llynya had acquired somewhat of the knack during her months in Deri, and would grow into more, but in this case it took only a somewhat knack to see beyond the surface. He was *sín,* a storm rising.

Her gaze faltered and she glanced away, struck again by the warning she felt and the disturbing awareness that he was not what she had expected. The man on the cliffs had looked to be a savior. This man did not.

Yet he was Rhiannon's son. 'Twas said Druids of old had called storms at will, conjured them to destroy their enemies, blizzards of snow and torrents of rain, thunder and lightning, winds to lift river water into an impassable veil, and fog so thick a man in the midst of it could not find himself.

Mychael ab Arawn was Druid.

She fingered a wisp of remaining fog and dared to look at him again, wondering. His gaze had not strayed from her, and she forced herself not to shy away. She should leave her perch and greet him, but some instinct kept her high in the elm. She had fallen into malaise at the end of the battle against Balor, and for sennights following the fight her mind had chosen not to remember anything of that day. In Deri, Aedyth had given her no choice but to recall the whole of it, and the first thing she had remembered was him, the archer with the unerring aim. The healer had told her Ceridwen's brother yet resided in Merioneth with the Quicken-tree, and so she finally had come north again. Redemption, if it was to be hers, could only be found by journeying through the time weir of the golden worms—and the way of that could only be found in the deep dark where the Yr Is-ddwfn had long ago engraved their knowledge on the walls. Mychael ab Arawn had been there. He knew the dreaded black maze, he'd survived the wormholes.

He had tasted time.

The truth of it streaked through his flaxen hair like a copper flame. The only way to get that anomaly was to drop oneself down a live wormhole. Nemeton, the Brittany bard, had been marked in such a manner, steel gray running through auburn. Dain Lavrans, the mage of Wydehaw Castle, had begun to show the signs before he'd gone north with Ceridwen, his chestnut-colored strands turning white in a three-finger streak down the left side of his head, and mayhaps there was one other who bore the mark, if he lived.

She let her gaze travel over Mychael again, his unkempt mane, the patched clothes of white monk's wool overlaid with Quicken-tree grays and greens, and the eyes that revealed a far from gentle mien. Ceridwen had told her Mychael had long been a hooded brother of Strata Florida, those of the creed "Thou shalt not kill," yet he had killed to save her. Was he still a monk then? she wondered. Or had changes come to him as they had come to her since that fateful battle?

He wore the blue woad of the Liosalfar, but no one had yet given him a Quicken-tree braid. She could do that for him, if she dared. No doubt she owed him a braid or two, or a half-dozen, and given a chance, she would start her twists and plaits within the copper strands of his hair. Given a chance, she would have a blazing streak of her own, a small price to pay to taste the shifting ethers of time and reclaim what she had lost.

Aye, *sín* or no, she had use of Mychael ab Arawn to save another reckless soul—Morgan ab Kynan, the Thief of Cardiff.

A shadow flitted between them, drawing her attention overhead. Nothing else in the tree moved. The doves had not ruffled a feather, yet she immediately found the shadow's owner.

"Shay." Her voice was soft, a bare whisper as she looked upward through the branches into a pair of eyes as green as hers, but far more innocent. He grinned down at her from where he sat on a limb.

"*Malashm,* sprite."

" '*Lashm,* Shay." Her eyes filled with sudden tears. So much had changed since she'd last seen him. She'd grown so old and in truth was a child no more. One salty drop spilled over to run down her cheek, and she swiped at it with the back of her hand. It seemed she cried for no reason at all anymore—one of the more annoying changes.

"Llynya?" He lowered himself to her branch and crouched in front of her, his long hair flowing over his shoulders. His smile faded. "What's this?" He took her chin in his hand and wiped away another tear with his thumb.

" 'Snothing." She squeezed her eyes shut and willed the tears to stop, embarrassed. She'd never cried in front of Shay before, except for once when she'd gashed her knee near to the bone while chasing after him in Wroneu. She still carried the scar from that escapade.

"You smell of lavender," he said, and she felt him lean in close, so close his breath blew across her cheek. Then came a touch, soft and brief.

A kiss? Her eyes opened. From Shay? Aye, indeed things had changed, and not for the better.

Unbidden by intent, she looked to the copse—and found it empty. A sense of loss enveloped her, a feeling as inexplicable as her tears, which had stopped as suddenly as they had begun. She wiped the last of them away, looking all the while to the overgrown birch where Mychael ab Arawn had stood.

He was gone, disappeared without a trace, and she'd not had the courage to so much as say hullo. Vexation thinned her mouth into a tight line. She needed better of herself.

"Rhuddlan is waiting at Carn Merioneth, and Moira has sweet bannocks for you," Shay said, breaking into her thoughts. He rose to his feet and took her hand to pull her up. "I'll race you to the postern in the keep's east wall." The challenge came with a grin, but before she could answer, a rustling of leaves below had him reaching for a higher branch and levering himself out over the limb on which they stood. "Good morn, Aedyth," he called down.

The old woman rose to sitting, brushing leaves off here and there as she looked up into the tree. "Good morn, Shay. Have you come to see us home then?" Her graying blond hair was plaited in a crown around her head with parts of the braid worked loose from sleep, but a tuck or two put the strands aright. Her eyes were bright, her fingers nimble, the signs of age showing mostly in the lines on her face.

"Aye, and give you first greeting. You made good time coming north." He dropped out of the tree and landed lightly on his feet in front of her.

"As if these old bones would not," Aedyth exclaimed in mock affront, accepting the hand Shay offered. Once on her feet, she brushed her skirts down. "If 'tis a race to the postern you want, I warrant I can give you one, if you would but even out the years a bit."

His grin broadened. "What would you have me do?"

"Drink the river dry and cross over the moon while I make straightaway for the castle."

"And I would still win," he boasted with an ingenuous laugh.

Aedyth shooed him off, smiling. The boy was right. She had not the will anymore to race, by far preferring to savor her steps no matter the prize at the end. The journey from Deri had not taken nearly long enough to suit her, but Rhuddlan's message had been clear. Winter was drawing nigh, and he wanted the girl in Merioneth posthaste.

Aedyth brushed again at her skirts, tsking under her breath. 'Twas more than the weather driving Rhuddlan, though that had been odd enough since Beltaine back in May. Ailfinn Mapp could not be found. The mage had not gone to Anglesey for the summer solstice, missing one of the great turnings of the year, and Aedyth knew from Moira's messages that Rhuddlan was beginning to fear Ailfinn was missing altogether. 'Twas an impossibility, of course, for someone who was so much a part of the Earth to be missing from it.

"Posh," she muttered.

For herself, she had planned on going many more years without having to deal with the mage. The wild boy who'd been in the copse was no doubt part of the reason Ailfinn was being searched out, but Llynya would not escape the mage's scrutiny.

Nor had she escaped Mychael ab Arawn's. Aedyth tsked again. There would be none of that, not an inkling. Madron had Druid plans for the boy, as if aught besides his past was needed to make him unfit for Llynya.

Trouble, trouble, trouble abrewing. 'Twas all against Aedyth's wishes. Llynya needed more time. She would have kept the girl in Deri through the winter and into the spring, and still would not have pronounced her strong enough to return to Merioneth, nor strong enough to face Ailfinn. 'Twas too soon, too soon.

Madron was yet at Merioneth and could be a handful all by herself for the mage. Few would e'er forget the last meeting between Ailfinn and Madron. Sparks, literally, had flown. As for Mychael ab Arawn, Rhuddlan would probably welcome some influence there other than his own, Rhiannon's child by all accounts having turned out to be as unmanageable as he had been unexpected.

From beneath the branches of the elm, Shay whistled and the doves fluttered off into the day, taking flight in a cloud of wings. Llynya swung down from the tree, landing as lightly as down feathers. The girl leaned forward to give her a quick morning kiss, and Aedyth returned the affection with a hug. "Be off with you then. I'll take this day's march at my own pace and enjoy Riverwood. Here." She reached into a pouch hanging from her belt. "Have some cake to break your fast." She broke off pieces of seedcake for Llynya and Shay.

They weren't children any longer, she thought, watching them take off into the woods. They had come of age. Aye, she was getting old—and with that came another thought far more startling. Mayhaps Ailfinn would think her too old to care for the sprite, to be the girl's guardian.

"Posh and fiddle." She dismissed the idea. Her hair was not so white.

No, the Prydion Mage would not replace her, or—the gods forbid—take Llynya from Merioneth. Not yet. 'Twas the Druid boy who had forced Rhuddlan to bring Ailfinn down upon them, and 'twas only Llynya's lineage sucking the girl into the storm.

Aedyth walked over to the place Mychael had stood and touched the birch with the tips of her fingers. Surprisingly, his presence was still strong, disconcertingly tangible, as if he'd left a trace of himself to mark a trail. She withdrew her hand, frowning. Few could recognize such a trace. Fewer still could leave one. The boy had not had such power when she'd last seen him in the spring.

She stepped back and looked around the copse. She'd been aware of the bramble when they'd crossed the river the night before, having recognized even in the dark the safety it would provide. In the light of day, she saw more than the Quicken-tree's handicraft was at work in Riverwood.

The lush summer they'd experienced in Deri had pervaded the north to an even greater extent. Leaves were thick and glossy and abundant, clustered on twigs and cluttering limbs. The trees were overgrown with new branches reaching out in every direction. She walked over to a nearby alder, then on to another birch, and lastly an elm, pressing her palm against each one. They all told the same story, of a fecund summer rich in rain and sunshine, and of thick, new layers of summerwood. The forest was bursting with life to an unsettling degree.

Aedyth let her gaze wander over stem and leaf, branch and trunk and blade of grass, taking the time to see each one. Not all was well. Birch bark showed fissuring and knots leaking sap where it should have been smooth. The leaves on the elm were more deeply toothed than they should have been, nearly lobed, with the teeth curving upward and reaching out. Hyssop flowers were too darkly purple and bunched together at the top of the plant, leaving two-thirds of the spikes bare. Curious, she knelt by the trunk of the elm and lifted the fronds of a fern.

A chill ran through her, and she dropped the frond with a gasped prayer. *"Shadana . . ."*

Rot underlay the rampant verdancy—black, putrid rot, a decay beyond any natural decomposition of green matter. She recognized it all too well, though she had not seen its like in many years, not since the Wars of Enchantment when the Dockalfar had called down a blight on the forests.

She took a step back and looked around her, seeing the copse through new, wary eyes. Mayhaps she'd been wrong. Mayhaps Rhuddlan had put out the call for Ailfinn Mapp none too soon.

Madron walked quickly through Riverwood, her Quicken-tree cloak veiling her in the mist-bound shadows of the forest morn, the hood pulled up to cover the loose flow of her auburn hair. Not all of Balor's cottars had run away when the keep had fallen to Rhuddlan, and she did well to take care.

Sunshine broke through the gloom in places, but did naught to lighten her mood. The day had barely begun and had already gone awry. Mychael ab Arawn had slipped free of her yet again. Recalcitrant, obstinate youth. She could help him, if he would let her, but he would forever go his own way, or Rhuddlan's, playing into the elf-man's hands as neatly as a hooked fish. Despite the Quicken-tree leader's interference, she would not lose the boy, not as she'd lost his sister.

She came to a small stream, a freshet, and lifted the hems of her cloak and dark green gown before stepping nimbly across and continuing on her way.

Shay and Llynya were running in the forest this morn. She'd let them pass her by a quarter league back. The two of them had appeared carefree, but for the girl at least, 'twas bound to be a fleeting state. The sprite's destiny was about to meet her head-on. Which brought Madron to her present problem and her woodland task, forced on her by the Quicken-tree and their damned brambling and tangling of the trees. 'Twould only get worse with the coming of Ailfinn Mapp—if the mage ever did come.

And if she did not, where did that leave Llynya? That Ailfinn had grown so powerful that she dared ignore Rhuddlan's summons was not out of the question. That she would desert her acolyte, flighty as the maid could be, was out of the bounds of reason. Yr Is-ddwfn aethelings were not so thick on the ground, and Prydion Mages even less so.

Nay, whatever promise Llynya had shown for the *magia myster-*

ium would not be lightly cast aside by Ailfinn Mapp. The mage would come, if only for the sprite—and just by her mere presence be a hindrance to Madron.

Rhuddlan would have Carn Merioneth slip into the mists, hide it completely from the rest of the world with his arboreal dabbling, and mayhaps after the debacle of Balor Keep he was right. Mayhaps 'twas time to let Carn Merioneth fade from the memories of Men, but a path had to be left open. One path must always be left open, for there were travelers besides Prydion Magi who needed passage into Merioneth. If Rhuddlan couldn't see the need for it, she could, and she would ensure that a path did stay open.

At the river, she turned south, following a worn track along the bank, her soft Quicken-tree boots leaving nary a mark. The Bredd grew narrower and deeper before it plunged beneath a giant's cairn of tumbled boulders on the southern edge of Riverwood, never to surface again. The waters of the river flowed down into caverns, winding through a labyrinth of corridors and passages before reaching Lanbarrdein, a cavern of near unimaginable size and riches deep in the earth. From Lanbarrdein, part of the river cascaded over a cliff into Mor Sarff, the Serpent Sea. The rest of the river disappeared into the deep dark, a place of mysteries and mazes that had never been fully mapped, not even by the Quicken-tree.

The boulders marked her father's, Nemeton's, southernmost path into Merioneth, a path he had laid with traces of magic, and 'twas with the *artes magicae* she had learned from him that she kept it open. She knelt close to the cairn by the river's edge and performed a ritual with fire, using the contents of the four pouches hanging from her belt. At the end of it, she spoke a few warding words and scattered forest debris over the small patch of scorched earth. 'Twas no safeguard against Rhuddlan discovering her trespass on his bramble, but 'twould hide it well enough from others. The Quicken-tree leader wouldn't countenance her breach, and if he found the path, he could undo her spell with little more than a flick of his wrist. As quickly as that the stems would begin to turn and the branches wind around one another.

Damned elf-man. He was forever tripping her up.

She reached for another handful of twigs and leaves, but inadvertently dug too deep and came up with black muck as well.

A soft curse left her lips. Here was Rhuddlan's true bane; the richness of summer had spilled over into rotting ripeness. Winter could come none too soon this year, nor the icy blasts of the north wind to freeze the blight from the earth.

She stared at the sodden remains of decayed vegetation, letting it drip from her open palm onto the ground where she'd made her elemental potion. Each drop sizzled and smoked as it hit the sanctified earth. Strange, wicked stuff, its presence in Riverwood kept Rhuddlan awake at night. Coupled with Mychael ab Arawn's heated, nocturnal pacings, Carn Merioneth never knew a moment's peace.

Rhuddlan was sending Mychael and the Liosalfar into the deep dark on the morrow to see what they could find. An ill-advised move, she'd argued. The youth's time could be better spent with her, exploring Druid wisdoms and teachings. How else was he to learn to call the dragons and take his mother's place? Or, she'd asked, did Rhuddlan now believe Druids to be as irrelevant as Men in the course he would take?

Damn Rhuddlan. He would have them all slip into the mists and no longer move even through the shadows of men's lives, and a graver error he hardly could make. For all his great knowledge of the past, Rhuddlan knew little about the future, and 'twas that aspect of the world that she would protect. The ways must be left open. 'Twas her duty and her desire.

As to the deep dark, she already knew what they would find: worms still churning, things still coming undone, the scrying pool lifeless and murky and useless for her needs. 'Twould take more than warriors and a wild boy to unriddle Riverwood's malady.

In truth, 'twould take the Prydion Mage, Ailfinn Mapp.

Another curse escaped her. She would have to be on her guard with that one running loose in Merioneth.

Leaning forward, she immersed her hand in the river and watched as the last of the black rot was washed into the current and carried downstream. Change and turmoil were afoot in the deep earth, a new chaos that she feared had been loosed when Ceridwen and Dain Lavrans had freed the *pryf,* a chaos that seeped upward into the light of day, bringing the rot and wildness. Five months had passed since the emerald seal had been broken and the gate of the *pryf*'s prison opened. Five months and still the worms turned deep in the earth, the frenzy of the *prifarym* having abated not one whit. Five months of things coming undone, and of Madron's growing doubts as to the wisdom of their deed.

Five months, and still Rhuddlan was a dragon keeper with no dragons to keep, and with no priestess from the ancient line of Merioneth to call them home. Rhiannon was dead. Ceridwen had taken herself north with Lavrans. Rhiannon's son, Mychael, could do it—she would swear by him—if he would but give himself over to Druid teachings.

The corruption thinned out into gelatinous strings before slipping over the last of the river rock and disappearing beneath the giant's cairn, returning from whence it had come. Mychael ab Arawn had been there, traveling the caverns and the deep dark alone for months before the battle for Balor, a feat no Quicken-tree could match. He'd seen fissuring in the damson shafts—dread augery—and met the old worm. He'd been in the wormholes and discovered the secret of dreamstone. And he'd survived, proving himself to be far more than she'd thought.

She knew the legends of this place above the Irish Sea, the stories born there and the stories brought from Eire. Mychael, named for the archangel of the Christian God, Rhiannon's unforetold son who had come into the world by sharing the womb with his sister. He should not be, except for some strange grace of fate and the magic arts of a woman long lost in time. Ailfinn would know the truth of it. One look would reveal the boy's forbidden origins to the mage.

Rhiannon must have been mad, or too far under the Christian yoke of her faithless husband, to have let a son be born from her womb. 'Twas what came from allowing love to make a match. With one set of ill-fated vows, Carn Merioneth had lost its firm hold on the past and been laid bare before the temporal world, a world that had destroyed what time had held inviolate.

Nay, Madron thought, Mychael ab Arawn should not be, but he was, and she would not lose him, not to Rhuddlan, not to Ailfinn Mapp, and not to the wildness reaching up for him from the depths of the earth. Without him she could not open the doors between the worlds and look beyond her time. Without him she could not take her father's place and be a watcher of the gates.

Chapter 3

Mychael returned to Carn Merioneth well after dark, flashing his dreamstone blade to make himself known to the guard at the postern gate. No other light shone the same clear blue. 'Twas as different from lantern flame or torchlight as crystal was from fire, and impossible for the Welsh, or the English, or any man to duplicate.

He had spent the rest of the day in Riverwood with Owain, a Welshman who had fought with the Quicken-tree and who had not left for Gwynedd after the battle for Balor, choosing instead to stay in Merioneth. They had found a trail of wolves and men running together in the northern woods and followed it as far as the Bredd, where the hunters had crossed the water. 'Twasn't the first time the strange mix of tracks had been found. Rhuddlan had long since doubled the scouts in Riverwood.

Owain had headed back to the keep hours earlier, yet Mychael had stayed out, letting the night come to him in the forest. He'd been restless since the morn and would have slept in the woods as well, wolves or nay, if not for the necessity of preparing for the coming journey into the caverns. Aye, that and mayhaps one other thing had brought him back inside the wall, a teller of tales with forest green eyes and shimmering curves.

Passing through the gate, he greeted the guard in the elfin tongue and resheathed his blade. Lanterns flickered throughout the upper bailey, casting amber light and shadows on the trees and the willow huts built by the Quicken-tree, the only structures left inside the wall. A few women were gathered about the hearthfire, serving the evening pottage, a not unpleasant stew of grains and berries. He and Owain had roasted squirrels over a campfire in the woods for their supper. 'Twas an act of barbarism to the Quicken-tree, but one he and the Welshman indulged in regularly.

Owain had served Morgan ab Kynan, a Welsh prince, and had been the captain of Morgan's warband during the battle of Balor. When the Boar of Balor had vanquished the prince into the abyss of the great wormhole, a saddened Owain had pledged his sword to Merioneth. A telling choice, for he'd picked no man—or Quicken-tree—to follow, but the land. 'Twas what Mychael had pledged himself to as well, including the land below Merioneth, where he knew his destiny lay.

Of the women at the hearthfire, 'twas Moira stirring the cooking cauldron. She mended his clothes when they needed it, and was the one he and most of the Quicken-tree went to when they were ailing. Her brown hair was plaited in a crown around her head, framing a face of gentle curves and rosy cheeks, but in her own quiet way, Moira wielded nearly as much power as Rhuddlan. Elen, next to her, was younger with darker hair, and was growing heavy with a child conceived during the Quicken-tree's Beltaine celebration. Three little girls sat by the fire, giggling over a game played with seashells and sticks, and Fand, a Liosalfar of the Ebiurrane clan from the north, lean and blond like the elder warrior she was, stood talking with Moira and Elen. The one he sought was not near, though he looked all around.

On his way to the lower bailey, he passed more Quicken-tree and Ebiurrane, some in groups, some not. He greeted a few, mainly the Liosalfar at the portcullis, and avoided others, keeping to the shadows.

Still he did not let any go unnoticed, and the maid was not to be found. Nor was Shay.

Well, there was his answer then, and he supposed they made a fine enough pair, though he doubted if Shay had much more experience with women than he did himself. Still, if that morn's adventure was anything to judge by, Shay was eager to learn, and the boy was a quick study. 'Twas no concern of his either way, he told himself, but Shay was to the deep dark on the morrow as well, and Mychael would as soon not have the boy mooning overmuch while they were below.

He passed through an open gate in the inner curtain between the baileys, heading toward the southwall on the other side of the great apple orchard. He kept a room in the tower on one of the lower floors. In spring, he'd awakened one morning to a shower of fragrant petals falling outside his window and known he'd truly come home. The orchard was as old as the demesne and made up of trees as mighty as any oak grove.

A stone chapel nestled against the seaside wall of the lower bailey, between the orchard and the fields of grass planted by the Quicken-tree, but Mychael had not had the courage to enter it. 'Twas a pagan life he led now, searching for his mother's gods among the wreckage of the ancient glory of Merioneth, and 'twas to this end that he devoted himself. Falling back upon the God he'd forsaken could do him no good.

Upon reaching the tower, he slipped inside and took to the stairs. 'Twas a matter of course that a man's weapons were sharpened before going into the caverns. Trig, captain of the Liosalfar, had been among those at the portcullis. Mychael would gather up his iron dagger and his leaf-bladed short sword and go work with the others bound for the journey ahead.

Llynya held her breath as she stretched out over the battlements, craning her neck to keep Mychael ab Arawn in view until he stepped inside the tower at the far end of the orchard. Even with moonlight and lanterns to see him by, and with her vantage point on top of the inner wall-walk, he'd been difficult to track across the wards. He moved like a flicker of shadow and light through the darkness, providing only an elusive silhouette. She'd lost him a time or two when he'd seemed to disappear into thin air, but now she knew exactly where he was.

She released her breath and dropped back down onto her feet.

Aye, she knew exactly where he was. She'd waited for his return the whole afternoon long, but again had missed her chance to speak to him by hesitating.

Or had she? No other had approached the southwall tower. He was alone.

The truth of that gave her pause. 'Twould be a simple thing to present herself at the door to his chamber, and she would have the privacy she needed for all she would say. Rhuddlan would banish her farther north to the Ebiurrane or south again to Deri if he divined even a hint of what she was about. To breach a wormhole was dangerous beyond reckoning and forbidden to all. To breach the time weir itself was tantamount to death.

Tantamount—but not death itself, and therein lay the nature of its terror. To pass through the weir and find no purchase on the other side was to spend eternity falling through the ages. If Morgan had survived the cutting blow that had sent him over the edge, she feared such had been his fate.

A chill rippled through her at the thought. She'd seen the flash of the Boar of Balor's blade and watched in horror as it had sunk into the Thief. She'd seen the blood fill Morgan's mouth—too much blood—and she'd been too late, too late to save him.

Sticks! She caught her lower lip with her teeth. Her hand came up to rub at a spot above her left breast. Damnable ache. Her place had been at his side. She'd been sworn to such not just once, but twice by Rhuddlan. Yet during battle she'd thought only of Ceridwen's safety, and for that mistake, Morgan had paid.

And so did she still pay.

She looked to the tower beyond the orchard, its walled rampart silhouetted against the moonlit sky. Mychael ab Arawn had walked the tenuous line between the tantamount and death. If she would do the same, she must deal with him. She'd known that from the beginning.

So what had stayed her? she wondered. She had no fear of men, but then neither had she ever had need of one—until him. Edmee, Madron's daughter, was not so wary of Mychael, but she was the granddaughter of Nemeton himself and like Mychael had her own share of Druid blood running in her veins. Edmee had confided earlier that day that Mychael tended to keep to himself, being even more of an outcast than others would make him. Yet Llynya had spoken with some at Carn Merioneth who were not at all comfortable with a man who had spent so much time alone in the deep dark; and others whose discomfort edged toward open hostility, like Bedwyr, blade-master of the Liosalfar. No Quicken-tree could have survived the isolation endured by Mychael, not for the months he'd spent, but—Bedwyr had been quick to say—it had not been so long since the Dockalfar, the Dark-elves, had lived in the deep dark, and wasn't there trouble in Riverwood?

The blade-master's accusations had fallen just short of naming Mychael ab Arawn consort of the ancient enemy. More foolishness, she'd told herself, yet twice her own instincts had warned her off her chosen course.

The Liosalfar tolerated him, for he was skilled with a bow and proving out with a blade, according to Wei, Trig's second in command. He had even mastered the art of the iron stars, throwing disks with sharp points like the rays of a star. They were an ancient weapon, not much in use since the Wars, but the Druid boy had taken to them. Shay called Mychael friend. Madron had use of him, dire use that it seemed she could not convince him of—this learned in another confidence from Edmee—and Rhuddlan would rule him, if he could. As for herself, she knew exactly what she would have from him; he knew the dark. She needed no other reason to search him out.

So what had stayed her? 'Twas not bodily harm she feared, yet twice she'd sensed danger in his presence.

Unexpectedly, he came back out of the tower, and a wash of relief ran through her. Her hand, still absently rubbing the strange ache, dropped to her side. He was not yet for sleep and dreams, and she would have no more hesitation from herself.

His long strides quickly brought him abreast of the gatestones in the inner wall. He passed through just below where she stood on top, heading toward the portcullis by the looks of the weapons hanging off his belt. She'd seen the Liosalfar there, grinding their blades to a keen edge for the morrow. On his current path, Mychael would pass by the keep's well. If she was quick, she could intercept him there.

In a twinkling, she was up and gone, before another warning had the chance to sound in her head and keep her from her fate.

Mychael strode across the ward, listening to the night wind sough through the tall grass, the mainstay of Quicken-tree meals. The sounds of laughter and shared conversations drifted to him on the breeze, com-

ing from the hearthfire and the portcullis at the far end of the bailey. All
of the Quicken-tree had voices like cool running water, and to hear them
mixed together whether in speech or song was to hear the sweet babbling
of brooks and the rushing tumble of rivers down mountainsides. He had
no place among them, and he oft wondered if they would stay when he
claimed the land as his own. His fight was truly not with them, nor even
with Madron or Rhuddlan, but with a nameless, faceless enemy he'd
sensed only once—the night he'd walked the cloisters of Strata Florida
and been beset by the vision. Heresy, to be sure, what he'd seen of the
pagan deeds threatening to damn his soul, yet the whole of it had drawn
him in and with every passing day tightened its hold.

All men fought the demons inside themselves, and the night of his
vision he'd thought the battle he saw was of a spiritual nature, and—
more blasphemy—that he'd be sainted in four hundred years for having
had it.

But the pull of the damn thing had been relentless and real,
dragging him back to Merioneth where he'd found dragon sign and
remembered dragon tales of old, things learned at his mother's knee,
long forgotten yet always known. 'Twas not sainthood awaiting him,
he'd realized, for if the dragons were real and the vision not a metaphor
for man's struggle with sin, he would become that for which he had no
heart, a warlord like his father, though far worse. In the vision he'd seen
himself wading through a river of blood that poured from the bodies of
his slain enemies, a sword in his hand dripping the same blood, and
above the destruction, the dragons screaming their victory across a night
sky rent by white light and sundering dark flame.

Aye, the dragons had called him home aright, not for sainthood,
but to fight. He who had been raised a man of peace in a religion that
relegated the beasts to myth was to fight as lord of a land he had not
claimed, against an enemy he did not know—or so he prayed.

What if 'twas the Quicken-tree he must purge from Merioneth?
The question came to him now and again. Could it be that they had
betrayed his parents and then found the new rulers not to their liking?
Doubtful, but possible. After the rout of Balor, no one else was clamoring
for the demesne, leaving a dearth of enemies.

To their favor, Madron abided the Quicken-tree, and her father
had died in the same battle as Mychael's mother and father fifteen years
past. Like him, she must have heard of Gwrnach's unholy death by his
son's hand and felt avenged. The son, Caradoc, the Boar of Balor, had

disappeared into the weir with Morgan ab Kynan, ending the Balor line. The other men of Balor had indeed been slaughtered, but not all by his hand. He'd killed only three and those with his bow, not a sword—and he'd killed them to save the maid, not for blood.

So 'twas not the battle behind him, but mayhaps one he yet faced that could make him a butcher. 'Twas what he feared more than death, this blood-drenched thing he could become, for therein lay the loss of God's will and the true heart of madness, should he live his life as a ravening beast.

As restless as his thoughts, the wind changed, slipping over the seaward wall and causing the fields of grass to sway to the east. He followed the rippling stalks, watching them crest in dark, golden waves across the bailey, until his gaze came to the keep's well.

His steps slowed.

She was there, the elfin maid, standing alone in a pool of light cast by a small lantern, drawing a bucket of water. He'd never seen a creature so fair, nor even imagined one—the dark tumble of her hair, more knotted than tangled, deliberately tied in a thousand intricate twists and braids and laced through with leaves; skin that shimmered, begging a touch; and a face that defied him to remain unmoved. Flowers were pressed into the Quicken-tree cloth of her tunic and leggings, bright stars of meadowsweet and rose petals as softly pink as her mouth. Woad tattoos encircled her wrist and twined upward around her arm in a pattern of runes and leaves, marking her as a warrior of the *tylwyth teg,* a Liosalfar, utterly pagan. And utterly amazing that one so seemingly delicate could fight. Yet he'd seen her wield a blade.

Five months he'd lived with the Quicken-tree and met many a pretty maiden, and he'd known that whatever he took from any of them, he would have to give like in return. So he had taken nothing. He would have none make a claim on him, however slight, be it for a kiss or more—until now. In Riverwood, at dawn, this sprite had held his gaze no longer than one moment, but it had been enough to ensnare him, for he'd seen a single truth in the verdant depths of her eyes: she was as wild as he, mayhaps even more so.

Reason enough to steer clear of her, he told himself, though he slowed his steps just the same. He needed no more wildness in his life. If he would take a woman, the commonest of sense and his heritage dictated that she would not be an untamed elf-maid. Rhuddlan needed no more suzerainty over him.

Aye, she was a complication he did not need, except for the kiss Shay had taken and he had not. He'd envied the boy that one brief touch of lips to fair cheek. He envied him still, but for himself he would have taken more, much more. He knew the way of a kiss well enough, the melding of mouths and the sharing of breath and where it could lead. Yet there was no quick tumble to be had with the elfin maid.

As he watched, she dipped a cup into the bucket and turned away from the well, unconsciously bringing herself into silhouette against the luminescence cast by the lantern, and he faltered to a stop. For an instant she looked as a dark flame cleaving the light, until the graceful continuation of her movement clarified the outline of her body—the limned rise of her breast flowing into her torso and the gentle curve of her hip, the slender length of her legs. There was naught of darkness about her, he told himself, disgusted at his wayward thoughts. The only darkness lay in his own black heart, for like the perilous dragon vision, she quickened his blood, though with a far different result. He was in truth a boy that he could be aroused so easily.

He had only to follow his course and the shift in the wind to arrive at her side. Instead he turned his feet to the north to skirt the well. He had come back to the keep to find her, and he had. He had wanted one more look, and it had been given. 'Twould have to suffice.

Llynya pulled the bucket up onto the rim of the well and balanced it there, glancing toward the field from whence Mychael ab Arawn would come. A not-so-chance meeting left a few things up to chance nonetheless, and a little care was not misplaced. She did not want him to pass by unnoticed.

She picked up a silver cup and dipped it into the bucket for a drink. The night breeze off the Irish Sea wafted over the outer curtain wall, caressing her cheeks and tangling through her hair, and setting the grass aflutter. She smelled the salt tang of it, so unlike the verdured winds that came down out of the mountains. Turning her face a bare degree, she happened upon another scent and stilled.

'Twas him, moving through the fields, his essence mingling with the grasses, so different from the *tylwyth teg*.

She closed her eyes, waiting, breathing him in. His was a richly layered scent, warm and animal, bespeaking a life beyond her ken, of years spent behind cloistered walls filled with smoking tallow candles and the pious chants of men. Faint but true, she read his history on the wind. The forest was there, winding through his days. The sea had come and gone in his life, and far and away beyond it all there was a scant strain of that which she sought—the ether of time, dark-edged and dangerous . . . *a tremor ran through her, sinew and bone, a stark shadow of fear cracking open an abyss at her feet. She leaped back, away from the sharp edge and into a pool of light*—and came up against the well wall. Water spilled onto her hand. Her eyes flew open.

"*Shadana* . . ." The prayer fell from her lips. She'd learned a bit of sight in Deri, naught to rival Moira's, but enough apparently to give herself a good jolt. Well enough warned, she chided herself, to go using deep-scent on a man-child of Merioneth, a Druid whether he willed it or nay.

He came out of the fields then, and the first sight of him confirmed the wisdom of caution. Gods, but he was wondrously strange. No two parts of him matched. Even his boots were made from the skins of two different kinds of animals. She recognized rabbit fur tufting out of his left boot and vair out of the right. His left stocking was mostly white monk's wool, his right mostly Quicken-tree cloth, the both of them patched and no doubt the cause of his elusive light-and-shadows stride. A wide leather belt worked with silver was buckled around his waist, holding his sheathed knives and a short-bladed sword.

He was going a bit awry of the path, and left alone, he was sure to miss the well.

'*Twould be better to let him go,* an inner voice whispered. She shunted it aside and called out, "*Malashm,* ho!"

He slowed to a stop and looked up to where she stood, hesitating for a long moment before starting in her direction. If he returned her greeting, she did not hear it. Mayhaps he nodded, mayhaps not. 'Twas hard to tell with the light against her and his face shadow-painted with woad. He stopped again not too far from her. There was yet an inch or two of empty space behind her, enough to accommodate a small retreat, though not enough to calm the racing of her pulse. Standing on a level with him, she realized it had been an intuition more powerful than cowardice that had earlier kept her on the wall.

No savior here, for certes, but mayhaps a man who indeed had spent too long alone in the depths of the earth. He was taller than she'd thought, lean and feral with an air of wary tension about him, and broader across the shoulders than any *tylwyth teg.* The stripe in his hair was startling when seen up close, a bright swath of copper and bronze glittering in the lantern light with an odd metallic sheen.

He was stone silent, standing at the edge of the light, and she wondered if he couldn't speak. Some wild creatures couldn't—though most spoke to her—and he was at least half-wild, if not more. His eyes were veiled by the dark of night, yet she felt his gaze tracking over her with a keenness that unnerved her.

She swallowed softly, wondering what she'd gotten herself into and how she would ever turn him to her need, or indeed even manage to escape the well if such proved necessary. He moved closer in a silent step, and she instinctively pressed back, her fingers making a warding sign. His gaze flickered downward, and when his eyes met hers again, he seemed to know more of her than she would have wished.

Sticks! What was she about? She would ask the world of him, to breach the gates of time and set her upon a path from whence she might never return. Warding herself against him was not the place to begin. Nor was it to her advantage to let him know a single step of his was enough to force her retreat.

He gestured toward the cup. "I would have a drink," he said, his voice low and gruff, as if in truth it did not get much use.

"Aye," she managed, clearing her throat and holding the cup out.

Their fingers touched when he took the silver mug, and she was chastened again to feel only warmth and not the least bit of sizzling power. Trig would have her wrung and hung if he saw her acting such. She was elfin Liosalfar, Yr Is-ddwfn aetheling, and the match of any man, even wondrously strange ones with a trace of magic about them.

Aye, there was that too. With him now in the light, she could see it. 'Twas the Magus Druid in him, a feyness in his eyes she'd also seen in his sister. Things were wont to shift in those blue-gray depths, and not just in shades of awareness. He had sight, and she wondered if that was how he'd seen his way clear to enter the wormholes.

When the cup was drained, he handed it back and wiped his mouth with his sleeve. "This morn, in Riverwood, 'twas your tale I followed to find you. Next time, bring your friends inside the wall if they would hear a story."

With that affront, he turned to leave, and Llynya nearly let him. Yet piqued or not, she would have him stay. In fact, she felt a powerful reluctance to have him leave, and hadn't she offended him first with her warding sign? Tit for tat—not such a good start for what she would ask.

"The birds are not mine to bid," she said, quickly finding her voice, "but do only as they will, not so unlike yourself."

"Aye," he agreed, stopping and returning his gaze to her. "I do as I will."

"And what of another's will?" she asked boldly. "If the need was great?"

He considered her for a moment, and to her surprise, the barest smile touched his mouth. "Rhuddlan has indeed grown wily," he said in his rough voice, "if he would send you to speak of needs."

A mystery of words there, but she divined their meaning enough so to feel warmth creep into her cheeks. What a strange thing for him to think, that Rhuddlan would barter with her company, and even stranger that the thought would bring a smile to his lips.

"I have not come from Rhuddlan," she said.

His smile faded. "I trust the witch of Wroneu Wood even less than the Quicken-tree man," he warned.

"Nay," she corrected him. "Madron has not sent me. I come on my own behalf."

At that, his brow furrowed. "Come for what?"

"You saved my life," she said, having long since decided on her opening gambit. "You're the archer from the damson cliffs, and I'll not forget what you did."

" 'Twas no—"

"Llynya!"

They both turned at the sound of her name being called. Llynya stifled a groan. She'd run out of time. 'Twas Aedyth approaching the well at a fair clip, her skirts hiked up to hasten her strides. The healer had not wasted her day either, speaking to all and sundry and learning enough to denounce Mychael ab Arawn as an unstable Druid boy. She knew the way of these things, the healer had said, and Llynya should listen. Rhiannon's son was not all that he seemed and was a good deal of what couldn't be seen, a darkling beast, Aedyth was sure, though none else had dared to name him such.

"Come away, girl," the healer called out. "I have looked the night long for you and would have you in your bed."

Double-sticks.

"Aye, Aedyth. I'll be there soon enough."

"Your soon enough will not be soon enough for me," Aedyth admonished. The old woman came alongside her and took hold of her arm. "Nor soon enough for Rhuddlan. He'd speak with you."

"Aedyth, I—"

"Enough, sprite," another voice interrupted. "Rhuddlan calls, and 'tis your duty to abide."

Mychael jerked his gaze from the girl to the darkness beyond the well and cursed himself for acting the besotted fool. He had been so intent on the maid, he'd not noted the man running up behind the old woman. 'Twas Bedwyr, the one who liked him least of all the Quickentree, and he had his hand on the haft of his knife, his message clear.

What did the old dog think? Mychael wondered. That he would ravish the girl?

Another glint of blade farther to the east caught his eye. 'Twas more than just Bedwyr calling him out, though he knew they dared go no farther. Rhuddlan would not have him hurt.

"What's this, Bedwyr? Trev?" the girl asked, her manner turning surprisingly imperious. "I need no escort here."

When the men didn't reply, but only finished unsheathing their blades, she went for her own knife.

Mychael grabbed her wrist before she could free the dagger.

The old woman gasped.

"Put up," he told the girl, even as he wondered who she was that Bedwyr acted so rashly on her behalf. " 'Tis for your protection that they act thus."

"And do I need protection from you?" she asked, pinning him with her gaze.

"Mayhaps." He spoke the truth and saw a fresh blush rise to her cheeks.

"Nay," she answered. "I think 'tis you who needs protection from them."

"And you would do the deed?" He released her with an odd reluctance, as if he might yet think of a reason to continue holding on to her. She smelled of lavender, luscious scent.

"Aye. I am Liosalfar, sworn to protect those in my keeping." The grim seriousness of her words and the gaze she leveled at him surprised him again. 'Twas no light thing she offered, and he wondered at the why of it.

"But still a chit who needs looking after," the old woman interjected, her mouth firming into a tight line. She gave the maid a tug, and this time the elfin girl moved.

Mychael stepped back and let her go, shifting his attention to the two men. Fools both. If he'd wanted to make away with the girl, it would have taken more than Bedwyr and one other to keep him from it. Had not the blade-master learned that much of him yet? For certes Mychael knew more of him, and now he would add another weakness to Bedwyr's tally. He would not forget that 'twas more than dislike the man felt, and that fear skewed the blade-master's judgment.

Bedwyr was with them to deep dark on the morrow and would bear watching. The caverns beyond the Magia Wall allowed little room for weakness, and fear was the dark's surest path to death.

Chapter 4

On a ledge high above the floor of a great cavern, and far below the land of Merioneth, Mychael knelt by a freshet of water and dipped his hand in for a drink. They were four days into the earth, three days past the Hall of Lanbarrdein, two and a half days beyond the Magia Wall, and into the home of the old worm on a scouting expedition to the deep dark. Not three paces from him, the stream poured over a cliff face and dropped into dusky gloom. His dreamstone blade gleamed brightly in its open sheath on his belt, spreading blue light into the mist roiled up by the falling water and glinting off the iron stars affixed to the leather guard that banded his right arm. A bow and quiver were slung across the pack he wore. An iron dagger, pattern-welded with a cutting edge of steel, hung ready at his left hip. His short sword was on his right.

Fires flickered along one wall of the cavern, dotting the darkness with yellow flames. He and Shay had set firelines to trap the old worm on the far side of the track Trig had chosen for the sortie. 'Twasn't the first time the captain had paired him with the young Quicken-tree to herd the beast off the trails so others could safely hone their skills in blind scouting the deep dark. He and Shay could blind scout caverns in their sleep.

They didn't trap the old worm every time they came below, but Trig was not wont to take any chances of late. Better to have the trail clear, he'd said. That meant setting firelines. Nothing could clog up a tunnel or a trail more thoroughly than the old worm. Although the smaller *pryf* could be prodded along with a dreamstone blade or sung into submission—wild though they'd become—the ancient one was where he was, unless stopped by fire.

Mychael heard the serpentine beast sliding in a slow rumble toward the other end of the cavern below, avoiding the flames they'd spiked with dragon seed, *hadyn draig.* The old worm knew better than to tangle with dragon matter.

Mychael brought his cupped hand to his mouth and drank. Water dripped off his chin, and he wiped it away with his sleeve.

A repeating arc of blue light cut through the darkness on the far side of the mist, catching his eye. 'Twasn't too far distant, coming from above a tunnel fire that was just starting to flame. Shay was finished with his last fireline. Mychael reached for his blade and returned the signal. 'Twas time to go. He dipped his hand in the stream for another quick drink before rising and loping down the passage that led away from the cliff face.

He and Shay had set their rendezvous point at a place where four tunnels converged in a cavern filled with animal paintings: graceful ochre and umber deer raced across the ceiling; a bear ran neck and neck with a bristling boar; a herd of bulls thundered in a swift curve over the top of one of the passages. All of them were fleeing a dark, hidden place depicted by slashed strokes of paint pouring out of a black crevasse.

When Mychael had asked what the images meant, Shay had made a warding sign with his fingers, muttering something about a place where even gods died. No matter how he pushed, the boy had not said more.

He'd found many such mysteries when he'd been alone in the caves. For those months, he'd been naught but a searcher following the path his heart set, a path that wandered through a world unlike any he had imagined. The Dragon's Mouth and the Light Caves below it had been as he remembered from childhood, but beyond the cavern of the scrying pool, at the end of the mazelike tunnels of the Canolbarth, was a cave of wonders he now knew was called Lanbarrdein, the Hall of Kings. 'Twas there he'd first held a chunk of bluish white crystal and felt it grow warm as it began to glow; and thus the fathomless abyss of darkness that had loomed in front of him—an abyss that he'd feared was the absolute edge of the earth from which all else fell into chaos—had been transformed into a heavenly palace wrought from the mother rock, alive with the light of dreamstone. And Lanbarrdein had been only the beginning of the wonders of the deep.

Yet for all that he had found, he had not found dragons.

Rhuddlan said he need not search, that the dragons would find him, if indeed he'd been called.

His jaw tightened. He had been called aright. This thing that churned through his blood, the restless yearning, had only grown in strength since his sister had freed the *pryf*. The last time, the night before they'd come below, it had been more than a calling. He'd felt the heat of it, the pumping of his blood freshly hot from his heart—wild, damned dragon heart that he'd feared since reading the red book Ceridwen had given him.

Fata Ranc Le, Madron called it, the Red Book of Doom, an inauspicious title, but accurate, for it certainly foretold his. He'd read it after Ceridwen and Lavrans had left, the sections in Latin and Welsh, and what he read had cost him many a night's sleep. A particular Latin passage had revealed a spell created by a long ago priestess, using dragon's blood to conjure a son out of the Druid priestess line of Merioneth. He'd been born of the Druid priestess line of Merioneth, and no son's name had been written in it until his.

Dragon's blood from his mother. That was what coursed through the paths of his body, what had filled him with a delirious dream four nights past. At the height of the nightmare that mirrored his vision, the heat had suddenly vanished, along with the delirium, and he had been left lying cold and shivering in his bed, beset by memories of the vision he wished had not been his.

Cursed blood. *Pryf* were dragon spawned, and he knew 'twas no coincidence that their stirring in the earth stirred him as well. The balance of power had shifted within the wormholes when Ceridwen and

Lavrans had broken the emerald seal. The holes he'd had access to, the smaller ones, had all closed up, been sucked back into the great wormhole, drawn by its growing strength and the steady hum of activity. 'Twas a lure for any man, a beckoning to come nearer and partake of its secrets.

He needed those secrets, needed the power conjured by the warm, swirling clew of worms that ringed the abyss and grew ever more golden the deeper one went, into the place where "whatever was" and "whatever will be" met and mixed. 'Twas there, in the timeless flux, that he'd found his only peace since coming north.

Rhuddlan had taken that away from him. The Quicken-tree leader had sealed the tunnels to the gate of time, forbidding anyone to go near the wormhole, saying it had gotten far too dangerous.

'Twas true. Mychael had felt that for himself, that the one great hole would as soon burn him alive as let him in, but the way would not be barred forever. Trig had taught him to read the ancient common tongue and elfin runes lining the passages of the deep dark, and told him that somewhere therein lay the keys to all the secrets of the abyss, though none had found them for a thousand thousand years: how to control the worms and the temperature fluctuations caused by their activity, how to direct their course and thus the course of the one who would enter the wormhole, how—in the end—to place oneself in time.

He could find the keys, he knew he could, and after the last bout of madness, he dared not delay. He would take what knowledge he had and begin his search. Unlike the Quicken-tree, he could stay below for sennights on end, following one hint of script to the next. Trig had shown him the way, how to read the marks in the rock and where things in the dark were not what they seemed but led to places stranger than what he'd already found.

Rhuddlan said there were times and ways to enter wormholes, and as a man bided the one, he must learn the other, or the rewards were not worth the dangers. Rhuddlan said he was lucky to have survived thus far. Rhuddlan said there had been only one dragon keeper in living memory of the Quicken-tree, and that was Rhuddlan himself.

Rhuddlan said. Rhuddlan said. Mychael had long since reached the point where he cared not what Rhuddlan said. He'd been called. The truth of it could not be denied, not even by the Quicken-tree man. He'd been called, and he had come. He would know why the wormhole and the weir gate and the dragons were all tangled in this maze of a puzzle that had become his life.

He reached the painted cavern before Shay, but not by much. A thin crescent of blue light appeared in the dark ahead of him, illuminating the curve of a passage that lay beyond the glow of his own dreamstone blade. 'Twas high on the wall above a scree slope that led down into the cavern.

Mychael leaned back against the wall and waited, breaking himself off a piece of seedcake and watching the curve of light slowly widen on the other side of the cave. He'd eaten a few unsavory things when he'd been alone underground, mostly tua—blind lizards—when he could catch the little beasts, but since meeting up with the Quicken-tree he'd been well supplied with food: seedcakes and catkins, strips of dried berry mash wrapped in green leaves—which they called murrey and which was not unlike the sweet pottage he knew by the same name—honey-sticks, acorns, apples. 'Twas all good fare, if a little short of meat.

"*Malashm,*" he called out as Shay ducked through the low opening and entered the cavern on his hands and knees. The crescent of the boy's dreamstone light expanded into a full, glowing circle when released from the tunnel, lighting up the herd of bulls above the passage and making them appear to move in the shifting blue light.

"*Malashm,*" Shay called back, signaling him before starting across the scree slope. The boy trekked over the pile of shifting rubble and rocks with a sureness of foot inherent in all the wild folk. Tightly wrapped chausses covered his legs down to short boots closed with silver rings. He wore a fitted shirt under his tunic. In dreamstone light, the clothes took on the look of liquid silver patinated with verdigris, and Shay's green eyes shone aqua.

As did Llynya's. Rhuddlan had sent her into the deep with Liosalfar, much to Michael's chagrin.

"Let's take the deer path," the boy said as he dropped to the floor. A leaf-bladed short sword was stuck in his belt, angling down his thigh nearly to his knee. "There's a connecting tunnel between it and Trig's route we can cut across. Save ourselves some time in catching up with them."

"Aye, we've taken too long as it is," Mychael agreed, pushing off the wall and heading toward the opening beneath the running deer.

'Twas the last day of their time below, and he was as ready as the next to begin their ascent. 'Twould not be long, though, before he was drawn back to the dark. He was always drawn back.

"Is that one of Moira's bannocks?" Shay asked, gesturing at the seedcake in Mychael's hand.

Mychael grinned and handed the food over. "I've got naught but a handful of acorns after this, so make it last."

"Aye, I will," Shay promised, then put the whole of it in his mouth in one bite.

Mychael shook his head, still grinning, and followed the boy out.

The passage of the running deer was high-ceilinged and broad enough to walk four abreast, a luxury in the deep dark, if one didn't mind the odd bit of worm slime. Shay and Mychael strode along its ample corridor, making good time. The first vibration hit them when they were a halflan from the painted cavern. 'Twas a sensation too familiar to be mistaken for anything other than what it was—the old worm on a run.

Mychael looked to Shay, who swore and dropped to one knee, laying his hand flat on the tunnel's floor. Mychael didn't need to use his hand. He felt the wave of power ripple up through the soles of his feet from the bare rock, a steady basso profundo trembling that quickly spread to every part of his body.

"Fireline broke and he's heading this way," the boy said, looking up with a sheepish grin. "Race you to the next tunnel." Before the words were out of his mouth, Shay had scrambled to his feet and was racing down the deer passage.

Mychael swore and took off at a run. 'Twasn't one of his firelines that had broken, nor was it the first time one of Shay's had, the boy's attention to detail being less than desirable.

'Twas a long way to a passage small enough to give sanctuary, nearly another full lan. Others were closer, but in the wrong direction with neither of them of a mind to try to beat the old worm to a safe hole by running toward him.

When the beast was less than a quarterlan behind them—and still picking up speed—Shay collapsed against the rock wall.

"Sticks!"

Mychael skidded to a halt opposite him. They weren't going to make it, not this time. Damn. His breath came in labored gasps. His body was doubled over from the stitch in his side. He looked across the passage and found Shay to be in the same pained, breathless position, except the Quicken-tree boy had a grin on his face.

"Fancy yerself as worm fodder, do ye?"

Mychael grinned back despite himself. Forget dragons and doom. Shay was going to be the death of him.

The old worm turned the last curve behind them, and the rumble of his movements rippled down into the tunnel where they stood, sending a fresh wave of vibrations up their legs.

"Fireline," Mychael gasped, still fighting for his breath.

They both dropped to their knees. Mychael pulled two sealed gourds off his pack strap while clenching his other fist around the haft of his dreamstone dagger, heating up the light. Shay did the same. Trig had drilled them a hundred times on the making of a fireline. There were seven steps:

One—heat your blades. Worms don't like light.

Done.

Two—draw a line across the cavern floor with your dagger, incising a shallow groove to hold the makings of your fireline.

He and Shay each carved a jagged slash on the floor, their steel blades scraping off each other when the knives met in the middle of the tunnel.

Three—pour a small amount of hadyn draig *out of gourd number one into the groove. Follow with gourd number two, shaking enough* roc tan *onto the* hadyn draig *to sustain a strong fire. Be careful!* Roc tan *has been known to spontaneously burst into flame.*

Mychael smashed his gourds against the tunnel wall, one after the other, and tossed the whole of them onto the floor. He looked to Shay and found the boy frozen in place, staring wide-eyed into the dark ahead.

Mychael looked too, and a queasy feeling rolled up from his stomach. 'Twasn't the dark that had frozen Shay. 'Twas the black face of the old worm filling up the hole and coming right at them. An odd smell pervaded the air, of worm and must and something burnt. He grabbed Shay's gourds and broke them against the floor.

Four, five, six—forget it.

Seven—there are three ways to successfully ignite a sulfur twig. First, holding the twig tightly between your thumb and first finger—

Mychael pulled a handful of the twigs out of a pocket sewn into his tunic and scraped them across the rock wall. He only needed one to light.

One did.

He threw them on the fireline, grabbed Shay, and ran like hell. A wall of heat slammed into them before they'd gotten ten paces. They stumbled, righted themselves, and kept on running. Behind them, they heard the old worm screeching and sliding, fighting himself to a stop, the sound of it like a cold iron bolt being forced into a too small hole, a deep, pained, heavy grating that echoed up and down the passage and spurred them on to greater speed.

Any march into the deep dark normally took two full days, and they'd gone two and a half beyond that, pressing forward from their last sortie. Trig was leading when he heard water in the distance, the rush and tumble of it as it fell over a ledge and splashed into a pool. The cavern of Crai Force was coming up and would be a good place to make camp.

He signaled a halt, and one by one the dreamstone blades behind him were extinguished, slipped into covered sheaths to conceal their blue light. He sheathed his own blade last, plunging the small band of Quicken-tree warriors into total darkness. A frisson of unease skittered up his spine. 'Twas something he never got used to, the complete absence of light this far down in the caves. The higher caverns and tunnels were riddled with veins of quartz that held dreamstone light for hours, life-sustaining light. The deep dark had naught but a darkness so coldly empty it sucked the life out of a man's bones. No Quicken-tree, not even Liosalfar, could survive in it for more than a fortnight, not even with dreamstones. The gates of time, the last outpost before the Magia Wall, were a refuge from the darkness, a sanctuary capable of reversing the ill effects of a too-long journey. Trig had abided there once during the Wars, letting the timelessness of the place seep into his bones and bring him around from a hazardous descent.

"Bedwyr," he said, and the man came down a short flight of stairs that had been cut into the rock. "Crai Force ahead at twenty paces. Take Math and Nia and scout toward the falls. Llynya and I will circle around to the south."

"What of Shay and Mychael ab Arawn?"

"They'll have the old worm beyond our track boundary by now, and know to return by way of the passages we marked. If memory serves, the cavern ahead is no more than a quarterlan long, too small for them to miss us." Trig had assigned the two to the firelines to keep Mychael and the blade-master from each other. He had enough to worry him, what with Naas's vision of five nights past.

"The ab Arawn boy would as soon live in the dark," Bedwyr said, his tone one of gruff condemnation.

'Twasn't the first time Bedwyr had complained, and if pressed, Trig would have agreed. Mychael ab Arawn had an affinity with the depths of the earth that went far beyond what any Quicken-tree could bear, and for certes he had an affinity with the timeless place that was the weir. The truth of that marked him clear enough.

"Make no mistake," Trig said. "Mychael ab Arawn is not a child. He's a man full grown, and we haven't seen the half of him yet." Not even close to half, if Nass knew what she was about. Trig had his doubts; Rhuddlan less so, but the old woman had barely spoken two words in the last fifteen years, and then she'd conjured a vision that was no more than a story any child knew and laid it at Rhuddlan's feet as if 'twas doom itself. Trig was holding judgment, but he was watching the boy as well.

Aye, he was watching the boy and every turn in the trail.

"Man?" Bedwyr snorted. "He and Shay are more like young pups than men, pups with no more sense than to follow their noses into trouble."

Trig recognized the fear in Bedwyr's easy dismissal, fear of the unknown, for Mychael ab Arawn was surely that. Many of the Quicken-tree had been unsure of taking him into their company, the stranger who had come to them from out of the deep dark in the heat of battle, a man raised among the hooded brothers of Strata Florida. He had not the gentle soul of his sister. Far from it. Trig had stood for him, though, and would again if needed. More than any other, Mychael ab Arawn had the right of their fellowship and, if necessary, their protection. He was the son of Rhiannon, the last seer of Carn Merioneth. He had proven adept at Druidic lore, and thus, like his mother, he was of use to the Quicken-tree—but the son was no meek thing to follow in anyone's footsteps. Madron despaired of ever turning him to her will or his duty. Even Rhuddlan was unable to tame the boy, but not for much longer. Ailfinn Map was coming, and there was not a boy or man alive that the Prydion Mage could not bring to heel.

The blood ran strong in Rhiannon's son, aright, mayhaps stronger than in any who had come before him. 'Twas what Naas had told them, that the boy would prove to have the stuff of legends in him.

"Dragon's blood," Trig muttered. 'Twas what set Bedwyr to twitching and what had kept himself awake for three nights in the deep dark and the night he'd spent above since the old woman had conjured her vision on the east wall.

Chiding himself for getting set in his ways, he reached out and unerringly clasped Bedwyr's shoulder, his senses of hearing and smell and a heightened awareness of proximity taking up where sight left off in the all-pervasive darkness. "We're a half day from the next crystal shaft. After we check it, we'll head back to Lanbarrdein."

Bedwyr agreed, mayhaps too quickly, calling Math and Nia forward to go on with him and leaving Trig to wonder if his second in command had grown overly skittish. Or mayhaps Bedwyr was only feeling the same unease Trig felt being so far down in the deep dark. Or mayhaps 'twas something else altogether. Damn vision.

They had been checking the western shafts, amethystine tubes of crystal, all summer. Now Rhuddlan was having them go deeper with every sortie, searching farther afield for trouble, when trouble was at their very door.

If Rhuddlan had let him skewer one of the wolfpack runners, they would have known a few things quick enough, and instead of looking for breaks in the damson shafts, they might be in the old tunnels far up under the northern ranges, smoking out skraelings. He had not forgotten where they lived, the dirty bunch, and should he live three lifetimes he would ne'er forget how they smelled. Foul, they were, pungent and odoriferous. He'd slaughtered hundreds in the last war and would do the same again, if they dared to mass on Merioneth's borders.

A sudden infusion of lavender brought his head around. Llynya had come up beside him, chewing on flower petals she kept in a small bag hanging from her belt. Trig had recognized the potion pouch as one of Aedyth's, but he could not fathom what benefit there was in chewing petals of lavender. He used them as a comfit, more often than not dipped in honey.

The sprite had made not a sound with her approach, the only clue of her nearness being the lavender, and for that he was grateful. Llynya had always been exceptionally light on her feet, and he was glad she still had one of her most intrinsic skills. Between her and Mychael ab Arawn, Trig doubted if they would leave enough of a trail on wet sand to be followed. In the caverns, they were both invisible.

He'd checked.

"Take the lead," he told her. "We're going to the south, away from the falls. Don't forget to read—"

"The marks at the end of the passage and just inside the cavern," she finished for him. "I have not forgotten, Trig."

Youth, he thought. Youth and impetuosity, and impertinence. She'd nearly drawn her dagger on Bedwyr, so Trev had said. Aye, and that must have given even the blade-master a start, to have an Yr Isddwfn aetheling set to flash steel.

A fresh burst of lavender told Trig she'd popped another bit of flower in her mouth. He would not have brought her so soon into the deep dark, but Rhuddlan had insisted, and surprisingly—for they seemed never to be of the same mind—Madron had agreed.

Llynya took the lead and he followed behind. At the end of the passageway, where it opened into the cavern, she stopped to read the marks in the rock with her fingers.

" 'Tis called Crai Force and is a quarterlan long," she said, and Trig nodded to himself. He had not forgotten. "The water is fresh and good and always runs, and in spring can flood the cave."

She continued forward, smoothing her hand along the wall.

"There're a few lines of history," she went on. "A couple of battles. Comings and goings. Who made camp in the cavern. Here's something interesting: Stept Agah, the last of the Starlight-born, was born beside the falls in the one hundred twenty-fourth year of the Twelfth Dynasty of the Douvan Kingdom. A bit before our time, eh, Trig?"

"Aye, before our time, sprite," he said, following her into the cave. The sound of tumbling water was louder in the cavern. A light mist filled the air. Off to Trig's left, Bedwyr gave an order, his voice echoing softly back toward the passage. There was no light, not so much as a flickering leak of dreamstone blade, and no sense of movement other than the Quicken-tree. All was as he had expected, yet something struck him as amiss.

"The Douvan Kingdom is mentioned again after—"

He reached for Llynya's hand, silencing her by pressing his thumb against the inside of her wrist. *There is danger in the dark.* She grew as still as he.

Trig turned, lifting his nose toward the center of the cave. With little effort he sorted through and discarded the green smell of the other Quicken-tree and Llynya's lavender. The various scents of earth were always the strongest ones in the caves, unless *prifarym* or the old worm had passed through. Neither had been there. The crisp, cleanly sweet smell of the water followed the earth smell. Beneath the water, he detected the scent of the rock. It came to him through his nose and left a faint metallic taste on his tongue. He licked his lips, exposing more of his tongue to the air. There was nothing more. Nothing. Nothing except . . . except . . .

He took a step deeper into the cavern, closing his eyes to direct his senses inward. There. At the edge of rock taste and earth smell lay the barest trace of something dry, and fine, and bitter. *Sha-shakrieg.*

Fear washed through him, sudden and icy. Spider people.

He released Llynya with a hissed command to fight and pulled his blade, throwing light into the cave. Instantly, a long, thin filament dropped out of the dark above him and wrapped around his arm.

"Bedwyr!" he roared as another filament caught him around the leg. *"Khardeen! Khar—"* His war cry was cut short by a filament wrapping around his throat. Llynya dashed in and slashed at it with her dagger. She freed him with a clean cut and twisted her body away before the next thread could catch her.

A scream of pure defiance tore through the air, and Trig whirled around to find its maker. 'Twas Nia, her body bound by a web of silken Sha-shakrieg threads, with more coming down out of the dark and wrapping around her, hundreds of them.

Bedwyr and Math were fighting their way clear of the threads entangling them, trying to reach her even as the sprite raced across the cavern floor. All to no avail. Nia began rising toward the ceiling, lifted upward into the dark by the unseen. She looked to be a star, a brilliant, shining, screaming star hanging by silvery threads, her body encased in a lustrous cocoon that reflected a thousand blue flashes of dreamstone light. Another filament snaked out of the dark and wrapped around her face, sealing her mouth shut and leaving naught but her final scream ricocheting through the cavern.

With a curse and a roar, Bedwyr cut the last of his bonds and let fly with his blade, hurling it beyond Nia to the darkness above her. Trig heard the knife hit home, and in seconds the shrouded, lanky form of a Sha-shakrieg fell to the cavern floor, trailing a silver filament.

A moment's silence followed the death, then the Sha-shakrieg dropped out of the dark and were upon them.

Chapter 5

An hour of walking brought Mychael and Shay to a place where they could hear a waterfall up ahead. They'd escaped the old worm by the skin of their teeth with little more than their pride scorched.

The green smell of Quicken-tree lingered in the tunnel they were in, a hint of freshness in the cool, damp air with an underlying scent of lavender that never failed to distract him. However did men survive with their wits intact outside the cloister? He did his best to keep away from her, but her damned lavender was everywhere.

Mychael palmed his dreamstone blade from out of its sheath and squeezed hard, reheating the dimming light to signal the others. Ahead of him, Shay did the same, but before they'd gone five paces, the Quicken-tree youth resheathed his crystal dagger with a flick of his wrist, covering the glowing haft and throwing himself into shadow.

"I smell something."

"So do I," Mychael said. "Liosalfar, and mayhaps supper, if we're in luck." He didn't mention lavender, as Shay was wont to speak of the girl all too often.

" 'Tis not Quicken-tree," Shay said.

"Are you sure?"

"Aye."

"Then what?"

Shay shrugged, looking ahead into the dark.

"Tua?" Mychael asked. For certes they had an odd smell.

"No, not tua." Shay glanced back over his shoulder at him. "Did you really eat tua?"

"Dozens."

Shay grimaced before sliding into the darkness on silent feet.

Mychael smelled nothing beyond the Liosalfar and Llynya, but he sheathed his knife to cool its light before following Shay. He'd been with the Quicken-tree long enough to know their sense of smell was keener than any hound's, capable of discerning knowledge from scent in ways beyond his ken. Something other than tua could be in the caves, yet in all the months he'd traveled beneath the earth, he'd found naught else of much substance. A few times he'd felt as though he was being watched, but he'd never seen anything, not even a trace of someone having been near. And he had looked, searched for anything or anybody that might help him find the dragons.

And, he vowed as another breath of lavender wafted to him, he would stay away from Llynya. The elf-maid stirred another brew to life in his veins and added fuel to a fire already racing out of control.

In camp he'd made a point of laying his bed as far from hers as possible, yet he kept awakening and searching out her sleeping form. Thus each night by the dying embers of the cookfire, he'd seen her sigh in her sleep and wondered at her dreams. He'd watched her hands unfold as she drifted beyond dreams into a deeper realm and wished he dared go near to see her thus revealed—with naught but the sweet essence of oblivion about her. And always, he traced the curves of her body with his eyes, following their mysterious paths into shadows he couldn't delve. He understood the physical longing inherent in love, but how could he be smitten with no more than what had passed between them? Or was it only lust that made him ache?

Not so her. She watched him like a hawk, true, but with a wariness in her eyes he well understood. He knew what he had become, and he knew his looks were far from a maid's desire. Those few who dallied with him in Carn Merioneth did it on a dare and never long enough to suit any need. That night he'd spoken with Llynya by the well was not the first time a maid had backed away from him with a warding sign.

Better to forget the girl and spend his days wandering the deep dark, where there were answers to be found without the distractions of lavender.

Shay stopped at the top of a rise in the tunnel and warned him of stairs ahead. Trig had said they would encounter such. 'Twas rough-hewn work left over from an age when the deep dark had been an oft used route, before the coming of the old worm. The sound of the water-fall grew ever louder as they descended the stairs, the passage leading them through a brief maze to the entrance of the cave, a looming empti-ness easily felt in the surrounding rock.

Mychael pressed his hand against the wall to read the marks that could be found at the beginning of every cavern in the deep dark. The cave named Crai Force was not so big, a quarterlan only. The water was good and tended to flood in spring. He walked forward slowly, with Shay a half step behind, smoothing his hand along the rock, expecting at any moment to hear the scuttling of tua. When he stepped inside the body of the cave, his expectations fell away. Shay had been right. Some-thing was wrong, and it had naught to do with tua.

"Meshankara mes," the boy whispered, drawing his sword. Battle was near.

Or just past, Mychael thought. The smell of fear and valor was unmistakable, even to him. He took Shay's hand and made a sign in his palm. How many?

Shay answered with two quick movements of his fingers. More than five. Less than ten.

Mychael slipped his iron dagger from its sheath. Only five could be the Liosalfar. He traced a cross on the boy's shoulder, left to right, down to up—they would search to the north, toward the falls.

Not fifteen paces in, they discovered Bedwyr, bound in some strange way and badly hurt. Shay dropped to his knees beside the older man and began slashing away at the bindings. Mychael pressed his hand to Bedwyr's neck, but could feel no more than the faintest flutter of life. He moved his hand farther down and felt the wet, sticky pool on Bed-wyr's chest.

His mouth thinned to a grim line. The battle had not gone well or Bedwyr would not have been left to die by himself in the dark, insensate and alone as the life ebbed out of him onto the cavern floor. For all their enmity, Mychael would not have wished such an end for the man. Shay cut the last thin fiber off Bedwyr's body and began murmuring strange words under his breath.

Mychael silenced the boy with a finger to his lips. They were not alone. He tilted his head to one side, listening beyond the weak sound of Bedwyr's dying breaths and beneath the rushing of the waterfall. He did not have a Quicken-tree's sense of smell, but his hearing was keen, and he heard something, a high-pitched, continuous hum seeming to come from above, beginning directly overhead and running to the north. Rising to his feet, he signed for Shay to stay with Bedwyr and set a course for the falls. Four other Quicken-tree needed to be found, mayhaps some who could be saved.

Quick and silent, he wove a path through the dripshanks hanging from the ceiling and jutting up from the floor, skimming his fingers over their smoothly rippled surfaces to mark his way and gauge his distance from Shay.

Bedwyr was dying, killed by an unknown foe. Four Quicken-tree were unaccounted for. He told himself a quarterlan cavern would make no easy end of Trig and the others, for a small cave could not hide much, even in darkness, but he feared the worst.

The noise came again from above, louder and closer, and he froze in place, not daring to breathe. His fist tightened on the iron knife. Whatever was up there, he'd not encountered it before, and mayhaps it was as good at blind scouting as he and Shay, needing little more than a scent or a sound to find its prey.

Or mayhaps 'twas a dragon.

A thrill of excitement coursed into his veins, speeding up his pulse. The beasts could kill. He knew that as surely as he knew the same awful truth about himself. But would they hum? In his dreams, they only ever screamed, letting out sky-scorching flames with keening cries that nigh cut through his heart.

The second noise faded to the north as had the first, and he followed, moving swiftly before he lost the way. He tracked it to a narrow arch made of two large dripshanks welded together at the top. Slipping through, he held his dagger at the ready. Spray from the waterfall misted the air on the other side, wetting the rock underfoot and dampening his face—and bringing to him a scent he'd feared he would not find . . . lavender.

She was near. He could only hope the others were with her and she was not alone.

Llynya crouched in the curve of a rock wall on the far side of the falls, having forded the stream to escape Trig's fate. Her captain lay bound and gagged somewhere to the south, completely wrapped in Sha-shakrieg threads. The same had happened to Math and Nia—but they'd taken Nia, hauled her to the roof of the cavern and stolen her away.

They'd killed Bedwyr. Llynya knew that for sure. She'd seen the silver bolt cut through the dreamstone light in a blinding flash and slice into Bedwyr's chest. *"Thullein,"* the bolt was called, named for the substance from which it was made, an ore mined by the Sha-shakrieg and forged in the far reaches of the desert with underling magic. Before the Wars they would come to the deep dark to dig for *thullein,* taking it back to the wasteland beyond. She'd been on her guard for nearly an hour, wracking her memory for bits and pieces of the Sha-shakrieg stories told around the campfires in Deri, and she'd come up with very little to cheer her. The spider people had been banished after the Wars of Enchantment, after their allies the Dockalfar had been overcome by the Liosalfar, which made the Sha-shakrieg unlikely to favor any Quicken-tree. 'Twas said elf shot, a precious stone mined by the *tylwyth teg* beneath the dragon-back of Mount Tryfan, was the surest way to kill them, but she had no elf shot arrows. Not many carried them since the Wars had been won. Rhuddlan had a quiver full, but Rhuddlan wasn't anywhere near the stick-forsaken deep dark.

A high-pitched hum streaked through the air above her, and she instinctively ducked, though logic told her a half-hand less of height would make her no more invisible when she smelled like a perfumery. 'Twas her saving grace, the lavender she carried, and had become a curse as well. She needed to keep herself so well infused in the caverns that she couldn't smell her way out of bed. None had guessed this newfound weakness, or recognized her need of the herbal for what it was. Rhuddlan would have forbidden her to come if he'd known, and Trig would have refused to bring her, both with good reason. How many Sha-shakrieg were in the cavern and their location was as big a mystery to her as why they had not already tracked her down and bound her. She could smell naught besides herself.

"Sticks," she swore under her breath. She was near as helpless as a babe, yet she dared not falter. Sha-shakrieg or no, if she could not master the labyrinthine heart of the darkness and find the written words of the Prydion Magi, the great wormhole would forever be beyond her reach.

When Ailfinn had first brought her to Merioneth, the trail she and the mage had taken from Yr Is-ddwfn had wound around the wormhole's outer walls, a trail hidden in the abyss of time. She'd felt the power of the hole then, swirling in the inner core just beyond where they walked.

The path she would take now was far more dangerous, for it wasn't that slip along the side into Yr Is-ddwfn, but a leap straight down the wormhole's throat. To survive the plunge into the flux of time took preparation. To not only survive, but to follow in Morgan's tracks, would take the knowledge of the ancients.

For certes Rhuddlan had not helped her cause. He'd sealed the eight tunnels leading into the wormhole with gossamer sheaths, one for each shimmering, pearlescent spoke of the weir gate, lucidly transparent but seals nonetheless. Seals she did not know how to open or break.

And Mychael ab Arawn would scarce look at her. 'Twas the warding sign she'd given him, she was sure, that had offended him beyond measure. In four days, she had not managed to speak one word to him, let alone enlist his aid. Every glance she gave him was met with his turning away, yet she found herself glancing at him more and more often. The Liosalfar did not shadow-paint themselves for descent into the caverns, and without the woad on his face he didn't look so fierce, but bore a deeper resemblance to his sister—silver-haired and golden-skinned and uncommonly fair of face, the way she also remembered Rhiannon, his and Ceridwen's mother. His eyes shone blue in dream-stone light, not gray, furthering her memory of the beautiful Lady of Merioneth. Long before Rhiannon had become a mother, she'd told her tales to Quicken-tree children. Llynya remembered a soft-voiced maiden and the enchantment woven by her songs and the melodies she played upon her harp. She remembered, too, the wondrous stories of faraway places and faraway times, of magical beasts and the women who tamed them, of wild, fell creatures and the heroes who slayed them.

'Twas with that same sense of enchantment that she oft found herself watching Rhiannon's son. He was no darkling beast as Aedyth had warned, yet Llynya could not help but wonder if he could be tamed to a woman's hand. Not hers, of course. Her future—what little there was of it—lay in a far different direction, and even if it had not, she was singularly lacking in womanly skills. No, 'twould be for another to give him the gentle succor of a female's touch, which he sorely needed. Any child could see that.

Still she would speak with him if she could, and try to win him to her cause, but even Shay had been unable to parlay a meeting between them. Trig, being captain, was an unlikely candidate for such a mission, and Bedwyr did naught but watch him with unconcealed animosity.

Or rather, he had watched Mychael ab Arawn. No mortal man concerned the warrior now.

The reality of her situation descended again. Mychael had saved her once, but none was likely to find her now. Even she didn't know where she was; she'd run blindly. She'd tried to cut Trig free, and Math. Threads had snagged her each time, not enough to hold her, but she'd lost her pack in the last tangling up, and with it her biggest stash of lavender. 'Twas best now to bide her time, to wait while the Sha-shakrieg made their retreat, which she thought the humming noises were a part of—the shooting of threads from one part of the cavern's ceiling to another in the making or unmaking of a web.

She started at a scraping sound to her left. 'Twas the second time she'd heard such beneath the rush of the falls. She peeked over the wall as she had before, squinting her eyes as if that would help in the darkness, but she saw naught and smelled naught, so she quickly scrunched herself back down into her damp cubbyhole, making herself as small as possible.

'Twas said spider people ate elf children if they caught them in the deep dark, and she wondered if they would recognize that she was no longer a child. Nia was not a child. They would not eat her, but Llynya shuddered to think what other tortures they might inflict. *Poor Nia!*

Her hand trembling, she dipped into her baldric pouch for a pinch of her herbal. She'd touched one of the spider people on her flight to the falls, stumbled over him, the dead one, and she'd thought to retrieve Bedwyr's blade. The Sha-shakrieg's clothing had been fine and soft in a way much different from Quicken-tree cloth, but when her fingers had brushed against his skin, her blood had run cold and she'd abandoned all thoughts of getting Bedwyr's dreamstone back. 'Twas only his arm she'd touched, and in shape 'twas much like her own, except bigger. In texture, 'twas not. He'd been covered all over with whorls, flat disks of spiraled flesh running up his arm.

Shuddering at the memory, she found a flower in her pouch and placed it under her tongue, not daring to chew. Mayhaps 'twould be a long time before she could replenish the sack, and without the smell and taste of lavender to hold her fears at bay, she would be overcome with despair.

Mychael had lost her scent, and something akin to panic set in. Trouble though she might be, he would find her. She should never have been brought so deep.

Another sin on Rhuddlan's head, for now Bedwyr was dead and the company overcome. He reached for his dreamstone blade, but stopped with his hand just above the hilt. Foolishness would not save her or the others. A flash of light to guide them might also get them killed. So near to the falls he could not hear any movement, but Llynya at least could not be far.

He turned to the south, stepping into the stream. Smooth, water-worn rocks made poor footing, but he waded in up to his knees, into water like liquid ice, and soon discovered why he'd lost her scent. A wall of rock or a huge boulder—he could not tell which—curved along the streambed on the other side, the top of it just within reach of his hand. If she'd gone beyond the great outcrop, 'twould be enough to block the fragrance of the lavender she chewed.

Taking care where he placed his feet, he followed the rock down-stream to where it turned back in upon itself and began rising out of the water to higher ground. 'Twas not a boulder but a wall three handspans thick, a gradually spiraling wall. He took up the faint trail left on the stone, and when he turned the last curve was suddenly upon her. The rich scent of lavender washed over him in the same instant that her blade flashed blue and slashed open the skin on his face with a bite of steel, cutting him high on the cheekbone.

'Twas instinct alone that enabled him to block her next blow. On the strike that followed, he captured her knife hand and lunged for the rest of her, grabbing her and pulling her hard against his chest. She struggled as if 'twas death she fought, but he held tight and forced her to drop the dagger. The clatter of steel and crystal on stone was a raucous backdrop for her breathless cursing.

"Not a child . . . s-sand eater. Let go of me. Bedwyr. Sticks! Filthy leaf-rotter . . . not a child—"

"*Llynya.*" He spoke her name harshly, tightening his hold and pressing his thumb against the inside of her wrist in warning. *There is danger in the dark,* he signaled, and despite the noise and light of her attack and what it might bring down on them, he swore most of the danger was in his arms. She'd nicked him on the wrist when he'd blocked her, and warm blood ran down his face. Curse him as a fool for forgetting she was Liosalfar and not a helpless chit lost in the dark. "Llynya," he repeated, and again pressed his thumb to her wrist.

She jerked her head up at his second warning touch, and the eyes staring at him in the fading glow of the fallen dreamstone blade were wild with fear. Her heart beat in a frighteningly rapid pattern against his chest. Her breathing was uneven. The icy mist settling in his wound was so cold, the bone beneath the cut ached, but 'twas no colder than the Quicken-tree girl. She was shivering uncontrollably, her clothes soaked through.

Are you hurt? He signed in her palm, but got no response before the last flicker of blue light died off her blade and plunged them once again into darkness. He was left with a vision of her stricken gaze and her fair face, of the dark mass of her hair falling down on her shoulders, twisted and braided and stuck through with leaves and twigs.

Llynya, he signed, and when she still did not respond, his own heart began beating too fast. Mayhaps he was too late. Mayhaps she'd already been alone too long and had begun her decline. She was not as strong as the others, not yet as hardened to the march and the weight of the darkness.

He swore to himself, at a loss. Shay would have seen the flash of dreamstone light and would come, but they could not stay where they were.

As if to prove him right, the crunch and scrape of some new thing in the dark sounded behind them, off to the east. Mychael whirled, keeping Llynya at his side.

The smell that came after the sound was enough to decide him. He swiped his hand up the side of her arm—*come*—and took off, determined not to be caught in the trap of the curved wall with God knew what readying itself for attack. He knelt for her blade and sheathed it with his own, never once letting go of her. She had no choice but to come with him, but whether she did it willingly or unwillingly, he couldn't tell. The strength of his grip overrode any effort she might make.

He wasn't going to lose her.

Swivin' dirt and light-sucking rock. 'Twas always the same. Dirt and rock. Dirt and rock. And a bit of worm flesh now and then. Christ save him, how long had he been scrabbling through the dark searching, ever searching? He'd once been strong and bold and feared. Now he was—what?

A swivin' dirt scraper. A leg dragger.

A leg dragger whose fortunes would soon be on the rise.

A groan strangled in his throat as he grabbed the next handful of dirt and rock and pulled himself up and forward in the tunnel. Some of the passages he traveled grew so narrow he had to crawl out of them. Such was this one, but this one was worth the trouble. He smelled lavender at the end of it. He'd been smelling it for days, here and there, and he was finally getting close, very close, to the source.

'Twas a woman. The underlying scent was unmistakable, and she was just ahead in the dark, in a cavern he'd left a few days past because of the strangers who had come, the newcomers. Swivin' odd they were, shrouded figures with bandaged faces come to dig in the caves for pieces of rock.

Fools, all fools. The treasure of the dark wasn't in the rocks. 'Twas in the holes, if a man had the strength to endure them.

He'd endured, so help him God. Caradoc, the Boar of Balor, had endured. And because he'd endured, the other ones, the dark soldiers, had found him and made their twisted promises to him. Skraelings they called themselves, and if he'd had them by his side during the battle for Balor, the land above would still be his. The smell of them alone would have been enough to send his enemies running. "Quicken-tree," the skraelings called the bastards who had slaughtered his garrison and left him to die in the bowels of the earth.

The sounds of the fighting had drawn the skraelpack south to where they'd found him half-dead on the shores of the black sea. A dirty bit of business they'd done there with the washed-up remains of his men, before they'd taken him back to their tunnels in the north. Foul, stinking places. He'd never known such stench, but they'd patched him together of a sorts. He felt a smidge stretched, a bit askew, not quite right, but he was alive and growing stronger and was no man's prisoner. When he'd had all he could take of the north and demanded they bring him south again—*south to the wormhole!*—by God they'd done it posthaste.

A grimace twisted his mouth as he took hold of his left knee and dragged his leg up closer to his body, readying himself for the next pull forward.

The newcomers were another lot altogether, wasting their strength hacking away at dirt and rock, working by the light of their yellow lamps for hours to gain even a small amount of stone.

He'd tried stealing a piece of their hard-won ore, thinking it precious, but he'd not gotten far before a thin, stinging rope had been thrown around his wrist, pulling him up short and forcing him to relinquish his prize. They'd be paying for that soon enough. The rope had disappeared nearly as quickly as it had come, but he'd been burned and had a scar to show for it. Bastards. They looked more to be fighting men than miners, so 'twas a fight he would give them. Skraelings would run ten leagues in a single night for the promise of blood, and he had sent word with the last pack of dark soldiers that had come south that blood was to be had.

Not many who came up against a skraelpack survived in one piece, literally. The night they found him, the stinking creatures had been chewing on his arm when he'd come to, and he'd sent three of them flying before they could get a good piece out of him. He had the scars from that bit of mischief too, teeth marks the size of tally sticks. The newcomers' swords were long and sharp, but not as long and sharp as skraeling teeth.

The green-smelling Quicken-tree had sharp swords as well, but their days were numbered—mark his words—had been numbered since the day Balor had fallen to the swivin' green horde. And then they had added torture to his torment by sealing the tunnels leading to the hole. He'd howled his misery then. Now he and the skraelings would kill them all—all but one. One he would keep alive, for the Quicken-tree knew much that he needed to know, much that he would know, if he could just catch one and ask it a few questions with his knife.

He hadn't as yet. Damn fast they were and tricky in the tunnels, impossible to track with any consistency, and the skraelings had been strangely reluctant to go after them. Wait, he'd been told. Wait and watch, and he would have all their skins as his reward. So he'd waited, and he'd watched, and he'd sent tidings of the newcomers. But his waiting was over. The Quicken-tree had made a mistake. They'd brought one who smelled of lavender, the scent so rich and sweet, 'twas impossible to lose her trail. He'd have her quick enough even without the skraelings.

A pox on all women. 'Twas Ceridwen ab Arawn, his own feckless betrothed who had cost him the life he'd known. Well enough that another of that fair rotten sex should return him to glory of a different sort. He would squeeze the secrets of the deep out of her, drop by perfumed drop, and bargain with her carcass if needs be for more. They knew. The blue-bladed bastards knew about the friggin' great hole, and they would know how he could get back in without being burned alive.

Wicked curse! He gritted his teeth and dug his hand into the floor of the tunnel. Then he pulled himself forward and up, shoving with his good leg.

'Twas always there in the back of his mind, those shifting shades of heliotrope and green flowing through the abyss, a swivin' siren's call. But every time he'd gone near, the heat of it singed and scorched, eager to consume him if given a chance.

Retreat was no less painful. When he'd first fallen into the hole, he'd despaired of ever getting out. Now he despaired of ever getting back in.

Redemption would be his. The cleansing waters, the blood of the Lamb, 'twas all there in the worm's mighty hole, and more, endlessly more, on and on into the promise of the Lord—the salvation of immortality. He'd had a taste, and he would have another.

There was a way back in, there had to be, and the Quicken-tree knew it. 'Twas why they'd killed everyone else, to keep them from knowing what power lay within the abyss.

He knew. He'd been there and been marked. 'Twas the bright copper stripe in his hair that had truly set the skraelings off him. Even the largest of them had grown wary upon seeing it. Wary, and then excited. Aye, 'twas the stripe that had saved him from their jutting, misshapen jaws.

He stretched his arm out again and touched cold, wet rock, not dirt. His pulse quickened. 'Twas the opening of the tunnel into the cavern. The smell of lavender was strong, so strong he knew that if he reached out with his hand, she would be there. His.

And so she was, for an instant. His fingers, stretched to their fullest, touched soft cloth, but 'twas the merest flick of it, a brush against him as she ran by.

No! He lunged for a better grasp, scrabbling out of the tunnel to prevent her escape, and was caught, his wrist bound by the quick burn and twist of a stinging rope before his shoulders had cleared the opening. The bastards! They had no right! He tried again, even knowing she was gone, and once more felt the lash of the intruders.

Swallowing his howl of rage, he jerked his hand free and sank back into his cold and lifeless hole. They would die. They would all die. Next time, he swore, there would be none to save her.

Chapter 6

Mychael ran with Llynya through the dark, skirting
dripshanks and pools, making his way toward Shay.
Something had been back there, something bigger than
a tua, and it had been after them, suddenly scraping
and scrambling, the stench of it bursting upon them in
a rush. If he'd hesitated a moment longer, it would
have caught Llynya. He was sure of it. They'd lost the
beast, if beast it be, in their wild dash through the
stream, but they were now both dripping wet, which he
feared would do the girl no good. He needed to get her
to a place where they could use their dreamstone
blades. The heat coming off a single crystal hilt more
than doubled when two were bound together. 'Twould
be enough to warm her, and mayhaps seeing the light
would ease her fear.

    The trail split ahead of them, with the path he'd
taken earlier heading across the cavern floor and another winding higher in a course of stairs up the wall.

He chose the stairs, keeping her close behind him. If trouble came, he would as soon have the high ground and a wall at his back—and the elf-maid at his side, fierce chit. He hurt like hell and was still bleeding. Half-frozen and scared witless, she'd cut him with a speed and a finesse he would be hard-pressed to better, ready in an instant to fight and, if needs be, to kill.

She knew what was in the dark, knew enough to be terrified. Sand eater, she'd called him, leaf-rotter, and cried Bedwyr's name. Only by the light of her blade and his touch had she recognized that he was of her company, a telling lack.

Sticks, indeed, he swore to himself. She couldn't smell friend from foe, let alone the hundreds of other things she needed to discern to keep herself safe in the deep dark. Like the old ones whose senses were no longer keen, she should not be allowed beyond Lanbarrdein. She belonged in the forests, not in the caves where the ability to blind scout meant the difference between life and death.

Leaf-rotter. 'Twas a coarse oath for a Quicken-tree to use, and he was sure it had naught to do with dragons, nor, he prayed, did the awful stench of the thing that had scrabbled after them. If dragons scraped and stank and lurked in fetid places, he was doomed.

They were nearing the place where he'd left Shay, when a high-pitched hum streaked across the black emptiness in front of them. He stopped and pulled her closer to his side. She did not balk, but followed his lead, keeping her one hand in his and holding on tight. Thus she clung and shivered and no longer thought to fight him. Thank God.

Her skin was soft, her fingers fine-boned yet strong as they clasped his. And the smell of her, lavender-breathed and something more, something essentially female at its core. No one at Strata Florida had thought to warn him about the scent of women, though they had warned of plenty else: the fire in women that made men burn, the lasciviousness of the female nature, and of mysteries too profane to be told.

Pointed ears and slender curves. Woad tattoos. Leaves and twigs in tangled hair. How many nights had he prayed that the monks had not lied?

He stared into the darkness ahead, waiting, the iron dagger grasped in his fist. If there was danger to others in the wild blood pulsing through his heart, he feared she would be the first to feel it. 'Twas more than simple lust she roused in him, he would swear it, though she roused him easily enough. He'd won and lost that monkish battle with himself enough times over the years to recognize its sweet edge, but the yearning he had for the girl went beyond lust—or so he'd thought. With her plastered up against him as close as anyone had ever been, her panicked breath warming his shoulder and melting his resolve, he wondered if in his inexperience he had simply underestimated the power of crude desire.

Shay had stolen a kiss from her in the guise of comfort. Dared he succumb to temptation and try the same? Dared he turn and draw her close and set his lips to her cheek? Soft skin there, to be sure, and not so far from her mouth. Would such a touch be enough to ignite the lasciviousness of her nature as the monks had warned?

Somehow he thought not. More than likely, she would gut him and be done with it. Aye, she was not one to be trifled with. She'd proven that the first night at the well, going for her knife against the blademaster himself. He should have taken greater heed.

The hum came again, farther away, and he wondered if they would not both be better served if he set his hand to getting them out of the cavern alive, rather than trying to immolate them with lasciviousness.

Monks, he thought. What could they know of women's natures?

"C-come," she suddenly said, slipping around him on the stairs and pulling him along by the hand. She was still shivering like a leaf in the wind. Not much fire there to burn a man, he granted.

In three steps, she led him off the stairs into a tunnel that twisted into the earth. 'Twas a novelty for him to be led anywhere by a woman, though Madron did her best to try. He followed the maid more out of a dubious impulse to stay near her rather than the common sense that told him she'd already gotten herself lost once and needed his help.

The tunnel grew progressively narrower and lower, curling in on itself, until they came to the end of it with him crouching for lack of headroom.

" 'T-tis safe to light the b-blades here," she told him, and he believed her. They were out of Crai Force. Holding both crystal hilts in his hands, he squeezed and ignited a lambent glow. The heat was slow to build, but 'twas there, coming to life between his palms.

A shuddering sigh escaped her, and she reached out with her hands, opening them to the light, warming herself as if he held a fire.

" 'Twas n-near frozen I was," she stammered.

With good reason as far as he could tell, looking her over. Her hair was sopping wet, her clothes sodden. Water dripped off the hem of her silvery green tunic, pooling on the floor. The warm puffs of her breath made small vaporous clouds in the cold air.

"Are you hurt?" he asked. She didn't look to have a mark on her—unlike himself—but that didn't mean she'd escaped her ordeal unscathed. Nor could she be any too happy that 'twas he who had found her. He doubted if she would have fought Shay so fiercely.

"Nay." She shook her head, and water fell from her leaves and twigs like a fine rain. "I am of a piece."

'Twas what he'd thought in Riverwood when he'd seen her in the wych elm, though he'd thought her of a far different kind of piece. Even knowing she was Liosalfar-trained had not prepared him for her skill with a blade. Her first strike had been like lightning coming out of the darkness. The ones that followed had been equally fast. Over the months in Carn Merioneth, he'd done his share of swordplay with the Liosalfar, and he'd not seen any as quick as the girl. With a blade in her hand, her speed defied belief, making him wonder if some other force was at work. Mayhaps her dreamstone dagger was *druaight,* an enchanted thing come up from the deeps of time. Madron had explained such to him, how the relics of an earlier age oft resurfaced as things of wonder.

He looked at the knives in his hand. His blade, Ara, shone more subtly blue than Llynya's, which leaned toward green. Not so subtle was the difference in the hearts of the crystals. The center of Ara's hilt gleamed white. Llynya's hilt held a shattered violet flame, the color lightening as it crackled up through the crystal, while remaining deep and unfathomable at the core. But whether 'twas enchanted or not, he couldn't tell. It felt no more unusual than his own glowing blade—a seeming magic to him, though Trig had assured him the phenomenon was as natural as rain. The way of it had simply passed beyond men's ken.

Once the maid's fingers were warmed, she leaned back against the tunnel wall and began searching through the pouches hanging from her belt and a green baldric bandoliered across her chest. She rummaged for a while before pulling out a soppy pinch of lavender and offering it up.

"It will ease you, if you like."

When he shook his head, she stuck the petals in her mouth. She was a mystery, aright, he mused, a mystery of terror and tears quickly overcome, of fast blades and flowers.

"We're safe here for the moment, long enough to get warm," she said, her head bent once more over her pouches. She must have had a dozen of them, but had lost her pack.

"Safe from what?" he asked.

"The Sha-shakrieg."

"Sha-shakrieg?"

Her gaze flicked up to meet his, and like Shay's, her eyes shone aqua in the dreamstone light. She held a piece of seedcake in her hand, and it, too, was the worse for having been dunked in the river. "Spider people." She put the seedcake in her mouth.

Spider people. *Sweet Jesu.* Mychael squeezed the blades tighter and cast a wary glance toward the tunnel opening. God's ballocks. She'd trapped them. 'Twas what he got for following his damned impulses. "What are spider people?"

"A wasteland tribe from Deseillign," she said around the mouthful. "They were allies of the Dockalfar in the Wars of—" She stopped suddenly, and he turned to find her staring at the side of his face where she'd cut him, where the blood still trickled down his cheek. Her own face paled at the sight.

He started to wipe the blood away with his shoulder, but she stopped him.

"Wait," she said. "Wait. I have *rasca.*" She reached for her pouches again, and he noticed her fingers were trembling.

"Are you sure you're not hurt?" he asked, hoping she hadn't just realized 'twas him tucked away with her in this far corner of the cavern. Mayhaps the light was only now strong enough for her to see. 'Twould be enough to startle anyone who felt a need for warding signs in his presence, to find him looming over her with a pair of daggers at the ready.

"Aye," she said, though the wavering of her voice belied the word. " 'Tis just a bit of the scare left in me. I'm not usually so skittish, but the spider people eat elf children, and it being a while since they might have seen one, I was afraid they would make a mistake and accidentally chew off my arm, or take a bite out of me before they realized I was full grown."

Christe. His jaw tightened, yet he felt some relief. Compared to spider people, he must indeed seem a savior.

"You should have killed me, if you thought that."

"I was trying, going for your throat. I don't know what's worse, that I missed, which could have been the death of me, or that I didn't miss a little more, seeing that 'twas you. Here, eat this." She came up with another piece of wet seedcake and gave it to him. He took the cake and found it sweet, still redolent of clover honey. The taste heartened him. Next out of her pouches was a small bundle of wrapped leaves tied with petioles, the *rasca*. He knew about the salve. Moira used it on everything from scrapes to breaks, and its soothing touch would be welcome.

"Come and sit, so I can tend you." She dropped to the floor to sit cross-legged in front of him, artlessly arranging herself in a tangle of arms and legs.

Obeying for reason's sake and not because she had told him to— for it seemed she had done naught but order him around since she'd regained her voice—he sat down and gave himself over to her ministrations. Mayhaps 'twas just her way of dispelling her fears, which he was all for, and the rewards of being this close to her were well worth the small annoyances. For certes the scent of the lavender she'd eaten was like the very breath of spring flowing into the cold, dark corner where they hid, and the view was unsurpassed. Her eyebrows were drawn close in concentration, two perfect black wings sweeping over long lashes and aquamarine eyes. For a moment, he'd thought she was going to cry again, but the crisis seemed to have passed, and without doubt she'd realized 'twas he who had rescued her. That knowledge heartened him even more than the seedcake.

She leaned in close, using the wet hem of her tunic to clean his face, and a length of her hair slipped over her shoulder. He watched it slide down and find a resting place across his thigh, where it dampened the leg beneath and made his mouth go dry. Aye, she stirred him, aright. Near ebony her hair was, a startling contrast to the fairness of her skin. He'd felt silk once, on a bishop's robes, and was sure her hair would have the same soft fluidity should he dare lift it with his fingers.

He did not, but he was sorely tempted to steal one of her leaves. She had arboreal badges to spare, not only in the live cockades of oak, hazel, and rowan in her hair, but in the sinuous tattoos twining 'round her wrist and up her arm. He could see long, curved willow leaves and pairs of lance-shaped ash leaflets winding through the elfin runes marking her skin. A delicately lobed oak leaf, glistening with river water and no bigger than the center of his palm, dangled precariously above one of her pointed ears—magical things, those, intriguingly pretty when seen up close, and faintly erotic.

He shifted uncomfortably on the floor. Could any Welsh maid entice him so?

With her fingers pressing the last of the *rasca* into Mychael's wound, Llynya stilled, startled into a moment of immobility by what she sensed. Her nose twitched. Not daring to move anything else, she kept her gaze on the herbal and the curve of his cheek, wondering at this unexpected turn and how it was possible that a man with a four-inch gash across his face who had been dunked in an ice-cold river from the waist down could be aroused—and the even greater improbability that it was she kindling his response.

Yet there was no one else about.

Mayhaps she'd changed even more than she'd thought. More likely, she was mistaken. Would be a rare wonder indeed if anything got through her nose in one fragrant piece.

Double-checking, she closed her eyes and gave herself over to her next inhalation. Warmth flowed into her slow and easy, a sweet-edged heat wrapping around her senses and tracing a path that led to a memory she had forgotten . . . *a cool spring night in the Mid-Crevasse glade, moonlight shimmering on the entwined bodies of a man and a woman.*

Her eyes opened, but this time the deep-scent vision did not all dissipate. The warmth stayed with her, settling into her veins and kindling her own response—a pleasant if undeserved respite from her guilt. Guilt that she'd cut him like that, when he'd saved her yet again. She was shamed by the deed. 'Twas the damned lavender making her scent-blind. Aboveground, she would have known immediately that 'twas him, but she could hardly admit to it. Neither was she likely to admit to the warmth she felt. 'Twas disturbing, and she prayed Mychael had not her nose for scents. As to the vision, she remembered the rest of it well enough, how Ceridwen and Lavrans had mated in the foresty glade, the salt-tinged musk scent that had drifted up into the trees, as if they'd made union with the earth herself. Aye, and she was a child indeed not to have foreseen such a possibility for herself.

Unbidden, her gaze drifted a few degrees lower, to Mychael's lips—soft skin caressed by his breath, a gentle indentation in the upper curve, the small nick of a scar near the rightside corner. He wanted to kiss her. In truth, he wanted more than a kiss.

And would she set her mouth to his? She knew kisses. Morgan had kissed her in the boar pit beneath Carn Merioneth, pressed his lips to hers in a sweet touch.

Aye, she was tempted to try kissing again, mayhaps overly so. The fascinating changes she sensed taking place in the small space between her and Mychael was a lure near impossible to resist. Beckoned by the breath warming their shared air, she moved a hairbreadth closer and sniffed ever so quietly, more a trembling of her nostrils. The scents were soft and rich with a restlessness not his alone. With a kiss she could taste the mystery of those scents, let them dissolve on her tongue and flood her senses. She had not felt the desire for such before, not with Morgan, and not from Shay's brief kiss. Was this, then, an enchantment of Rhiannon's son? Some Druid charm?

A warning sounded in her mind, making her pull back a bare degree. Sticks! He was far more dangerous than Aedyth thought, for she feared she could be caught in this spell. Was her heart not already racing in anticipation?

Proof enough of the folly of the deed, she told herself, that she could be so easily swayed from her course. She knew what came from kissing—at the least, ever more kissing. Ceridwen and Lavrans had done little else after the night at the glade. Always kissing, they'd been, and it took no great gift of sight to realize a man was less likely to drop a lover down a wormhole than a Liosalfar. At the other end, a kiss was no light thing. In truth, she oft wondered if 'twas Morgan's kiss that had set her on her present course, for that kiss had bound them in a way they should not have been. Better to be forewarned of Mychael ab Arawn's surprising charms and leave him alone.

She moved back to where she'd been and took his chin in her hand to scrub at a recalcitrant spot. The *rasca* had stopped the bleeding and would keep the wound from putrefying. "I could teach you how to block the strike I used," she said, feigning ignorance of his state and applying common sense to her own.

"I did block you." He showed her the proof, the bleeding cut on his wrist.

She released his chin and turned his wrist into the light. Not only had she sliced his face open, but his knife hand too. She'd probably ruined any chance she'd had of getting him to help her. He'd saved her and she'd done naught but hack into him.

" 'Tis no great wound," he said, pulling away.

She shook her head, denying him. "No, I sliced you open well enough. The arm's not so bad, but your face is a mess." She returned her attention to his cheek. "The cut's a deep one, an even swipe from stem to stern. Most would have let up on the high end, but Trig taught me to wield a blade when I was scarce old enough to . . . well, scarce old enough to hold one, but he's going to have my hide for this bit of work."

Mychael's pride, which had gone amissing while he'd been mooning over Llynya's leaves and hair and eyes, rankled back to life under her bold summation. Sliced him open well enough, had she? Wasn't he the one who had saved her? And what had that long look at his mouth been all about? When she'd moved in closer, he'd nearly kissed her. Now he wished he had and saved himself her thoughts on how well she'd cut him up.

Aye, he knew the way of a kiss, but he did not know the way of her. He was beginning to think the fragile loveliness that so enchanted him was more illusion than fact. Mayhaps the warrior he'd discovered in Crai Force spoke more truly of her nature. Warning enough for him to take heed where she was concerned.

"The captain could stitch you closed," she went on, "but if 'twas me, I'd wait for Moira." She paused for a moment, and her voice grew less sure. "Truth is, archer, neither of us comes out good in this."

Especially him it seemed. Cut by a maid with a bloodthirsty blade and a sweet mouth.

"Where neither of us comes out good is in this rock-bound trap," he said. "We're getting out of here." He made to rise, but she stopped him with her hand on his leg. It was enough to freeze every muscle in his body. Had the girl no sense at all?

"Nay, you don't. Stay put while I finish. 'Tis safe here. Shashakrieg prefer the open caverns, where they can throw their wicked threads to make webs."

Webs. That's what he'd heard, the slinging of webs across the cavern ceiling, not dragons.

"And the other?" he asked, relaxing when she removed her hand to bind his wrist with a bit of gauze pulled from another pouch. It, too, smelled of *rasca*. "The thing on the far side of the river that scrabbled up out of the dark? What does it prefer?" They weren't safe. He was sure of it.

She shook her head, dislodging another shower of water droplets. *Jesu.* Every move she made was designed to enchant, and he was a fool for noticing.

"I know not what that was," she said. "Tua?"

"No tua ever smelled like that."

"Mayhaps not," she agreed. "But the walls were written on along the stairs, marking this place as a sanctuary of old, when the track was well used."

Sanctuary? This? He looked around the barren walls, his spirits sinking. 'Twould be better to die of wildness than to spend the last of his days in such a place. He reached out and pressed his palm to the rock behind him, checking, and thankfully felt nothing. The Dragon's Mouth called to him more strongly than this lost hole.

"Whatever safety this place held is long past," he told her.

Her gaze lifted from his hand to his eyes, and one of her eyebrows arched a fraction higher than the other. "You can read the walls without marks?"

He shrugged, dismissing the skill. Madron knew he could follow her father's path. She was the one who had explained the traces of magic to him. Until then he'd thought 'twas something in the air that made one place feel different from all the rest, or mayhaps something in him. Now he knew it was Nemeton's doing.

"Is that how you get into the wormholes?" Her voice had become a whisper filled with equal parts awe and hope, neither of which he found auspicious. He preferred to keep the wormholes, and his knowledge thereof, to himself—a preference Rhuddlan cared not one whit to honor.

"No," he said with no intention of elaborating. Madron and Rhuddlan offered naught but warnings when it came to wormholes, but Mychael knew when the holes were safe to enter, feeling it in a way far more graphic than he felt Nemeton's magic. The bard's marks were subtle, there for an instant and then not again. The power coming out of a wormhole was not so coy. The holes said enter, or they said beware, and since the freeing of the *pryf,* the weir gate always and only said beware.

"No?" She sounded vaguely disappointed, then even more curious. "There is a way of it, though, isn't there? One you could teach?"

"Teach?" He cast her a narrowed glance. Mayhaps he had not seen the truth of her even yet. Not an enchanted forest faerie or a Liosalfar warrior, for if she sought those swirling depths she was simply crazed. They would eat her alive more surely than any spider people. She had to know that. No Quicken-tree was allowed below who didn't know the dangers of wormholes.

"We could make a trade," she went on.

"For what?" he asked incredulously. She had naught that he wanted except a kiss, but a bargained for kiss was worth nothing. Cloistered as he'd been, even he knew that much.

She quickly reached for her pouches and began emptying them. "I have treasures."

Twigs, acorns, and bits of grass spilled onto the tunnel floor, followed by wet wads of feathers and thistledown. A few crystal shards rolled free.

He looked at the piles of matted fluff and miscellanea, and his patience ended. She'd cut him and enticed him and mocked him with her offer to teach him how to block her strike. Wasn't he the one who had disarmed her, taken her knife away from her? Who would have been cutting whom then, if that had been his purpose?

And now she'd proven herself no different from the others. Everyone wanted his knowledge of the wormholes.

"I have no need of your simples, girl, and we've lingered here overlong."

"Girl?" She glanced up at that, and there was no mistaking her ire at his rude dismissal. "Have you heard of the Dangoes, *boy*? Or the Pillars of Manannan? Do you really know all that is in the deep dark, and can you find what you want without knowing?"

"If it exists, I can find it. Which is more than I would suppose of you. Does Trig know you can't find your way in the dark?" He was not looking for a companion on his search, and if he had been, she would be the last he'd choose. She muddled his brain more surely than wine. And how did she know he was looking for anything? Rhuddlan and Madron were the only ones he'd talked with—or rather, been forced to confide in. The Quicken-tree man was not one to let a stranger or a secret linger in his domain; and dangerous as she was, Madron was his only likely ally.

Whatever argument Llynya had been ready to offer next died on her lips.

Aye, he thought. They had come to the crux of the matter, which for all his fascination with her was not about a kiss.

"Does he?" he asked again, though he knew the answer.

"I can find my way," she said, and changed the subject by dipping two of her fingers into the remaining salve and smearing it on his face wound. "Now hold still."

He wasn't dissuaded. "You're scent-blind. You can't smell friend from foe, or north from south, or danger when it's upon you." He winced at the roughness of her healing touch. Moira did not hurt a person so. What a fractious elf the girl was. For certes he had to have been mooning not to have noticed her faults before.

" 'Tis a passing thing." She made her admission brief and scooped up another dab of *rasca*.

He caught her hand when she raised it to his cheek. "Then until it passes, you should not be allowed beyond Lanbarrdein. Bedwyr lies dead in the dark, and I would not have the same happen to you. Nor would Trig."

"Trig doesn't know." She pulled her arm free with a quick jerk even as he released her.

"He will soon enough."

"Not if you keep your silence. A simple promise could—"

"Promises made in the dark are easily broken in the light of day," he told her, then immediately wished he hadn't. The words had naught to do with what she'd asked; they were oft-quoted advice for the love-lorn, which of course she was not. Nor was he, he added in silent disgust. The trouble he suffered from, while not all lust, was most decidedly not love.

"Mayhaps," she answered, "but I would have yours."

Sweet innocent. She nearly swayed him with the hesitancy of her request, as if she knew his promise might come with a price, but his course was clear—and did not include her.

"No."

Her mouth tightened, and after wiping the last of the *rasca* back onto its bed of leaves, she began retying the petioles. "Some say you ought not to run free with the Liosalfar in the caves."

He knew that to be true. Bedwyr had been one of them, but if she would bluster at him, she'd have to find a heftier threat to wield.

"And soon they will say the same of you."

She had no immediate reply to that, and for a moment he thought he and common sense had prevailed, but she gathered her wits and proved him wrong yet again.

"I would stand with you, Mychael ab Arawn."

Not so much as a flicker of emotion inflected her words, but 'twas the first time she'd spoken his name, and he was not unaffected. Just as quickly, he renamed himself a fool. 'Twas idle banter at best. Rhuddlan would not listen to a lavender-addled maid should the tide of opinion turn against him.

"I stand alone." He always had, since he'd been five years old and ripped from family and hearth, and he saw no end in sight until Ddrei Goch and Ddrei Glas were at his side.

"So will I, if needs be," she said, pinning him with her gaze. Emotion aplenty inflected that statement, and it was all coolly convincing. She was the warrior again.

Stubborn wench, he thought, stifling an aggravated sigh. No Quicken-tree alive would choose to travel alone past Mor Sarff. Except for this one, it seemed, the one least likely to survive the journey.

"Why?" he asked. "What calls you so strongly into the dark?" She'd already gotten herself lost and half-frozen and frightened, and was scent-blind into the bargain. The spider people were still skulking about, and she knew she was their preferred first course. So what compelled her?

No answer was forthcoming. Silently, she repacked her acorns and fluff into the pouches, her movements stiff with unconcealed frustration. There was a truth to be found in her, and 'twas obviously not what he'd been thinking these last five days, nor was it what he'd thought in the last hour.

His gaze skimmed the contours of her face, and for once he did not allow himself to be misled by her delicate beauty. Rather, he noted the furrowing of her brow and her eyes, grown old before their time, and the resolute line of her mouth as she bent to her task. The years did not lie as tenderly upon her as he'd thought. The sadness he'd first seen months past in the oak grove above Carn Merioneth, and again in Riverwood, was still with her, a sadness that had begun when Morgan ab Kynan had been defeated by another's blade.

Aye, she'd lost a friend.

Or had Morgan been her lover?

The sudden question formed all too clear a picture in Mychael's mind, and he swore to himself. He'd been ludicrously naive. He had known Morgan, and the Thief's easy way with women, and Llynya was of age. Both Ceridwen and Lavrans had still been mourning Morgan's loss when they'd left to go north.

The elf-maid must be mourning too, and mayhaps contemplating a foolhardy venture into the wormhole that would surely bring her death. Did she think she would find Morgan in there? His expression grew grim as he watched her pull the last pouch closed by its double loop and tuck the ends into her belt.

"There is no margin for error in a wormhole, Llynya," he said, restraining himself from grabbing her and shaking some sense into her. "None, especially in the weir gate. No safe passage if a traveler missteps, and the cost of failure is higher than any sane soul would choose to pay."

"You are here," she countered, her chin lifting.

'Twas true, but she did not know the price he'd paid for his dalliances. Moira and Madron had seen the scar that ran the length of his body, an extension of the blaze in his hair, his gift from the wormholes.

"By the grace of God I survived, but I would not trust your life to the same. Nor would Rhuddlan. You know as well as I that the wormholes are forbidden to the Quicken-tree." And there was the end of it. Rhuddlan had forbidden him the same, but he felt no compulsion to obey. He was not Quicken-tree.

"I am only half Quicken-tree," she said, sending his unvoiced argument back at him with a hint of challenge, as if she dared him to gainsay her to do whatever she willed.

A fierce chit, aright, he thought as he rose to his feet, sure to give someone trouble. He'd been wise to avoid her up to now, and as soon as he got her out of the caves, he'd take to doing it again. No good could come from trailing after her. He'd meet someone else to kiss, someone who was not in love with another.

"And the other half?" he asked, handing back her dreamstone blade.

"Yr Is-ddwfn." She stood up and took the knife.

Mychael had heard the name before. 'Twas another tribe of *tylwyth teg,* the same as Ailfinn Mapp, the mage Rhuddlan searched for, and mayhaps explained her pointed ears.

"Then I'll make sure Rhuddlan also forbids your Yr Is-ddwfn half from coming below."

" 'Tis not so easy to forbid the Yr Is-ddwfn."

"Mayhaps not," he conceded, sheathing his own dreamstone blade in preference of the iron dagger, "but I'm sure Rhuddlan is more than equal to the task." No maid, however brokenhearted and bent on self-destruction, would get past Rhuddlan. Nor would she get past him. With a gesture for her to follow, he started back down the tunnel.

*   *   *

Llynya stared after him, crossing her arms over her chest and bringing the warm crystal hilt of her blade close to her heart. Arrogant sapling, she thought, soaking up the soothing light. He had called her *girl*. She was Liosalfar. Hadn't the truth of it been running down the side of his face? No girl could have cut him so well. No girl could have cut him twice.

Mayhaps no girl would have cut him at all.

There was a thought, was there not? Mayhaps she'd wounded his pride more deeply than his cheek.

They had not gotten off to a good start, but pride could be mended, wardings apologized for, wounds healed. Gods, since first seeing him she'd done naught but make her task more daunting. If there were another to whom she could turn, she would abandon Mychael ab Arawn out of hand, but there was no other. 'Twas either him or no one, and his trick with the wall proved him well worthy of better effort on her part.

Of course, he'd turned down her treasures too, proving he was unacquainted with the value of such things. Madron's Druid had much to learn.

The archer's blue light faded as he turned a corner, and she took off after him. She would not fail this side of her own grave in conquering the time weir of the great wormhole. Mychael had told her nothing she had not already known, neither of its forbidden nature or its dangers, and she was dissuaded by neither. 'Twould take another's peace to steer her from her course—and the Thief of Cardiff had not found peace.

She balled her free hand into a fist to keep it from a sudden trembling. Gods save her, she feared Morgan was still falling. The sensation of it would come upon her at the oddest moments, visceral and fearsome, and change even the brightest day into darkest night. No amount of lavender could save her then.

'Twas because of her last fight that Morgan had been lost to this world, to his world. She had deserted him, left him to face the Boar of Balor alone instead of fighting by his side as Rhuddlan had sworn her to do. She'd left him to slay a hairless devil-priest, but the nightmare of Morgan's falling had not left her. She had to find him, as much for her own salvation as his.

She caught up to Mychael at the end of the tunnel, and they

stepped out onto the stairs into a flood of dreamstone light. Below them, Shay, Trig, and Math stood on the cavern floor with their blades held high. The joy she felt at finding them safe was quickly dispelled when her gaze fell to Bedwyr at their feet. The sight of the old warrior lying motionless in death nearly undid her.

There had been so much death of late, death and trouble and an unraveling of the threads of life. Time was when autumn had meant gathering the earth's bounty for the long winter months of storytelling in Kerach—the Quicken-tree wintering ground. Summer had been a time of the sun *in excelsis* and warm, lazy days for doing what one pleased, and spring a time of glorying in the supreme magic of blossoms.

The glory had been short-lived this year, lasting barely long enough to greet the dawn of Beltaine before the Quicken-tree had descended into battle, and naught had been the same since.

They tracked the Sha-shakrieg for a half day deeper into the dark, hoping to catch them with Nia still alive, but such was not to be. The spider people had left Crai Force by way of a passage hidden behind the waterfall. The trail was rough-floored, cold, and damp. They did not blind scout, but kept their blueknives glowing strong and hot, forging ahead across ice-crusted pools and coming out through another sheet of water that poured from a hole above them into a damson shaft of cave-like proportions—and 'twas there they were forced to concede defeat.

A web had been strung across the narrow end of the shaft, a thickly spun obstruction. Trig approached it with caution. The others followed.

"What is it?" Shay asked, coming up beside the captain.

Mychael wondered the same. He'd not seen its like in all the months he'd spent in the deep dark.

"A war gate, the bastards," Trig said, tight-mouthed. He'd been cut across the face and one eye, a purple welt attesting to the stinging lash of the spider people's fighting threads. Other cuts marked his arms, and his hose were torn.

Mychael stepped forward and felt the web. 'Twas made out of wide, strong strips of material, darkish gray, tattered along the edges and not at all like true spider silk. The web itself was divided into eight triangular pieces put together and woven around and around with a double spiral. The outside edge was attached to the damson shaft by dropped loops, a sticky substance holding the threads to the jagged protrusions of amethystine rock. Four wide threads crossed all the others, three going straight from the ceiling to the floor and the fourth cutting diagonally across the three. Two thinner threads were knotted around where the diagonal and the middle vertical thread met.

Shay pulled a knife to take to the ominous thing, but Trig caught the boy's wrist before he could strike.

"Leave it be," the captain said. "Unless ye would bring the Shashakrieg up out of the wasteland to the very shores of Mor Sarff. From there 'tis but a day's march into Merioneth, and they well know the way."

"But what of Nia?" Shay demanded.

"Aye, Trig, what of Nia?" Llynya also asked.

"The two knots on the web are for the two deaths," Trig said, ignoring the hint of rebellion in their voices. "One on each side. 'Tis a sign of fair balance. They don't mean to kill Nia."

"So we just let them have her?" Shay did not sound willing.

"Not even a Liosalfar captain can pass a war gate without permission from Rhuddlan," Trig said, not sounding any more willing to leave Nia.

Behind them in the cavern, Math called out, "Trig. Come quick."

Shay and Trig retraced their steps to where Math knelt on the floor, leaving Mychael alone with Llynya at the war gate.

The elf-maid turned back to the web and slanted him a look. "I am not a Liosalfar captain," she said. "Are you?"

Trouble and more trouble, he thought. He understood what she wanted. He understood why, but when she lifted her blade to the web where Trig could not see, he grabbed her hand and spoke to her under his breath. "Trig is right. We have one lost and one dead, and I would not have more. Rhuddlan will gather a fighting force, and we'll return."

Her gaze slowly lifted from where he held her, and her eyes met his through the jacinth light.

"You cannot keep me from what I must do," she said, and he knew she spoke not of the war gate, but of the wormhole.

"I can keep you from this," he said with utter certainty.

Her gaze slid to the thickly spun web, then back up at him. "Aye. For now 'tis best," she conceded, and he let go of her knife hand. She did not immediately turn and leave as he'd expected, but continued looking at him as if she would say more. When she did not, he tensed.

She was thinking something, but he'd be damned if he knew what. Finally, after what seemed like a small eternity, she turned on her heel and left him at the gate.

He let out his breath. 'Twas the last time he dealt with her. He swore it. Whatever tears he thought he'd seen were long dried. Whatever concerns or imaginings he'd had of her had all been misplaced. She didn't need a hero. She needed a keeper, but 'twould not be him. He would stay with the Liosalfar to the surface and see her banned from the caves, then would come back on his own.

The elf-maid stopped next to where Math and the other Liosalfar knelt on a smooth stretch of the shaft floor. Her shadow rose above the others on the far wall of the cave, a slim darkness fragmented by the dreamstone light streaking through the crystals in a chaotic pattern. Only one place on the wall was free of the confusion.

Mychael lifted his blade higher, tossing light against the patch of darkness. Llynya knelt with the others, removing her shadow from the chaos, but the darkness remained. A crack or an opening perhaps? To one side he detected an unusual flat surface of rock, a chiseled plane, and on it mayhaps a mark.

The Liosalfar changed position in their search, and the entire rock face danced and weaved with the light and shadows thrown by their dreamstone blades. With the new patterns of chaos, the dark place disappeared. Had it been no more than a trick of the light then?

He tried to find it again and couldn't. Still, 'twas a place he would remember and return to when he could.

He walked over to where the others knelt on the floor. In their rush toward the web, none had noticed the glasslike shards scattered across the water-smoothed rock next to the stream. This was what Math showed them, and 'twas what led them to the break hidden in the jagged peaks and valleys of the rich rock encrusting the rest of the floor.

'Twas why they'd come to the deep dark, to see if other damson shafts had broken like the one Mychael had found before the battle for Balor.

Trig muttered something under his breath and leaned forward to put his hand in the gaping crack. His fingers no sooner breached the surface than a chill ran up Mychael's spine. 'Twas hard to see clearly in the shifting light of dreamstone blades, but he would swear a wisp of darkness tore away from the blackness deep in the fissure. It reminded him of nothing so much as the picture in the painted cavern, and like the graceful ochre deer and the thundering herd of bulls, he wanted to run. Another wisp tore away, and this time there was no doubt of its rising up out of the fracture. Trig let the smoky stuff flow over his hand, feeling it with his fingers. A foul curse escaped him. Math made the sign Mychael had seen Shay make earlier. The boy was doing the same. Llynya was motionless, staring into the new-fledged chasm.

Looking grim, Trig rose to his feet and eyed them one by one. "We're three days past Lanbarrdein," he said, "and must make it back in two. The Sha-shakrieg would not risk their lives to come to the deep dark and then leave without *thullein*. Carrying the ore will slow them down. With haste, we can return and catch them before they reach Deseillign." His gaze shifted to the web, and his jaw hardened. "We'll know then why they crossed the Magia Wall into the deep dark, breaking the treaty forced on them five hundred years ago when they lost the Wars of Enchantment." With no more said, he raised his hand into the air, giving the command to march.

Math followed him out, then Shay. Mychael made sure Llynya went before him. She gave the war gate a brief glance, but made no more move to disobey.

At the edge of the waterfall, Mychael looked back too, his gaze searching the wall and finding naught. Then he looked to the seeping crack in the floor. A faint burnt smell wafted up from the fracture with the smoke, reminding him of the broken fireline when the old worm had come at them, for it bore a similar scent. 'Twas redolent of rot and decay, and the chill rippled through him again.

He turned and followed Llynya, plunging through the running water to the path beyond, knowing 'twas no good thing he left behind.

Deep in the shaft on the other side of the war gate, Varga of the Iron Dunes, leader of the Sha-shakrieg, watched the Quicken-tree leave. The Liosalfar had seen the breaking of the earth, as he'd intended. 'Twas far worse in the south, the tunnels there filling with dread smoke, the portent of doom, the coming of Dharkkum—unless it could be stopped.

Skraelpacks from Rastaban had passed the eastern edge of the Rift into Deseillign a month earlier. The same were ranging west, where a Sha-shakrieg troop had found debris from a skraeling encampment in the outlying *thullein* basin. The Quicken-tree would feel their bite soon enough and know the danger that was awakening.

The Liosalfar had an Yr Is-ddwfn aetheling with them, proving that old alliance still intact. Fair tidings, mayhaps, and fair tidings were in short supply this day, especially for the Lady Queen of Deseillign.

He looked behind him to where two of the company spun a death web for the Lady Queen's youngest brother. Senseless loss. His soldiers were already talking of revenge, a sure course of destruction he would not allow any to take. There was but one enemy for them to fight.

On the far side of the shaft was the warrior they'd captured, a woman. Silver threads wrapped her from head to foot, except for the opening across her eyes and nose. Thus she watched, but could not cry out. She hid her fear well for one so young, too young to have known the Wars of Enchantment and thus too young to know much of Sha-shakrieg or skraelings.

Taken unaware by the Liosalfar stumbling into their mining oper-ation, Varga had seized the woman more out of reflex than deliberation, but he'd quickly seen the opportunity she represented. Her capture would bring the Light-elves down on Deseillign in full force, and lead-ing them into battle would be Rhuddlan, the Elf King. He would come to free the woman from the ancient enemy of the *tylwyth teg*.

Such a path was not without its dangers. The Lady Queen had not sanctioned the taking of hostages, and for certes not any Quicken-tree Liosalfar. She did not take kindly to those who would usurp her rule, and there was no one she hated more than Rhuddlan, the Scourge of the Wasteland, who had once sought to destroy her. Her hate went no deeper than Varga's own, but he did see reason, and he saw Deseillign's doom if they fought on alone. They needed the Elf King. For now was a time of need, when ancient bonds must be renewed, dreamstone crystal and *thullein* reforged, and the Magia Blade resurrected from the ashes of war.

Now was a time for dragons.

Chapter 7

The ragged band of Liosalfar came up out of the deep
dark onto the sands of Mor Sarff, the subterranean sea,
with no more than a day and a half having passed since
the battle with the Sha-shakrieg. Black waves of the
rising tide rolled up onto the shore and washed at their
boots, dampening feet grown sore with the relentless
march. They'd eaten little and rested less, pressing forward, knowing Nia's only chance lay with their quick
return.

Mychael was the last to leave the tunnel. By all
rights, 'twas Trig's place, but both Trig and Math had
succumbed to the thread poison embedded in their skin
within hours of leaving the damson shaft. The *rasca*
they'd used to treat the wounds had worked but little
against the wounds inflicted by the Sha-shakrieg
scourge.

Mychael had seen the captain's first stumble and
had not waited for a second before dropping to the rear

to guard their retreat and urge the others onward. Thus far, no one had questioned the pace he'd set. Neither Shay nor Llynya had dared in his present mood, and Math and Trig had no strength for dissent. Only blind stubbornness kept the two of them going.

"Shay," Mychael growled, gesturing toward the damson cliffs. The boy nodded and veered off from the group, holding his blueknife high to light the crystalline rock face. The cliffs began to glow a deep violet-blue, and soon they could see the pearlescent bore holes ringing the headland, eight in all, the tunnels to the gates of time, the entrances to the great wormhole.

The Liosalfar had stopped there on their descent six days past, checking the gossamer seals of ether Rhuddlan had put on the tunnel gates to keep the *pryf* from getting back into the weir. Except for the clew of golden worms that never left the swirling depths of the abyss, the *pryf* were needed in their nest. No dragon would come to an abandoned nest—so Rhuddlan had said—but five months of freed *prifarym* had brought them nothing but wildness.

Wildness everywhere and not a dragon in sight.

Mychael slogged through the wet sand, gritting his teeth against exhaustion and the flame of heat licking at him from beneath his skin. The damn stuff had come upon him in his sleep when they'd made a brief camp after the previous evening's meal, slipping into his consciousness on the fleet, fiery wings of a dream—and on the breath of war.

Sha-shakrieg. Spider people. He feared he'd found his enemies, the source of his river of blood.

He ran his hand back through his hair, then wiped at the sweat beading on his upper lip. He'd had the elf-maid's kiss in the dream, before it had turned into a nightmare, a kiss and much more, but the sweetness had been short-lived, ending in the flames that had found purchase in his veins.

She should not have been a part of it, that remnant of the fiery vision that had first come upon him in Strata Florida. Down to his bones, he knew no good could come to her from him, but since their closeness in Crai Force when she'd tended him, he hadn't been able to shake free of her. The feel of her soft skin lingered on his fingertips like Nemeton's magic. The scent of lavender met him at every turn, whether she was near or far. For certes she'd marked him somehow, no doubt with her elfin magic in hopes of bending him to her will.

Christe. As if he would have any will left when the fire finally took him and the shadows rose into legions. Against that day, her will stood no chance a'tall—and neither did he without Ddrei Glas and Ddrei Goch to fight by his side.

And he was doomed to fight. The surety of that truth tightened around him with each passing breath. He would fight. There would be blood. He'd taken the bait of the dragon lure, and the price would be paid.

A thin curl of pain raced down his arm, one of many threatening to undo him. He stopped it with a swift clench of his fist, swearing beneath his breath. The blood-churning madness had never before come upon him in the caves. That it had now was no good sign, and worse yet that Llynya had slipped into the heart of it. He had to get to the surface. The Quicken-tree thought him immune to the heaviness of the dark. They were wrong. He felt it, and with the fire running through his blood, 'twas near unbearable. He needed sky above him, before he was crushed by the flames and the dark and the sheer weight of the earth surrounding him.

Aye, the madness was upon him, and delirium as well. Specters had hounded him out of the deep dark as surely as any spider people. He'd felt eyes upon him, seen fleeting shadows disappear behind him on every turn of the trail, heard scuffling where no one was to be found. And the smell. They'd brought the rotting smell of the black smoke up from the deep dark with them. It haunted his steps.

He looked to the front of the group. Llynya and Trig were carrying Bedwyr's body with the maid in the lead. Math plodded along beside them, his head hanging low, one arm limp at his side. With the light coming off the cliff face, Mychael saw the purple festering of Math's wounds and the unnatural stiffness on the right side of the man's body. The spider people possessed baleful weapons, poisoned threads and razor-sharp bolts of *thullein*. He knew not what Rhuddlan would come up with to fight them. Llynya spoke of elf shot, while Shay wondered if enough of it still existed in the world. The mines beneath Tryfan were said to have long since been played out.

Mychael had thought the mines only legend, the stuff of his mother's stories. She'd been a master tale-teller, weaving words together with her voice and a delicate power that had forever engraved them upon his heart, stories of the iron-spined, dragon-backed ranges in the north and the mountain halls of the Douvan kings, of dragons and caverns filled with treasure, and of an age of elves and men. Since his return to Merioneth, too many of those tales had proven true for him to doubt the others. With war upon them, mayhaps he would yet see the wonders of Tryfan.

"Wonders," he muttered to himself. 'Twas hell seeking him out, not wonders.

Up ahead, Math staggered, falling behind, and Mychael swore again. God's blood, but he would not lose more Liosalfar, and they could not carry another. He lengthened his stride, then broke into a run when Math's knees buckled.

"Llynya! Hold!"

The maid looked back and, upon seeing Math, loosed her grip on Bedwyr and came running. Mychael reached the man first, with Shay close behind.

"Sticks," the boy whispered, sinking down on his knees next to his fallen comrade.

Mychael thought worse, but said naught. Math was pale, his muscles tight with pain, his eyes squeezed shut. Strange words poured out of his mouth.

Delirium, Mychael thought, the beginning of the end for them all. "What's he saying?"

" 'Tis a prayer for the dying," Llynya answered, dropping down next to Math and pressing her hand to the young man's forehead.

"He's dying?"

"No." She smoothed Math's lank dark hair back off his brow. "But he thinks he is. 'Tis an old tongue of the *sídhe* he's speaking. He'll feel better when we're out of the caves."

He wasn't the only one.

The maid ran her hand down the side of Math's face, tenderness guiding her touch as she bent over him and cooed soft words of solicitude—and all Mychael could think was that if Math wasn't dying right then and there, he might want to consider it for the kind of attention he was getting.

"Give him your lavender simple," he ordered gruffly, "and get him to his feet. If he wants to pray, he can do it in Merioneth."

A quick glance passed between Llynya and Shay, as if each thought the other should speak up on the side of reason. He quelled Shay with a look the boy knew well enough not to misinterpret. The maid, damn her, defied him.

"Math needs rest, not just simples," she said, her chin lifting with determination. "We all do."

Wrong, he could have told her. He didn't need rest. He needed to get out of the swivin' caves before they ate him alive.

"If the Sha-shakrieg had been following us," she went on, as if he didn't already know the truth of it, "they would have attacked before we reached Mor Sarff. We're safe here."

The hell they were.

"Get him to his feet," he growled, repeating his order to Shay, who knew better than to disobey, "or give him to the mother ocean. We're moving out of here, and we're moving out fast."

Left alone, Trig stumbled to a halt. He tried to steady his breathing to clear his mind and think. Pain scoured a deep line across his face where he'd been wrapped by a Sha-shakrieg fighting thread. The eye it had crossed was near blind. *Rasca* was no balm against the spider people's poison. The wound burned like fire on his skin, but the threads had not been steeped to a killing strength, or both he and Math would have died in Crai Force.

Aye, dead they should be. Curious, that. He'd never known the Sha-shakrieg to take half measures.

He looked up, instinctively turning his face toward the light, and realized they'd reached the damson cliffs and Mor Sarff. He should have known; the smell of salt was strong. 'Twas not far now. He lowered the rest of Bedwyr's body to the beach, then watched as water lapped at the shroud they'd made of their cloaks. Behind him, he heard voices.

"Ah, and come on now. Open up, Math." The sprite was bent over the warrior, putting something in his mouth. When Math ate it, she closed her pouch and shoved her shoulder under his. Along with Shay, she got the fallen Liosalfar to his feet.

"Llynya!" Mychael ab Arawn roared from up the beach, and Trig saw her stiffen. "Llynya!" he yelled again.

With obvious reluctance, the sprite left Shay to struggle on alone with Math. She did not look well. Her face was drawn, her strides unsteady as she climbed the beach toward the headland. Mychael had pushed them hard, mayhaps too hard, but Rhuddlan would be pleased to know he had done what was needed.

Trig's gaze drifted back to Shay and Math. The threads had

slashed open Math's tunic and burned a line up his arm and around his neck, marking him with the purple poison from the bia tree, wicked sap of the wasteland.

"You won't," he heard the sprite say a moment later, her voice edged with an angry tremor. He looked up the beach. She was faced off with Mychael, her feet planted in the sand, her arms akimbo. "Nobody's questioned you so far, but you'll not get away with that."

Mychael's back was to him, and Trig couldn't hear his muttered reply, but he saw Llynya blanch, and he thought he had better rein the boy in. They had nothing left to give him, either in speed or strength. Mychael had gotten them to Mor Sarff in record time. No more could be asked.

Before Trig could move, Llynya stalked off, coming back to the water's edge. An angry flush colored her cheeks.

"Help me get Bedwyr farther up the beach," she said upon reaching him.

Aye, Trig thought, she was right. His second should not be left in the surf. 'Twas well past time for rest and food. Mayhaps someone still had seedcake to share, and catkins' dew.

Nay, he remembered. There would be no catkins. They'd drunk the last of it when they'd made their rough camp. He would send Shay on ahead for more . . . and for reinforcements. Aye, for reinforcements. That was the important thing. Another damson shaft had broken, fell tidings, and the day's trek had taken an odd turn, even withstanding Mychael's foul mood. He'd liked not the feel of the tunnels on that last stretch up to the sea. Eyes had been watching, and even through the dense scent of the bia sap, he'd detected the stench of skraelings. That they dared to come this far south was proof of more than trouble brewing.

Aye, he'd send Shay on ahead to Merioneth. The boy had strength to spare, and Trig trusted he would stay out of trouble, given the seriousness of their circumstances.

"Trig?" He felt a hand cup his chin and looked up to find Llynya leaning in close and staring into his eyes. "Can you hear me, Trig?"

"Aye," he said gruffly, and pushed her hand away. He was not so far gone as that. "Come on, then."

Between the two of them, they carried Bedwyr higher up on the shore, laying him at the foot of one of the trails that wound up the dark cliffs, leading to the *pryf* nest. Math was leaning against the rock face

with Shay supporting him and looking uncomfortably cowed. Mychael
had drawn his crystal dagger and was pacing a trough in the sand in
front of the cliffs, looking up at the nest twenty feet above them.

The open catacombs writhed with the movements of the worms.
Light from the crystalline headland shone on their slick greenish black
bodies, revealing which tunnels were active and which were open. The
trick in getting through the *pryf* nest was in choosing the right trail from
the beach to get to an open tunnel. In times bygone, before they'd been
sealed in the weir, the *pryf* had been easy to herd. Now 'twas a good day
to make it up to the nest without having a worm come rushing down the
trail and sending everyone scrambling for the beach. Like all creatures
that had tasted the weir, they wanted back in the hole. The only thing
keeping them out was Rhuddlan's seals.

"Shay, take Math up. Hold to the left," Mychael ordered, pointing
out a path. "Llynya, go with them."

The two young men started out, but the sprite didn't move. She
had a stubborn set to her mouth, though not enough to offset the wariness in her eyes. 'Twas not the path worrying her, Trig knew. Any one of
them would have chosen the same. Still, she was hesitating and looking
to him.

"Go on, girl," Trig said. "Mychael and I will carry Bedwyr."

Her gaze shifted to Mychael, seeking something the boy was unlikely to give. Assurances had not been his strong suit on the trek.

"Go," Mychael said, dismissing her with a gesture and a harsh
tone. "You'll not want to be part of this."

The sprite turned and fled, leaving Trig to wonder what Mychael
meant. 'Twas not like Llynya to run off if she had something to say. He
wished his mind were clearer. There would be no time for rest and food
if they started up to the nest now. He should order a halt, for everyone's
sake, even Mychael's. Mayhaps especially for Mychael. There was an
unhealthy edginess about the boy.

Mychael looked at him then, turning away from watching Llynya
as she reached the others. Trig found himself staring at a stranger's face
framed by a mane of disheveled yellow and copper-colored hair. The
caverns were cool, the shore of Mor Sarff even more so, yet sweat dampened Mychael's forehead and cheeks. His skin was flushed, his muscles
tight with strain, and when their eyes met, a cold, hard knot formed in
Trig's stomach. He instinctively made a warding sign . . . *Shadana.*

The younger man noticed the flicker of movement, and his mouth twisted in disgust. "I thought better of you, Trig."

He'd thought better of himself too, that Bedwyr's worries were overblown and that Naas's vision would come to naught. He'd been wrong.

"Then ye have not seen yerself this day." Trig knew men's gazes, knew what lurked behind the dark centers, and he saw chaos in Mychael ab Arawn's, the heated frenzy of Ddrei Goch's breath stirring in the boy's spine.

For all the frenzy of his gaze, Mychael eyed him dispassionately. "In truth, I have seen too much of what I am and fear it not near so much as what I shall become."

Aye, Trig thought, holding back from making another warding sign. Naas's vision *had* spoken true, and there was reason to fear. The grim portent of the boy's words spoke of at least a measure of sight. Rhiannon must have known. Yet if those women of old had sent their blood down through generations of novitiates until such time as one bore a son, their plans had gone dangerously awry.

Trig looked at the ragged hem of the Welshman's tunic, at the monk's wool leggings he wore and the Quicken-tree boots. No ancient priestess would have condoned the raising of one of her acolytes in a Christian monastery. They had fought the hooded brothers and their bloodstained God on every quarter. Nor would the Druid women have liked any better the giving over of him to the Quicken-tree—with good reason. Rhuddlan would use the boy as well as any, if he could. With Mychael by his side, the Quicken-tree leader need not wait for time to take Carn Merioneth beyond the reaches of Men. Time would come to him, drawn by a dragon-born seer on the night of Calan Gaef. Except the dragon-born seer had not been trained by the one who bore him, and more likely than not, Rhuddlan would set him to the task anyway and they would all be swept into a vortex without end.

Trig stifled a curse. Madron had created this stew. She'd stolen Rhiannon's children during the battle fifteen years ago and hidden them away behind the Christ's sanctified walls where no Quicken-tree dared go. For her trouble, they must all now deal with a man whose loyalties were torn and whose powers not even he could control.

And the look of him, with that fire dancing in the depths of his eyes . . .

Trig tamped down his surging unease, refusing to call it fear, and reached for Bedwyr. He had not blanched at the dark smoke in the broken damson shaft. He would not let himself be unnerved by a fledgling. Still, there would be no argument or orders for rest and seed-cakes. 'Twas best to leave as quickly as possible. With that goal in mind, he took hold of Bedwyr's shroud.

"Leave him be," Mychael said.

"Ye can't carry him alone." Trig bent to the task and was stopped by a forceful hand on his shoulder.

"Leave him on the sand," Mychael said, the command spoken through gritted teeth, with naught of a request about it.

The cold, hard knot in Trig's stomach grew even colder. Damn the boy for his gall, that he dared to challenge a Liosalfar captain. Priest-ess creature or nay, Arawn's son went too far if he thought to rule here. Trig had been blooded in battle before Mychael's father had been born, before his grandfather.

Shaking off Mychael's hand, Trig straightened to his full height, wincing at the pain the effort caused. "The Quicken-tree do not leave their dead in the dark."

"I am not Quicken-tree, old man. Leave him."

Old man. Trig bit back an oath and reached for his blade. Before he could find his knife, Mychael grabbed his hand and pulled it up between them. The pain near put him to his knees.

A snarl curled Mychael's lips. "I can still smell the black smoke where it touched you, Trig. Would you have it taint us all? We're leaving Bedwyr and making our run to Merioneth. If you would have it other-wise, gainsay me with your steel."

Out of the corner of his good eye, Trig saw the flash of the crystal blade in Mychael's other hand. He was half-blind on his left side, and though he carried daggers on both sides and had a longsword, Mychael's dreamstone would win the day before he could draw any of them. The only question was where the boy would strike . . . and how deep.

He held Mychael's gaze and feared the answers he saw. The mad fool might kill him, and that would do none of them any good. Swallow-ing the bile of defeat, he muttered a curse and pulled away, and knew that he was no longer captain of the Liosalfar. Nor did he deserve to be, if he wasn't quick enough to overcome a nestling, even if 'twas Ddrei Goch's. He, a hero of the Wars of Enchantment, had been taken without a fight, but that was the only shame he'd bear. The boy could cut him down where he stood, but he was not leaving Bedwyr on the sand, not with a skraelpack lurking so near.

He shifted his one-eyed gaze to Mychael. "I'm puttin' him in one of the tunnels. Ye might or might not 'ave noticed we was being followed, but those that was doin' it like nothing better than a bite o' tylwyth teg."

That made the boy blanch. "Bedwyr is no child," he said.

"The stinkin' beasts don't care if 'tis mutton or lamb when it comes to Quicken-tree flesh. Dinna ye smell 'em?"

The boy slanted his gaze to the path they'd taken up from the dark, proving that he had.

" 'Skraelings,' they be called," Trig said, "and twisted, evil men they be. I've been smelling 'em for two lan."

From his expression, so had Mychael. "Do what you will with Bedwyr, but be quick about it."

Trig was quick, smoothing his hand over the curved arch of the nearest tunnel to find the signs of the lock while Mychael watched, then sliding the crystal hilt of his blade into the notches keyed by Rhuddlan. When the ether, a pearlescent gossamer sheath that covered the entrance, lifted away from the sand, Mychael helped him slide Bedwyr inside. Trig removed the blade from its last notch in the rock and the sheath fell back into place, truly a death shroud for the old warrior, and not one that skraelings or Sha-shakrieg could breach.

They turned to leave, and Trig's attention was drawn to Llynya. The sprite was standing at the bottom of the path, uncommonly still and watching them with an intensity that made Trig uneasy. 'Twould do neither of them any good should she decide to come to his defense against the boy. Yr Is-ddwfn aetheling or nay, he would not give her much of a chance against Mychael on this day. When he walked toward the path and her gaze did not shift, he realized it wasn't him at all that held her attention, but the tunnel gate.

Mourning for Bedwyr, he thought, as did they all.

Late. They had been too late. Skraelings run like the wind for blood, they'd said. Ten leagues in a single night, they'd said, and then the craven bastards had taken a sennight and missed their chance at the shrouded strangers and a whole friggin' mess of Quicken-tree—and the lavender woman who would be his.

Couldn't be helped, Wyrm-master, they said. Needs to wait for Slott of the Thousand Skulls.

Wyrm-master. He, Caradoc, the Boar of Balor, had been reduced to Wyrm-master; and he, too, waited for Slott, the thousand-skulled cretin who had caused the delay and cost him the lavender woman.

The skraelings had brought him something for his leg, a roughly wrapped package offered with a sly nod. He took the bundle and limped over to a bench hollowed out of a wall in the rough and dirty cave they'd brought him to. 'Twas a day's march from the wormhole, on the same northern route they'd taken in the spring. The skraelings sat all around the cave, some on other benches or outcroppings of rock, some on the floor at the edge of a murky pool. Smoke from their fires wafted in the cross-breeze flowing down from a vast cavern two days farther north. Rastaban, they called the cave, Eye of the Dragon. The place had been long abandoned the first time he'd seen it, with piles of bones half turned to dust and great swaths of cobwebs hanging like cathedral curtains from giant stone chairs and the huge, thick pillars flanking them. Each bench in Rastaban was big enough to sleep three men. Stairs had been carved from the cold rock with risers as high as his knees, leading up into the fathomless dark of the ceiling. And now 'twas to Rastaban they would return.

A few of the skraelings were still scavenging food from out of the rat cage no skraelpack traveled without, roasting the vermin on the tips of the same pointy sticks and swords they used for murder and mayhem. Most were finished feeding and had taken to picking their teeth with the bones.

A more motley bunch he'd ne'er seen. The man to his left was pasty-faced, so pale the veins showed beneath his skin, blue rivers running under a bulbous nose and lumpy cheeks and into erratically placed wisps of hair. Caradoc had seen a few others like him. Next to the fire a group of three dark men, their skin different shades of gray ranging from fine ash to charcoal, played a game of knuckle-bones. Greasy black hair stuck out from under their iron helmets.

The most cunning of the troops by far were the greenlings, called such for the green tinge to their skin. Two of these were cooking rats over the fire. A third was spitting one of the pale, eyeless lizards that inhabited the caves. Two more milled from one group to the next. There were twenty skraelings in all, five more than had taken him north in the spring. Each of them had teeth of unnatural length and sharpness for a man, but men they were, or mostly so. To call them beasts would have been an affront to the animal world.

Aye, only men had eyes that darted and shifted with a skraeling's speed and suspicion. Only men wore knives and daggers though they had fingernails the size and shape and toughness of bear claws.

He recognized four of the pack from the spring: Blackhand Dock, a tall greenling with black claws curving out from the tips of his left-hand fingers and yellow claws curving out from his right; Igorot, whose ash gray skin was as smooth as river rock, except where the side of his face had been burned raw and healed badly; Beel, the ugliest, the pasty-faced one, the one he'd caught chewing on his arm when he'd come about on the beach. Beel was missing one of his teeth from that encounter. Caradoc had kept it as a dagger and had it shoved in his belt. The last that he knew was the captain, Lacknose Dock, a greenling.

The ragged edge of Igorot's sleeve revealed three black bands around his forearm and a nasty scar that could be naught but a brand, a fresh and weeping one, in the crude shape of a thunderbolt. All of the greenlings were marked with muddy blue lines and a finer, well healed version of the thunderbolt brand. Beel was branded, but not tattooed. Igorot was the largest in the troop, the one who had carried him most of the way north before.

Caradoc hadn't liked being away, hadn't like it a'tall. The worm-hole had a hold on him, and he'd suffered for not being near the swirling abyss. But he'd made it back, and the skraelings had returned, and together they would track down the Quicken-tree and force them to unlock the seals and show him the way back into the hole. That was his reward for watching and waiting and sending word. Then the power would be his again and the skraelings could go to hell.

He unwrapped the package they'd given him, and a ripple of unease circled around the cavern. Beel grunted and moved away from him on the bench. Thus 'twas with care that Caradoc peeled away the outer layer of leather to reveal a leaf-encased pot. One by one he lifted the leaves and watched them crumble into dust. The thing was old, very old—plunder from a long ago war, they'd told him—probably too old to do him any good. The pot was made of clay and was cracked in a hundred places, and it crumbled away as well when he removed the last layer of leaves. All that remained was a hardened lump of some transparent golden resin, smoothed into a flat-topped ball by the pot.

He started to taste it, but Igorot made a harsh sound and gestured toward his leg. Caradoc put it there instead, inside his chausses next to his wound, and lo and behold, the pain immediately lessened. Not so much at first, but enough to note the difference. Slowly, the stuff melted against his skin. The faintest smell of the forest drifted up to him, a fragrant, leafy ribbon winding through the foul stench of the skraelings.

Igorot and the others moved farther away, taking their knuckle-bones to the other side of the fire. Beel heaved his bulk up and trundled to the far end of the cave. Only one came near him, the captain, Lack-nose Dock, whose mostly missing nose had been replaced by a silver half-cone.

The greenling stopped by the bench and reached out for a handful of Caradoc's hair, grabbing up in his long-clawed fist the copper stripe that ran through the dirty yellow strands.

"We go now to Slott, Wyrm-master," Lacknose Dock said, and tugged on the length of hair.

Caradoc jerked free with a snarl and rose to his feet. 'Twas about time. He would bargain with Thousand Skulls and be done with under-lings.

Lacknose Dock did naught but smile, a fearsome, toothy thing, and, growling a set of orders, led the way out of the cave.

Chapter 8

Rhuddlan strode across the upper bailey of Carn Merioneth, a full quiver held tightly in his fist, his destination the ancient yew by the northwest tower. The
Liosalfar had brought sore tidings up from the caverns
this night: Bedwyr dead and Nia captured; Trig and
Math wounded; Sha-shakrieg back in the deep dark—
and worse.

Worse, aye, enough to bring an end to them all:
damson shafts cracked and smoking, and skraelpacks.

No skraeling would venture into the caverns of
Merioneth on a dare or for treasure. Nay, they only
came for blood, and only when driven by a master. The
trick for Rhuddlan would be to find out who wielded
the whip.

As for why the spider people had returned, he
had to look no farther than himself. Many years had
passed since the price on his head had lured Sha-
shakrieg into the deep dark, yet he had known they

would come again, a new set of warriors to test their mettle against the Scourge of the Wasteland. He oft wondered if spider children still sang songs of Rhuddlan's Retribution and his march to the Salt Sea. The day he burned Deseillign to the ground and poured a hundred years' worth of the Sha-shakrieg's water into the sands had been the end of the Wars of Enchantment, just as the Wars of Enchantment had been the end of so much that had gone before—or so he'd thought.

He would burn the skraelings out of the caverns, if needs be, but the smoke rising from the crystal seals would require another's intervention—Ailfinn Mapp's. The seals were the Prydion Magi's most ancient watch, and he feared only a great distance or great travails could have kept her from her duty.

Throughout the castle grounds, the Quicken-tree were hanging lanterns on their willow huts and in the trees, bringing a semblance of the stars down to earth on the crisp autumn night. While the Liosalfar awaited him at the yew, others moved here and there, tending the groves they had planted in the spring, saplings of oak, hawthorn, and hazel, of rowan and fir brought from Riverwood. Lilting evensongs filled the air, sung to keep the young trees warm the whole night long, to entice three years' growth out of one. Honeysuckle and elder had been planted along the inside of the wall. Wild grasses had been strewn throughout the wards and had reached the golden ripeness of their first harvest.

There was no rot inside the great wall of Carn Merioneth, but Riverwood was decaying at an alarming rate. The bramble would not be enough to save it, and now Rhuddlan knew why.

"Owain." He greeted the man striding toward him from across the bailey.

"When did Trig get back?" Owain asked, falling in beside him. The man's rough-hewn face wore age beyond his years and scars of battles past. He was stocky and dark haired, larger than any Quicken-tree, which had proven a boon when they'd fought Balor, a boon soon to be needed again.

"Early this eventide," Rhuddlan answered.

"Morgan?"

The Cymry captain always asked, holding out hope that one day when the Liosalfar came up from the caves they would have tidings of his prince.

"No," Rhuddlan replied. "War and worse."

"I've not come across worse than war."

"You will shortly, if you choose to stay," Rhuddlan said grimly. "Are there still villeins south of the Dwyryd?"

"Aye, but they'll be gone a'fore winter sets in too hard."

Owain had proven to be an invaluable liaison between the *tylwyth teg* and the few of Balor's cottars that remained. In the aftermath of battle, when the Quicken-tree had claimed Carn Merioneth from Caradoc, the keep and castle grounds had been looted and pillaged by both the free men and villeins of Balor, an action encouraged by Rhuddlan. He'd wanted nothing of Caradoc's and for a fortnight had kept his soldiers well out of sight in the caves. The deserted castle had been easy pickings for even the faintest-hearted serfs. The thieves had not been inclined to stay in the demesne and await their new lord's displeasure.

As to the farms, Merioneth's legendary bounty had perished under Balor's rule with the *prifarym* sealed behind the weir, until naught but the most meager subsistence could be wrung from the ground. There had been little to hold the people of Balor to the lost keep, especially in the spring when winter stores had grown thin.

"And the band of thieves seen lurking in Riverwood a sennight past?" Rhuddlan asked.

"Wei and I set 'em a running, and for certes they'll have tales to tell."

Rhuddlan knew that many who had fled Balor had tales to tell of the strange new ruler in Merioneth. For the rest, time and the bramble would do the deed as Carn Merioneth slid farther and farther from men's minds. The forest would grow and become impassably dense, until men remembered only that 'twas easier to get to the sea by going north or south around the woods, until Carn Merioneth became no more than a memory. Within the span of those years, any remaining cottars would die, their children would leave, and according to Madron, a vital link would be lost between this world and the other, between Men and their gods.

Rhuddlan had once thought so too, that naught but the passing of time tamed a land's gods, and he'd been willing to enhance time's passing and thus disappear more rapidly into a veiled existence embodied by myth—an inevitability he'd foreseen long ago for the *tylwyth teg*. Men, he'd reasoned, would find another way to manifest the natural laws, or they would break those laws and suffer their own demise.

A time of Quicken-tree and the other clans, of *Fir Bile* and *aes sídhe,* would come again, a time when the voices of trees would be heard once more, a time when to lay one's hand upon the earth would be to feel the heartbeat of the Mother, a time when stones would speak of Deep Time.

Aye, he'd thought all those things and reasoned himself right in his decisions, no matter that Madron did not agree. This night, Trig had proved him wrong. Waning gods needed to fear another force besides time. It came padding into his woods on wolves' feet and snaked out of the ground on wisps of smoke, and if left unchecked would destroy them all.

Too many years had passed since he'd looked beyond the borders of his own lands. For too many years he'd given way before the world of Men, feeling the end of the Fifth Age drawing nigh. He'd been wrong. The last battle of enchantment had not been fought.

Together, he and Owain neared the yew tree where the Liosalfar were waiting. Trig was with them, along with others of the Quicken-tree, three Ebiurrane, and Madron.

"How's the boy?" Owain's naturally hoarse voice took on an edge.

"He's well enough," Rhuddlan said, knowing Owain asked of Mychael. The two had formed a bond, the older man and the younger one, both Cymry, the one trained in battle, the other learning. "Moira has him. He's tired and needs stitching, but fared better than most."

The truth of that was easily seen in the welts running across Trig's and Math's skin. The wounds had turned purple, and Rhuddlan knew they burned and ached far worse than a knife cut. A thread had caught Trig across the face, singeing a line through his left eyebrow. Hair would not grow there again.

The worst of Math's wounds were around his neck and down his arm. He was being cared for by Aedyth and Elen in a lean-to not far from the yew. Unlike Trig, a grizzled silver-haired warrior who had long since been beyond the limits of suffering, the younger man's eyes had been glazed with pain when they'd reached the surface. Trig's eyes had shown only anger. Nearly three days had passed since the battle in the quarterlan cavern, and the worst of the thread's damage was done. Soon naught would be left but the scars.

Rhuddlan looked toward the lean-to as they passed. Aedyth was pulling Math's long dark hair up and away from his neck and applying a fresh coat of *rasca* and salves. Under the healer's guidance, Elen was bandaging the young man's arm with dark green Quicken-tree cloth, the purest available, without a trace of the older silver threads running through it.

Like to heal like, Rhuddlan thought, for the base material of the cloth and the Sha-shakrieg fighting threads was the same, the larval silk of *pryf*. The Quicken-tree used the silk in its natural state. The spider people carried theirs deep into the wasteland, to a place far past Deseillign where poison bubbled up from the ground. There they let it steep through the cycles of the moon before winding it up into deadly whorls.

No Liosalfar had been marked by fighting threads since the Wars of Enchantment, when the Sha-shakrieg had fought by the Dockalfar's side, not since Rhuddlan had earned his own such scars.

Rhuddlan stopped at the yew and faced the warriors who had gathered to await his orders. He saw Llynya scoot farther into the shadows, as if that would hide her from his gaze. She would have to be watched, with skraelings loose in the land. Kneeling, he shook out the quiver of arrows, letting them fall on the grass beneath the tree. One of the Ebiurrane, a fair-haired woman named Fand, her face marked with a diagonal stripe of blue woad, leaned in and chose the first arrow. Its shaft was straight and true, born in the heart of an ash tree and marked with runes. Its flights came from the black wingtip feathers of snow geese, its deadly point from beneath the dragon-back of Tryfan—elf shot.

"I will go to Llyr in the north, and tell him the tale told here this day," she vowed, then rose to her feet and in a twinkling had melted into the shadows and was gone.

Llyr had lost both a son and a daughter in the Wars. Rhuddlan knew he would come.

A Liosalfar of the Quicken-tree, Prydd, chose next. Brown haired, he was past the stages of youth, entering his middlin years. "To Brittany, Rhuddlan, as ye command," he swore, holding up an elf shot arrow. "To the Daur-clan, to tell them of Sha-shakrieg in the deep dark and skraelings, and of worse to come." He stood, and Rhuddlan dismissed him with a nod.

Too many years had passed since he'd last seen any of the Daur-clan. Rhuddlan knew not if they would come, or even if Prydd would find them. The seas had changed and pushed the Daur-clan farther inland on the continent. Rhuddlan had seen for himself how the ocean had risen up and swallowed the forest of Mount Tombe, making it an island surrounded by quicksands and coveted by Christian priests. Nemeton had been the last traveler from Brittany, and he had been Druid, a man, not *tylwyth teg*.

Madron walked out of the shadows of the yew and knelt by the scattered arrows. Rhuddlan tensed. He knew what she was about, and he would not allow it.

Graceful fingers grasped an arrow, and the white silken sleeve of her kirtle flowed down across the top of her hand. "To Anglesey," she said, meeting his gaze. Her eyes were green like a Quicken-tree's, but she claimed no lineage other than that of her Druid father. Her hair, a burnished auburn, was held back from her face by a gold fillet wrought in the same pattern as the golden crests emblazoned on her butter-colored gown.

"Aye, the Druids must be warned," he agreed, albeit reluctantly and not without a trace of warning. "But I would as soon send another. I have need of you here."

Madron was well versed in Druidic lore and capable of manipulating natural things—a witch, he'd heard men call her in an absurd underestimation of her skills—but she was no warrior like Fand to be sent alone on a mission, not with war brewing.

"None know the path as well as I," she countered, barely concealing her irritation with his veiled command. That she tried at all, Rhuddlan considered a hopeful sign. In truth, she was not his to bid. Anglesey was as much her home as Merioneth, or the cottage she'd left in Wroneu Wood, and he'd long since lost any rights he'd once had as her protector. She had stayed with the Quicken-tree in Merioneth more for their daughter Edmee's sake than because of him, accepting that 'twas better for the girl to be among her own than to lead the solitary life of her mother.

For himself, he was glad to have Madron near, whether she was his to bid or nay. The summer had provided many opportunities for indulging in her company, a contrary pastime that both appeased and intensified his longing for what they'd once shared. Few were as quick as Madron, and she'd learned much in their years apart. Much that had surprised even him.

"Nor do any make paths as well as you. Not even your father could set such a blaze to the earth," he said, effectively telling her that he knew of her efforts to keep an opening in his bramble with her spells.

"Nemeton but marked a path. You conjured a beacon with your bags of stuff."

She had the grace to blush, for Madron was ever graceful, even at her worst. That he could discomfit her at all, he took as another hopeful sign. For too many years she'd been as stone with him.

"Did you leave it be?" she dared to ask, her blush notwithstanding.

"Aye. For you. For now. Anyone who uses your path will find himself delayed, but not harmed."

"Fair enough," she conceded, relinquishing the arrow. "You know, in truth, that we are not at cross-purposes."

"Nay, we are not," he agreed, then turned and called a Quicken-tree youth forward. "Tages, take this to Anglesey and find the old men who live in the caves. Tell them the tale of what the Quicken-tree found in the damson shafts, and then it's to Inishwrath with you. I would have tidings of the troll fields on the island. No change is too small to report."

Tages swore his oath upon the elf shot arrow and went the way of Fand and Prydd. Rhuddlan continued around the gathering, sending various men and women of both the Quicken-tree and the Ebiurrane to warn clans in the far north and the west, south, and east, and with each of them he sent word for Ailfinn to come nigh. He needed the mage as well as an army.

Shortly before midnight, the last messenger left the confines of Carn Merioneth, a fleet form sliding silently through the postern in the wall and heading for Kings Wood across the border in England. Being closest, the Kings Wood *tylwyth teg* would be the first reinforcements to arrive in Merioneth.

Madron took her leave, heading toward the lower bailey. To check the boy, Rhuddlan was sure. Others in the group spread out to find what rest they could before the march. For him there would be no rest. He would leave before dawn with a handpicked troop to recover Nia, and to reconnoiter the deep dark and see what inroads the enemy had made.

"What else would you have me know, Trig?" he asked, turning to the elf-man who waited by his side.

Aedyth had fashioned a patch of green leaves for Trig's left eye. The other stared at him with an emotion Rhuddlan couldn't name.

"Ye said the boy would test me," Trig said, "and by the gods, he did. 'Twas not me who left Bedwyr by the dark sea."

"Was blood let?" Rhuddlan asked with misgiving. 'Twas no time for him to lose the old warrior as his captain, and Trig would not have left Bedwyr without a fight.

"Nay." Trig shook his head. "He flanked me with his blade drawn before I could so much as find me knife."

Rhuddlan shifted his gaze to the hearthfire and back to Trig again, releasing a sigh. 'Twas also no time for Trig to be losing his edge. " 'Tis not like you to be caught with your guard down."

"Nay."

"But without any blood being drawn . . ."

"Nay, Rhuddlan. 'Tis over. Your new captain lies in the lower bailey. If he lives the night, no doubt he'll serve you well."

"He had no wounds other than what Llynya inflicted. Moira will heal those quick enough."

" 'Tis not his wounds that threaten him," Trig said. "He's what Naas told ye—quickened in his mother's womb by priestess blood, and dragon spawned. A nestling no more, he's cooking in his own fire this night."

Rhuddlan glanced toward the lower bailey in time to see Madron slip through the open arch in the wall. His instinct was to follow her, but his common sense bade him stay and hear Trig out. She knew the boy better than most. Indeed, when he'd told her what Naas had seen, she'd shown no surprise and said naught but that there was a little of the dragon in all of them.

'Twas Rhuddlan's fear, the dragon in the boy, for 'twas more than a little. Many nights this summer past he had watched Mychael pace the ramparts, oblivious to storms that had sent the Quicken-tree into their huts. He'd seen the moments of frenzy in the boy's eyes, and he'd seen the scars that marked the boy's body from his repeated attempts on the wormholes—and his fears had grown.

Rhuddlan had been a dragon keeper until he'd sealed the weir gate to protect the *pryf,* thereby sending the dragons far out to sea. They'd not come near him or Merioneth since, but they called to the boy, and 'twas to the boy they would come if they ever came again. When that happened, Rhuddlan knew his time would be at an end, the old king passing to make way for the new.

Mayhaps he was ready. Mayhaps. But the boy was not. The boy

was wild and growing wilder. Now Trig had seen the roiling up of power in Mychael, the dragonfire, but whether it would work for the Quicken-tree or against them, not even Naas could tell.

"Nay, Trig, your work as captain is not yet done," he assured the older man, keeping his fears to himself. If the darkness was rising, the *tylwyth teg* needed Ddrei Goch and Ddrei Glas more than they needed Rhuddlan of the Light-elves. The question was if they could survive Mychael ab Arawn. "In the morn, we'll set the boy to a task to put him back in his place."

"And what place would that be?" Trig asked with a skeptical lift of his eyebrow.

"For now, 'tis behind you in battle and bent to my will."

"The boy don't bend too well."

"No," Rhuddlan agreed. "He doesn't."

Clapping his captain on the back, he sent Trig on his way, then crossed over to the portcullis to choose his weapons for the morrow.

He knew the Earth. He and the *tylwyth teg* spent their lives in the flow of her most subtle rhythms, shifting effortlessly from one season into the next with the trees, one eon into the next with the living rock, revolving with her around the Sun and basking with her in the celestial light of the Moon, forgetting nothing. Nemeton had prized them for what he'd called their bit of knowledge, which Rhuddlan had in the beginning thought to be an absurd conceit. *Earth is all,* he'd said. *To know her in all her wonders is to know the heart of the Mother.* And so Rhuddlan had believed, until Nemeton had directed his gaze toward the heavens and told him that before Earth there had been Chaos, and it had come from afar.

Rhuddlan knew the story of the Starlight-born. 'Twas written on the first page of each of the Seven Books of Lore, lest any forget. The surprise had been that Nemeton also knew the ancient tale and had brought it to bear on an age long removed from the terror.

The Douvan kings of the Twelfth Dynasty had lived in a second age of chaos long before the Thousand Years War. In their time of direst need a child had come to them out of the deep dark to wield the Magia Blade—Stept Agah, the last Dragonlord. That story, too, was old, even in the reckoning of elfin time, a telling of battles and plagues and a shadow across the land, of armies of wolves and *uffern* trolls, of sweeping sickness scouring the ranks of men and elves, and of the black, reeking vapor—portent of Dharkkum—that had hung like a pall between heaven and earth, until Stept Agah had called the dragons and overrun the plaguing armies. The beasts had devoured the darkness, and the Prydion Magi had once again forced the remaining smoke and effluence into the chasms that lay deep below the surface, sealing them with damson crystal wrought with words of power.

But beasts of war are ever hungry . . . and once roused to battle, the dragons were wont to ravage the land unless ruled by the Magia Blade. In all his long life, Rhuddlan had never seen them fight. They came to the nest on Mor Sarff to breed and spawn and die. They were born in the nest, a secret place beneath the *pryf*'s labyrinth accessible only through an underwater tunnel, and they died in the same.

Now the crystal seals were breaking. He needed Ailfinn to tell him why, and if the worst proved true, he would need the dragons to fight—the dragons and Mychael ab Arawn.

Descent . . . descent . . . descensus—*He was falling, falling like an angel from the grace of God.* Kyrie, eleison. *Lord have mercy, Lord have mercy . . .*

Mychael lay spread-eagled across the rugs Moira had laid for him in his solar. His tunic and shirt were off, his braies loose. One of his chausses was missing, leaving his left leg bare, and still the heat burned him.

The Quicken-tree woman had long since stitched him and left him alone for his night's sleep, but there would be no escape into sleep for him this night. The first incandescent flash had finally broken through his will and flamed to life even as Moira was smoothing the last of her *rasca* down the scar running the length of his left arm, torso, and leg. If she'd felt it, she didn't say. He'd noticed no difference in the healing touch of her fingers when the heat began. Thankfully, she'd left before the changes in him had become too visible. He'd never told her of his fearful malaise. She knew about the scars. 'Twas enough.

Madron knew. She'd seen the scars, and she'd offered him potions. Potions to cool the flames. Potions to ease his pain. Potions to soothe his soul. Potions, no doubt, to make him hers.

Ceri had not trusted her, but he trusted in Ceridwen. In his hands he held his sister's gifts, a green stone she'd called "Brochan's Great Charm," and the *Fata Ranc Le.*

He should not have let his sister go so quickly to the north. She was the touchstone to his past, blood of his blood, but she suffered no dragonfire. Mayhaps she could heal him. For certes the Quicken-tree's old healer, Aedyth, would have naught to do with him. Moira's *rasca* helped, but only to a point far short of relief.

There was one other spoken of by the Quicken-tree, a mage summoned by Rhuddlan who had not yet answered the call, whose touch it was said could raise the dead, whose simples were as the elixir of life itself, whose enchantments put Madron's to shame. Ailfinn Mapp was her name. A Prydion Mage, they said, someone who knew the secrets of the ancients.

Naught could be more ancient than dragonfire, and if the mage kept the secret of his bane, he would know it. But she did not come, no matter how many messengers Rhuddlan sent at the turning of every moon.

Nay, he thought again, he should not have let Ceridwen leave him so quickly on his own. Yet with disaster looming, 'twas best she was well out of it and away. Away to the cool north. *Thule.* Land of the frozen wastes. Farther north than any man had ever gone. Did Dain Lavrans also burn with inner fire to long so for the farthest reaches of coldest winter?

Ceri had spoken of a palace to be carved from ice, and of a boy-child to be born there. Mychael wondered what manner of man would come from out of the arctic landscape, home of the fierce north wind. And would he ever meet his twin's son? Or would he die an ignominious death bathed in sweat and burning in madness before the child was even brought into the world?

Another wave of heat washed through him, and he gritted his teeth, clenching the red book to his chest to keep from being swept away by the force of it. Only God knew how much of himself he would lose if he let go. He feared it would be more than he could bear.

A rock-crystal lamp lit the interior of the tower room, the colors of its flames dancing over bare stone walls and a roughly made table. Above him, a half-thatched roof of woven willow wands became an arborescent cathedral bathed in flickering light and shifting shadows. Stars and the moon shone through the loose weave.

". . . mercy," he whispered for the thousandth time, struggling against the endless tide of fire. But God in His wisdom denied him.

His mouth was parched. A flask of water lay not an arm's length from him, and another of catkins, but he dared not let go of his talismans to reach for either. His very existence was balanced on a knife edge, suspended over a fiery abyss.

An abyss. A fathomless canyon carved into his heart by the dragons, grown deeper each time he'd lowered himself into a wormhole. When had he first heard their cry?

In Strata Florida on a winter night when he'd walked the cool cloisters alone and been beset by a vision.

When had the wildness first come upon him?

So very long ago—but not like this.

Never like this.

How could the dragons not be upon him when he felt their flames scorching a path down his body? 'Twas the vision all over again, with Ddrei Goch and Ddrei Glas raging across a night sky, weaving trails of fire with their breath, and the shadows of his enemy marching from behind, wave upon wave of fear-begotten foes taking form out of the darkness. Sha-shakrieg and skraelings.

Only he could hold them all at bay. Only he—and the sword he'd been given did not fit his hand.

The muscles in his arms twitched and shivered with the force of his grip on the red book and the charm. They never yet had kept him from the inferno that burned inside him, but he held on. He needed will and yet more will to keep him from his feral doom, strength of will to hold on until the wild madness passed. For as surely as it would come in the dark heart of the flames, the wildness would pass.

All things passed in time. *In time.*

"Time." He muttered the word as a curse, forswearing his pleas for mercy. The wormholes had beckoned, and he'd succumbed. Still they'd kept their great secrets from him. He knew nothing of time, except that burning with an inner fire could give a man a glimpse of eternity, an eternity of damnation—for what was the fiery abyss that reached for him if not hell itself?

His breaths grew shallow and quick, like the panting of an animal. His gut cramped, doubling him over with a weak cry of protest. The next sound to breach his lips was a keening moan . . . and so the wildness began. *Christe, Christe, Christe, eleison . . .*

Chapter 9

Llynya made her way through the willow huts in the lower bailey, eating a warm honeycake she'd gotten from Moira at the hearthfire. Moonlight shimmered on the curtain wall, beckoning with the promise of solitude and an unencumbered view of all the stars in the night sky. Mayhaps she should climb to the battlements. The meeting under the yew would be finished soon, giving leave to more private discussions she wanted no part of, especially if they included Rhuddlan or Shay.

Rhuddlan would have naught but scolding on his mind and punishments too onerous to bear. While Trig had made an accounting of Mychael's mishap, the Quicken-tree leader had turned his brief but thoroughly chastening gaze on her. She had thought herself full-grown, until Rhuddlan's glance had proved her otherwise. Despite all she'd been through, she was still the sprite, and still in hot water up to her neck. In hindsight, she'd been damned lucky no Sha-shakrieg had gotten his teeth into her.

As for Shay, her longtime companion in adventure and mayhem had become appallingly solicitous and disgustingly overconcerned for her welfare since the battle with the spider people. If 'twas up to Shay, she would not be allowed beyond the wards. Her great worry was that he would convince Rhuddlan of the same, yet she dared not argue for her continued freedom. Better to lie low this night, assume the best, and stay discreetly to the rear of the column on the morrow. She would camp with the Ebiurrane in Lanbarrdein and with luck, Rhuddlan wouldn't even know she'd made the descent. And thanks to Trig, she now knew how to open the seals on the tunnels leading to the wormhole.

"Bagworms," she muttered. She'd been as well into the thick of the battle with the Sha-shakrieg as any and been the least harmed. Even Rhuddlan had noted that, though he'd not given her much of the credit for her unscathed state.

Coming abreast of the stairs, she angled her steps toward the wall, then changed her mind upon seeing the bent form of Naas on the battlements. The old woman toiled night and day to bring down the curtain, planting her seedlings in every rocky chink. She wasn't given much to talk, but this night, Llynya was inclined toward none.

With the ramparts taken, only one place could ensure her privacy, the apple grove in the farthest reaches of the lower bailey. 'Twas the oldest part of the castle grounds and had been the least changed by the Boar. The southwall tower where Mychael had taken up residence was close by the orchard, but she could avoid him easily enough.

Keeping to the darkness and the shadows cast by flickering lanterns, she passed huts of different shapes and sizes. Some were thatched and daubed for wintering over. Not everyone had been going to the winter grounds this year, and now mayhaps none would go. Hushed voices speaking of nighttime things slipped through the woven willow wands as the wild folk bedded down. In some of the huts, lullabies were sung to charm children into dreams.

Let others sleep this night, Llynya thought, continuing on. She would look to the stars and gaze at the moon, celestial orb rich in elfin lore and magic for a woman's taking. She needed magic, more magic than she held, earth magic she could take into the deep dark.

Mychael ab Arawn had proven an unlikely ally. Crazed man. His mood had grown dangerous on the march up to Carn Merioneth, leading him into mutiny on the shores of Mor Sarff. By anyone's figuring, wounded or not, Trig was the captain, and he'd been against the decision to leave Bedwyr at the Serpent Sea, but he'd been no match for Mychael. Neither was she. On the sands leading to the gates of time, the archer had shown himself to be exactly what she'd seen in Riverwood. *Sín.* A rising storm of fury.

Neither she nor Shay had jumped into Trig and Mychael's short-lived battle, and not because of a sense of divided loyalties. They'd both been too wide-eyed and dumbstruck to move before it had all been over. If she was to stay in Rhuddlan's good graces, 'twas probably best to distance herself from the archer. Yet he'd read the walls with his hand. In all her life, she'd seen only Nemeton do such a thing.

He hadn't spoken to Trig of her scent-blindness, another point in his favor. Below Mor Sarff, they had all been too intent on reaching the surface, and after Mor Sarff, Mychael and the captain had not spoken a word to each other. Bad blood had been spilled there, for certes. Rhuddlan would want to speak to Mychael, but Rhuddlan was headed back to the deep dark before dawn. Moira had taken Mychael up almost immediately when they'd finally surfaced, and Llynya hadn't seen him since, neither at the meeting nor the hearthfire. If he slept, he was sleeping through his last chance to expose her. She could only hope it so.

Strange man, to turn so suddenly fierce. She'd thought him a sapling in Crai Force cavern, but no sapling could have daunted Trig, and no sapling could have made the run from the deep dark to Merioneth in two and a half days with two wounded and one dead. They might have lost Math without that speed. Aye, Mychael could make a powerful ally, but there were definite dangers to weigh.

Upon reaching the apple grove, she swung herself up into the nearest tree. Immediately, a familiar and comforting lightness suffused her limbs. She was home. The leaves in her hair fluttered ever so slightly, and a smile came to her mouth. Her ears twitched. These trees remembered her from the spring. They had been a haven for her then, awash in blossoms and open to her tears, cradling her in boughs laden with fresh green leaves. Before Aedyth had taken her to Deri, she'd spent her days sheltered in their shadow-dappled branches.

Her tears were gone now, and the blossoms had yielded fruit, moonlight limned apples, their golden roundness edged with crescents of lunar silver. She picked one and took a bite, her teeth sinking into sweet, crisp flesh. Moira had told her the trees had been planted down through the ages by the Anglesey priestess. They had refined the juice of the apples to a love potion of unsurpassed potency and used it to bind men to them in times of danger. At least a garrison's worth of men, so one story went, had been lured to the coast by songs of enchantment set loose upon the wind. After filling the mortals with magic drink, the women had marched off with them to do battle with a monstrous creature. Few of the men had survived the slaying of the beast, according to Moira, but those valorous few had lived the rest of their lives in peace and plenty, blessed by the favor of the priestesses.

No such potions worked on *tylwyth teg,* nor did any such poisons, priestess brewed or nay. If it grew upon the earth, it flowed through elfin blood. 'Twas only the damnable desert brew that laid them low. Llynya took another bite of apple and began making her way deeper into the grove, alighting from one bough to the next, heading for the middle of the fruitful copse. In the tallest tree's topmost branches, she made her bed and settled in to watch the sky and let the moon's light soak into her pores.

The first keening moan was no more than the barest whisper on the breeze, an underlying dissonance more than an actual sound. She might have missed it except for a tingling in the tips of her ears.

She rolled over and brushed aside a veil of leaves, looking to the southern end of the bailey from whence it had come. Or so she thought. When next she heard it, 'twas from over the great wall, clearer, louder, yet faint with distance. Pushing to her feet, she balanced herself between one branch and the next and looked out to the sea. Long breakers were rolling in toward the cliffs, their white froth shining in the moonlight. Farther out, on the edge of the horizon, almost past where the curve of the earth cut its scythe across the sky, a thin streak of green fire edged in red flickered in the night. Then all was gone, both the keening cry and the colored lights, and naught remained to delineate where the blackness of the heavens sank into the last reaches of the ocean.

A movement on the wall drew her gaze, and she looked to find Naas staring out to sea, her aged fingers making some unknown sign. 'Twas no warding like Llynya had ever seen. On each hand the woman's third finger was bent into the palm, while her little finger came forward to make a circle with her thumb. Naas was extending her hands out as if in offering—but an offering of what? And to whom?

*   *   *

Caradoc and the skraelings had marched for two days, through tunnels and caves that grew ever higher and wider, but no better smelling, despite the stacks of oak planks filling some of the caverns. An odd cache, he'd thought, until farther caverns had revealed their even odder purpose. The skraelings were building ships.

Other skraelpacks had joined them from out of connecting passageways, some carrying bags of rivets and spikes, or thick skeins of withies for lashing. They'd made their first camp in a cave filled with the skeletal beginnings of half a dozen halvskips, and the troop had grown to a hundred strong.

And still they came. That morn, a single portal had disgorged enough of the beastly creatures to double their ranks, and they had doubled again at the next cavern. Somewhere along the trail, wolves had joined the horde. Caradoc could see them sliding like shadows through the pack of marching feet, dark wisps of terror with far less beastly-looking men at their sides. He thought he recognized one or two men from Balor, but the crush of the crowd made it impossible for him to get more than a fleeting glimpse of any one face.

There were more than enough soldiers to squash the Quicken-tree. Yet even more came, pouring out of every hole in the dark, until he began to think there were too many.

The growing corps bristled with halberds, pikes, and lances. Greenlings favored bows and short swords. Knives and daggers there were aplenty, and staves, iron-spiked caltrops, war flails, axes, and hammers. The clash of metal and thumping of feet created a raucous din, and soon the jostling in the narrower passages turned into shoving matches. One such test of wills ended in a grunt and the collapse of a white-faced skraeling to Caradoc's right. Without a pause, the man was trampled beneath the hobnailed boots of the marching soldiers, but not before Caradoc saw the foot-long gash in his side and Igorot wiping his bloody blade across the front of his hauberk.

A quick signal passed between the greenlings, and Lacknose Dock, still in the lead, shouted above the burgeoning roar, *"Grazch! Kle, drak, dhon, vange!"*

The count was taken up and down the lines—*"Grazch! Kle, drak, dhon, vange! Kle, drak, dhon, vange!"*—and order was restored, with feet marching in rhythm and the strident noise of skraeling voices grating on Caradoc's ears.

Piles of fresh bones and hollows afloat with rancid offal in

Rastaban's outlying tunnels warned him of even more skraelings to come. His gut churned into an angry knot. He'd been played false. He'd asked for a scant hundred skraelings, a garrison to replace the one he'd lost, and they'd brought a whole friggin' army down on his head.

The wind picked up as they neared the triple arch entrance to Rastaban, carrying the sound of hundreds—nay, thousands—more voices raised in the skraeling war chant. *"Kle, drak, dhon, vange! Har maukte! Har!"*

He tried to slow his pace, every instinct he had telling him to retreat, but Lacknose Dock grabbed him with a viselike grip and hauled him forward into the shadows of the archway's pillars. Fear overtook him then, and he tried to break free. Lacknose did but tighten his hold, aided by Igorot's mighty hands. 'Twas thus he entered the Eye of the Dragon, bound on one side by a metal-nosed greenling, and on the other by a burnt and branded grayling.

The wretched scent of burning flesh assaulted him in the cavern, a redolent wave of carnage so strong it near put him to his knees. Thousands of skraelings filled the vastness of Rastaban, all of them stomping in rhythm to the chant. The ground trembled beneath Caradoc's feet. The sound crashed into the walls. The air itself shook with the force of the cries—and at the far end of it all, ten times the girth of any skraeling in the cavern, sat Slott.

Slott of the Thousand Skulls—human skulls and animal skulls, each one of the little bone-white things braided into the giant's hair, hundreds of calcified ribands twining through wiry locks and weighing down his beard.

Caradoc faltered at the sight. A ring of fiery braziers encircled the dais where the monstrous beast overflowed his huge stone throne. Against Caradoc's will, and over the harsh sounds of his threats, Lacknose Dock and Igorot half-carried, half-dragged him down a great flight of stairs into the cavern hall. As they crossed to the dais, the chant died down into murmurs, and then silence. The only sound to be heard was the clink and clatter of the thousand skulls as Slott swung his big head down to spy him with a milky black eye.

Hunched as the giant was in the chair, his arms reached past his knees. His knuckles scraped the ground. Hairs the size of bristles stuck out of the backs of his hands. A matted brownish black pelt covered the rest of him, including his long, twitching tail. Slott wore no shirt or tunic or shoes, only a vest made of stretched skins, some furred, some pale and hairless, some gray . . . some tinged green. Salt crusted his beard and made white streaks on his skin and clothes. Strings of bladdery kelp clung to the skulls twisted into the greasy strands of his hair.

His face was broad and smashed-looking, his lips overly large and glistening with drool. Warts the size of potatoes clustered along the curve of his nose—and Caradoc realized with a bolt of terror that he had seen the beast before. Aye, he'd seen Slott in the wormhole, where futures were written and pasts collided, where all of time stretched out in an infinite banquet, where the histories of all who had ever been or who would ever be ringed the abyss in a golden swirl. The giant had been there, a fleeting image stretched thin by the speed of the light running through it, but there nonetheless, too large to remain unseen in the chaos of faces, too horrific to forget.

"Bow to the Troll King," Lacknose Dock growled, pushing Caradoc to his knees. "Abase yourself and swear fealty to your lord. Now!"

"My lord," he gasped, encouraged by the twist Igorot gave his arm. Everything was wrong. Wrong. He was to have no master. None. The power of the wormhole was to be his.

"Swear by the Stones of Inishwrath," Lacknose Dock demanded, his nose flashing silver in the torchlight.

"By the Stones."

"*By the Stones!*" Slott roared in a voice so harsh it near took the skin off Caradoc's face. He drew back in the wake of the Troll King's breath, choked by stench and fear.

The skulls rattled and jangled as Slott turned his head and bore down on him with his keener eye.

"Caerlon!" the king called, and from the other side of the dais a tall greenling strode forth, fair of face and with no long, sharp teeth, no long, sharp claws.

"By the Stones, lord," Caerlon said, dropping down onto one knee, his short brown hair falling across his forehead.

"Am I not risen from the smoke and the rock?" Slott asked, each word sounding like a sloppy tumble of bricks caught in a backwash.

"Aye, lord. I took the smoke myself to Inishwrath to break the power that steeped the king's host in deathlike sleep. To unbind the dire enchanting art of the spell that was cast in the Wars. To set you free, lord."

"Why?"

"When the smoke arises the skraelings shall have a king. Such has it been told since the Wars."

"And what would a king have?"

"Glory, sire."

"And what is the greatest glory?" The giant reached out and with two huge fingers pinched the copper stripe running through Caradoc's hair.

"Time, milord," Caerlon said, rising with a short bow and putting on a thick leather glove that had been hanging from his belt.

Slott handed the greenling his scepter, and upon noting it, Caradoc felt his last shred of hope seep out of his pores. 'Twas a thick shaft of iron with a zig-zag bolt of lightning welded to the pommel. 'Twas the brand, the instrument of carnage.

Caerlon turned to the nearest brazier, and Slott pushed his face closer to Caradoc's, each of his stinking breaths like a cold north wind sent to freeze a man's bones. Even Igorot and Lacknose Dock backed off, though they still held him.

"Would you steal my glory, skraeling?"

"I—I am n-no s-skraeling," Caradoc stammered, feeling a wet warmth run down his leg.

Slott leaned even closer, and a dark flame came to light in his eyes. "You soon will be," he promised in his guttural rasp, "and whatever you've taken, you will give back to me tenfold."

Caerlon turned from the brazier, his gloved hand holding the red-hot scepter. A wan smile crossed his lips.

Caradoc began to struggle, desperately. Igorot and Lacknose Dock seized him with renewed force, forcing him to the floor, his arm outstretched in homage to his lord.

The brand was pressed onto his skin, and the stones of Rastaban echoed with his screams. Then he heard nothing.

"Wyrm-master," Slott said contemptuously, rolling the ragged, little man over onto his back. He smelled of roasting meat. "I should eat him."

"No, milord," Caerlon advised, kneeling beside the prostrate form. "Not this one. See?" He lifted a swath of hair, and copper strands fell through his fingers along with the gold. "He is as was long ago foretold, Troll's Bane, born of Merioneth, a golden-haired youth with an auburn blaze marking him as a traveler, a—"

Slott grunted. "He is not so young."

" 'Tis a relative thing, sire. For the span of his life, nay, he's not so young, but compared with your great years, he is but a babe."

Slott accepted the explanation with another grunt, and Caerlon continued.

"—with the strength of a thousand men—"

"He's lame," Slott interrupted again.

Caerlon released the slightest breath of exasperation. "Aye, milord. He's lame, but I had some salve given to him, and by all accounts he's getting better."

Slott waved him on.

"—and the knowledge of time." Caerlon shook the copper strands. "Such is the heir to Stept Agah's sword, the Magia Blade. We have him, milord, and now he's sworn to you."

"Why not just eat him and be done with it?" Slott licked a finger and smudged it around on the man's cheek before sticking it back in his mouth.

Caerlon positioned himself more carefully between his king and the unconscious morsel.

"He has worth, sire, ever so much more worth than supper." He saw the doubt in Slott's keen eye, and in the milky one too. "Revenge, milord," he quickly elaborated. "Is not your lady-wife still frozen in stone on the shores of Inishwrath?"

"Aye." Slott's brow furrowed and lowered into a hairy ridge.

"With this one, victory will be ours, sire. Whatever knowledge he has taken from the weir, whatever power comes to him through the dragons, can be ours. With the son of Merioneth to mark the way, we can go back, the whole horde, and win the Wars of Enchantment."

Understanding dawned in the Troll King's gaze. "I am only half-awake, Caerlon," he admitted.

"I know, sire. But we have returned to Rastaban, and the ways are open into the deep dark. The damson shafts are breaking, and the fell smoke of Dharkkum rises from its ancient prison, the promise of darkness for a dark lord. And is that not you, sire?"

"Aye," Slott agreed in a low grumble. "I am the darkest lord."

"And dear dark lord, victory shall be yours. Whoever wields the blade rules the dragons, and now you rule the blade-wielder. Have him hold the dragons in check. Let Dharkkum destroy what it will and wipe the earth clean of our enemies. Even now the Sha-shakrieg venture forth, the wretched betrayers, and Light-elves search the deep dark for broken damson crystals. We shall have them all, lord, the spider people and the Quicken-tree, the Ebiurrane, the Daur, the Kings Wood, the Red-leaf, the Wydden, and the wicked Yr Is-ddwfn. All who denied us before shall die in darkness."

"What of us?" the troll interjected, looking doubtful.

"We won't be here, milord," Caerlon said, brightening with a winsome smile. "We'll be in the past, fighting the Wars, and when this day dawns again, we'll unleash the dragons on our side, to clear the world for the Troll King's Dynasty."

Slott leveled his gaze on Caerlon. "How long was I asleep on Inishwrath?"

"Five hundred years, sire."

"And you woke me because you saw hope in this?" He poked at the golden-haired man.

Caerlon hesitated but a moment, then said, "And in the aetheling."

Slott's gaze instantly sharpened. "Aetheling?"

"Aye. From Yr Is-ddwfn. All the signs are here, milord. And with Dharkkum to come, and the blade to be reforged—"

"Why would they send an aetheling now?" Slott interrupted.

"To better battle the darkness, Lord," Caerlon supposed. "To stand by the bloodling son of the priestess line and call forth the starlight. To fight by the side of the one who wields the blade, or mayhaps to take the blade herself and bring the dragons to heel in the doorways of time. Mayhaps they make a bid for the future, sire, just as we must make our bid for the past."

A bid for the past. Caerlon made it sound so simple, Slott thought. Blades and dragons, aethelings and priestesses. Except it wasn't simple. Slott remembered that well enough, how things had gone awry in the Wars. How the lines had broken and the Quicken-tree had gotten through to Deseillign. How the Lady Queen's house had been destroyed and the Sha-shakrieg had deserted in droves to save her. How the Dock-alfar had all gone mad and left him with nothing but skraelings and his own too few trolls to carry on the fight.

How the Prydion Magi, aided by their Yr Is-ddwfn aethelings, had turned him and those he loved into stone.

No. War was never simple—and naught but victory ever sufficed.

He again nudged the fallen man. Wyrm-master.

"Stept Agah wielded the blade as a Dragonlord," he said to Caerlon. "Not a Wyrm-master."

" 'Tis but Lacknose Dock's jest," Caerlon said, shooting the captain a withering glance. "I recognized the man for what he was right off, but Lacknose Dock dared to doubt and call him Wyrm-master."

No, Slott thought again, war was never simple, and in those last months of battles, he remembered oft wondering if Caerlon had gone as mad as the rest of the Dockalfar.

Take an army into the past to win a war long lost? 'Twas madness itself—but then, what was war, if not madness? And what was madness, if not the coming of Dharkkum?

A slight shiver sent a tremor across his shoulders. With his sorcery Caerlon had devised a crack in the damson crystal shafts. Clever, clever Caerlon, to bring the wrath of Evil Incarnate up from the bowels of the earth on them. But could the elf-mage control what he had wrought?

Slott slanted a hooded glance in the elf's direction. Time would tell.

He looked down at his freshly branded vassal and gave the man a testing push with his toe. "The aetheling will die, if she has naught but this to fight by her side," he said.

"Aye, lord," the fair greenling agreed, a faint smile curving his lips. "We can only hope it so."

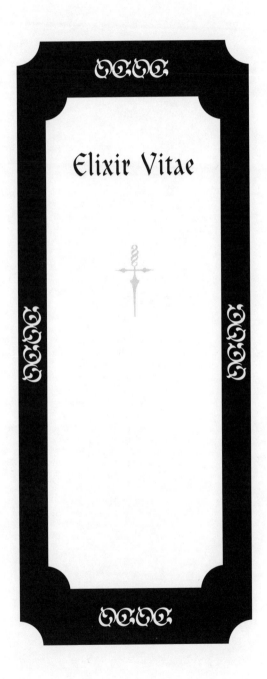

Elixir Vitae

Chapter 10

Dawn crept into Riverwood from over the mountains, gliding into shadows and grykes and transforming night-drowsy dew into sunstruck drops of brilliance. The almond scent of warming meadowsweet filled the air, along with the fresh, rushing sound of water.

Nennius stopped every few feet along the banks of the Bredd, the light licking ahead as he observed some new twist in the foliage. Long stretches of the wood had been made impassable by the twining and winding of shrub branches and flower stems, grass stalks and petioles. Even the tree limbs appeared to be reaching for one another, closing in and battening down the woodland hatches.

He lifted his hand and fingered an intricate plait of willow scrub. 'Twas not nature's work. Magic was afoot.

Behind him, his horse chewed on a bit of grass, tearing it out of the ground and waiting patiently with her heavy load. He'd not left his books on the island, but had proceeded carefully, bringing everything he might need to devise his journey home. He'd also taken the precaution of shaving his head. The wormhole had marked him with a blazing white stripe through his coal black hair, making him instantly recognizable to anyone who knew the consequences of passing through a weir gate. He'd entered the land of such a gate, and he would not have himself revealed and his purpose discerned before its time.

An azure damselfly swooped in to hover over the autumn-yellowing leaves, then darted to the south, leading Nennius's gaze to a giant's cairn of boulders tumbled across the river. Staring at the dam through the tangled coppice in which he stood, he cursed under his breath. The river disappeared beneath the cairn, and the track winding along its banks had been his hope that morn. He'd spent two days bushwacking paths to no good end, searching for a way through to the castle on the cliffs. His camp beneath a gritstone crag high on one of the mountains gave him a clear view to the sea, but had shown him no route through the damnably tangled forest.

There'd been fires the night before, and runners leaving the keep by the light of the moon. They had headed in all directions, unhindered by the bramble that so thwarted him. The thought had come to catch one of the runners and by his own patented means extract directions through the maze of trees and bracken. He'd been stayed only by the fleet-footedness of the bastards, certainly not by any compunction. He would kill them all, inside the keep and out, if it would further his cause.

Fucking primitive people with their rough earth magic. Gruffudd's demons. Nemeton's princely wild folk. He would show them magic. They'd probably constructed some damn religion around the great worms. That religion had not survived, he could assure them of that, but it would be one more obstacle for him to overcome when he reached the castle—and he would reach the castle.

He looked again to the pile of rocks barring his way and noticed a faint lightening in the near shadows. Tugging on the mare's reins, he strode farther down the river, until he came to a clear space where the brake and bramble turned back in upon itself in a leafy arch. 'Twas not a large opening, but he was well pleased for having found it. An odd scent was in the air, of burnt earth and something rare. He knelt down and sifted his hand through the dirt at his feet. There were burn marks on the ground, and a few scorched leaves lying about. He sifted through the soil again and brought a handful to his nose. The odd scent deepened around him, winding its way out of the burnt smell in ever-increasing strength.

Chrystaalt.

He sniffed again and smiled. Dear Gruffudd had indeed brought him treasures beyond imagining to have led him here. Someone in Merioneth had power he could use. Nemeton had written of universal salts, but Nemeton was gone from this time. Could it be that he had left a peer behind, someone with access to his paraphernalia and goods? Someone with the knowledge to use them?

Nennius looked up, his gaze scanning the woods around him. He knew there were scouts in the forest, but for the most part, they let the trees do their work for them. An itinerate trader with a brace of donkeys had come up the road from Cymmer Abbey a day past. Nennius had watched from his morning camp as the trader had tried first one worn path and then the next to make his way through the woods. He had given up at midday and continued on to Castell Aber la.

The scouts had left Nennius alone as well. Yet he wondered: Did they know of this small breach in their green rampart? 'Twas neatly hidden in the shadows of the giant boulders, right along the edge of the river. Not many would come this way.

He rubbed the chrystaalt-scented soil between his fingers, then withdrew a scrap of parchment from a pouch on his belt and twisted the loam inside it. He made two more such packages from the burnt earth, careful not to miss any. A bit of incongruous rot fouled his third measure. He scraped off what he could, then twisted the parchment closed and stored it with the others. Given time and even a rudimentary still, he could recover the pure chrystaalt and add it to his own hard-held grains. Or mayhaps he would discover the one who had burned it and commandeer his supply. Any traveler was better off for being fortified with chrystaalt. For the journey he intended, even a small quantity could mean the difference between merely a rough passage and a trip through the vortex of hell.

Worms, enchanted woods, and chrystaalt. Another smile curved his mouth. Merioneth was truly a land of plenty, and all of it there for the taking. His taking.

*   *   *

'Twas warm and fragrant, the world of dreams, and smelled more like apples than not. Llynya shifted on the bough that held her and let the warmth of morning sunshine take up where moonlight had left off in the night. He'd kissed her in her last dream—Mychael ab Arawn—and tasted of catkins' dew. Quite sweet, his mouth had been, quite sweet.

"Bagworms," she muttered, not opening her eyes in hopes that yet another dream would come her way—one without the plaguing archer in it. He'd cast some Druid spell on her, no doubt, that thoughts of him came to her so easily and so often, bothering her even in her sleep.

She stretched and rolled onto her side. The lazy drone of bees drifted up from the herb garden below, along with the mingled scents of marjoram, thyme, and sage, and through and above it all ran the redolence of lavender. 'Twas not such a sore affliction, her need for lavender, except in the deep dark.

The deep dark.

"Sticks!" Her eyes flew open, and she immediately squinted. The sun was a bright ball of full morning light shining down into the bailey. "Double-sticks!"

She swung to a sitting position and made quick work of straightening her clothes. She needed a pack to replace the one she'd lost in Crai Force. She needed provisions, including a supply of lavender. Gods, but an elf shot arrow or two would have been nice.

She squinted up at the sun again. Aye, she had some catching up to do. Rhuddlan had been gone for hours.

"Ho, there!" A lilting, singsong voice cried up from below, and her spirits sank. She'd been found before she could make good her escape. "Llynya, ho!" 'Twas a Quicken-tree boy, Gwydion, waving wildly up at her. His hair was as black as coal with a stubby braid sticking out above his left ear. She lifted a hand in a desultory greeting, the mood of which was completely lost on the small interloper. "Trig wants ye at the p'cullis posthaste."

His message delivered, the boy ran off, skipping and leaping through the orchard. No doubt there had been the promise of a honeycake for a job well done.

She sank back down onto the apple tree boughs, releasing an aggravated sigh. Her goose was cooked, and mayhaps her gander too. The portcullis was a grim place, a gaping maw of iron teeth and murder holes. 'Twas not where she would choose to go of a morn, even if she didn't have other more pressing plans. The long way around would take her by Aedyth's hut and the hearthfire, though, and she could gather the needed lavender and food.

Resigned to her posthaste summons and hoping for a menial task—for she could yet catch Rhuddlan in the caves—she swung down from her branch and dropped to the ground, landing with practiced lightness. To the west was the herb garden, and she detoured from her path to pick some sage.

A small stone chapel stood between the curtain wall and the neat rows of herbs, its masonry banked with thyme and overrun with creepers turning scarlet with the shortening of the days. The pink, clustered flowers of the thyme were abuzz with bees. The sage was farther to the north and less well frequented. She bent and pinched off a couple of gray-green leaves for her pouch and a couple to chew. The chapel was not a place of the priestesses, who, like the *tylwyth teg,* had worshiped with the trees. Aedyth guessed that it had been built by Gwrnach, father to the Boar, as the Boar himself had shown no bent for holy things.

Aye, Llynya thought, her mood souring. Caradoc had shown no bent at all except for the unholy, and that he had relished. If he had survived his descent into the wormhole, she would yet have his gullet slit by her blade—for 'twas he who had sent Morgan to his doom.

Three had fallen beyond the graven rim of the weir that day, Lavrans, Morgan, and Caradoc. Only Lavrans had arisen, found and pulled to safety by Mychael. The other two had been lost. Where they'd gone, or when, or whether either had survived their wounds were questions that had been left unanswered, and reasonably so by Quicken-tree standards. But she was Yr Is-ddwfn, and in an age long past the Yr Is-ddwfn had used the gates of time and the weir of the wormhole to travel with an ease unknown to others before or since. They had known the secrets sought through the ages of men. The old priests on Anglesey looked to the stars to re-find the ways. Llynya knew her oracle was not to be found in the heavens, but was carved in stone and lay hidden in the labyrinthine heart of the deep dark. She would find the walls written on in an Yr Is-ddwfn hand, and through them make her way into the weir. She would find Morgan, and if the chance arose, she would kill Caradoc. She'd given his hairless devil-priest, Helebore, to the old worm to crush, and if the Boar did not die easily on her blade, she'd do the same to him.

Tucking a bit of sage in her mouth, she left the chapel grounds and struck out across the bailey. The smell of honey wafted to her on the air, coming from some cook's baking. Children played in the sunshine and scampered through the wild grasses, while older girls and boys shooed them off and worked at the harvest. Llynya recognized the richly amber *jhaen* grass used for seedcakes, and the rust-colored redbuck best eaten as morning porridge. Less abundant were the long stems of *kel* with their drooping white panicles and blue-green leaf blades, a rare gift from Naas. All would be hand-threshed and winnowed.

With a season of work, the Quicken-tree had turned the wards of Balor into nascent meadows and woodlands. Most of what had been inside the wall, she'd been told, had been burned at the summer solstice for an Alban Heruin festival of uncommon brightness. By all accounts, the unkempt buildings of wattle and daub and thatched roofs had taken to the torch with ease. Those in the lower bailey had been torn down and dragged into the upper ward to make a pyre for the abominable keep. Only the worst of the lot remained untouched, the boar pits and Helebore's chambers. Naught but time could sanctify those foul catacombs with their endless maze of tunnels running through stonework and earth alike.

Talk had been going around even in May of a will-o'-the-wisp in the tunnels, sighted by the children more often than not. Llynya hoped to see it one day herself, though why a will-o'-the-wisp would choose such a mean dwelling was beyond her comprehension. Mostly they were forest phenomena.

She passed near the postern tower in the west wall, rounded a halfwall, and stopped. Her first instinct was to sneak back behind the halfwall and find another route, for Mychael ab Arawn had made no quick getaway that morn either.

He was sitting on a low bench in a patch of sunshine, his back resting against the great stone curtain, his legs splayed with a bucket on the ground between them. A water ladle rested against the wooden slats of the bucket, and as she watched, he brought it to his mouth for a long drink, spilling a good bit of it down the front of his much patched tunic. The second ladleful was poured over his head in a steady stream, not the first he'd dispatched in that manner from the looks of him. On his third try, he dispensed with the ladle altogether, bending over and using his cupped hands to splash his face before running his fingers back through his hair.

Wet, he didn't look nearly as fierce as he had on the shores of Mor Sarff, she mused. In truth, he looked fair peaked.

A child's laughter drew her attention toward an adjacent gallery arch, and quickly enough, the boy Gwydion came bounding through with half a dozen young hounds leaping about him and nipping at his heels. Trig's bitch had whelped in early summer, a litter of black pups carrying the blood of Rhuddlan's mighty hound, Conladrian, in their hearts. The boy giggled as a pup latched on to his hose and near dragged his braies down. Another nipped the first, and they all went tumbling, the whole of the ruckus heading straight for Mychael. Llynya caught his pained look at the impending invasion and couldn't resist the inner dare to saunter over.

Gwydion landed at the archer's feet in a pile of pups when she was but halfway there. She heard Mychael swear, a sweet, chiding curse, and saw him reach out to tousle the boy's hair. Gwydion laughed and prattled on about the morn's adventures, and between each "Mychael, ye know this," and "Mychael, ye know that," the archer graced the child with a smile, a warm curve of mouth and flash of white teeth that near made her stumble—her, the lightest-footed elf in the forest. The word "p'cullis" was the last she heard, before Gwydion was off again with the dogs.

"*Malashm,*" she said, hunkering down and helping herself to a ladleful of water, wondering if she dared hope for such a smile for herself. 'Twould do her heart good, but such wasn't to be.

Mychael ab Arawn did naught but squint up at her through one eye, then let his head fall back into his hands with an audible groan. Moira had worked a fine piece of stitchery on his cheek, using only the greenest threads. Llynya knew the woman well enough to know he'd been fed as well, but up close he looked worse than peaked. Gold and auburn strands of hair stuck out wildly from his head, run through with his hands and glistening with the water he'd poured over himself. Morning sunlight limned his face, giving him a wanly luminescent look, as if the light shone through his skin, not on it. Besides the stitchery on his left cheek, which had left him bruised, there were other bruises she could not explain. Blue smudges of weariness colored the skin beneath his eyes.

What had he done in the night, she wondered, to have worked himself into such a state? For certes, his brief encounter with Gwydion may have cost him more strength than he had to spare.

"You look like Christian hell," she said, deliberately glib to hide her concern. Her bluntness got her another bleary-eyed glance. She reached behind him and plucked a sprig off the pennyroyal growing up the wall. "You might take a chew of this."

He brushed the pungent leaves away with an indecipherable grumbling.

He looked feverish and uncommonly pale for one who had been in the caves less than a sennight. She stuck the pennyroyal in her own mouth, chewing it up with the sage, and gave him a closer scrutiny. What she saw only increased her alarm. His tunic was half unlaced and torn across the shoulder; his chausses were loose and sagging. A livid mark on the inside of his left wrist snaked out from under his sleeve and across his palm, and she wondered how far up his arm it went. Whatever fury he'd had on the march had burned through him well and good. He was no longer a storm rising, but a storm spent. If Trig had a use for him at the portcullis, she hoped it wouldn't require quick thinking.

Then again, Trig might have something really awful in store for him. Naught had been said during the meeting the night before of the mutiny at Mor Sarff. With only her and Shay to witness, she'd been relieved that the subject hadn't come up, but it would. Trig would have his due. Better that the captain had taken it out of Mychael's hide on the sands than this morn, when he didn't look to have much left in him to take.

She glanced over her shoulder into the yard. Mayhaps 'twould be best if he wasn't sitting out in the middle of the bailey where anyone who was looking could find him. True, he'd already been caught by Gwydion and summoned, but the boy had gone in the opposite direction of the portcullis. If reporting back to Trig had been his chore, he'd forgotten, and if naught else, she could buy Mychael an hour or two to pull himself back of a piece. 'Twouldn't hurt to put herself into his better graces either—if such was possible.

"There's an old fosse outside the wall that overlooks the sea," she said. " 'Tis hedged with a deep hazel brake. I could take you there, and Trig need ne'er know whether the boy found you or not."

"I'm not afraid of Trig," came the muttered reply.

Of course not, she thought. He didn't have enough sense to be afraid.

"Would you like some honey?" she asked, pulling a honey-stick out of a packet tucked into her belt.

He shook his head without bothering to look at her offering. 'Twas fresh clover honey packed inside a rough horsetail stem. She stuck it in her mouth and dug into one of her pouches for a pinch of lavender. 'Twas the last she had, and it had bits of stem and leaves mixed in with the petals. 'Twas still a potent simple, and good for whatever strange malaise ailed him, she was sure.

Holding the lavender in her palm, she took the honey-stick out of her mouth and squeezed a glob onto the sweet-smelling debris. She worked the whole of it into a small ball and gave him a measuring glance. 'Twould do him good to eat it. The trick was getting it in him.

He might bite her head off, or worse.

But she was Yr Is-ddwfn Liosalfar, was she not?

Aye, she thought, she was a warrior from the kingdom across the timeless sea.

Still, 'twas with a cautious hesitancy that she reached up and took hold of his hand, pulling it away from his face. Her trouble brought her under the close regard of two very bloodshot eyes.

" 'Twill do you good. I swear it," she said in a coaxing manner, even as she wondered what she was about. Spent or not, he was still a storm, and 'twas usually no undertaking of hers to coax storms into the palm of her hand.

Daring all, she pressed the sticky stuff against his lips and instantly knew she'd made a mistake. He did not bite, but opened his mouth to take the lavender and her fingers inside. Startled, she made to pull back, but could not. He caught her hand in his, holding her still as his lashes swept down across his cheeks.

Sticks! She scarce could breathe. His tongue was unexpectedly soft . . . and warm . . . and wet, and the slow slide of it across her skin, sucking the honey off her fingers, sent a wash of heat flooding down her body. *Double-sticks!* She had not known that one stroke of the Druid boy's charmed tongue would weave such a dangerous spell.

"La," a voice exclaimed. "What's this?"

Llynya whirled around, jerking her hand free of his. A guilty blush stole up her cheeks. Her heart was pounding.

Two of the harvesters had come upon them, Massalet, a young Ebiurrane woman, and Edmee, Madron's daughter. Gods, Llynya thought. Edmee would not miss much. Her friend had one side of her silvery green tunic hitched up through her belt and was carrying a birch basket full of raspberries. Massalet, brown eyes all atwinkle, held a wooden bowl full of cream.

Both maids were smiling broadly—much to Llynya's mortification—and Edmee set her basket down so she could make words with her hands. Llynya's blush deepened. She and Edmee had devised the language years ago, basing it on the silent signals of the Liosalfar, and she understood Rhuddlan and Madron's mute daughter all too well.

"Moira would have you eat these," Massalet said, interpreting for Mychael and trying hard not to giggle, "in case ye canna make a full repast of Llynya's fingers."

"Be gone with you." Mychael's voice was hoarse and gravelly, revealing a fatigue that went far beyond what Llynya had seen in his face, but she dared not look at him again. She wanted to run, felt the need of it twitching in her heels, yet felt equally compelled to stay. Damn Druid. He had ensorcelled her. Hadn't she told herself to beware of his kiss?

But who would have thought he would kiss her fingers?

"Oh, aye, we'll leave ye be," Massalet said, grinning, undaunted by his gruff demeanor. "Just be sure ye eat something besides the sprite." With a laugh, she set the bowl down on the bench and took off. Edmee, however, was not so easily dismissed.

Finger sucking? she said, giving Llynya a lift of her eyebrow and the barest hint of a smile as she settled the raspberry basket next to Mychael. She was fair-skinned with auburn hair like her mother, and had eyes as green as rowan leaves. *The ab Arawn boy and I have been studying the Druid wisdoms together since May, and he's not tried to suck my fingers.*

Just as well, Llynya thought, sending her friend a vexed look that she hoped disguised her inner turmoil. Though Edmee's hearing was fine, Llynya answered her in their silent language, hoping Mychael would simply ignore them. *I was administering a simple, nothing more.*

Edmee's grin broadened as she gestured to the berries and cream, offering them to Llynya. *Nor, as far as I know,* she continued, *has he been sucking on anyone else's fingers, though a few would be willing.*

Llynya ate some berries and drank some cream and didn't taste either. Neither did she deign to answer the quip, guessing Massalet was one of the maids holding herself forward for the archer's attention.

Has he kissed you yet? Edmee asked.

"No," she blurted out, then cast a glance at Mychael. The intentness of his gaze on her was far worse than Edmee's gentle teasing, and she quickly looked away. She was ready to run away as well, no hesitation.

He will, you know, Edmee continued. *Once a man has sucked your fingers halfway down his throat, he's going to want a kiss.*

"Oh, sticks and bother," she said, though she already knew the truth of it. Hadn't she sensed as much in Crai Force? *Look at him, Edmee. Does he look to be in any condition to kiss anyone?*

Edmee considered the question for a moment, slanting a glance at Mychael. *He looks in need of a kiss,* she finally signed. *But I would that it was not you who gave it to him. He's—*

Mychael's hand shot out and covered her fingers. "You go too far, silent one."

Llynya near expired on the spot, her mortification complete.

If Edmee was surprised by Mychael's reading of their hands, she gave no sign other than her considering gaze.

"Tell your mother I would speak with her today," he added, releasing the maid.

Edmee rose to her feet, and Llynya scrambled to hers, not wanting to be left alone with him. Gods, what had she and Edmee been about? Speaking of kissing in front of him as if he were blind. Trig had taught him the Liosalfar signals. He'd even used them with her. To discern the rest of their language was not so much for the quick-minded.

Trig. She near swore. 'Twas well past time for her to get to the portcullis.

Edmee signed a repetition of Moira's instructions for Mychael to eat, then with a teasing smile was gone, walking back toward the harvest fields. Awkward in her haste to do the same, Llynya handed Mychael the cream and muttered something about hoping the lavender helped, all without once looking at him. Then she took off, only too glad to escape.

Mychael watched her leave and wondered if traces of the previous night's madness yet flickered through his veins. What else could have compelled him to such a rash act? He'd tasted her, slid his tongue around her fingers and sucked the honey from their tips, and if not for Edmee's untimely arrival, he would have had his kiss. He'd heard the catch in Llynya's breath, felt her pulse racing. There had been no resistance in her, nor any lascivious fire, only a soft giving he could have drowned in.

He'd near died in the night. Whatever was happening to him, he no longer had the strength to control it. Worse, 'twas Madron who had saved him, filling him with some nameless potion and chanting songs that had taken him away from his pain—taken him from his dark and fiery vision to a place outside the flames. Aye, he'd risen above it and looked back and seen himself still lying in his tower room, swathed in shadows and sweat. Whither he'd gone he could not say, but a cool, waveless sea had been close on one side of him and a dense mist-laden forest on the other. Though a pale sun had shone above it all, to the west there had been night, a dark lake of sky with the rind of the moon and blue-white stars floating in it, stars unlike any he'd ever seen over Wales. In all that stillness, naught had moved until the lure of the west bade him take a step. To the dark he'd gone, following the shore, cloaking himself in moonbeams and feeling time shift with the sand beneath his feet. Into the dark he'd gone, a traveler clothed in white, treading a path marked by starlight.

After a long hour the wind had come up, rising over the water, swirling about him and turning his gaze from the moon. From across the sea he'd watched the witch blow her breath into his mouth—not a kiss— and thus cool his blood even more. With the last of the heat gone, he'd returned, awakening as if from a dream.

Except none of it had been a dream. When he'd finally stirred at dawn, he'd found a half-empty phial holding a dark concoction nestled in the bedclothes. He had it with him, secreted in a pocket Moira had sewn in the lining of his tunic. He would ask Madron what it was she'd poured down his throat, and what his price would be for having drunk it. For the witch's brew would have a price; there was no doubt about that, just as there was no doubt about its effectiveness.

Aye, the damned stuff had worked. The Druid woman would have him yet.

He turned his gaze to the field of grass. So would Llynya have a price, one he'd already begun to pay. The taste of honey and lavender lingered on his tongue, and the taste of her skin. He'd been mad indeed to set his mouth to any part of her. Still he knew he would taste her again.

From up on the wall-walk, Madron watched Mychael slowly get to his feet, obviously still aching from his ordeal by fire. Dragonfire. She'd stayed with him until dawn, until she was assured he would suffer no added ill effects from her potion. Thus she'd spent the night sitting by his side reading the *Fata Ranc Le*.

The boy had not let anyone near the Red Book of Doom since Ceridwen had given it to him. Where he kept it hidden had been beyond Madron's ability to find, until she'd watched him return it that morning

Balor's boar pit, not a place she would willingly go. Last night, blessed fate of its own, he'd had the book in his room, open and ready for her to peruse at her leisure.

Disappointingly, no more of Mychael's fate had been revealed beyond his place in the priestess line and the circumstances of his birth. Proof enough that like Madron, he was a carrier of the book, not a part of it. Such was the book's magic, set into it by she-whose-name-could-not-be-spoken, the greatest of all the Prydion Magi, that when an heir laid his or her hand upon the *Fata Ranc Le,* their fate would begin to reveal itself on the pages within, and the book would pass into that person's hands. Sometimes bits and pieces came to light within other stories, if the fates were entwined. Sometimes the stories were short, barely a page. The book was highly illustrated and ofttimes illuminated, making it a thing of beauty. Many of the languages in the *Fata* had died or been lost, and not even her father had been able to read all of the stories.

'Twas a rare pleasure to hold the book again after so long a passage of time. Seventeen years earlier, Madron had taken the Red Book from the Hart Tower in Wydehaw Castle and put it in the scriptorium at Usk Abbey. Nemeton had feared he could no longer protect either her or the *Fata Ranc Le,* and had exiled them both to a Christian house. His other great book, the *Prydion Cal Le,* had not been seen since his death.

'Twas at Usk, at her father's behest, that she had written Ceridwen's story into the *Fata*'s pages to ensure that the future would pass as he had foreseen. No one else would have dared such a breach of the hallowed pages. Except mayhaps a Prydion Mage.

She smoothed her hand over the worn red cover and opened the book again to the last written-upon page, revealing the new fate the book had acquired since Madron had written Ceridwen's. How it had gotten there was a mystery. No Prydion Mage had ever gone to Usk to write the story, and neither had her father. And if by chance the book had come into contact with one of its fated heirs, why hadn't it passed on?

That Mychael's story had not appeared was a sore burden. She would know if the boy lived or died, if he would have sons or daughters to carry on the Merioneth priestess line, if the dragons would come when he called, or if his dragon-tainted Druid blood would be his doom.

The book had told her naught. Without such guidance, she would be hard-pressed to help him beyond what she'd done in the night.

Beautiful wild boy, she thought, watching him make his way across the bailey. He had one arm wrapped around his middle, his hand soothing the left side of his torso where the dragonfire was wont to run rampant. *Did that long ago priestess conjure you only for you to die before you meet the fate for which you were born?*

Chapter 11

Trig barely gave her a glance when Llynya finally made it to the portcullis. A group was already gathered, Liosalfar mainly, with a few untried youths hanging about the fringes and sitting in a haywain. War was the order of the day, and Trig was firmly in charge, dispatching scouts and assigning watches to a cadre of the more experienced warriors—those who had fought in the Wars. Each of the border scouts was given a horn of tightly curled silver to sound in warning or if in need.

Shay spotted her immediately, giving her a short wave and walking over. Bits of chaff littered his hair and stuck to his tunic, making her wonder if he'd chosen to sleep in the haywain the previous night. 'Twas not a bad berth. She'd done it herself a time or two when the nickering of Rhuddlan's mares was the lullaby she needed.

"Where have you been?" he asked, a note of concern in his voice.

"I stopped by the chapel," she said, offering him a sage leaf out of one of her pouches, hoping to distract him from the blush she still felt on her cheeks.

He stuck the leaf in his mouth. "You've a cream mustache and berry stains on your lips."

She shrugged nonchalantly and wiped her mouth with the back of her hand, relieved by his inattention to more personal details. "So would you, given the chance."

"Well, you almost missed *your* chance. Trig's called for an expedition to Tryfan." Shay's eyes lit with excitement. "Twenty of us are to go and see what we can find. Wei is leading, and he's already picked me."

An expedition to Tryfan, she thought. Gods, but there was the chance of a lifetime.

"To mine for elf shot?" she asked, her blush forgotten.

"Aye, and mayhaps a chance to explore."

"The mountain halls are said to be bigger than Lanbarrdein, with stone thrones twice as high as a man."

"They'll not be as rich, I'll bet."

"Not in dreamstone or rubies"—for Lanbarrdein was encrusted with both—"but mayhaps in something even more wondrous, supposing they could be found." And there was the catch, she thought. Legend said the mountain fastnesses of the Douvan kings had been sealed for all time, ne'er to be opened again. Even so, here was adventure on a high scale indeed, to mine for elf shot.

"Come with us, Llynya. You know Wei would be glad to have you."

He was right. 'Twould take no more than a lift of her hand and Wei would have her with them on the journey north. In easier seasons, they'd traveled many a league together. He knew her strengths and probably her weaknesses too—except for the lavender simple.

She searched the crowd, looking for the elf-man, and found him by the iron gate, instructing two boys in the making and fletching of arrow shafts. Naught else would be needed to complete the weapons, except for the elf shot points he and his party would bring back from Tryfan, if any could be found.

" 'Tis far safer in the north you'll be, sprite."

Something in Shay's voice brought her head around. 'Twas more than the patronizing air he'd taken with her lately, the one she found so damned rankling. His face was drawn, his eyes dark with worry.

"Wei and I were the ones who carried you away from the weir after the battle of Balor," he went on, quietly insistent, "and after this last go 'round in the dark, I think you should steer clear of the caverns. There's something down there, and I fear it means you no good."

"I'm not afraid of the Sha-shakrieg." 'Twas only a small lie, for at the worst she was no more afraid of them than any other Quicken-tree.

" 'Tis not the Sha-shakrieg I'm talking about."

"Then what?"

"I cannot say exactly, but . . ." His voice trailed off, and though he shrugged, he did not smile. Nor did he retract his words.

"I've not known you to be prescient, Shay."

" 'Tis not prescience to sense something that's truly there, and in Crai Force, while I searched for Trig and Math, I sensed something else in the dark besides Quicken-tree and spider people. Did you not feel it too?"

Aye, she had sensed another presence in the furtive scrabbling she'd heard, and mayhaps in a raspy rhythm of disturbed breath.

A cold shiver wound its way down her spine. Had she heard breathing, she wondered, while she'd huddled by the falls? Or was her memory playing tricks on her? Had something grasped at her tunic as she and Mychael had run? Or was she building a troll out of Shay's fears?

There was danger in the dark. She could not deny it, but she did not need an elf child's nightmare of *uffern* trolls to find where hers lay. Descent into the weir of the golden worms would be her undoing—or her salvation.

"When does Wei leave for Tryfan?" she asked.

"After the midday meal," he said with noticeable relief. "We're taking Rhuddlan's mares and will meet at the stable."

"I'll see you then." She clapped him on the shoulder in good-bye before making toward the portcullis and Wei.

She'd made no promise really, and given enough time Shay would figure that out. He would certainly know it when they left and she was nowhere to be found. Her duty lay elsewhere.

"Wei," she greeted the Quicken-tree man. His hair was near as pale as Trig's, a mix of blond and gray showing his age and falling past his shoulders. His sleeveless tunic revealed iron-bound muscles and a lifetime's worth of tattoos: his initiation into a leaf clan, *daur* for Wei, the oak clan; his name in ogham down the inside of his right forearm and in the runes of the ancient common tongue down the inside of his left. All warriors had been marked thus in the Wars of Enchantment. High on his shoulder was a rowan leaf, identifying him as Quicken-tree, and below it the sign for Deri, where he was to be buried.

"Sprite." The elf-man looked up from his apprentices and smiled. He had a long, narrow face, his skin burnt brown by the sun. "Ye look none the worse for wear. Too quick for 'em by half, I'll bet."

"Too quick, or not worth the thread to burn me."

"Kept your guard up, did ye?"

"Aye."

"And didn't stand still like a fear-froze rabbit?"

"Nay, I didn't."

"Then ye were too quick for 'em by half."

"Mayhaps," she conceded, "but 'tis true that they didn't seem as interested in me as the others."

"You're young for a Liosalfar. Could be they thought ye were yet a child." He turned and caught a fletched shaft tossed to him by one of the apprentices. Wei looked it over, running his fingers down the smooth wood, then over the feathers.

" 'Tis what I thought too, Wei, but"—she paused, glancing at the two boys before lowering her voice—"don't the spider people eat elf children? Why wouldn't they have grabbed me for their spit?"

A broad grin spread across Wei's face, warning her of what was to come.

" 'Tis a mother's tale only, sprite," he said, chuckling, "conjured by women to keep their chicks firmly underfoot. Aye, and it did the trick during the Wars."

He laughed and patted her cheek, and she found herself twice humiliated in one day—and all before morning was done. Then his gaze caught and held hers, and his expression grew serious.

"You're Yr Is-ddwfn Liosalfar, Llynya, and faster than all the others tied together. Anybody tries to eat ye, ye gut 'em with your blade, girl, and if one comes after that, ye gut him too. 'Tis why ye carry iron dagger, dreamstone knife, and leaf blade sword."

"Aye," she agreed, knowing 'twas true. "But Bedwyr, he was . . ." She stopped, her gaze shifting away. Bedwyr had been fast. They both knew that too. The blade-master had been the one to teach her the Falcon Strike and the Bear's Feint. He'd been the fastest in Crai Force to throw a blade, and for that he'd died.

Wei lifted her chin and used his thumb to wipe away the tear rolling down her cheek. " 'Tis a truth without end, sprite, that warriors die in war. We'll all be missing him, and when the Liosalfar bring him home, we'll sing him back to the mother."

He released her to catch the next fletched shaft tossed his way and looked it over with a discerning eye, rolling it in the sunlight to see if 'twas straight.

She wiped her face with her sleeve. Damn tears.

"I'm to Tryfan," he told her. "If ye want a sennight of mountain travel and can carry a stone's weight of elf shot, you're welcome to come."

"I would sorely love to see Tryfan," she said, having no trouble conjuring just the right amount of wistfulness in her voice. "But Trig has use of me, and I've dallied long enough. Step lightly, Wei."

"Aye, sprite. We'll all be steppin' light, though not as light as ye, I trow."

With a short wave, she was off and heading toward Trig.

Now there was a gruesome sight, she thought, Trig with his green leaf eye patch and purple scars. Math was still under Aedyth's care in one of the willow huts. The captain needed no such coddling.

He saw her coming and dismissed the Liosalfar by his side.

Llynya grimaced. She should not have taken so long and she hoped to the gods that she didn't look like she'd been crying. Swallowing hard, she lifted a hand in greeting. "Ho, Trig."

"Llynya." He gave her a baleful look out of his one good eye. Strands of gray glinted like silver in the long fall of his fair hair. A five-strand plait was tightly braided down the left side of his head. Trig had all the tattoos of the Liosalfar from the Wars as well as a captain's wavy double stripe around his wrist. Woad hazel leaves wound up his arm. The rowan tree marked him high on his shoulder, and beneath it was the sign for Deri.

Given his grim mood, she thought it best to talk fast, before he could pronounce her task or her doom.

"I've spoken with Wei and would go to Tryfan, if you'll give me leave, Trig." 'Twas a hasty plan, but better than naught.

"Ye think to usurp my rule too, sprite?" If anything, his glare grew even darker.

She blanched. "Nay, Cap'n." She stood a little taller and met his good eye a little straighter on. 'Twas no good sign for him to speak of the mutiny so openly, and did not bode well for the day.

"Then ye'll listen before ye speak. The mountain trek is no easy—" He halted in midsentence, his gaze shifting to a place just beyond her left shoulder. She knew what had caught his attention even before she looked. The tightening of his jaw gave it away, as did the tingling she felt on her nape. She did glance back, though, and 'twas as she'd feared. Mychael had roused himself and, still looking like Christian hell, was headed straight for them.

She clenched her hand into a fist, not wanting to stay and face him again, but not daring to leave. Mayhaps her luck would change and Trig would dismiss her as he had the Liosalfar.

She shifted her stance, hoping to draw his attention and a gruff "be gone with ye," but the captain's gaze was unwavering.

"Trig." Mychael's gravel-voiced greeting announced his arrival. He stopped beside her, and Llynya did her best to ignore the blush crawling up her neck by staring resolutely at her boots. Ignoring Mychael was impossible. She tingled with awareness of how close he stood. Her ears twitched. Her nostrils quivered.

"Boy," the captain said, and she winced. 'Twould not be a bygones-be-bygones meeting.

"I was turned back from the Light Caves at dawn," Mychael said, every word seeming to cost him. He would have fared far better, she thought, if he'd taken her advice and gathered a bit of strength before facing Trig. "The sentries on duty said 'twas on your orders."

She looked up at that. She'd never known there to be sentries at the Light Caves, and she never would have guessed that Mychael had been up and about at dawn, or that he would have had no more sense than to go back down into the caverns in his condition. He needed a keeper.

He glanced in her direction, as if drawn by her own wayward gaze, and she was struck anew by the wildness of his parti-colored hair and the stark beauty of his face. Her blush deepened all over again. He wanted to kiss her. She sensed it even now.

"Aye, 'twas," the captain confirmed.

"You know I should be with Rhuddlan," Mychael said, his attention back on Trig. "I can lead him to the war gate."

"Rhuddlan can smell a war gate at four lan, boy. He'll not be needing ye to find it."

"Then I would go for myself," Mychael insisted, which got him naught but more of the captain's cold, unwavering stare.

Looking at them, Llynya wouldn't have believed the archer capable of imposing his will on Trig. Battle-scarred and tattooed, the captain was every inch the warrior, with the added advantage of a good three stone on the younger man—most of it in muscle.

"Ye'll not be goin' below for yerself," Trig said with an unbreachable finality. Then he turned his fearsome gaze on her. "Nor will ye, sprite. And if either of ye think to drop yerself down some hole in the hills or in Riverwood ye believe I don't know about, ye better think again."

Mychael said naught, only meeting Trig's gaze and looking like a good wind would blow him down.

Though his was no doubt the wiser course, Llynya could not accept such a dismal edict in silence. "Trig," she protested. "I—"

Mychael spoke quick enough then, even as his hand grasped her shoulder to silence her. "She'll not be going into the deep dark. Will you, Llynya?" The squeeze he gave her, though not physically discomfiting, was reminder enough of what else had transpired between them.

She squirmed away and shot him an annoyed glance he did not acknowledge. Plague archer, she thought. He was that and more if he thought to rule her, and a double plague to make her breath catch and her mind to wander where it should not go. He was naught but trouble—for himself as well as her.

"Aye," Trig said. "She'll not see the deep dark again until she can smell friend from foe and count Sha-shakrieg and skraelpacks with a whiff."

"You—" She whirled on Mychael, but was stopped by Trig.

" 'Twas not the boy, sprite. I would have figured it out myself, if not for the thread wounds sappin' me strength. 'Tis Rhuddlan who forbids ye in the caverns, but he gave me leave to use ye as a scout in Riverwood. As for ye"—he turned to Mychael—"Rhuddlan's orders are clear. Ye are to Lanbarrdein in a day's time. If ye'd be a captain, it will be of Ebiurrane pack ponies. A string was spotted this morning coming down from the north, led by Tabor Shortshanks himself. They'll make the castle walls by early afternoon. If any can get the beasts laden in half the time and headed down a dark trail, 'tis Llyr's pony-master. He knows ways in and out of Lanbarrdein others couldna even guess, and none save him ever got a pony past the old worm when we needed them in the deep dark. If it comes to that, he can do it again. 'Til then the hall must be provisioned, and a camp set up to supply those goin' below."

Mychael knew Tabor Shortshanks and his noxious ponies. Tabor had led a pack train down from the Ebiurrane summering grounds in late spring. Mychael had gone back north with them—and with a few pains along the way. Tabor was good company, well versed in elfin lore and full of a thousand tales that he took great delight in telling, but the ponies were another story altogether. An *uffern* breed claimed in the last Wars and not fully turned to an elfin hand, they bit, bold as brass when the urge took them, desiring a mouthful of man as if naught else could get the grass taste out of their teeth. The shaggy brutes kicked too, their sharp hooves striking out at seeming whim, but always hitting their mark, which more times than he cared to recall had been his shin. The thought of taking them into the caves and being trapped with them in the narrow passages of the Canolbarth was enough to churn his gut.

He met the captain's gaze, a protest on his lips, but was fore-warned by the glint in Trig's eye. Dissent would be dealt with by a heavy hand, and Trig had the heaviest when he was of a mind to use it. 'Twas by no accident that he was captain. As to what had happened on the beach by the Serpent Sea, the madness had put him up against the older man, and only the work of thread poison had left him unscathed. He pledged vassalage to none in Merioneth, but he owed Trig his allegiance. Better to take his punishment in pony bites than lose a friend, if Trig could still be called such.

"To Lanbarrdein on the morrow, then," he said, conceding, if only somewhat. From there he would do as he wished. He, too, knew a few ways in and out of the Hall of Kings he'd never seen the Quicken-tree use.

'Twas a chance he had to take.

The captain nodded, satisfied with Mychael's answer, but apparently with little else about him. "Yer a mess, boy. Llynya"—he shifted his attention to the maid—"take him to Aedyth and have her put somethin' together to get the green baggish look off 'im. When he's set, come back here for yer post."

She blanched, albeit slightly, and opened her mouth as if to say something, but was stopped by a shout from one of the guards on the battlements. The captain looked to the great wall. 'Twas with more effort that Mychael dragged his gaze from Llynya to the top of the portcullis. Pwyll, a young Quicken-tree, stood atop one of the gate towers. The boy made a quick sign, and Trig nodded.

"Go on with ye, then," the captain ordered, returning his attention to them.

Mychael stepped aside to allow Llynya the lead, having no wish to linger in Trig's presence. Apparently of the same mind, she turned on her heel.

Trig watched them go, then lifted his gaze back to Pwyll. The boy made another sign, more urgent, and Trig called for Wei.

Once on the wall-walk, Pwyll directed their gazes to the southern end of Riverwood.

"It started not more'n a moment afore I called you," the boy said, pointing at a line of trees along the river. The upper branches of the alders on the banks of the Bredd were leaning oddly against the wind, the top leaves of the coppice fluttering in opposition to the prevailing breeze. A faint scent of danger mingled with alder wafted in over the wall.

Trig needed no more to tell him what was amiss. "They've caught something."

"Some*one* more like," Wei said, "and no cottar."

"Aye," Trig said. "We best go see what they've got and what we can make of it."

Chapter 12

Mychael followed Llynya along the path she chose, through the fields toward the tower gallery in the eastern wall. At its other end the gallery emptied into the lower bailey, where Aedyth's hut stood in a copse of saplings. Trig had given an order, not made a request, but Mychael had no intention of obeying. Aedyth would probably as soon poison him as not. Moreover, he was still hurting from the night and Madron's concoction yet ran through his blood. God knew what another dose of some female's herbal might do to him. The maid looked a bit mutinous herself, her mouth a thin line, her gaze steady on some distant spot—avoiding his. Her strides were long and determined; the quicker to get rid of him, he was sure.

Tall stalks of *jhaen* warmed in the morning light, filling the air with the scent of ripe grain and brushing their shoulders as they passed. The harvesters were working the west side of the field, their voices a silvery murmur beneath the swaying of the grass.

Llynya was not like the other girls in Merioneth. Seeing her with Edmee and Massalet had sent that point home with a clarity that had been missing the other times they'd been together. No flirtation ever fell from her lips, even on a dare. He'd seen no smile cross her mouth except for the one she'd given Shay's doves. Not even Shay had been graced with such. As for himself, under circumstances dire or benign, she looked at him with naught but a darkly serious gaze, and if she ever laughed, it had not been where he could hear it. Odd for one known as sprite.

Was the loss of Morgan so great?

It troubled him to think so, and not because he would have her for himself, though there was that. He knew the pain of loss. He'd lived with it unabated throughout his childhood, the gnawing ache in the middle of his chest, the hard lump in his throat that inevitably led to tears. As a child in Strata Florida, if perchance he fell asleep dry of eye, he'd awaken before dawn and find his cheeks wet with tears, for his heart never forgot the deaths of Merioneth even when his mind wandered from grief.

He looked down at the solemn warrior by his side and wondered if she cried herself to sleep at night. He fervently hoped not. He'd seen no tears those nights in the caves, yet she didn't smile, and she never laughed, so pretty and serious was the elf-maid from the Yr Is-ddwfn.

"I'd not be going to Aedyth for simples, if I were you," she said, breaking the silence with a warning.

"Why?"

"The healer thinks you're a darkling beast, and there's no telling what she might give you."

"Aye, and she's right enough." His easy agreement garnered him a pair of raised eyebrows and a sidelong glance.

"I'd not go believing everything I hear about myself either, were I you." 'Twas an admonishment, as if she knew better than he which rumors to hold and which to belie.

She was piqued aright, but 'twas not his fault, not totally. She'd been found out and banned, and unlike him, her chances alone in the dark were near to naught.

"There's herbs aplenty in the east tower," she continued, then paused for a long moment as if in indecision. "If it suits you, I can mix you a simple as well as the healer." This last was spoken quickly, with barely disguised reluctance.

He grinned. Poor chit. She'd have naught to do with him if she could, but her conscience couldn't leave him to old Aedyth.

"Aye, your simples suit me better than most," he told her.

Color flushed her face, entrancing him. No rose blushed as prettily, and no girl ever for him. He would have her for his own, he realized of a sudden, whether 'twas love or not that held him in her grip.

"Trig let you off damned lightly for mutiny," she said, keeping her gaze forward even as her blush deepened.

"Better to ask why Rhuddlan let me off. Naught happens here except by his order."

She glanced up at that, her gaze going straight to the stripe in his hair. "Aye. I guess he has reason enough to keep you safe."

Side by side, they passed under the arch of the gallery, a narrow hall running ten yards along the inside of the great wall. Square windows looking onto the bailey lit the murky interior, showing gray stones damp with seepage. Green moss grew in the roughly dressed cracks. A yard down the gallery's length, a stairwell opened up into the east tower.

" 'Tis not Rhuddlan or Trig who concerns me," he said. "Nor Aedyth if it comes to that."

"Nor anyone, I'll bet." He barely heard the soft muttering as she turned into the tower.

He followed close behind, his grin broadening. After the brightness of the sunlit fields, he was briefly blinded by the dark, and the thought came to him that he was ever following her into dark and winding places.

In the next instant, as he turned the first curve in the stairwell, all his thoughts deserted him. Light from an open doorway in the room above spilled partway down the stairs, and by the grace of God and an errant breeze a bit of her bare leg flashed above the tops of her hose with each stride she took. He froze on a narrow step, staring up at her, transfixed by sudden yearning.

Christe. The breath left his lungs. The petals of meadowsweet and rose in her raiment glittered as if with dew. Thus she sparkled, and shimmered, and beckoned, tripping up the stairs with light steps, showing that silky skin. He swallowed hard, resisting the urge to reach out and touch her.

She'd kill him for certes.

Aye, he warned himself, taking off after her before she could disappear. Sticking his hand up her skirts or pouncing on her like some lust-crazed drake was unlikely to gain him much, being too crude even for one of his inexperience. And there was her knife to consider, and her present mood, neither of which boded well for an illicit caress or tower dalliance. In his forest imaginings, there had usually been a certain amount of desire on the wood nymph's part (actually, an inordinate amount), a creature so beguiling and seductive she had burned through every ounce of his (admittedly fragile) will and had her way with him in every manner he could devise.

But that had been before he'd seen Llynya lying in a tree bound with river mist. Naught in his imagination had ever compared to the reality of her.

"Nay," he belatedly said, recalling her accusation that he was concerned with no one. "There is one I think about overmuch of late."

The words were no sooner out than she made an abrupt about-face on the stairs. He nearly ran into her. Unfortunately, he was far too quick to run into someone accidentally, and she was far too surefooted to stumble, even on narrow, rough-hewn stairs.

"Who?"

He'd trapped himself. He could hardly tell her that 'twas she he thought about day and night. That he'd awoken that morn without the scent of lavender about him and had felt, along with all his other aches, a distressing sense of loss; or that the taste of her fingers had done more to restore him than any simple.

Or that the sight of her bare leg was enough to turn him into a lusting beast.

When he didn't answer, he sensed a stiffening in her stance.

"Massalet?" she demanded, standing far too close for reason to take hold.

Kiss her, was all he could think.

"If she's made you a promise," Llynya went on, " 'twill come to naught. An Ebiurrane man awaits her in the north."

"And you? Who waits for you?" *Kiss her.*

Surprise widened her eyes. "No one waits for me. I am not for any man," she said as if the fact was self-evident and inviolate.

"What of Morgan ab Kynan?" The question was hard to ask, but he would know.

"Morgan?" Her eyes widened even farther, and so help him God, he saw her ears twitch. "What sayeth you of Morgan?" The angels themselves had never sounded so innocent.

He was not fooled. "I say if you think to look for him in the time weir, 'tis death you'll find, not love."

Her face paled in the golden light curving down the tower wall. "You know naught of which you speak."

"I know more than you think and would have you hear me out," he said, growing earnest. He mounted a stair between them, bringing them on a level, face-to-face. "The path is not easily trod, Llynya. The light blinds your eyes and skitters across your skin. Ofttimes it sears in a screaming bolt. Thunder roars in the weir, and the air is so heavy, it near bursts your lungs to breathe it. Even if you can bear all of that, there are still the winds to contend with—fierce and sudden, coming at crosscurrents from all quarters, a destroying tempest that could rip a man in two. Verily, I tell you, all of love is not worth such a journey."

"I am stronger than you think," she said, but in truth sounded no more convinced than he.

"Even if you survived the descent, there is no surety of what you would find." Frustration edged his voice. "The weir changes all. Naught goes in that comes out the same."

"The stripe in your hair?"

"Aye, and this." He lifted his arm and pulled his sleeve up to reveal the pinkish bronze skin that ran along the inside of his forearm. He had not planned to show her the scars, but the loss of vanity was a small price to pay if it dissuaded her from her course.

Delicate fingers smoothed across the welted skin. "Does it hurt?"

"No longer, except when—" He stopped himself, and her gaze rose to meet his.

"Except when?" she prompted.

He shrugged and gave a negligible shake of his head.

She returned her attention to his arm, her fingers sliding off the scar to unmarked skin and back again. " 'Tis warmer," she said, looking up again, a question in her voice.

"The heat of its making returns sometimes."

"Like last night?"

He hesitated only a moment before admitting the truth. "Aye."

She pushed his sleeve farther up, past his elbow to the curve of his bicep. The scar continued. "How far does it reach?"

"From my skull to the soles of my feet."

In disbelief she lifted her gaze to his, then without preamble pushed aside the torn corner of his tunic. The scar arced across his shoulder. With hands gentler than he remembered, she followed the faintly metallic trail up his neck and behind his ear to where it aligned itself with the copper strands in his hair. When she reached for the hem of his tunic, though, he restrained her by grasping her wrist. Vanity might have fallen, but he would still have his pride. Her exploration, however gentle, had its consequences, and he would not have her know that her slightest touch was enough to rouse him.

"You'll not find the love you had, Llynya." His voice was rough as he felt himself teetering on the edge of an abyss, made vulnerable by her scent and her touch and the sight of her close enough to kiss.

Her gaze slid away from him. " 'Twas not love I lost when Morgan fell, but honor."

Honor? Confused, he let his hand fall back to his side. With the release, she turned up the stairs, taking the steps two at a time.

When the curve of the tower took her from sight, he scrambled after her. "Honor? You would die for honor?" Any joy he'd felt at knowing she was not pining away for love had been shocked out of him by the rest of her admission.

"There is worse than death to fear," she retorted.

He swore, a crude word she should not know, though the startled look she cast over her shoulder told him she did. 'Twas true what she said about death. He knew it well enough, but she should not. He should have kissed her when the thought had come to him, for now all he wanted to do was shake her.

They made the first landing with its open door spilling light into the shadows and kept on up the stairs. Moira's drying room was on the top floor. He'd been there a few times when the older woman had sent him to fetch something for her. The second landing was dark, the door to the topmost solar closed. Someone had strewn hyssop on the floor, and the pale scent of oranges rose up from their footsteps as they crossed to the door. Llynya reached for the latch, but he covered her hand with his, keeping the door closed.

"Honor?" he asked. "What honor?" Then a thought struck him, and his hand tightened on hers. "Did Morgan dishonor you? Is it vengeance you seek?" He would go after the Thief himself if that was the truth.

"Nay. He kissed me, true, but there was no dishonor in it, only a certain . . . ah, I don't know . . . sweetness."

Jealousy, as pure and galling as anything he'd ever felt, pierced his heart. Morgan had kissed her.

"Then where was honor lost?"

"Morgan was in my keeping, twice by Rhuddlan's orders. I should have been by his side to block the Boar's final blow."

"You did well to survive," he told her vehemently. "No one holds you responsible for what happened to Morgan."

"I need no one to tell me where my responsibility lies." Her chin lifted. "I am Yr Is-ddwfn. What passes for Quicken-tree honor will not suffice for me."

Arrogant, stubborn wench. "Does Rhuddlan know the high regard in which you hold him?" he asked, straining to hold his own anger at bay. "Or the lengths to which you'll let your foolishness lead you?"

"Nay, and if he did, he would banish me from Merioneth, which suits neither my purpose nor yours."

His purpose. Had she divined it then? Impossible, unless she meant his purpose with her. Aye, and she did aright. He could tell by the color suffusing her face. She knew he wanted her—and she was not running in the opposite direction.

Nay, she was not like the other girls in Merioneth. She was not afraid to be alone with him, yet of them all, she had more reason to be afraid. For that alone her banishment would not suit him, to have her exiled from the land where he was held by visions of war and dragons. He feared his days would be devoid of all light if there was not even a chance of coming across her in the bailey.

The realization brought him no pleasure. Had he truly become so besotted in less than a sennight? Morgan had kissed her, and she'd thought the Thief's kiss sweet. Now she dared him, Mychael, to have her banished if he would, and lose whatever chance he might have for a kiss himself.

Was she so sure he wouldn't do it? Was he so easily read?

Aye, he probably was, and that thought gave him no pleasure either. Only one thing could give him pleasure.

Damn. He stood before her, and his frustration grew until there was no help for it. He bent his head and pressed his mouth to hers, and a sorrier excuse for a kiss he couldn't have imagined: lips chilled by the dank cold of the tower, an unyielding body, harsh words lingering in the air. It was a hopeless kiss—yet she did not pull away. She took his clumsy kiss and by the sheer grace of her acceptance turned it into more than it was. Her sweet breath blew against his skin, softly, so softly, and the tension ebbed out of him. He stepped closer, so her body brushed against his, and sighed at the relief given him by the light pressure. She opened her mouth, and he fell headlong into desire.

Shadana . . . shadana . . . Llynya had wondered about his kiss since Crai Force, and now she knew. 'Twas a thing of heat and power. The change in his body temperature had been almost instantaneous with the touching of their mouths. The muscles in his arms, at first relaxed, were tightening beneath her hands, gathering strength as he moved closer. With his last step, she felt the hard warmth of his body pressed fully against her. 'Twas unlike anything she'd ever known.

And the taste of him. Gods. She'd opened her mouth and been flooded with a tidal wave of sensations. His tongue had swept across hers and she'd been drenched with an aching sweetness. He was all instinct and no finesse, devouring where she would savor, filling her with an overwhelming number of scents, each of them telling of a need beyond her understanding. Yet she felt it too, the inexpressible longing inherent in his body's movements. The difference between them, she quickly discovered, was in the level of daring. Where she would have balked, he pressed forward, inexorably pushing her farther than even an ounce of common sense would have allowed her to go. His hands slid from one forbidden caress to the next, with her own deflecting moves a half step behind, until she'd been touched everywhere. Or so she thought.

When his hand slid under her overtunic and above her hose to bare leg, the kiss changed. His groan echoed in her mouth, and 'twas all she could do to keep her feet beneath her. His hand, so warm on top of her clothes, was like a brand beneath them.

"Mychael," she gasped, pulling her mouth from his.

He did naught but take the opportunity to kiss her cheek, and her jaw, and her brow, murmuring her name while his other hand was busy at her waist. Her belt slid clattering to the floor, and she knew she was lost.

In a trice, his hand was under her shirt, his palm cupping her breast. Her clothes pushed up, her laces coming undone, she was falling at breakneck speed into uncharted territory.

Into heaven. Mychael was awash in wonder. He'd never in his life held anything as delicate and alive as the woman in his arms. The taste of lavender filled his mouth and infused his senses. Her skin was soft, so soft he feared the roughness of his hands would mark her somehow. Thus he was careful, molding her breast with a gentle palm, feeling the slight weight and falling deeper in love just for having touched her.

She smelled of flowers, hot flowers, like a riot of them blooming under a fiery summer sun. The perfumed redolence rose from her skin; he could taste it on her. Elusive violets and gillyflowers, sweet woodruff and peonies, lavender and lilies mingling together in an intoxicating scent. It went to his head like wine, swirling through reason and longing and mixing one with the other until he knew not where the first left off and the other began. Her heart raced beneath his hand, echoing his pulse where his wrist lay against her skin. He'd never been close enough to feel another's heartbeat, yet he was not nearly close enough to her.

Not nearly.

He pressed himself against her, his chest to her breast, and felt her melt into him, the soft giving way of a woman to a man. He pressed lower, a slow thrust of his hips; she gasped, and liquid fire ran into his loins. The scent of flowers deepened around him, making it harder to think beyond the fierce, running edge of desire. He thrust again and heard her breath catch in her throat. Again, and her fingers clutched at his shoulders.

He slid his hand farther up her leg, pulling her tighter against him, reveling in the silky slide of her skin, until he reached the apex of her thighs and felt her braies. Softer than Quicken-tree cloth they were, yet not as soft as what lay beneath, verily at his fingertips.

The intimate awareness washed through him, dragging a rutting heat in its wake. He was burned by it and worked feverishly at his own belt and braies to free himself. She moved to stop him, another protest of "No" on her lips, and in the confusion of hands and rough linen, her fingers found him—and did not pull away.

'Twas enough.

With no more movement on her part, he was stripped of all vanity and pride, his life's seed spurting out of him in equal measures of ecstasy and shame. The last left him, and she slipped from his embrace with a shocked expulsion of breath. Snatching her belt up from the floor, she disappeared down the tower stairs on silent, soft-booted feet. Naught but the sound of his own ragged breath echoed back from the surrounding stone.

Groaning, he leaned against the door, his head held in his hands.

Humiliation seeped into his every pore even as his body pulsed with the exquisite aftermath of being brought to climax by her hand. Gods! The crudeness of what he'd done appalled him, as well as his total lack of control. She'd touched him and a floodgate had opened, releasing every pent-up longing he'd ever had. He had not known it could happen so suddenly, so intensely, or be triggered by no more than a single touch.

Her touch.

He swore through gritted teeth and hit the door. He'd made an utter fool of himself and had probably horrified her beyond all forgiveness. Mayhaps his luck would improve on the journey to Lanbarrdein and one of Tabor's ponies would mortally wound him. A quiet death in the caves was no more than he deserved.

Yet for all his humiliation, the release she'd given him had been sweet, so very sweet. And for all that she'd gone, she'd not left him until the deed was over.

Chapter 13

Nia smelled the desert long before she felt the heat of it winding down into the caves. Her nerves were on edge, her strength and her courage faltering from the long, hard march. She'd done her time in the deep dark, but the Sha-shakrieg had done naught but descend from the damson shaft, and by the third day of her capture they'd gone deeper than she would have thought it possible to go and still live. Even now, after two days of climbing, she was not sure if she would survive the lingering malaise that had beset her on the steep descent—or the memory of what she'd seen, and felt, and heard in those far depths.

The nadir of their trek had been crossing a tide-pulled sea via a narrow causeway of stone. Far below the path, waves had crashed into one side of the cliff face. Salt spray from the wind-whipped water had lain in pools along the track, making every step a treachery. On the other side of the causeway, a huge ice cavern had loomed up out of the darkness. Glistening blue-white dripshanks the girth of a hundred men hung like grim sentinels at the cavern's entrance. By the light of the Sha-shakrieg's torches, she'd seen frozen waterfalls gushing out of the cave's inner walls, flows of blue-green ice roiling up from the floor, and a ceiling encrusted with slender white icicles.

"The Dangoes," the man in front of her had said in the common tongue. Varga was his name, and he was the leader, the one who held the rope binding her wrists. Naught else had been done to hurt her, though 'twas not for lack of enmity. Strange, frightening beings, the spider people were bound from head to toe in layers of brown cloth with gray gauze wrapped around their faces. They seemed of elfin or human shape—descended from a common ancient race, mayhaps—but only their dark eyes could be seen, watching her every move with hostility and a wariness she didn't understand. What did they think she could do against so many?

They'd thrown an extra cloak over her before they'd gotten to the causeway, yet 'twould have taken more than a cloak to keep the cold horror of the place from seeping into her bones. The vast, frigid cave smelled of death, of cold beyond the grave reaching out to hold life hostage in an icy grip. Passing the mouth of the cavern, she felt the caress of unseen wintry fingers, one across her cheek, another curling around her ankle. Light gusts of wind, she thought, until whatever spirit ruled the cave tightened its grasp—the better to pull her off the track and down into its gaping maw. Her cry brought Varga to her side with his torch. He swept the fire between her and the cave, and in the arc of sparks and flames she saw wisps of icy vapor twined and gnarled like old bones. Varga's quick action freed her, but fear had gotten a hold with that arctic touch and would not release her.

A true wind came up behind them as they followed the long, sinuous track over water and ice. Its frigid draft set the icicles in the cavern to singing, an eerie resonance of the earth's breath blowing through frozen strings. "Ice music," someone close to her muttered while making a warding sign. Varga walked on, pulling her behind, seemingly unaffected, but others of the spider people tightened their wraps over their ears for protection against the otherworldly strain.

The song floated out over the track to the sea, wordlessly melodic, its notes rippling through the raw air and running like ice water down her spine. Madness lurked in the song, the promise of a sweet, sleeping death to lure the weak or unwary, or those too tired to go on, whether their weariness was from the march or life itself. She was not so far gone as that and set her mind to other things, trying to block the eldritch tones. They were halfway across the causeway when a new melody came into play, and the fine hairs on her nape rose like hoarfrost. She stopped, unwillingly, her attention drawn and held by the glacial cavern.

The fey, mournful howl of the new song grew in strength, echoing off the giant pillars of ice and drowning out the sound of the sea crashing into the rocks below. She stared into the black reaches of the cave, frozen in fear with a prayer on her lips, until a hand grasped her arm.

With a start, she looked up and found Varga near. She could see naught of his wrapped and shrouded face except for his black eyes peering at her. His hand on her arm was like enough to hers, including being chafed red with the cold, but she saw what lay beyond the loose cuff of his sleeve, and she flinched. He immediately loosed her arm.

" 'Tis naught but your hound loose in the dark," he told her in his muffled voice, nodding toward the cave where the unearthly cry still rose from its depths.

"I have no hound," she said, her breath making vaporous puffs in the air. Then she knew and gasped a name. "Conladrian."

Varga shrugged and motioned up the trail. Nia followed, but cast a look behind. Conladrian, last seen in the mists pouring out of the weir gate. 'Twas Rhayne he must be mourning, his littermate, younger sister laid low on the shores of Mor Sarff by Caradoc. How was it he lived in this faraway place girt with ice and darkness?

The Dangoes. She repeated the name silently, and a shiver set her to trembling. She would not forget.

That had been two days past, and now 'twas heat she felt, building ahead of them and pressing against the chill of the caves. Bedwyr had been killed in Crai Force, but the others had survived. She'd seen them in the damson shaft and heard their plans. Their leaving had been hard to bear, but she was Liosalfar and knew Trig had spoken with wisdom. They had been outnumbered twenty to one, and Trig would have sensed the greater force. Rhuddlan would mount a rescue, but by her best reckoning, she put him just beyond the Magia Wall. She was on her own and had gleaned little information to help either herself or the Quickentree.

The Sha-shakrieg had argued in the damson shaft after the Liosalfar had left. Blades had been drawn and the company near split a dozen ways. One faction had cleaved to the dead boy they'd carried out of Crai Force. Others had made to follow the Liosalfar, but Varga had held them back, and miraculously held them all together. Rhuddlan's name had come up many times. In the end, Varga had prevailed, and they'd begun their trek toward Deseillign, carrying the body and their leather packs filled with *thullein*.

The sound of rushing water came to her on the next turn in the track, a great fall of it, and around the next turn came the light—bright and unbearable after the darkness of the caves, cast in shades of yellow and orange. The colors, she soon realized, were not of the light itself, but from the surrounding rock. Varga slipped a protective layer of gauze over her eyes before leading her on. She noticed all the Sha-shakrieg doing the same, pulling their gauze bandages up to dull the light. The landscape changed quickly from mostly horizontal to toweringly vertical, from the grays and browns of the deep earth to a thousand shades of orange and umber, to yellow, gold, and ochre, and to red in all its hues. Sheer-sided slick-rock canyon walls rose ever higher on either side of the gorge they followed, with a pale ribbon of blue-lighted sky showing in the opening above. In places, water ran down with the light, rivulets of color wetting the stone and illuminating the richness of the striated colors. Ahead of them, she could hear the thundering of the falls growing closer.

Pools of crystal-clear water marked one side of the path. Small and intermittent at first, they soon grew larger and closer together, until they began running into one another in a trickling cascade. Green plants sprouted up at the edges of the pools, and moss showed around the banks. Yet for all the beginnings of vegetation and the stream, 'twas the smell of the desert she sensed most keenly, dry and fine and slightly bitter. The sand, when it came, was at first no more than a few wind-driven grains littering the floor. By the time they began switchbacking into another descent, it had become a thick layer drifting into the canyon's nooks and crannies.

The falls gradually came into view, a line of silver rimming the edge of a canyon wall and growing wider as they rounded the curve, until finally the sheeted veil of water was before them. A heavy mist billowed into the gorge, dimming the light. The desert scent was drowned by the smell of water. Looking about her, Nia could see the trail had come out on a great rift that stretched for miles in either direction. The falls dropped from a promontory hundreds of feet above the trail and plummeted back into the earth through a mighty chasm hundreds of feet below them. In width, the chasm was half the length of Carn Merioneth's eastern wall, with rivers joining it at different heights. Canals stretched out in four directions from the lake formed by its rushing waters, and far in the distance, across a barren landscape of endless sand, she saw towers floating on the horizon.

"Deseillign?" she asked, pointing to the east. She would know her doom.

Varga shook his head. "No. Wadi Bishr-dira. The towers you see are pillars of rock shaped by the wind. Their heavy capstones keep them from being completely worn away. Deseillign is twice as far as can be seen from here."

Wadi Bishr-dira. The name echoed softly inside her. Varga used the common tongue when speaking with her, the language of all lands, but his voice had warmed when he used his own language to speak the name of a place he knew. She looked back out over the empty plain. Like the canyon walls around her, the desert was shaded in many colors. Clouds scudding across the sky threw shadows on the rise and fall of dunes and the rare scattered outcropping of rock. There was naught of what she knew, no trees, no mountains, no free-running rivers. It was the land of her enemies, yet the land itself was part of Earth, and she sensed the same power moving through it as moved through Riverwood or Wroneu. What stories did the night winds tell across the desert? she wondered. Of what did the sands whisper beneath the burning sun?

A group of black-cloaked guards waited nearby, while the rest of the Sha-shakrieg troop continued on down the trail, silent except for the creak of their leather ore packs. Varga called one of the men over and spoke to him in a low voice, then pulled a parchment from a pouch on his belt and handed it to the soldier. When the soldier started back down the trail at a run, Varga turned to her and pulled the gauze away from her face. Then he lowered his own, though only from his eyes.

"You should eat," he said, handing her a tough strip of the mashed and dried leaves that had been their rations on the journey.

She accepted the food, her hand out, and noticed an odd shimmering blue cast on her skin. Curious, she looked up, past the clouds, and her breath caught in her throat.

"The vault of heaven," Varga said. "The light of the Star still burns above Deseillign."

Nia knew what it was, but she'd never expected to see it. Far above the clouds, looking truly like the sky, was the roof of rock that encased the underground realm of the Sha-shakrieg, a cavern so vast as to deny that description, a country stretching from the Rift to the wasteland, a full thirty days' march wide.

The light flooding the subterranean desert came from the masses of crystal lodged in the rock, remnants of a star that had fallen to earth. Spread across the dome in a clear, mineral venation, the crystal burned with the fires of heaven, unquenched for a span of time beyond even the memories of trees. Only the rock itself had lived as long.

She moved her hand through the chroma, watching the starshine play upon her skin. That it could sustain a Light-elf, she had no doubt, if just barely. For all its bright beauty, 'twas not as potent as the daystar. Locked in the earth for millions of years, its life force was waning. She wondered if the Sha-shakrieg knew their time was running out—as would hers, if she could not escape.

She turned to Varga. "How many days' march to the city?"

He considered her carefully through the slit he'd made in his bandages. His eyes were not so dark as she'd thought, but closer to brown, very thickly lashed and deeply lined at the corners. "For them"— he gestured at the troop winding its way down to the desert floor—"two days by caravan. With the Lady's leave, you and I will go back."

"Back?" she repeated, startled.

"To Merioneth, to Rhuddlan's court that I may speak my piece."

Hope rose in a rush. He was taking her back. Alone. Whether 'twas brave or foolish, she cared not, though from what little she knew of him she thought that foolishness was not his wont. Yet with only him to guard her, she had a high chance of escape—even if her chances of survival were not nearly so good. She'd been underground for nine days without the sun's light to lift the weight of the darkness, and had only five more before the toll would tell. Beyond that was the unknown. No Liosalfar had stayed below more than a fortnight since the Wars of Enchantment.

She looked out to the crystal-streaked sky above the sand valley of the Rift. The starlight would help, but mayhaps not enough. Five days to get to the Dragon's Mouth. Alone, she could do it, if she was not injured in the escape.

Near as quickly as she allowed her hope to rise, 'twas dashed. Varga carried only her pack, but signaled for another of the black-cloaked guards to bring him one of his. Unlike the ore packs, the guard's pack jingled and clanged. Inauspiciously, she thought. Her foreboding proved justified when Varga reached into the pack and pulled out a wild tangle of chains. Rusted and barbed with a line of hooks, they had the wicked look of fetters.

"What are those?" she asked in a voice edged with anger begat of fear.

"Running shackles. Your odds of escape will not improve for being left alone with me." The clinking of iron underlay his curt explanation.

"I'll not run with those on my legs."

"You'll run," he said, calmly assured, untangling the looped metal links one from the other. "And over the middle stretch, you'll wish you could fly."

Bastard. She cared not what he said. If he bound her with chains and irons, the journey back through the caves would take longer than she could survive.

Something must have shown in her face, for his next words offered encouragement. "I know how the deep dark weighs on the Quicken-tree, and that you've been at least nine days down. With it eight days back to the light, you'll be dead, or at least halfway there three days before we get to the Dragon's Mouth. So we'll not go back the way we came. There are shortcuts through the great caves, none swifter than the ones we'll take, and few more hazardous, but we'll cut the three days we need off our time."

"We'll cut even more if you do not shackle me."

"We could," he agreed, "but you're Liosalfar, and I remember enough of the Wars to take extra care."

"What care?" she chided in her anger. "You risk certain death to go to Merioneth."

Unbelievably, he appeared to smile beneath the gauze. "Not so certain as all that. Rhuddlan will not underestimate the importance of what has brought me out of the desert."

Nia's ears pricked up. Here was the answer that had eluded her all these last long days. The Wars were centuries past, the realms of enchantment at peace. Those who had battled for supremacy, the Dock-alfar, had fought to their death, each and every one, ensorcelled by their mad leader with a bloodspell gone awry. No contact had been made between the Quicken-tree and the Sha-shakrieg for five hundred years— until Varga had captured her in the dark.

"Why did you come?" she asked.

Varga gave the Liosalfar warrior a measuring look and was reassured by what he saw. He'd stopped drugging her that morn, replacing the lightly poisoned rope he'd used on her wrists to keep her manageable on the trek. He'd dared not continue with it. He needed her strong for the run they would make to Merioneth, and within a half day's time, she was rebounding in health and vigor. The dullness had gone from her eyes, leaving them a pure, clear green, the color he'd oft seen Quickentree eyes in battle when they shone as bright as their dreamstone blades. Her hair was a dark chestnut brown, proving her young, barely out of swaddling clothes by *tylwyth teg* standards, yet she was tall and leanly muscular and old enough to have been carrying daggers and a sword.

The answer to her question held risks, but also rewards. If he could bring her to his side, the shackles could be left off and her chances of making it home would increase tenfold. For all that the Liosalfar had seen the smoke and the broken damson shaft, after the debacle in Crai Force not even Varga of the Sha-shakrieg wished to walk into Merioneth without a hostage. 'Twould do him far better not to have his captive dead in his arms when that day came, if there was to be a hope of an alliance.

In a matter of days, the *thullein* they'd brought home would be forged into blades and given an Edge of Sorrow by the desert smiths, with one blade made more deadly than all the others combined. No skraeling could withstand even the weakest of the desert smith's swords. With the Lady's leave, he would offer the swords to Rhuddlan in return for a fighting force. Together they could put the skraelings in a vise.

And still it would all be for naught.

A foul curse lodged in his throat. *With the Lady's leave*—The curse escaped him in a low hiss. Her long-held hate would be the death of them all. Rhuddlan had nigh destroyed her once, but the King of the Light-elves was her only hope now.

The great crystal seal on the abyss in Kryscaven Crater had been broken by enchantment, and 'twas from there that the mortal danger arose. Dharkkum. None could withstand it, not skraelings nor trolls, nor the fell mage who had wrought such malevolence.

To win the battle against the all-consuming darkness of Dharkkum they would need Rhuddlan's dread beasts, and they dare not draw the dragons down upon themselves without a lord to rule them. The King of the Light-elves was a fair dragon keeper, or had been before Merioneth had been lost and the nest emptied, but to wield the Magia

Blade took the fire and fury of youth, and Rhuddlan had near as many years as Varga himself.

The aetheling he'd seen in Crai Force had fire in her, starfire. 'Twas in her blood, but the bloodlust fury for the fight was not. He'd watched her fight, and aye, none were faster or cleaner with a blade. Warring with dragons, though, took madness, and he'd seen naught of that about her. There must be another laethling, a Dragonlord, and that one, he knew, would be Rhuddlan's bane.

"Do you know the story of the Starlight-born?" he asked in answer to the Liosalfar's question.

"Bits and pieces, aye," she said. "They ruled the Douvan Kingdoms, but that was a long time ago, too long ago to be remembered."

Yes, she was young, he thought.

" 'Twas even before the Thousand Years War," she said, adding the reference as if he might need one. He smiled beneath his mask of gauze. He'd had a child once who had been as young as she, but no more. All his children had been lost in the Wars of Enchantment.

"The Thousand Years War gave the elves two kingdoms of their own, that of the Liosalfar and the Dockalfar," he said. " 'Tis said the Wars of Enchantment had their beginning in the ending of the Thousand Years War."

"Aye, I've heard the same."

"Such is often the case with wars," he went on. "One leads into another. For the Starlight-born 'twas the same, but the span of time between wars was far greater, encompassing whole ages. The time between the Thousand Years War and today would be naught compared to those ages. Time enough for all the world to forget the war that came before and to be unprepared for the war that comes again."

"War is coming?" He heard the quickening in her voice and took it as a good sign. She would fight, as would Quicken-tree and Ebiurrane and Yr Is-ddfwn, and all of the *tylwyth teg,* fight for their lives.

"War, but unlike any you have known, unlike what any of us have known—Sha-shakrieg, Liosalfar, and those of Men who trade in memories even more ancient than the Douvan Kingdoms."

"You don't know much of men, if you think they see beyond their bellies and the short span of their lives," she said, arching one of her eyebrows to make her point.

A warrior, he thought, but no scholar. Yet for what he needed, 'twas the warrior who would do.

"They are there," he promised her, "in every corner of the world. Holy men and women who guard the secrets of the past so that they will not be forgotten, whose sacred duty is to their gods, but whose sacred trust is the knowledge left by those who came before, age after age since the world began. Rhuddlan knows them in your land, even as the Lady of Deseillign knows them in hers."

"You speak of an alliance?" She sounded incredulous, and both of her eyebrows rose, as if she thought him crazed beyond saving.

"Aye."

She dismissed him with a rude noise.

Hiding a smile, he shrugged out of her pack. "It is in my best interest as well as yours to return to Merioneth as quickly as possible. If you think on it, you'll know I speak the truth. You'll not be guiding me into the heart of the Quicken-tree stronghold, as I already well know the way. And there'll be no surprise to your kind. Rhuddlan is not one to forget his old enemies, and on the war gate I left him a sign that I would return. He'll remember enough of knotwork to read what is there, and remember me well enough to know that if I'd meant you harm, I would have left you *en chrysalii* for him to find with the message."

Her gaze, so bravely contemptuous before, filled with fear. Yes, she understood what he'd said, even if she'd never seen the ancient torture. Mayhaps the Quicken-tree told their campfire stories as well as the Sha-shakrieg. No child of Deseillign did not know of Rhuddlan, Scourge of the Wasteland.

"So I offer you a truce," he said. "Your word against these." He lifted the chains, and light glinted off the razor-sharp barbs.

"Aye, and you've got it," she said after only a moment's hesitation. How truthful she was being remained to be seen, but even if her agreement was half a lie, 'twould be enough to see them through. The route he planned would leave her little time or inclination for escape.

"Good." He pulled a leaf-wrapped seedcake out of her pack and held it out to her, but when she reached for it, he didn't immediately let it go.

She lifted her gaze to his in question.

"You're Liosalfar," he said, as if reminding her.

"Aye."

"And strong?"

"Stronger than those who are not."

He released the cake and gestured with a lift of his chin. "Show me your arm."

Another short hesitation followed his request. Then she stuck the cake between her teeth and pushed up her sleeve, showing him the tattoos he'd hoped to see.

"Good. Good." His gaze tracked the hazel leaves embedded in her skin and the single rowan leaf high on her shoulder. The mark for Deri was below. Her name was in runes between her elbow and her wrist. Nia. "Have you been through the Kai Crack?" he asked, naming a crawlway off the main passages in the Canolbarth.

Her eyes narrowed suspiciously. "You know much of Liosalfar training if you know of the Kai Crack."

"Every man knows his enemies. Rhuddlan could tell you more of me than my own captains."

She seemed to give that some thought, then nodded. "Aye. I've been through the Crack and a couple of other squeezes besides."

"Then you'll not have any trouble with the Grim Crawl."

She looked dubious. "Grim Crawl?"

"Ghranne Mekom in my language, a squeeze that bypasses the Kasr-al Loop. To take a hundred soldiers through is too slow, even provided that you have a hundred who won't freeze up in the tighter spots. But two travelers can cut half a day going that way. Don't worry. It's not much worse than the Crack."

The skeptical look she threw him did much to increase his confidence in her. No one who had struggled through the tight and narrow crawlways called "squeezes" underestimated their danger. Getting stuck in a tunnel so small that the ceiling pressed down on your back while the floor pressed up against your chest was a real threat, and the natural urge to panic in that situation spelled death.

"How do we cut the other two and a half days?"

"We'll gain a half day roping down into the Mindao River Slot. The water isn't running too high. We'll get wet, but we won't be washed over the falls."

Her eyebrows rose again, even higher, but she made no protest. "And what do we have to do to save the other two days? Leap a flaming gorge? Climb one of these canyon walls with our bare hands?"

'Twas his turn to hesitate. Unlike with the other two shorter routes, he had no reassurances to offer with the third. They would drop down off the trail into jeopardy, and the threat would deepen around every turn until they reached the Magia Wall.

"No," he finally said. "Though you may wish it were so. The third route lies through the Dangoes."

She visibly paled, and her fingers moved in a quick sign. He said nothing, but knew it would take more than a warding to keep them safe. From the look of fear in her eyes, so did she.

"Eat your cake," he told her, "and I'll tell you the tale of the Starlight-born as it is written in the *Elhion Bhaas Le.*"

"You know the Indigo Book of Elfin Lore?" she asked, a bit of her fear giving way to surprise. She was not easily cowed, nor for long, he was heartened to see.

"Aye, the very same. Listen well, for such a time as it speaks of is now."

And so he began. The story was an old one, the oldest, for it told of the beginning, of the star and the darkness, of the Ages of Wonders and the Dark Age that had followed. The story told of the Prydion Magi and the Seven Books of Lore—and it told of the making of the dragons from a star-metal cauldron and how the mighty serpents had devoured the darkness.

"But beasts of war are ever hungry," he said, drawing the story to its close, "and even as the dragons spawned their first brood on the shores of the nether sea, the magi forged a peerless sword to rule them, its edge tempered with star-wrought metal, its hilt crowned with stones of light. A bloodspell was then cast over the people of the Earth so that forever after those who could wield the blade would come forth in time—Aethelings of the Starlight, bound by celestial ether." He finished and looked at her. "Stept Agah was such a one. 'Tis said he was bound to the blade by a Chandra priestess and though he died, the sword yet delivered its killing blows."

" 'Tis a *druaight* blade that will fight when its master is dead," Nia said, a note of apprehension in her voice.

"Aye, and it takes a *druaight* master to wield such a sword."

Nia lowered her gaze to the trail, hiding her fear and the sudden pounding of her heart.

She knew an aetheling, the only one, Llynya.

*   *   *

In his private quarters above Rastaban, Caerlon stood in front of an opening that looked out on the court of the Troll King. Below, Slott ranged through the assemblage, a mountain of flesh and hair and clinking skulls, and long, twitching tail. Near the west wall, Lacknose Dock was readying a troop for a morning raid into Merioneth. They would leave within the hour and make Riverwood by the next day's dawn. Blackhand Dock had taken a force of skraelings and a wolfpack into the deep dark the previous night. With Sha-shakrieg daring to breach Quicken-tree territory, time was running short. An alliance between the old enemies was unlikely, but Caerlon was not taking any chances. Every possible obstacle to victory had thus far been removed—*every possible one*—and he would not let delay be his undoing. The aetheling had returned from Deri less than a fortnight past and with all else ready, 'twas time to bring her into the fold. Whether aboveground or below, he would have her, a succulent boon for Slott, before he rid the world forever of her kind.

One other troop had been sent the day before, a skraelpack to Tryfan, led by Redeye Dock. The Quicken-tree would go there for elf shot, but Caerlon was going to give them a taste of war.

He turned from the opening toward the room. Light from the torches and fires in the great cavern spread an orange glow around him, revealing curved, stone walls and Slott's newest vassal sleeping on the floor.

Wyrm-master. A despicable name for one held so dear, yet Caerlon himself had to admit that Rhiannon's son was less than inspiring. In truth, he looked far different than Caerlon had imagined him, far worse, even with the clean tunic and hose Caerlon had procured for him. Yet the stripe was there, and he was golden-haired, and he'd been found in the deep dark, where no other man could have survived. His coming had meant the end of Caerlon's long wait—five hundred years of wait. "Troll's Bane," the man was called, and as had been told, the breaking of the damson crystal seals had drawn him nigh.

Bloody hard work that had been. A thousand spells Caerlon had cast, nine hundred and ninety-nine of them for naught, each requiring rare configurations of metals and stone and crystal, before he'd been able to put so much as a hairline fracture in one of the seals. But he had prevailed, and the crystals had cracked. Half a year past, even the mighty seal on Kryscaven Crater had given way before his sorcery. 'Twas then he'd begun amassing his army from the ranks of men, one warped soul at a time, in readiness for when the final breaks began and the smoke arose, the dark effluence of another age that had power over the enchantments of the Prydion Magi.

Below walked the proof of it. When he'd taken the smoke to Inishwrath and poured it over the rocky headland that had been Slott, it had released the Troll King. He'd brought Slott home a fortnight earlier to strike fear in the hearts of the Quicken-tree and the Sha-shakrieg—and the friggin' skraelings. He'd needed a king to hold them in check before he dared gather all of them together in Rastaban, just as he needed the golden-haired man to hold the dragons in check; for as sure as the darkness came, the beasts would come to destroy it.

So there the great sword wielder lay, branded and lame, and not so young as Caerlon had thought he would be. Sworn to Slott he was now, and no longer Troll's Bane. Naught was left to keep Caerlon from his desire—the weir gate, the great wormhole. So he had read in his closely held book, and so he believed. To fall into the future took no great skill, but no redemption awaited Caerlon in the future, no glories to overcome his shame. For that he needed the past. The dragons could place him there, the book had revealed, him and all his host in one great breach of power. Brought to heel in the doorway of time, Ddrei Goch and Ddrei Glas could turn the worms, all of them, the whole golden clew, and open a window onto the Wars of Enchantment, onto a time before the death of the true king, Tuan of the Dockalfar, the sovereign Caerlon had failed with his bloodspell.

Mad, Caerlon remembered, his hand tightening into a fist. They'd all gone mad, the Dockalfar, to a man, woman, and every child, and in their madness died with his potion running through their veins.

No smoke could bring the old bones of the Dark-elves to life. Naught but a return to the past could do the deed, and soon Caerlon would hold the reins of time. The way of it had been revealed by the one he held below. Fitting justice, for she was the one who had betrayed him with the bloodspell. She had written on a page where there should have been naught, and thus he'd gone one step too far in his conjuring. The damning ink had faded from his sight even as the Dark-elves drank his draught, and he'd been too late to stop them.

Cursed Ailfinn Mapp. Cursed, cursed mage. She'd dared to deface the *Elhion Bhaas Le,* the Indigo Book of Elfin Lore, and the Dockalfar had paid the price.

Now she paid, and when the Quicken-tree all lay dead about her, he would count her penance done. Until then, she was his to torture, as she had been since she had come to Merioneth and found him lying in wait.

He'd known she would come. Though a thousand years should pass, she would come for the book he'd stolen. Her book. The *Elhion Bhaas Le.*

It had been a fortnight had passed since he'd gone down to see her. There had been no time, what with his business at Inishwrath, and the calling of the skraelings from all points north and south, and the bringing in of Troll's Bane. No doubt she was languishing on the edge of death, for that was where he kept her, suspended between life and death, heaven and earth, in a place where no skraeling dared go, a place where the twilight sleep of forgetfulness reigned—the oubliette of Rastaban.

Aye, he would go see her and take her some foul sustenance, and upon his return he would unleash Lacknose Dock to sniff out the aetheling in Riverwood.

Chapter 14

The forest was asleep when Mychael struck out from the castle for Bala Bredd, a small lake high in the mountains, the source of the River Bredd that wound through the wooded glens of Merioneth. He and Owain oft went there together, though the older man had declined to leave a warm and cozy bed this night for a trek into the hills.

Tabor Shortshanks had indeed reached the curtain wall early that afternoon, and he and his ponies would be rested and ready for the journey into Lanbarrdein come morning—only a few hours off. The pony-master had been pleased that Mychael would be his companion, far more pleased than Mychael was himself. He'd already been kicked once and stepped on twice while helping Pwyll and a couple of others unload the packs, and he doubted he would fare any better in the caverns.

Llynya had not been there to help with the ponies. Nor had she been at the hearthfire for the feast Moira had ordered in Bedwyr's honor. The old warrior's body had been brought up from Mor Sarff and on the morrow would be taken to Deri for burial at the base of the great mother oak.

Elen and two kitchen boys had baked loaf upon loaf of *kel* bread for the feast, and well into evening the upper ward had still smelled of hot ovens and fresh manchets. Seedcakes had abounded, soaked in honey and smoothly crunchy. Redbuck pottage had been served with blackberries and cream from the cottars' cows. The largest cauldron on the fire had held a great stew of porray herbs and vegetables: leeks and neeps, wild lettuce, wurtys, peas and purslane. Nuts and murrey had rounded out the meal, along with platters of Moira's delicate mushroom pasties.

It had been a feast for kings and Mychael had barely eaten a bite. Next to the elf-maid's kiss, food held no allure. He had spent the day searching for her in every nook and cranny and bailey tree, inside the castle walls and out, wanting to make amends, wanting to see her again, even if 'twas only an apology he would have on his lips and not her kiss. But it had proven to be true that a sprite who did not want to be found, could not be found.

He had waited in the ward for twilight, thinking for certes that the singing would draw her out, that she would brave his presence out of respect for Bedwyr. He'd been wrong, and that pained him, for he knew only a great loathing could have kept her away. No doubt the only reason she hadn't run right off in the tower was because she was too young to have known what was happening. When she had realized, she must have been horrified in the least, and at the worst, frightened.

All the more reason he needed to talk to her. He would not have it on his conscience that he'd forever put her off love. Despite what was certain to be naught but an embarrassment to himself, he had to assure her 'twas nothing but his own foolishness she'd suffered. Aye, the longer he thought about it—and in truth, he'd thought of little else all day— he'd practically attacked her. He was lucky to still be of a piece.

The singing was behind him now, the sound of lute and lyre, of bodhran drums and silver flutes and Quicken-tree voices. Tabor's voice could be heard above the rest, singing a lament for Bedwyr. The sweet, clear notes of the pony-master's song and the soft din of the accompanying music traveled on the night wind, slipping o'er the stone curtain and into the forest, yet fading farther away with each long stride Mychael took through the trees.

A scout line had been set up all along the river, and as he neared the Bredd, he grew more cautious. 'Twas not an easy thing to elude Quicken-tree scouts, but the last thing he wanted was for some youngish elf on his first patrol to startle at a broken twig and blow his horn. He would never reach the lake then.

To the south was the arbor copse where, Mychael had been told, the trees had captured a monk. Mychael had considered going to see the stranger, but time was short, and he would as soon spend it at Bala Bredd.

He reached the lake with the half-moon full risen. The final stretch was a rocky climb through a cascade of boulders and the small streams that gathered 'round them before running down the mountain-side. As he neared the top, the boulders gave way to a boggy fen with a string of beaver ponds marking where the water flowed out of a small vale and the streams began.

The lake was bordered by a great forest on the north and west, the last outpost of Riverwood. On the east, the steep scree slopes of Glyder Mawr rose to a towering summit spiked with pinnacles of stone. An island floated in the middle of the lake, with a precarious bridge of fallen, half-submerged trees linking it to the westernmost shore.

The island was Mychael's destination. 'Twas haunted, according to local legend and with good reason. Strange noises could oft be heard sighing and hissing through the island's trees. Clouds of mist would sometimes appear at the base of its rugged limestone cliffs and then glide, ghostlike, out over the water.

Tonight was one of those "sometimes." A whole bank of dense fog lay about the cliffs and their environs, parts of it wisping off to float on the lake. The wind was carrying odd sounds with it across the fen.

Mychael grinned, recognizing the faint hiss of steam coming from the geyser pool at the heart of the island. The spring that fed it was running high to have made such a fog. There would be hot water aplenty.

He was across the tree bridge and had dropped onto the island's sandy shore when he heard the crack of a breaking branch behind him in the forest. He instantly crouched down, his senses alert, and peered across the moonlit lake into the woods. A gust of wind came up suddenly and blew through the trees, their limbs dipping and swaying. Nearly as quickly as it had come up, the wind was gone. After waiting a good while and seeing and hearing nothing more, he turned away and headed into the trees, making for the pool.

Llynya watched him from the low bough of a trembling pine, still not believing that she'd broken one of the tree's branches. Yet there the thing was, right under her foot with half of it sticking out from beneath her boot. The tree trembled again, up from the roots and down every limb, shaking her and stirring up another wind. It wanted her gone, but she dared not leave its cover until Mychael was good and away. She'd followed him, wanting to know where a Druid boy went of a cool dark night, but she didn't want to be caught sneaking along behind him.

"Sticks," she swore at herself, dropping out of the tree when he finally disappeared into the island's small wood. A branch brushed up against her backside with a light swat at the same time as a pinecone bounced off the top of her head.

"All right, all right," she muttered, brushing herself off. Such had never happened to her. She was the sprite, the light-foot, the one whom all the trees had graced with a leaf for her hair, not some clumsy oaf who went crashing through the forest. The trees expected better of her.

The day she'd returned to Carn Merioneth, Mychael had kept to the forest well into the night, and she'd wondered where he had lingered. If he knew about Bala Bredd, she figured 'twas likely he'd been here that night as well. 'Twas a healing place, where the wild berries grew and gave fruit nearly up to the winter solstice, what with the pool to keep the bushes warm. Those of the world of Men avoided the vale, though not strictly because of the mysterious hot spring. Rhuddlan had long claimed the lake as his own and woven a warding around the island, enough to make Men uneasy when they first stepped upon the fen, or if they set foot on the western slope of Glyder Mawr.

Riverwood held its own enchantment, of the deep forest and of old growing trees that had long listened to the Mother. There were parts of Riverwood where even the bravest of men felt the ponderous weight of arboreal eyes and the warning to beware, and one of those parts bordered the western shores of Bala Bredd.

A shrubby margin of brambled hazel, hawthorn, and bracken rose up on the hills to mark the beginnings of the lake forest. She could not speak for the hawthorns, but the hazel trees were old beyond their time, their long life a gift from Rhuddlan for some ancient deed. The lake forest birklands were her favorite. Made up of lofty golden beech trees and the occasional giant sycamore, they were lovely places to while away an afternoon or an evening, especially when a full moon dappled the leaves with silver. 'Twas like a fairyland then, with the light dancing all around.

When she could no longer detect movement through the trees on the island, she made a quickety-split dash across the bridge. Mychael was no doubt heading for the pool at the base of the cliffs. If he was going for a swim, he really should have a lookout, so 'twas just as well she'd followed him out of the castle.

In truth, she'd been following him all day, keeping him in sight while keeping out of his. Her fascination with him had doubled over on itself half a dozen times since being with him in the tower. She was thoroughly dismayed with her reaction to a single bout of kissing—and thoroughly smitten with him, she feared.

He'd spent a terribly long time with Madron in her hut that afternoon, before Tabor had arrived with the ponies. When Mychael had finally left the Druid woman's quarters, Llynya had seen him slipping a phial into his breast pocket. A simple, no doubt, and she dearly wanted to taste it and discover what Madron had given him. Some witchery potion for certes, mayhaps a cure for the dragonfire that was wont to lick beneath his skin, mayhaps something to more securely bind him to Druid ways—or to Madron herself.

Llynya didn't like the thought of that a'tall. She'd gone back to the tower while he'd been unloading the ponies and made him a simple of her own, the dose she'd promised him in lieu of Aedyth's. She'd left it on his tower-room door, but he'd not gone back to his room before making his escape through the postern gate.

He'd gone to see Moira that afternoon too, and come away with a bundle of Quicken-tree cloth he'd taken with him when he'd left Carn Merioneth.

Fool boy. He should not be wandering beyond the curtain wall by himself after dark. Nigh onto most all of the wolves had strangely disappeared out of Riverwood four days past, but there was aught besides wolves to fear. And if he was going for a swim, he'd be even more vulnerable, in the water without weapons, naked as a newborn ba—

She pulled herself up short, a blush full-blown on her cheeks. What was she thinking? She couldn't spy on him if he was naked.

On the other hand, if he was naked, she dared not spy on him, if she was to keep him safe.

"Bagworms," she muttered, caught betwixt and between and annoyed at herself because of it. She'd seen plenty of naked men of all shapes and sizes and ages, from the newest babes to the oldest warriors. With Moira and Aedyth, she'd done her share of tending to aches and pains, and she'd swum in Bala Bredd with a dozen or more naked Quicken-tree and not thought a thing about it, because nakedness was not thought of by any of the *tylwyth teg.*

But Mychael ab Arawn was not *tylwyth teg,* and she'd ne'er kissed a Quicken-tree man the way she'd kissed him. It changed everything, that kiss, and to secretly look upon him naked with lust in her heart would be as close to Christian sin as she hoped ever to get.

And truly, it was lust she felt for him. She'd held him in her hand and felt the spell of sex magic rise up in both of them, the power and the heat and the longing, until his had spilled into her palm. It had all gone too fast, but she'd thought of little else all day—and of how such kissing could have come to a far different end, one in which she had not run away.

Aye, she wanted the Druid boy for her own, and mayhaps that was the biggest change in her. She no longer could have sat in a tree all night and blithely watched over lovers in the glade below, not without thinking about Mychael and his kiss.

Her only hope, then, was to catch him before he got in the pool, smooth over the part about following him, and convince him to return to Carn Merioneth posthaste. Thus she took off into the woods and arrived at the pool just in time to see him dive—bare naked—into the water. The curses of "sticks" and "more sticks" fell from her lips. Thoroughly frustrated, she paced the shore, waiting for a chance to catch his attention, determined to make a clean breast of it. She'd followed him, aye, but for his own good. She'd seen him naked, aye, but purely by accident and not for long, and with the mist and the night, she'd not seen much. Truly, not much at all.

Her foot landed on something soft, and she stopped to see what was cushioning her step. 'Twas his clothes.

Of course, she thought with an exasperated sigh. They lay in a haphazard pile near a small ring of stones, a fire ring. She knelt down and brushed her bootprint off his tunic and, in the brushing, felt Madron's phial. She paused, but for no more than half a moment, not long enough to give her reticence a chance to bloom into restraint before she had Madron's gift in her hand.

Settling comfortably onto the leaves and pine needles carpeting the ground, she crossed her legs, rested her elbow on her knee, her chin in her hand, and gave the phial a good looking over. 'Twas sheathed in a leather casing—cow's leather, poor thing—with the top sealed by a round of beeswax, a typical configuration of Madron's. The leather was an abomination, as always, but Madron was Druid, not *tylwyth teg.* Llynya sniffed around the seal. The beeswax came from a hive in the northernmost reaches of Riverwood, where the bees harvested sweet clover and heather, and she wondered that Madron traipsed so far afield.

Carefully, she rolled the beeswax up to reveal the potion. 'Twasn't much to look at, darkly green with bits of whatnot floating on top, but the smell was enough to set her back. Herbaceous and pungent, it reminded her of nothing so much as one of Dain Lavrans's concoctions, *aqua ardens,* water that burned. The mage had ever been distilling something in his lower chamber, and often enough it had been *aqua ardens.* The herbs in the potion were mainly of the cooling variety.

Cautiously, she touched a little of the stuff to her tongue. Naught happened at first. Then it warmed, giving her a tingly sensation. The warmth spread as far as such a small taste could go and cooled. The basic infusion was refreshing, mostly benign, except for a couple of ingredients: a hint of mushroom spore she knew to come from an ancient faerie ring in Wroneu Wood, and a salt she could not precisely define. The herbs were potent enough to be helpful, but not harmful. On the whole, the potion had about it the taste of Moira's *gwin draig,* dragon wine, yet with an edge Llynya was not sure the Quicken-tree woman would countenance—except mayhaps for a Druid boy. Moira and Madron oft had their heads together over one simple or another, and this one could very well be a compilation of the two women's. There was naught of a binding spell about it, and for all its potency, she did not think it could hurt him. Someone should be with him, though, if he ever decided to use it. Men were not oft prepared to go where mushroom spore might take them. 'Twould be best if he wasn't alone if that time came.

Her curiosity satisfied, she resealed the phial and returned it to the pocket of his tunic. The white wool from his much-altered monk's habit was patched and worn, roughly woven and scratchy beneath her fingers. Moira's patches of quilted Quicken-tree cloth were luxuriously soft and thick in comparison, and Llynya found herself wishing all his clothes were so fine. She folded everything in a pile: tunic, shirt, a buckled baldric, chausses, braies, and reached to set the cloak on top. 'Twas a good piece of Quicken-tree cloth, dark green shot through with silver.

But 'twas more than just his cloak, she realized when she lifted it. Moira's bundle was wrapped inside. She took a peek, wondering what the other woman had made him.

A flash of purple caught her eye at first look. She was ever inclined to investigate things like flashes of purple and, it seemed, anything having to do with Mychael ab Arawn. So she lifted a piece of the cloth and discovered, to her surprise, that Moira was more prone to binding spells than Madron. The Quicken-tree woman had finished the edge of the cloth with intricately knotted braidwork known to weave a binding fate. The stitches along a seam were fine and delicate, worked one over the other, then back again to recross, the whole of it making a never-ending knot in one of Moira's strongest patterns. Then there was the purple.

Llynya lifted another length of the cloth and discovered a tunic sleeve, a marvelous sleeve more like her own than what any of the Quicken-tree wore. To get a better look, she shook the tunic out, and a cascade of wild iris rippled down into her lap—purple petals delicately veined in saffron yellow, calyxes and stems intact, sword-shaped leaves woven into the cloth like verdured blades.

The plants graced naught but the outside of his left sleeve, from shoulder to wrist with each corolla pressed into a perfect fleur-de-lis. More of the sword-shaped leaves had been woven as narrow panels into the front of the tunic and as a stripe down one of the chausses, their supple greenness contrasting with the cloth. 'Twas wondrous and strange that Moira should make him such clothes.

Llynya smoothed her fingers over the tunic. 'Twould keep him warm, much warmer than sheep's wool, and the shimmery green cloth would hide him in the forest as well as it did any of the *tylwyth teg.*

The sound of a splash at the far side of the pool drew her head up. He was swimming through the shadows where the cliffs angled out over the water, but even the added layer of darkness couldn't hide the pale gold of his hair. He levered himself up onto a rocky ledge for another dive, and moonlight ran down the length of his body in a silvery stream.

He was beautiful, she thought, bathed in mist, the steam curling around his feet and legs and twining about his torso like a silken veil. She brought a handful of his clothing to her nose and watched as he dove, entering the water even more quietly than he'd left it. The scent of violets came to her from his tunic, telling her his clothes were worked in iris even down to the roots. The cloak smelled solely of him, of man and musk, and she brought it closer to her face.

When he surfaced about midway across the pond, she raised her dreamstone dagger and tightened her hand around it to make the hilt flash, identifying herself as Quicken-tree. The colors of the crystal would tell him 'twas Llynya of the Light-elves. She planned on staying until he left, so she would as soon let him know he wasn't alone. To her surprise, after a moment he flashed her back. 'Twas then she realized he was not nearly as vulnerable, nor as naked, as she'd thought. A quick check proved his belt and dagger sheath nowhere to be found.

"Rotters," she swore under her breath. She'd been on a fool's errand. He'd been running with the Liosalfar for nearly half a year. He did not need her protection. No doubt he could handle wolves and skraelings, the Sha-shakrieg, and a whole band of marauding thieves and cutpurses with one arm tied behind his back. Yet now that she'd so blatantly announced herself, she couldn't very well leave, not without looking even more the fool. So she sat herself down by the fire ring to brave it out and silently condemned herself as a half-wit ninny.

He slipped beneath the water and did not surface again until he reached the rocky ledge that made up the shore. The pool was depthless, or at least the bottom had ne'er been touched by a Quicken-tree. A pillar of rock did rise to within ten feet of the surface in the center of the pool, and 'twas from there that the geyser sometimes blew out its steaming, mineral rich brew. Mostly the hot water bubbled out of the pillar without reaching the surface, making the pond warm and pleasant for swimming even when snow was piled all around—none of which occupied her thoughts nearly as much as the sight of him rising out of the water.

"Malashm," he said, wiping his face and then slicking his hands back over his hair.

"'Lashm," she said on a half swallow. The water glittered on his skin and ran in rivulets down his lean, angular body, defining the muscles in his arms and chest. Small waves lapped at his abdomen and broke on the silver and leather belt buckled around his bare waist. The hilt of his dreamstone dagger glowed blue and white beneath the surface of the pond, lighting the jut of the hipbone from which it hung and probably more, if she'd dared to look, which she did not.

He didn't seem the least surprised to see her, or the least self-conscious about his undressed state, which disconcerted her almost as much as the way he looked, like a pagan water god ascending from his kingdom in the mere.

"Is everything aright at the keep?" he asked.

"Aye," she managed to get out, then wished she'd prevaricated a bit. Of course he would think she'd been sent by Trig to find him, and for certes she'd given herself away by admitting there was no emergency that had sent her out in the middle of the night and that demanded his speedy return.

He was quiet for a moment, his gaze holding hers across the water. His right hand had settled around his dagger hilt. His left was splayed across his midsection in an absent caress that did damnably odd things to her insides every time her gaze slipped the least bit. No doubt he was mulling over her reply and realizing she'd come of her own accord and not on orders—a fact proven by his next question.

"Are you staying for a while?" he asked, cocking his head as if he was not quite sure what to make of her being there.

"A while," she said as nonchalantly as possible, as if she had merely happened by with no particular plans.

"Would you watch this, then?" He unbuckled his belt and laid it on the rocks, dagger and all. "I'll swim better without it."

At her nod, he dove back into the water with a graceful arc and swam again to the far side of the pool.

Left at a loose end, she could think of nothing more sensible to do than build a fire and gather a goodly pile of sticks and fagots. The air was growing cooler and had a certain crispness that ofttimes heralded snow. 'Twould probably not reach Carn Merioneth or the lower reaches of Riverwood, but Bala Bredd was a mountain lake, and the mountains could well be dusted by morning. She lifted her nose into the night and closed her eyes. Aye, there would be snow, and soon.

He finished his second lap of the geyser pool and started another, swimming with powerful, even strokes—back and forth, back and forth—until the fire was crackling and she'd long since stretched out on her back on a makeshift pallet of their cloaks, to watch the stars rather than him. Now and then she wondered if he would swim the night away, but mostly she let the rhythm of his strokes fade into the background as she tracked the wanderers across the heavens and waited for his return.

Chapter 15

The wind had picked up by the time Llynya awoke, rising out of a drowsy slumber to find Mychael sitting across the fire from her, finishing the last of a handful of raspberries and looking very elfin in his new clothes. Firelight danced along the shimmering cloth, picking up the colors of the flowers and the leaf blades, and giving them a faint metallic sheen to match the copper stripe in his hair. The line of his scars had been clearly visible earlier in the moonlight, but had done naught to take away from his appeal. He was marked, but with time, the magic elixir of life. It suited him well.

"Hullo," he said, looking over when she stirred and extending his hand with the berries.

"Nay, thanks." She shook her head at his offer and eased her shoulders with a stretch. Some protector she was, she thought, sleeping away while he walked all about, drying off and changing clothes, buckling and unbuckling his baldric and belt and probably snapping all kinds of twigs and branches while he'd picked his berries.

"I didn't mean to wake you," he said.

She thought she detected a teasing note in his voice, and sure enough, when she glanced over, a grin was curving the corner of his mouth.

Much to her irritation, she felt her cheeks grow hot. Bothersome boy.

" 'Tis rare work Moira did on your tunic and chausses," she told him, pushing herself up to a sitting position and ignoring his gibe. "Not many *tylwyth teg* can weave whole plants into their Quicken-tree cloth."

"Not many of them break the branches of trees they're hiding in, either," he said, and his grin broadened, warming the cool gray depths of his eyes. "What's the matter, sprite? Losing your touch?"

"Touch. Posh." She set about tucking a few straying braids back into the tumble of her hair, as much to hide her blush as to accomplish any tidying up.

" 'Twas you I heard, then. Banging and clattering through the woods behind me."

"I've ne'er banged and clattered in my life," she declared in mock affront.

"Aye," he agreed, opening a gourd of catkins' dew he'd brought with him to the fire. " 'Twas what I told myself, that it couldn't possibly be you, but mayhaps an old, lumbering boar bear, or a staggering hart with his rack all tangled in the bracken, or mayhaps a great questing beast the likes of which bay at the moon. But there's no beast here, only you."

He was clearly enjoying himself, and so was she for all her show of discontent. 'Twasn't often that he smiled, and even less often, if ever, that he teased, yet he was teasing her.

"And there you are wrong," she assured him. "There's a questing beast here, come to Bala Bredd to devour the fruits of the forest. Mayhaps she'll come for you next, when the raspberries run out, so you'd best eat your fill and be gone."

His grin flashed again, and he laughed. "I've oft searched for questing beasts in the woods and never yet found one, so I think I'll wait and take my chances."

The sound of his laughter so surprised her, running through her like clear, cool water, that her pulse quickened and her ears pricked up and twitched forward. She could do naught but gaze at him, dumb-struck—gaze and yearn for his kiss. For that was the trick, wasn't it? And the real reason she'd come? To steal a kiss from him, if she dared.

She could have quickety-splitted one off him, but a quick kiss was not what she wanted. She wanted one of those slow, wandering-all-over kisses he'd given her in the tower. And now she wanted another kind of kiss, one with laughter in it. Sweet mystery of desire, to want to kiss, and touch, and taste his delight, to press her lips to the teasing curve of his smile and sigh and laugh with him, sharing the same warm breath. Aye, the truth of it was very clear when she sat this close to him. She'd come for a kiss.

But how to go about getting one, that was the vexing question. They'd been arguing in the tower just before he kissed her, but she had no heart for arguing this night.

He'd nearly kissed her the time she'd cut him in Crai Force, but she knew that had been "in spite of" and not "because of" her dagger work. Nay, she did not want to hurt him, not ever again.

What she wanted was to kiss him, once, twice, thrice, and on and on, until the sun rose over Glyder Mawr and silvered the scree. Given her reaction last time, though, she doubted if he was still inclined to kiss her.

Sticks and rot, she thought, her mouth tightening. There had to be a way besides Massalet's flirting. She'd never flirted with a man in her life. 'Twould make her feel a perfect fool. 'Twas best, mayhaps, to try to win his friendship, and then, as a friend, she could outright ask him for a kiss.

"Does your cheek pain you a'tall?" she asked, her concern real even if her motives for asking were highly suspect.

"Not much," he said around a yawn. Putting his hands together, he stretched his arms out in front of him. Lean, supple muscles flexed and contracted beneath his tunic. At the apex of his stretch, he groaned, a soft, intimate sound, an animal sound full of animal pleasure. The vibrations of it echoed through her, and she near melted on the spot.

"Moira put something on it," he continued, relaxing from the stretch and taking up the catkins. "Something besides *rasca* to take the pain away. 'Tis mostly her stitches I can feel anymore, not the dagger cut."

They sat for a while in companionable silence, so companion-able—what with the fire crackling and the wind soughing through the trees all cozylike—that Llynya nearly convinced herself they'd already reached a stage of friendship. Then she did a quick review of their encounters over the last sennight and decided that although there was some sort of relationship between them, it could not yet be classified as friendship.

"I've seen some of the Quicken-tree move in that special fast way you did in Crai Force with your blade," he said, looking up from the fire, his eyebrows drawn together in thoughtful confusion. "But none of them are as fast as you. Not even close. I remember 'twas like a lightning strike when you cut me."

" 'Tis called 'quickety-split,' or 'tlas buen' in the elvish tongues," she said, struggling with a twinge of guilt. Rhuddlan might still have her wrung and hung for cutting one of their own. "The Yr Is-ddwfn aethelings have always been the fastest of all the tylwyth teg. The Quicken-tree have lived too long in the world of Men, for eons and eons I s'pect, and there's been marriages and such between the two, sort of like the one between your father and mother, who though she was not exactly elfin was the closest I've ever seen a priestess be. Near faerielike, she was, a rare faerie blodau, not one of the little woodland beasts. The mingling up has made the Quicken-tree and the other clans stronger in some ways and weakened them in others, but they can still run circles around men."

"You knew my mother?" he asked, leaning forward, his sudden, eager interest reminding her of his long-ago loss. She nearly reached out and touched his cheek, but held herself back. Under no circumstances could her feelings for him be misconstrued as maternal.

"Aye, and I loved her too," she said, glad they shared such a bond, though she'd not seen Rhiannon or gone to Merioneth for years before he'd been born. Ailfinn and she had wandered far and wide after leaving Yr Is-ddwfn, returning to Merioneth only to find it had been lost to Gwrnach. "She told the most wondrous stories and played the sweetest harp. You could hear the stars singing in Rhiannon's harp. She had soft hands, and a soft, soothing voice, and her hair was like a beautiful golden cloud. I ne'er saw hair like that again until Ceridwen came to Deri. I gave her a thousand braids that night to keep her safe." She paused, stirring the fire with a long stick and giving him a sidelong look. "You know, you could use a braid yourself, a fif braid. 'Tis one of those fair, subtle things that bind you to the trees."

"Binding, knotting, braiding, and brambling," he said, smiling again. "The Quicken-tree are ever weaving the world together. To what end do I dare bind myself to the trees?"

"Well, you'll walk through them a little easier, if they know you're there," she explained. "Most times they don't bother with a man. Men's lives move too fast for trees to care much about, but if you're *fif* braided, kind of like how all of them are wound up together on this patch of earth or another, they'll notice you more, and sometimes they'll talk to you a bit."

"Talk?"

"Aye."

"About what?" he asked, his voice rising on a note of incredulity.

"This and that," she said with a lift of her shoulders.

He stared at her for a long time before the doubt faded from his expression. "They talk to you, don't they?"

"Aye, and Rhuddlan, and Madron, and most any of the *tylwyth teg* who take the time to listen."

A sigh escaped him as he looked up at the trees. The dark crowns of pines, and oaks, and a few straying beeches carved out their silhouettes against the night sky, curving around the pond in an uneven horizon.

"A *fif* braid will tie me to the Quicken-tree as much as the forest, won't it?"

"Aye," she confessed.

He lowered his gaze from the trees back to her. "Some of them would not be so glad to see me walking into Carn Merioneth with my hair braided."

"Naas gave you a dreamstone, and Moira made you a suit of clothes with a whole wild iris woven down the sleeve," she asserted, stirring up another batch of sparks. "No matter if Rhuddlan himself wanted you gone, he could not go against those two."

Another smile curved his mouth, but 'twas wry, lacking any semblance of delight. " 'Tis not Rhuddlan who would have me gone. I think he would as soon I was reborn a Quicken-tree so he could be my uncontested liege lord with full power over me."

A turn of events he was not inclined to allow, she'd realized days past.

"He's fair enough as a liege lord, but the braid will make you no more his than you are now," she assured him. " 'Tis a protection for you, is all, and it only ties you closer to the Quicken-tree because they are all tied close to the woodlands and meadows, to the fens and grykes, mosses and moors. I heard tell once of an Ebiurrane who went so far north there were no trees, no green living thing. One night, she became lost in a blizzard of fierce snow and ice. At dawn, when she was nearly frozen stiff with the cold, she heard the trees of home calling her. She heeded their voices and was guided to safety. If you ever needed sanctuary in the forest or out of it, the braid will make it easier for the trees to guide you."

"A *fif* braid will help the trees mark me a path into sanctuary?" he asked, looking up from the flames, his eyes dark with the keenness of his gaze.

"Aye. They know the way from every which place to every other and e'en the places in between, like Yr Is-ddwfn."

"Yr Is-ddwfn? The place where you're from, is it a sanctuary, then?" His curiosity was fully alight now, and of asudden she realized a misunderstanding had taken place. She could have kicked herself for not being more careful.

"Aye, I suppose it's a sanctuary of sorts," she told him, backing off a bit from her tinker's pitch for the braid. Aedyth thought him a darkling beast, but Naas had told her a different story that afternoon while they'd sat on the wall and watched Mychael and the others unload Tabor's ponies, a story of priestesses and dragon's blood, and Mychael's searching of the Dragon's Mouth for a map of Nemeton's.

Neither treebound refuge nor Yr Is-ddwfn could protect him from himself, and the dragonfire that burned through him was implicitly his, a bloodspell from Ddrei Goch and Ddrei Glas conjured in an ancient time and running through his veins.

"It's a sanctuary of learning and some might say of enchantments," she went on, avoiding an outright blighting of his hopes. "The Prydion Magi found it near the end of the Dark Age, though they believed it to have been there even in Deep Time. 'Twas the dragon spawn, the *pryf,* who opened the path to Yr Is-ddwfn through the wormhole."

"I've been in the wormhole," he reminded her, "and I never saw a path."

"You wouldn't have, unless you'd been taught, even if 'twas right in front of you. Ailfinn Mapp, the great Prydion Mage, tried to teach Nemeton how to find the path, but for all that he learned, he was ne'er able to learn the way to Yr Is-ddwfn."

"So Yr Is-ddwfn isn't Nemeton's sanctuary?" he asked with a

furrowing of his brow, coming around to the truth quick enough on his own.

"Nay. But mayhaps I could teach you the way there," she said on a hopeful note, thinking she really should kiss him. She knew she could cheer him with a kiss. "Most anywhere, a thing is either there to see or it isn't, but the path to Yr Is-ddwfn has a trick to it. There's a place not very far inside the rim that looks to be either here or there, and if you squint just so"—she demonstrated with a crinkling up of her eyes—"and soften your gaze so you're not staring too hard"—and she did just that, peering at him while actually trying not to see him so much as to see through him—"you'll notice there's a wee bend to the rock, and if you can find your way 'round that bend, which I'll be the first to admit can be a bit troublesome on account of its not being too solid as rock goes and with the worms swirling all around, well, if you can do that, you're practically there, and once there, you'll be surprised to find it's not very far from here. Not very far at all."

She opened her eyes and found him watching her with equal parts of puzzlement and amusement.

"Well, that is how it's done," she said in her own defense.

"I've no doubt," he said, "but I think I know why the Druid never mastered the trick. I don't suppose you have a less tricky method for finding the sanctuary that was Nemeton's?"

"Nay," she admitted. "Naas says Madron has turned Merioneth apart trying to find her father's journals, for therein lay his maps and such, but naught has come to light."

"Naas says?" he repeated doubtfully. "Naas never says anything. She doesn't even talk to Rhuddlan."

"Well, she talks to me. We've been friends from when I first came to the Quicken-tree."

A grin twitched the corner of his mouth. "The trees talk to you. Naas talks to you. The chickadees and the doves talk to you. Is there anything or anybody who doesn't talk to you?"

"There was a man once," she said, leaning forward and smiling herself, "but now he's talking to me too."

He blushed, much to her delight.

She scooted closer and slid her fingers through a length of his hair. His blush deepened, warming his skin and her fingertips, and once again she was struck by his beauty—by the high angles of his cheekbones, and the fine, near delicate line of his nose, by his dark lashes, and the equally dark arcs of his eyebrows, so in contrast to his fairness. He looked more from the far north than from Wales, from beyond the North Sea where his white-gold hair was common among men, where his cleanly carved features were not so unique. His eyes, so palely gray, held the barest rim of Ceridwen's blue. Around the pupil was an even thinner line of amber. 'Twas the amber line that was wont to light with flame when the heat was upon him as it had been on the beach at Mor Sarff. This night he did not look so fierce and fiery, only warm from his swim, his body relaxed and at ease. This night he was a man who laughed.

Fascinated by the changes wrought in the waters of Bala Bredd, she lowered her hand and touched the small white scar at the corner of his mouth. "How did you get this?"

"I stumbled in the garden at Strata Florida and cut myself on a rock," he said after a moment's hesitation.

'Twas her touch, she knew, adding the husky edge to his voice. His temperature rose about them both in heated awareness, caressing her skin with the scents of desire and longing. She'd been wrong to think he didn't want to kiss her—for he indeed wanted a kiss, a kiss and more.

She glided her finger over the scar before removing her hand. "How old were you?"

"No more than five or six. 'Twas the day Moriath took Ceri away from the monastery. When the monks locked the gate behind them, I panicked and went off running, trying to find another way out. Everywhere, the walls were too high for me to breach, until I found the garden. A small gate at the end of it lay open onto the fields, and I could see the road they'd taken." A trace of his smile returned. "I nearly made it, but by the time I picked myself up from the ground, bleeding like a stuck pig, Brother John had caught me, and he didn't let go of me again until I was twelve and too big for him to handle."

Llynya had heard tell long ago about Rhiannon's daughter being at Usk Abbey, but no one had spoken of a son. It had been Ceridwen herself who had told Llynya that her twin brother was in Strata Florida.

"Was it too awful, being in such a place?" she asked, repressing a shudder. "I've heard they tie women to stakes and burn them, and that they keep their God alive in vats of wine and bits of bread and eat and drink his flesh and blood."

" 'Tis true, but no one was ever burned at Strata Florida. Our abbot did not abide by those ways. As for the wine and wafers, 'tis not as cannibalistic as it sounds, but is meant as a form of worship."

"I would as soon sing the Mother's praises and walk gently in her woods."

"Aye, it seems a good way," he agreed, "and one more suited to my nature, though in truth I suffered less harm at the hands of the monks than I have since coming home to Merioneth."

"You could go back," she said, and immediately regretted the words.

"Nay." A shake of his head sent the silky length of hair she'd handled sliding over his shoulder. "I thought so once, but no more. Most men know naught of the enchantments living beyond the forest's edge and beneath the hills they call home, and mayhaps that is the way it should be. They rarely pass into the realm of the *tylwyth teg,* and those brief trespasses are accounted as 'magic' and nothing more. But I would not go back and close my eyes to what I've seen." He angled a shy glance in her direction. "That morning at the river, I thought you might have wings, so fey did you seem with the mist rising all about you, talking to a flock of chickadees."

Aye, he wanted her aright.

"No river faerie me," she denied, mayhaps too quickly, feeling a rare bout of shyness herself. She'd thought she was the only one entranced that morn. As to the other, wings weren't so far removed from her family line that her shoulder blades didn't tingle now and then. "Come. Let me give you a braid to bind you closer to the trees. I swear they'll do you even less harm than the monks."

He nodded, and she took up a handful of his hair, pleased to finally be doing him a good turn. Working from the bottom to the top, she finger-combed the flaxen strands until they slipped like sunlight through her hands. His hair was straight and fine, not a wild tumble of curls like Ceridwen's. The texture made her work both easier and more difficult. Fine strands were less apt to tangle up with one another, but more apt to slip free of the plait, especially when from the top of his head to his shoulders his hair was any number of lengths. 'Twas also any number of colors, all blond, from yellow and honey-gold strands to subtle swaths of lighter hues, of silver and palest ivory.

Parting off a small section, she began plaiting a five-strand sinnet, half blond, half auburn. With the crossing over of the outside lengths toward the middle he would have a parti-colored braid and the most unusual plait that had ever been seen from Riverwood to Wroneu. For his added protection, because he was not *tylwyth teg,* she slipped a silver ring from one of her baldric pouches into the braid about a third of the way down. At two-thirds, she added another, small ring worked with runes, and started twisting in a green and silver riband of Quicken-tree cloth. Nemeton had never taken a *fif* braid. Lavrans had done such only for the fire festivals, and those had been before he'd dropped into the weir and his hair had changed.

That only left one other who could have compared.

She made another pass with a length of auburn hair and riband, her smile fading. Wherever Morgan was, she doubted if anyone had thought to give him a braid; and if the truth were told, she doubted if Morgan were anywhere at all, but was yet suspended in some awful limbo far away in time and space. She knew little enough of what happened inside a weir, and Aedyth had known even less. Ailfinn knew. Ailfinn knew everything, but though the mage had been expected in Merioneth all summer, she had not yet come. Llynya hadn't felt the Thief falling since leaving Deri, which might have been a fair portent, except for the unsettledness in the vicinity of her heart that had not left her since he'd disappeared into the wormhole.

Nay, Morgan had not landed someplace in time, not yet.

As she neared the end of Mychael's braid, a gust of leaves—oak and birch, hazel, and a few straying rowan—swirled up around the fire, encircling them in an autumn dance of scarlets, ambers, and yellowing greens. The wind held the leaves for a moment before they drifted back to earth, falling about Mychael's shoulders and in his hair.

"The trees are glad to have you, whether Aedyth will be or nay," she said, finishing the braid with another silver ring and bit of Quicken-tree cloth pulled from her baldric. Thinking of Morgan had taken the lightness from her mood. Yr Is-ddwfn wasn't Mychael's sanctuary, but Nemeton's map—if it could be found—might lead him to a place where he could escape the fate of his dragonfire. Her escape awaited her in the wormhole, and Mychael had all but promised her that the wormhole, if she dared its graven rim, would be her destruction. For certes his deep descent of the weir had not been accomplished without risks and harm. She, too, would have to go deep, far deeper than the path to Yr Is-ddwfn. That morn, Mychael's skin had still burned with the heat of the wormhole scars. Could she bear the same, if such was to be her fate?

Nemeton's skin had not been marked, and he had breached the wormhole more than once in her memory. The Druids were ever ones with a potion, and mayhaps he had prepared himself before going into the weir. Madron would know. She had always been at her father's side, conjuring with nature's bounty. But 'twas unlikely that Madron would tell Llynya any secrets, especially any concerning the wormhole. The weir gate was the Druid's bailiwick in Madron's estimation. Like the first Prydion Magi to discover its special properties, the Druids had sent travelers through. They watched the gate for such travelers to return, and on one night per year, Calan Gaef, they watched a priestess of Merioneth open the doors between the worlds and look into the depths of the temporal flux. 'Twas because their lives were so briefly mortal that they hungered after time, Rhuddlan had explained.

The priestesses were all gone from Merioneth now. Ceridwen had been the last, and by most accounts she'd not had near the power of the priestesses of old. That there had been no one to train her was part of the problem. That she'd shared the womb with a twin brother was considered by both Moira and Naas to be the greater cause of her lack of skills.

Mychael—the wheel ever turned and came back to him.

"If the braid dismays you, you're welcome to unplait it," he said, reclaiming her attention, his voice concerned.

She looked up and realized she'd given herself away with her gloomy musings, changing his mood as well as hers. "Nay," she said. " 'Tis not the plait."

"Then what?"

In answer, she took his hand and turned it over, revealing the scar along his inner wrist and palm. She slid her fingers up the pinkened skin and was surprised to find it the same temperature as the rest of his arm.

" 'Tis cool," she said, glancing up. "The fire is gone."

"Bala Bredd has a magic of sorts. 'Tis why I come."

"Aye, there is more healing in the waters of Bala Bredd than in others. Still the pool must need one of Moira's rejuvenating infusions, if you must swim for hours on end to find relief."

"A good soaking usually suffices," he admitted, absently tossing a twig into the flames. "The swimming was for your benefit."

"Mine?" She didn't understand.

His eyes held hers for a moment, before he tossed another stick on the fire. "I looked for you everywhere today."

"I know," she said. "I watched you search Carn Merioneth from hither to yon and back again from morn to night, pretty much following my trail."

"Jesu," he swore softly under his breath, glancing up. "Were you so afraid I would find you?"

"Not afraid, just unsure of what to say, or do after . . . after you . . . we . . ." Her voice trailed off in confusion. Her gaze faltered. Picking up the hem of her tunic, she smoothed a meadowsweet petal so that it would better reflect the firelight.

"I only wanted to apologize," he said, "and explain . . . if I needed to." There was a question in his voice, a question she couldn't bring herself to answer. When she said naught, he sighed and went doggedly on. "Not that I've had much luck explaining it to myself. You can be certain I never meant to embarrass you."

"Nor I you," she assured him in all earnestness, looking up.

"And I would never hurt you," he vowed. "I swear this on all the gods that ever were, or will ever be."

"I was not hurt." She hesitated slightly before asking, "Were you?"

"Me? Hurt?" His look of surprise lasted briefly before transforming into chagrin. He swore again and covered his face with his hand. "Nay, sprite, I was not hurt."

"I know 'twas not the normal course of things," she hurried on. "I feared when I touched you that I might have hurt . . . you, when you . . . you—" Words failed her again. She had witnessed all manner of couplings each Beltaine, but she'd never heard a name put to any of them, and she—silly chit—had not thought to ask. Nor, she now realized, had she really seen too many of the particulars. She'd thought there was plenty of time still before mating became of any importance.

Time had run out, though, for she was alone with Rhiannon's son in the soft, dark night, with the wind and the starlight wrapping around them, the moon shining down, awaiting a kiss she feared she might not get.

" 'Twas foolishness, nothing more," he said, breaking the awkward silence and making to rise. "Come, let's get you home, before Aedyth sends out scouts."

She stopped him with her hand on his wrist, holding him. "I'm no child to do as Aedyth wishes."

"Nor are you yet a woman for me to do with as I wish," he said gently, tousling her hair.

She could have hit him for that bit of condescension, but only out of her own frustration. When he rose to his feet, she scrambled up beside

him, unwilling to let him walk away while the scent of desire was in the
air. For all his misplaced gallantry, he still wanted to kiss her.

" 'Twas my fault, wasn't it," she said, "that things went so awry in
the tower."

"Nay," he said. "The fault was all mine." He turned to leave, but
she reached for him again, her hand light on his arm. His gaze came
back to her, indulgent and faintly curious.

"I ran when I should have stayed . . . when I wanted to stay.
You taste truly wondrous, Mychael ab Arawn," she said, "like forests,
and rain, and dark, thundering clouds. Like salt water from a faraway sea, like honey warmed by the sun, and I . . . I had hoped for
another kiss." She was treading onto perilous ground. To put words
to desire was a binding spell, an incantation of seduction well known
in *artes magicae*. She did not want a spell to be what held him, yet
she would have him know the truth of why she'd followed him.
"One kiss, no more. I swear."

As she spoke, his countenance changed from curiosity to an expression she couldn't interpret beyond the tension bracketing his mouth.
His eyes were dark, unreadable without the firelight to illuminate their
depths. Slowly, he brought his hand up to cup the curve of her jaw. His
fingers spread across her cheek.

"You ask for a kiss, one kiss and no more?" The question was
laced with resignation. "One kiss, when I would give you a thousand."

He was so close, she could scarce find her breath, while his
breath—sweet draft—warmed the air between them. If she'd asked for
too little, if that was what had put the sadness in his voice, she would
gladly take more.

Daring all, she rose up on tiptoe, bringing her mouth near to his.
"Even a thousand kisses must needs begin with one," she murmured,
then brushed his lips with her own, a gossamer kiss. As if moved by her
touch, his other hand came to rest on her waist. On her second kiss, he
met her partway, and his hand slid to the small of her back. The third
kiss was his to take.

Mychael opened his mouth over hers, his arm tightening around
her, inexorably drawing her closer and closer. *Christe.* He was going to
drown in her. He could tell, could see it coming, yet naught could have
kept him from accepting what she offered. Kisses. A thousand of them.
Taking her home would have been the right thing to do, considering her
innocence, but he didn't have the strength to take her home when her

hand was tunneling through his hair. And God's truth, when her body pressed against him and her mouth clung to his, she didn't feel innocent.

Nay, he didn't have the strength to take her home. He only prayed he had the strength to take her slow.

To that end, he did naught but kiss her, and kiss her again, losing himself in the wet warmth of her mouth and the taste of lavender. Her tongue played with his and a hot-edged sweetness poured through him, leaving fire in its wake. Her teeth grazed his lips and nipped at his chin in soft, teasing bites, and he wanted to devour her with the same, to put his mouth on her everywhere, to taste and discover. She was the river nymph of his woodland idylls, the enchantress of his waking dreams, the one he'd conjured so many times with a stroke of his hand and an aching need to be loved. In all his dreams, though, the nymph had not been as beautiful as the woman he held in his arms. No fantasy had ever been so delicately formed. No man had ever imagined the wild tumble of braids and leaves and loose strands of hair that framed her face in such silky disarray.

He ran his mouth over her cheeks and brows and lashes, wanting to infuse himself with her, with the fragrance of flowers rising from her skin. She was every green living thing, winding around him, tying him to her with tendrils of desire, binding him with pleasure. And 'twas then, within the heated tenderness of her kisses, that the first truth of what she'd done with the braiding of his hair came to him. She'd bound him to the trees, aye, and in return the trees were binding him to her.

As the sweet sap of lust rose in him, so did the sap rise in the pines and birches and oaks. No metaphor, but a true rising. He could smell it, though autumn was upon them, and he could smell the same happening to Llynya, could smell the intensifying scents of roses and sweet wood-ruff on her skin, the scents of meadowsweet, violets, and peonies, flowers long out of bloom, but redolent in the late September night—because she was aroused.

Kisses alone would not suffice for the sprite. Innocent or nay, she wanted him with the same degree of longing he felt for her, and he wanted to have her lying beside him, taking him in, her arms wrapped around him, her mouth kissing him, dampening his skin, her hands touching him, inciting him with pleasure. He wanted to know what it was to have a woman, and she was the woman he would have. No half measures would do. He wanted no more to be alone—and neither did she.

Thus it was empathy, not boldness, that brought his hand to her belt and loosened the buckle; the desire to soothe and not just desire that guided him as he loosened her hose from *en coulisse* and let them slide down around her ankles. With a single tug, her braies unwound from around her hips and drifted into a soft pile at their feet. He broke his kiss to slip her baldric over her head, then reclaimed her lips and began unlacing her tunic. She could have stopped him at any time, but she did not. In truth, her own hands were not idle, and as she was half undressed, so was he. He felt the chill of the wind on his legs when she loosed his chausses. She had his tunic unlaced before he'd finished with hers. He shrugged out of it and tossed it aside.

When her tunic slipped, verily of its own accord, off her shoulder, revealing the rise of her breast, he put his mouth on her and took his first taste. *Sweet heaven.* His groin tightened, and his hands slid around her hips to the warm, bared curves of her buttocks. He held her thus, within the circle of his arms and mouth, and felt as if he'd taken her inside himself.

Her hands tangled in his hair, holding him. "Mychael." His name was a benediction, a sigh, not a call for restraint. He'd come to Bala Bredd to heal, and she'd come for love, and between the cool night air and the thick clouds of warming mist rising off the pool, the two were proving to be the same.

He cupped her face with his palms and kissed the corners of her lips.

"I would lay with you, Llynya," he said, speaking his heart's truth. After the debacle of the morning, he would not have her mistake what he wanted, and regardless of what he felt, he'd not push her further without hearing the same from her.

"Oh, aye," she breathed against his lips with another gossamer kiss, and a warm flush of anticipation coursed through him.

Taking him by the hand, she pulled him down with her onto the soft pile of their cloaks and discarded clothing. He went willingly, readily, and with a silent warning to himself not to overwhelm her. He was considerably bigger than she and unschooled in the ways of love, and a definite streak of nerves ran through his excitement—a receipt for disaster, if he did not take care.

Yet when he looked at her, he wondered if 'twas possible to touch her and not be moved to take the greatest care. Moonlight shimmered on her bare skin and wound through her tattoo, silvering the blue leaves on her shoulder as she worked off her boots and hose. When she finished, she shrugged out of the rest of her tunic, letting it slide into her lap, and the pale light ran like quicksilver down her arm, limning the runes and ogham marking her as Liosalfar.

'Twas a sobering sight. He knew what she was, yet the full display of her tattoo seemed at odds with the rest of her, with the fineness of her bones, with the softness of her breasts and the slender curves of her legs. Battle was coming, and given a choice, he would not have her fight.

He ran his finger down the full length of the tattoo, following the path of leaves and vines to her wrist.

"A warrior," he said, failing to keep a rueful note out of his voice. "I wish it were not so."

"Would you have another then?" she asked. He glanced up, startled by her question. Then he saw the flash of anger in her eyes and realized his mistake. "A harvest maid, mayhaps?"

A warrior, aright, he thought, not daring to release the grin he felt twitching at his lips.

"Nay, sprite. I would have no other than you, ever." 'Twas true. He knew it the moment he spoke the words, and he didn't understand it any more than she appeared to believe it, considering the look she was giving him.

"Edmee told me Massalet followed you like a dog all summer long." Her eyes were definitely green, and not just in color, and that amazed him almost as much as having her sit across from him naked, arguing.

"For certes she happened to be in the same place much of the time," he admitted.

"And?" she prompted, looking more the Liosalfar and less the doe-eyed nymph with every passing moment.

He quickly checked on the whereabouts of her dagger, thinking he should never have stopped kissing her long enough for a conversation to begin. The dagger was safe, a good foot and a half closer to him than her.

"And I never noticed her enough to make her anything but snippish with me. You ken 'snippish,' don't you, sprite?" His grin slipped free, and she was on him in a trice, pushing him over with a soft "oomph" of effort.

Fast she may have been, but she was no match for his strength. He caught her in his arms and rolled her over into the cloaks in one easy motion, pinning her with a soft laugh and a leg thrown across hers—and as simply and quickly as that, Massalet was forgotten.

Every fiber of his being was suddenly and totally focused on Llynya and the rush of arousal pulsing through his body. She'd said she would lay with him, and the time had come. Separated from her only by his braies, he rubbed against her and watched as her eyes darkened.

With the slightest move, her legs parted, allowing him to nest closer, and a groan escaped from deep in his chest.

"Aye, you ken," he murmured.

"Aye, Druid boy. I ken what you're about." A mischievously sensual smile curved her mouth. She teased him with another small move, and his own smile met hers. They would manage, he thought. Aye, they would manage.

Snowflakes drifted down from the sky to land on her lashes, and he kissed them off. They cooled her cheeks, and he warmed the fair skin with his mouth, cradling her head in his hands.

Her kisses were no less ardent, roaming at will across his face and down his throat to his shoulders, each one touching him someplace far deeper than the surface of his skin. When her hand caressed the lower part of his chest and drifted tantalizingly across his abdomen, he stilled, his muscles instinctively contracting in invitation, creating a space for her hand to delve lower.

When she didn't, he brushed her cheek with his mouth. "Please."

She shook her head.

He thought he knew what stayed her, a thought she confirmed with her next words.

"Nay. I would not have this end, not just yet."

A pained grin crossed his face. 'Twas a fair enough, if rather faithless conclusion. Yet they were far from any ending, and he would have her know it.

He lifted himself a bare degree to meet her gaze, and realized with an odd sense of fascination that their hair had become entwined, his pale yellow strands winding down around one dark braid, her rich sable locks twisting upward into gold. Even as he watched, a slight breeze lifted another dark curl and started it twisting around the riband she'd worked into his braid.

Swearing silently to himself, he tore his gaze away from the enchantment only to meet another when he looked into her eyes. Forest green and lit deep with reflected starlight, the dreamy desire in them was his final undoing. She was open before him, soft and giving beneath him, and all his thoughts tumbled into one that had naught to do with "slow."

Filled with a sense of urgency, he tugged off his braies, and fully naked, fully aroused, he lay back down, half over her. He was a carnal beast; he knew it, and she incited his lust with damnable ease. The only surprise was how much tenderness there could be in lust, for she incited that in equal measure.

Her breath caught as his fingers slid through the soft hair at the apex of her thighs and into that most mysterious of all the female regions, the source of endless speculation among the less pious novitiates, known to him only by the Latin, *vulva*.

"You're so soft," was his first awestruck discovery, followed quickly by a harshly groaned, "you're wet."

The realization washed through him with a force far greater than any he could control. In a single move, he covered her, pressing against her damp nest of curls. He was awkward, she was kind, and when he finally pushed up inside her, he feared her pleasure was forgotten in the exquisite intensity of his own. He came all too quickly, but to save his life could not have conjured a regret. 'Twas God's plan, he was sure, for the second time she was already halfway to completion before he'd hardly started. When her climax came and he was suspended for those few glorious moments in the flow of her release, he knew he'd been changed forever. By the third time, his confidence was high, the rhythms were his, and his goals were clear in his mind.

Llynya had no such goals. Passively replete, sated with wonder, she was amazed when he came to her again—and her amazement did naught but increase. Stamina, she realized some time later, was a gift and a pleasure all its own. There were pinnacles to be reached and fallen off beyond where she'd already been, and one by one, he took her to them, always holding himself back, always pushing her a little higher, until whatever barrier she may have held between a man of Men and a Yr Isddwfn aetheling disappeared. He became one with her, a part of her. She felt the exchange taking place, powered by the primal thrusting of his body. His life's seed, the damp moisture of his kisses, his sweat, all of it seeped into her, inside and out. She melted with the infusion, turning wanton in her need.

Licking his face, she tasted him down to the bone and felt a love so intense, she feared she could die of it. She breathed him in, every scent he'd ever had, and was caught in a whirlwind of flames. For a fleeting instant she was afraid, but his arms were around her, holding her safe. For a fleeting instant she heard a keening cry coming from deep in the heart of the fire, but then 'twas gone and all she could hear was Mychael whispering a litany of love in her ear. When she could take no more, he stopped moving. Buried to the hilt of his shaft inside her, he grew utterly still, and within the space of a breath, from the deepest place of their joining, a wave of pure erotic bliss rose up and washed through her, a dark ocean of pleasure that swept her away.

She clung to him in the aftermath, shocked by the tears running down her face. He kissed her over and over again, murmuring her name, his body bonelessly limp beside her. Their legs were entangled. His arm was across her in a protective gesture, a useless gesture—for naught could protect her from him.

Was it love they'd made? Llynya wondered, watching him sleep in the cool light of a nascent dawn. Or had it been something else, something more elemental than love—if such was possible? She finished pulling on her second boot and nimbly ran the ties through the silver rings, bereft of answers.

'Twas love she felt for him, she knew that. She looked at him and ached with love, and therein lay a danger all its own. More so than Morgan, a thousand times more so, she'd bound herself to Mychael, and now she needed to unbind herself before any damage was done. She was going down the wormhole, going deep, and she'd not have him suffer for her deed.

Rising to her feet, she took one last look at him. His face was soft in sleep, his breathing even, his hair a tangled mess of gold. She'd heard the dragons and felt their fire when he and she had been joined. Their essence ran deep in him, creatures awash with seawater and universal salts, winding through him with every breath, winding through her as well with each breath they'd shared. The dragons had cried out to her through him, and she'd known then what she'd heard in the apple orchard the night Naas had walked the ramparts, her old white eyes looking far out to sea. The dragons were coming. Coming for him.

The end of his quest was nigh. Soon he would have the beasts to heel.

With effort, she resisted the urge to kiss him and took off into the forest. She needed Ailfinn. Only a Prydion Mage would know how to untangle such a mighty spell as they'd woven in the night.

Chapter 16

So there he was, Llynya thought, staring down from her high perch at the man held captive in Riverwood and the mare grazing by his side. Early morning light filtered into the alder copse that held him, revealing thick twinings of branches, boughs nesting together into impassable walls, and the dense weave of shrubbery that left him no escape. The man had entered the forest three days past, setting the trees to trembling and filling the woods with warnings of danger. Day and night the leaves fluttered *Beware,* until Merioneth felt beset all around. Wolves and their kith ran free through Riverwood along with all manner of cutpurses and robbers, but not he, and Trig wanted to know why. To that end the captain had succumbed to necessity and brought her down to the river with the morning patrol. The man had answered no questions put to him, and Trig would have her match her deep-scent skill against his reticence.

Damn grateful she was to be let out of Carn Merioneth, if only for an hour or so. Mychael ab Arawn had started a turmoil in her heart that she scarce could bear. She'd sent prayers of thanks to the gods when he'd left for Lanbarrdein the day before, for there had been some doubt that he would.

She'd expected him to be angry when he awoke and realized she was gone. She had not expected the storm that had descended on Merioneth with his return from Bala Bredd. He'd stood in the bailey and cried her name, until not a soul in the castle could doubt what they had done.

She'd weathered the storm by hiding on the wall-walk with Naas. And then he'd left with Tabor, and the storm had passed, except for the havoc wreaked on her heart.

She'd done the right thing, of that she had no doubt. Her only doubt was whether she would survive it. Ailfinn would come, though, and set her free.

Until then, she would be haunted by memories of Bala Bredd. Already they slipped into her dreams and wound through her days, remembrances of his touch, his kisses, until all she wanted was to put her mouth once more to his and fall into the wondrous wonder that was Rhiannon's son and no one else. She wanted him pressed against her, to feel the lithe strength of his body and the heat of his skin. She wanted to taste him and feel his breath flow into her. She wanted to kiss him and love him again—and she wanted it with a fierce ache she couldn't assuage. No one else would do. She, a Liosalfar warrior, had become little more than a love-bit maid, a sorely love-bit maid. Pitting her skills against the Riverwood captive's wits would be a welcome diversion from the sorrows of such love.

Trig had warned her that the captive was a bald Culdee like Helebore, but to Llynya's relief, all similarity ceased with his religious bent and his pate. The monk in the alders had fine white teeth he'd bared at the scouts, and a firm mouth he'd used to voice his threats, of which he had many, some so bloodcurdling—especially those detailing the methods of evisceration he would apply to each and every one of his captors that he caught—that a few of the younger scouts had not held up. 'Twas another reason Trig had been forced to bring her. Having been blooded in battle, she was unlikely to falter under a frightful diatribe no matter how gruesome.

She climbed to another branch to better her view. Below her, the monk sat on a downed limb, his finely arched eyebrows drawn together in a fierce scowl, his dark eyes flashing in icy rage. 'Twas a wonder to her that the trees had held him at all. From what she'd heard, he'd done everything except rip the alders out by their roots to get free. He'd thrashed about the enclosing coppice until Trig had feared for his safety, though all to no avail. The forest would have him for its own, until Rhuddlan released him. How he'd gotten in with the bramble nearly complete was apparently a question Madron would answer. Trig had found faint signs of enchantment not far from the alders, on a path leading to the giant's cairn where the Bredd flowed into the earth.

Nay, he was not like Helebore, Llynya thought, looking him over. The man's body was not crooked and bent, but strong and straight. His face was not wrinkled with age and stained with debauchery, but was fashioned with clean, angry lines. 'Twas no young man's face, but 'twas not so old either, despite the loss of his hair. As a child in the woods, she had used a child's form of deep-scent a few times on men and found that those who skulked through forests usually had hearts full of hunger or fear, depending on whether they were the hunter or the hunted. The monks traversing the woods were equally divided between piety and avarice, incense and ale. Some few had lust on their minds. She'd come across a group of lepers once, and they'd smelled of slow death, rotten flesh, and pain. Moira had shooed her away and then gone back with *rasca* to tend them. Princes smelled of battles fought, pilgrims' thoughts were of the Christian God. Traders smelled of the road and their goods. 'Twould be interesting with her now greater skill to see what this one was about.

He knew they were there, a half-dozen of them hidden in the trees. She could smell the awareness on him, see the subtle cocking of his ears and the tension in his muscles, held so still beneath his brown cloak.

She slipped down another branch to bring herself closer to him, and Trig signaled a warning. The man, too, shifted in his alertness, his head coming up a bare degree. No fool, this, if he'd sensed her silent step.

She had a bit of lavender in one of her baldric pouches, but not enough to set her apart from what grew wild in the woods. She'd not needed it of late. 'Twas as if Mychael's kiss had turned her mind from malaise—though she would be the last to suggest that the turn had been for the better. A fine choice it was between malaise and lovesickness, for the two were much alike, except one could be ameliorated with lavender and the other by naught but a kiss.

As for the man, he smelled clean and of the forest, rare enough for a monk. The Quicken-tree had brought him seedcake and catkins each day, and he smelled of those too. The trees had given him plenty of room to prowl. He'd paced a path from one end to the other of his arboreal prison, and the scents of crushed vegetation rose up around him in a green swirl.

She inhaled more deeply on her next breath and let her eyes drift closed. He had distilled salts on him and dried meat—her nose wrinkled in distaste—which explained the smell of blood. His wineskin held grape of uncommon strength; the scent alone was nearly intoxicating, fruit with a sharp, pungent underlayer. His heart held little more than an all-consuming anger. He had pouches of herbs, some she recognized and, oddly, some she did not. After the herbs came the first trace of deep-scent, a redolent mélange of spices from faraway lands, saltwater seas, and the smell of dust coming off an endless, winding road. A pilgrimage, she would have thought, except the spices she smelled were from beyond any point of Christian pilgrimage. They spoke of the east to her, a place far, far away, past the goddess mother mountain and the great grass plains, a place where no man of Wales had ever gone.

Curious, she leaned closer. The leaves around her fluttered in warning. She wondered at that and anchored herself more firmly to the branch. Slowly, she breathed him in, one layer after another, her nose sifting through the thousand mundane scents of life and his more exotic wanderings, until she came to the end of them into a space of nothing.

Absolutely nothing.

Not even the smell of his anger was in that space.

She opened her eyes and gave him a quizzical glance. Was he blocking her? And if so, how? Her training was only half-completed at best, but Aedyth had not mentioned any way to block scent. Llynya tried again and did no better. He had an angry present, a few rich and exotic years before that, and then nothing, as if his life had barely begun.

Strange, she thought. No man stepped full grown onto the earth's stage. Every man had a past—except this one.

Reason enough, mayhaps, for the trees to tremble and keep him from Merioneth.

From the other side of the clearing, Trig questioned her with a hand signal. Unready to concede defeat, she shrugged and made a motion to wait. Riverwood had captured a fine mystery indeed. Death stole a man's future. What could steal a man's past? Naught that she could think of, for even if a man forgot himself and all that had come in his life, his past did not forget him. It clung to him, a gossamer sheath impressed upon his soul.

She looked at the captive more closely, wondering. He had a present, and his future was proven by his every passing breath. Within the protective copse 'twas certain he would live to see another day. 'Twas only his past he'd lost.

Or escaped.

"Shadana," she whispered, drawing herself back with sudden understanding. 'Twas time. He'd lost his past by coming through time.

A surge of excitement coursed into her veins, and in a twinkling she'd dropped down another branch. There should be a scent somewhere. Hadn't she smelled as much on Mychael? The faint trace of ether from out of the weir that yet lingered on him? If what she thought was true, this man should have even more, not nothing.

At her movement, the alderwood captive suddenly turned, staring up into the thickly woven tree branches. She stayed perfectly still, balancing on a supple limb, watching him. With his head now in the sunlight, she could see what forest shadows had hidden from sight—he was not bald, not truly, not like Helebore had been. An all-over stubble sprouted on his pate like dark spring grass. His head had been shaved.

For piety's sake? she wondered. Or for subterfuge?

Just how great a threat was this man who had worked so hard to find a way through the bramble, and whose lack of hair disguised what she knew should be there—the telltale stripe of the weir?

She closed her eyes and took a breath, quickly discarding the initial scents, working her way toward the void. Be careful! she warned herself, remembering what had happened at the well with Mychael.

But nothing happened in that empty space that lay beyond rich spice and road dust. Nothing.

Frustrated with her failure, and more than a little irritated with the monk, she stepped to the next lower limb, barely above him now, barely out of his reach. Around the glade, a half-dozen arrows were instantly nocked into bows with a simultaneous swoosh from quivers and click of ash on yew. Out of the corner of her eye, she saw Trig's glare and his signal to get back up into the trees, a signal she ignored at her peril— but ignore it she did. She would know this man.

Nennius felt the sudden rise of menace in the glade, recognizing full well the sound of bows being drawn, just as he'd recognized that one of his captors was probing him in a strange way, touching him with the perceptions of an extra sense. That one lurked too near. Mayhaps 'twas time to give Nemeton's wild folk a taste of fear.

He slowly rose to his feet, his hand slipping inside his cloak for the dagger sheathed on his belt. They'd been too quick before to impale, but after three days of listening to them scurrying about the trees, he knew which way to toss his blade. He would have this one. His hand closed on the haft.

"Who are you?" An imperious feminine voice sounded from above, freezing him with his knife half-drawn. "And what brings you into Riverwood?"

Regally disdainful, haughty beyond wisdom, and full of reckless courage—he knew that dulcet-toned voice.

"State your purpose, stranger," she blithely commanded, and his heart raced. Memories tightened in his chest. He scarce could breathe. How could it be that she was here? In this time. In this place.

She had been walking away from him, her cloak billowing in the wind, the sun glinting off the golden strands of her hair, the sand rising off the dunes.

How close had she still been when the vicious storm had hit and sent time snaking off its course, sucking him back to this primitive age?

"Speak your name now."

"Nennius," he croaked, then remembered she would not know him by such. "Corvus," he amended. "Corvus Gei."

Only she, of everyone he knew, had never trembled at the name. After all these years, would she still deny him his due?

"What brings you to Riverwood, monk?"

Monk? Did she not recognize him then, even by name, the underworld lord of the whole friggin' parsec? The weir was a conflagration that could nip and sear a man's or a woman's memories, but even with him dressed in plain brown robes, he would have expected some spark of recognition from her. They'd spent so much time at each other's throats.

"Show yourself, Avallyn Le Severn," he demanded, using his own imperious voice and taking a step forward.

Six arrows shot into the ground at his feet, coming from all sides and forming a barrier between him and the tree that held her. The sound of six more being nocked and drawn quickly followed. His nemesis had always inspired an obscene amount of loyalty.

He'd followed the river with her name from its source to the sea when he'd first come to England, thinking the river was the reason he'd been led to Wales, the land of the Cymry. But the river had revealed nothing of the weir, nor of why it held her name, the royal bitch he would have once given his life for.

Love he'd offered her, and been denied.

"Avallyn," he warned again, searching the tree above him, looking through leaves and limbs for a glimpse of her. A green shod foot came into view, a boot with silver rings interlaced at the short cuff. A length of slender leg followed, with a tunic made from the gray-green cloth all the wild folk wore. He strained to see her face, his breath held against the damn hope building in his chest. Could it really be that she'd been snatched out of time along with him?

"How long have you been here, monk?"

His hopes rose even higher at her question. The wild folk knew exactly how long he'd been there, three days. The alders had no sooner closed the path than the scouts had converged on him. Yet she asked, and in her mouth, the question took on new depth.

How long had he been there? Long enough for his fortune to have been stolen and his armies dispersed or taken over by one of his rivals, probably Strachan, the filth, or Van the Wretched. Long enough to have learned patience, a virtue he'd singularly lacked in the future. Long enough to have planned his return and the deaths of those who had sent him here.

Aye, he'd been in the past long enough.

"Sixteen years," he answered her, and at that she shifted her position in the tree, revealing her face between the leaves. She was marked with a blue stripe, a diagonal line of paint crossing from her brow to her chin, as on the others he had seen. Still, for a moment the similarity of features fooled him: the shape of her nose, her mouth, the angle of her cheekbones, the curve of her brow and cheeks and chin. Then the differences became clear. Hair that should have been light was a rich dark brown and full of a wild mélange of sticks and leaves. Eyes that should have been gray were green and far too innocent to be Avallyn Le's. The woman herself was slight, hardly more than a girl.

Disappointment settled in him like a lead weight.

"From through the weir?" she asked, too young to control the excitement in her voice.

"Think what you will," he told her, turning away, unable to bear looking at her. Pain clutched him, clawing its way up out of the abyss where for sixteen years he'd kept it sealed with silent fury. Death it would be for all of them. Her voice, her damn voice had tricked him into a moment of hope, and for that they all would die.

Avallyn!

He sank back down onto the fallen branch, his shoulders slumping forward, his chin dropping to his chest. The wild girl wanted to probe him, did she? Well, let her look her fill. Let her poke around in his mind and tremble at the terrors she would find there.

He relaxed his guard, his hands coming up to cover his face. Son of a bitch. *Avallyn.* Time was mocking him, sending her likeness through a stranger.

He had to get back.

Llynya heard his muffled groan, smelled his suffering, and wondered if the man was mad. Emotions had crossed his face like quicksilver, from rage to wonder, to an unknown victory that had lit like fire in his eyes, and then to ultimate defeat.

"Why are you here?" she asked, and received naught for a reply. "Are you lost?"

The last question elicited a strangled cry from the monk. Deranged, for certes, she thought, but yet of another time, and she would know from whence. The trees did not lie. He was a danger.

Daring to go a step beyond caution, she took a breath and held it, a tried and true method for strengthening deep-scent. Breath after gently held breath, she searched through the void for a hint of something more, and was near ready to pass out or give up when the something more came to her. 'Twas faint, so faint, a mere sigh passing through the vast emptiness, not even enough to name as a scent. 'Twas enough to follow, though, and she did, drawing it deeper inside herself. Within the moist confines of her lungs, the scent ripened to a full breath of the ether. Success. The grasp of the timeless stuff wound around inside her, tenderly at first, a welcome relief from the hard search, but soon it tightened. She gasped a fresh breath—too late!—trying to release herself and could not. From full breath it strengthened into a wind, taking harder hold, and from wind to storm—*sín*—pulling her inexorably in its wake, racing her toward the dark edge that suddenly loomed up ahead. No void at all, she realized with growing terror, but a fathomless canyon snaking across the inner landscape of the man's past. Light streaked past her, shooting up out of the abyss. One final bolt burst upon her mind in a blinding flash and she was over the edge . . . falling . . . falling . . . falling through time.

Nennius heard a pained gasp and jerked his gaze to the trees to find the wild girl slipping from the branch. He lunged for her, and 'twas to him she fell before one of her own could reach her. The others came streaming out of the alders, dropping down into the clearing with bows drawn and swords at the ready, but his blade was at her throat before they landed.

She stirred within his fierce embrace, coming around from her little journey in his mind. He'd been probed by better—in truth, he'd had his memories ransacked and raped more than once, before he'd learned to wall them off—but he'd ne'er been invaded by one with such a light step. A skill such as hers could prove useful, if he lived long enough to use it.

His gaze raked the cadre of soldiers surrounding him. Nemeton's wild folk were taller than he'd been able to discern with them in the trees, fair featured and slender. One had long pale hair. The others were dark like the girl. All had blue-painted faces. Sunlight and shadows mixed across the shifting colors of their clothing, allowing them to fade into the backdrop of the forest. He could scarce keep all six of them in view.

"Hold," he growled, drawing the girl tighter against him. She struggled and he stopped her with a bare bite of the blade against her jugular. Not enough to cut, but enough to assure her of the possibility of death.

"Ye draw yer last breath when ye draw her blood," the pale-haired man said, unsheathing a dagger with his left hand even as he held a sword in his right. Both were deadly looking blades, razor sharp, each edge glinting with a streak of light. In the dagger, the light continued on into the crystalline hilt and flashed from between the man's fingers, violet edged in blue. Nennius had not seen its like before.

"I'm taking the girl and leaving. Try to stop me, and she dies," he swore, pressing closer to the alder tree at his back. The light from the crystal hilt was preternaturally bright, near as bright as the sun. He wanted to raise his arm in front of his face, but dared not remove his dagger from the girl's throat.

"And where ye be goin'?" the pale-haired man asked, coming a step closer, the fool.

Nennius pushed his knife a hairbreadth deeper into the girl's skin, and the man stopped. "The weir gate, the wormhole," he ground out. "She'll take me there."

A quick look passed between his opponents, and in the next instant the crystal appeared to shatter, filling the glade with a thousand sharp, swirling daggers of light. They stabbed into him, and he cried out, dropping the girl. He tried to escape by turning away, but could not. The light was everywhere, glancing off every leaf, every limb, in a dazzling, dizzying display. It flowed over him and cut into him and forced his gaze back to the very heart of the blade. A pulsing brightness flickered to life in the hilt's core, the gleaming crests of waves on a storm-tossed sea. They crashed against a rocky shore and dragged him under into darkness with the moon's pulling tide.

Llynya looked at the man collapsed beside her, still shaken from what she'd seen in his memories and ever so grateful for Trig's timely cast of dreamstone sleep.

"Disarm him," the captain said to the others, striding forward. "Check him from the top o' his head to the bottoms of his feet and take every weapon ye find." He knelt by Llynya and smoothed his palm over her brow, checking her. "Ye slipped."

'Twas a show of concern and a condemnation all in one, and as much consideration as she was going to get. She could have told him she'd done far more than slip, but that admission would do naught but work against her. She'd proven rash enough for one day without letting him know she'd once again leaped before she'd looked and near done herself in.

"He's from another time, Trig. I saw it through the deep-scent. He's been through the wormhole."

Trig's gaze narrowed on her. "Aye, and that must 'ave been a pleasant trip for ye."

"Scary at first," she confessed, "but then it evened out." Evened out into more of the endless fall, a weightless traverse of space and years, the same that she felt when her connection with Morgan grew strong and threatened her with despair.

She knew how to find him now. She'd seen the way of it in Nennius Corvus Gei's memories. The paths of time clung to the monk, if monk he was, soft shreds of knowledge twined together into a wavelike ribbon that connected him from where he'd been to where he was.

Morgan would have left such a trail.

"So he's a traveler," Trig said, looking the man over. "I knew Nemeton's daughter was in this. Mayhaps 'tis Madron I should bring out to question him. Like her father, she's ever been waiting for one of the lost magi to return."

"He's no mage, Trig. He's got violence all around him, through and through."

"He's got naught to do with skraelings either," the captain said. "E'en I can smell that much. Well, we'll not learn more 'til he wakes, but for certes there was reason enough for the trees to hold him and reason enough for us to do the same. Pwyll and Lien." He turned to two of the scouts. "You take the day watch on him. He'll come 'round quick enough, and we've got more than him to worry about. Llynya, it's back to Merioneth with ye. Kynor, go with her. The rest of ye, up in the trees. We'll check the border to Afon Mawddach."

Downwind, Lacknose Dock watched the Quicken-tree emerge from their brambly copse and take off to the south. Grumbling started in the ranks as the greater Liosalfar troop disappeared into the trees, grumbling he silenced with the baring of his teeth and a hand signal that promised death to any who disobeyed his orders. Frey Dock, his second, reinforced the promise with a threat of his own. Caerlon had sent them into Riverwood for one reason, to get the aetheling. When the skraelings struck the holds of the Quicken-tree, it would be in force, from all directions, with total victory as their goal, a victory Caerlon had told them would be theirs if only two of the warriors could be captured aforehand and taken out of the fight.

Lacknose had delivered the mewling Wyrm-master, and the aetheling would soon be his. Blackhand Dock had lost in making his bid for finding her in the deep dark, yet there would be battle and blood aplenty once Caerlon had his final prize.

"Caerlon the Clever," Lacknose muttered to himself. Too clever by half, and too clever for any of their goods in the Wars, but the twisted princeling had finally conjured something aright. He'd brought them Slott from Inishwrath. There was naught like the Troll King to strike fear in the hearts of men and elves, and while skraelings had once been the former, there was no doubt that the Quicken-tree and all their kind were still of the *tylwyth teg*. A thousand nights of sweet supper they would make for the Thousand Skulled One, until the great king was Slott of the Two Thousand Skulls.

The Light-elf warrior he sought strode out of the copse with another Quicken-tree, a young one, and Lacknose signaled for his soldiers to move out. Two Liosalfar had been left with a prisoner in the alders. He set four of the skraelpack to their murder. Quick and silent, they knew, the way they'd killed the two Quicken-tree scouts to the north that morn without a warhorn blown. By nightfall, Rhuddlan's captain would know he'd lost the day's battle with five dead; until then, he wouldn't even know his border had been breached.

Lacknose fingered the phial hanging off his belt. Caerlon's smoke potion had rotted through the bramble with the same ease as it rotted through the undergrowth of Riverwood. A fine weapon it was and a fine bit of strategy to rot the trees right out from under the *tylwyth teg*.

Careful to keep downwind—for Quicken-tree noses put a dog's to shame—Lacknose, Frey, and the one other Dockalfar, Ratskin, guided the skraelings on a parallel course with the aetheling and her companion for a quarter league. Divide and conquer, isolate and destroy, was the Dockalfar's method. The trees thinned out the farther they moved from the river, and as they approached a small clearing, Lacknose knew the time and place for their ambush had come. He lifted his hand to signal the attack, and a horn blast broke the forest silence. 'Twas an elfin warhorn, calling the Quicken-tree to arms and battle. The Liosalfar maid turned with her sword drawn, and the horn sounded again, coming from the alder copse.

Impossible! he swore to himself, that two young Quicken-tree could outfight four of his blooded skraelings. With a low growl, he sicced his minions on the aetheling and her scout.

"*Khardeen!*" she cried, seeing him and his soldiers rising up out of the forest gloom and bearing down upon her. "Kynor! To the trees!"

The first horn calls were joined by others from the south, but even a hundred horn blasts would not save her. In a trice she was surrounded, before she and the boy could make to the nearby birches, and Lacknose would have had them both—the aetheling for Caerlon and the boy for Slott's supper—if the girl hadn't pulled an elfin trick.

"To Merioneth! Quickety-split!" she said to the boy, then herself disappeared into the woods in a twinkling, breaking through the skraelpack line before the scurvy beasts even knew she'd moved. The boy did the same, heading west to the castle on the coast. The aetheling had gone south, and Lacknose went after her, calling for Frey and Ratskin to follow. Dockalfar or Liosalfar, the trick was the same, and no skraeling could do it. Nor could one fleet-footed sprite outrun three Dark-elves. The boy they would have another day.

Llynya ran with her sword drawn, not daring to sheathe it. Leaves of gold and green swirled across the ground in her wake as she leaped low-slung brambles and dodged trees with the speed of a falcon. Half fly she did. Wind tore across her face and spread her hair out behind her. 'Twas a pace she couldn't keep, being far better for running circles around men than outrunning Dockalfar.

Dockalfar! And skraelings in Riverwood.

Skraelings, while deadly, could not catch a Quicken-tree in the forest except on the end of an arrow, and then only if they moved with due speed. Kynor had a good chance of making Merioneth, but she was fearfully close to being caught by the three Dockalfar who had taken after her.

Out of the corner of her eye, she saw the Dark-elves split up to flank her. In a lightning-quick dash back to the north, she changed direction, but three were too many to escape. They countered every move she made and began drawing close, tightening their circle. When there was no place left for her to run, she turned to fight, her sword in one hand, her dreamstone dagger in the other.

"*Shadana,*" she prayed, trying to watch her back and her front and both sides at once. She'd ne'er seen Dockalfar before—all of them supposedly having died in the Wars—and they were more awful than anything she'd imagined, sharp-toothed and dirty, with a faint green cast to their skin. The biggest one had no nose, only a rough piece of silver to cover the hole in his face. Trolls, she might have thought, *uffern* trolls, except for a certain fey cast to their faces and their speed. For certes naught but an elf could have caught her.

But the smell of them! Murder and mayhem and rot. 'Twas all she could do to keep from retching.

The two smaller ones slipped coils of rope from across their shoulders, while the bigger one sidled closer, sword in hand. She lashed out at him with her long blade, forcing him back while trying to keep the other two in sight. She darted and dodged, but on her fourth parry with the noseless elf, the other two snaked their ropes around her wrists and dragged her to the ground.

"Sticks!" She squirmed and cursed and got in a couple of good kicks before they were able to bind her ankles. Her heart was beating so fast 'twas near to bursting. Captured. She'd been captured. She swore again to keep the sob from escaping her throat.

The noseless one took her dreamstone dagger and pushed her hair up away from her ears. He let out a pleased grunt at what he saw. His gaze locked with hers.

"Ye should'a stayed in Yr Is-ddwfn, aetheling, with the rest o' yer pointy-eared kind." He spat on the ground and rose to his feet, leaving the other two to finish trussing her up after Ratskin had taken her sword. They wrapped a length of dirty cloth over her mouth, and she almost fainted from the explosion of rank and fetid smells.

"Lacknose," one called out. "She's turnin' blue."

The big Dark-elf came back and looked at her. "I'd turn blue too, Ratskin, if ye wrapped yer filthy food sling over me mouth. Frey, get it off her."

Like the other two, Frey was blond-haired, but was missing an eye. Ratskin had all his parts with the addition of soft gray hair growing in patches on his face. Some dire happenstance had befallen them that they were all thus disfigured.

Frey took the sling off her, but immediately replaced it with his own only slightly less rancid one. Ratskin's he used as an extra binding around her legs. Ropes bound her arms to her torso.

The horn to the north had grown silent, but Trig's yet sounded from the south, the calls moving toward the alder copse. He would pass her by, unless the smell of the skraelings alerted him. The skraelpack had caught up with her and the Dockalfar. She could see them gathering 'round Frey and Ratskin, peering over the Dark-elves for a look at their prisoner.

They were terrifying to a soldier, their teeth barely contained within their overlarge jaws. A few wore mail hauberks. Others had boiled-hide gambesons sporting spiked bosses to protect them. Each was fully armed with spears, daggers, and swords. Two of those leaning over Ratskin had morning stars looped over their belts. A few others, she realized, were female, as equally armed as the men and with no more pity in their gazes.

Lacknose growled an order in a language she barely recognized as derived from the ancient common tongue. 'Twas harsh in his mouth, a scramble of hard letters and short sounds, but the skraelings responded as one, falling into line and heading toward the river. Frey slung her over his back like a sack, and everyone made way for him to take his place at the front of the pack.

A new chorus of horns sounded from the west, from Carn Merioneth, answering Trig's call. Kynor, she fervently hoped.

"That puts 'em on two sides of us, mayhaps three," Ratskin grumbled.

"He's right, ye know." Frey looked to Lacknose. "And every scout they 'ad in Riverwood is headin' in this direction by now."

"Aye, but we'll not be in Riverwood for them to find," Lacknose said. "There's a hole into Lanbarrdein not a quarter league hence. We'll lose them in the dark." With a barked command, he doubled their pace.

Doomed, Llynya thought. She was doomed.

Nennius stood over the four dead soldiers, his breath coming hard, his arms throbbing from the force of the blows he'd delivered with killing strength. The sword he'd borrowed dripped blood at his side. He shook his head, trying to clear the last of the pale-haired man's friggin' enchantment from his brain. He'd come back to consciousness in his alder prison with naught but two scouts left to guard him, two who were obviously not up to the deed. Behind him, the two wild boys were sprawled in the grass, wounded, but not dead.

One—Pwyll, he was called—had been shot in the leg with an arrow. Poisoned, by the looks of the wound and the boy's face. He'd gone white with sweat dampening his dark hair and pouring off his brow. He'd been the first to fall from his perch, and 'twas his sword Nennius had taken. The other one, Lien, was more sorely hurt. He'd fought a brace of the enemy in the trees and jumped to Pwyll's rescue when two more of the smelly brutes had broken through the alder wall. Thus they'd fought side by side, Nennius and Lien, and killed all four of the soldiers while Pwyll had blown his horn.

The other wild folk were returning. Their warhorns echoed through the forest, coming closer, but Nennius doubted if they would arrive in time to save Lien. The scout was losing blood from a sword cut on his side, lots of blood. An hour earlier, Nennius would have finished the boy off himself. Now he stood and watched and hoped the scout would live. To his practical advantage and to save his own skin, allies had been made out of enemies. 'Twould be a shame to lose them nearly as quickly as they'd been converted.

One of the deformed attackers twitched, a death spasm, and Nennius stuck him again for good measure. Then he walked back to the boys, collecting the food they'd brought to him at daybreak.

Holding first one and then the other, he gave them each a drink of the sweet, fresh-smelling water they had plied him with each day. Pwyll managed to swallow. Lien could not. For himself, Nennius took a swig of brandy off the flask he'd carried from Ynys Enlli. Stiff stuff, it probably would have killed the scouts on the spot, and he wanted them to live.

Aye, he dearly wanted them to live.

To that end, he took Pwyll's crystal dagger and made a swift incision on the boy's thigh where the arrow protruded. Once he'd located the barbs, he extracted the arrowhead with a minimum of damage. He poured some of the sweet water into the wound—the stuff had a quality about it that made Nennius believe it could do naught but help—and bound the wound with a strip of cloth he cut off Pwyll's cloak. Suturing would have to wait.

For the other boy, there was not so much he could do. He cleansed the gash in Lien's side with the sweet water, bound him with green cloth, and wrapped him in his cloak to keep him warm before sitting down beside him. 'Twas thus Nennius arranged himself to be found by the returning wild folk, with a blooded blade lying across his lap and a dying wild boy cradled in his arms.

Chapter 17

Caerlon followed Redeye Dock through the northern passages leading into Rastaban, cursing him all the way.

"Skraelings." The word was lodged behind his clenched jaws. "You left him with skraelings. Imbecile! Cretin! The rotting skraelings *eat* Quicken-tree. If they've eaten this one, your hide will be the next one to lengthen Slott's vest, your rotting thick skull the next one to hang from his braids."

The threat was real. Caerlon's hand was ready on his knife. If there was naught left but the young warrior's bones when they reached the small cavern ahead, Caerlon would drop Redeye like a stone, sever his throat, and let the skraelings chew on him while he bled to death.

They rounded the last turn, and Caerlon held his red-hearted dreamstone high. A rush of relief washed through him. The Liosalfar was still in one piece.

"Grazch!" he ordered, and the two beast-men watching the prisoner backed off from the trussed bundle lying in a heap on the cavern's floor.

Caerlon strode forth and with a flick of his blade cut the rope securing the hood over the Quicken-tree's head. He pulled the hood off, and a long dark fall of hair tumbled out over the Liosalfar's shoulders. Like black silk it was, with a *fif* braid twisted into one side. Fierce green eyes flashed up at him, and a thrill of nervous pleasure went through Caerlon to his core.

"Get him to his feet," he ordered, and Redeye hauled the Liosalfar up.

He'd been poorly handled. Caerlon could see it in the bruises marking the boy's face. His hands were bound behind his back, and he'd been cut, a slash across his chest. The blood had already dried and crusted on the Quicken-tree cloth, proving the wound not too deep.

"When did this happen?" he asked Redeye, pointing to the slash mark.

"In battle, milord. They've lost no skill since the Wars. We were hard-pressed."

Of course they'd been hard-pressed, Caerlon thought in disgust, a skraelpack of fifty men against twenty Quicken-tree.

"Their losses?"

"Two dead, five wounded, and this one captured."

Caerlon hated to ask, but he was their leader and needed to know. "And how did you fare?"

"Twenty-two dead, milord, including the five I finished off myself."

Caerlon nodded. A badly wounded skraeling was a dead skraeling. 'Twas all Caerlon could do to keep his army in rats. There were no rations to be had for those who could not fight.

"Where's the elf shot?"

Redeye gestured, and one of the skraelings lumbered toward them with a pack. He spilled the contents on the floor. Naught but elf shot was there, the black, highly lustrous stone used by the Quicken-tree and other clans of *tylwyth teg* for making arrowheads. Caerlon had harbored a hope there might be more.

"Preparing for war?" he asked the Liosalfar. He expected no answer and got none. "How was Tryfan? Still full of good stone, I see."

He ran the toe of his boot across the pile on the chance he might have missed something. No, there was only shiny black stone.

"No luck finding the Douvan Throne Room, eh?" Too bad, he thought. The riches of the Douvan kings were legendary, but more than one kind of magic had sealed the mountain fastness. Rumor had long held that naught but the passage of years would open the Throne Room's doors, bound as they'd been by a time-cast spell.

With a long-suffering sigh, he signaled for the skraelings to repack the elf shot. They had to be killed, of course. He couldn't take any chance of Slott learning about the Liosalfar captive. He had his hands full keeping Wyrm-master off the Troll King's plate. The Quicken-tree sapling wouldn't last through the introductions, let alone supper, and Caerlon would have discourse with the boy.

"Redeye," he said when the skraelings were bent to their task. He made a killing motion with his knife.

The Dockalfar understood the need and nodded. Redeye had knocked the boy out cold a halflan from Rastaban and told the other skraelings from Tryfan that the captive had died. Caerlon would have to reward him for that bit of brilliance, even as he resented that Redeye knew his weakness.

He turned to the prisoner. Five long centuries he'd been without a suitable companion. Five long centuries spent in the company of his books, a few deformed Dark-elves, and the brutish offal of Men. Nay, he would not lose his prize to Slott's insatiable hunger.

Where to keep him, though, posed a problem. There was only one place safe from the rattish nosiness of the skraelings—the oubliette. And it was occupied.

"Take the pack to my quarters," he said to Redeye, keeping his gaze on the Liosalfar. "I'll gift the elf shot to the Troll King, Slott of the Thousand Skulls, at the evening's feasting."

Fear flickered to life in the Quicken-tree's eyes, and Caerlon smiled, satisfied.

"Aye, milord." Redeye gave a short bow of his head and herded the skraelings out of the small cavern.

"What's your name, Light-elf?" Caerlon asked his prisoner, expecting an answer this time. When he got none, he stepped behind the boy and slashed his sleeve open from shoulder to wrist, marking a line of blood on the young warrior's skin. One look told him what he wanted to know.

With the tip of his blade, Caerlon turned the boy's head to meet his gaze. A pleased smile curved his mouth.

"Welcome to Rastaban . . . Shay."

"Tabor! Hold up!" Mychael called out, then gritted his teeth and shoved at the pony standing on his foot. "Swivin' beast. Move!" Tansy was her name, and she no more resembled a buttonlike flower than did he. 'Twas a delusion of Tabor's. He called all the rude beasts by sweet names. Saffron, Twitch, and Hollyhock, Eyebright and Heartsease, and the damnable Tansy were the last of the bunch to be taken up out of the caves. If an assault was to be made on the spider people and the bunch called skraelings that Rhuddlan was searching out, the Hall of Kings was ready.

Mychael could not say the same for himself.

She'd left him. Damn her.

She'd left him on the shores of Bala Bredd without so much as a by-your-leave. 'Twas Trig alone who had dared to approach him in the bailey that morn, Trig alone who had kept him from tearing Carn Merioneth asunder to find her.

Just ahead on the trail, a wall of luminescent flowstone marked a narrow route leading off a main passage of the Canolbarth and back toward Lanbarrdein, the third such that they'd passed and the last to be had. 'Twas the reason he'd come, to give Tabor the slip and go on alone, to lose himself in the deep dark. Yet when the first little-used passage had loomed into view, a dark opening with a bit of wind blowing through it, he'd not had the heart for it. 'Twas too steep, he'd told himself, and with the water that ofttimes slickened its floor, the most dangerous of the three. He would wait for the next.

The next, when they'd reached it, had held no more allure than the first. Something about the smell had dissuaded him. A faint trace of *pryf* had been in the air, making him believe that mayhaps the worms had broken through into the passage from their nest. *Pryf* in a passage were not necessarily dangerous. They were not wont to run over people or grind them up like the old worm, but they could definitely get in a person's way and cause countless delays.

The smell had not been skraelings. He and Tabor had both been on the lookout for sign of them and had seen naught this side of the Hall of Kings. The skraelings were all in the deep dark. But the third passage was upon him, and instead of taking his pack and making a run for it, he was calling out to Tabor.

"Ho, boy!" the lanky pony-master called back. The man's eyes were bright, his lean face creased with a smile. A tousled fall of youngish brown hair was loosely braided down his back, belying his age as his name belied his long-limbed stature. He wore a dark green vest over his gray Ebiurrane tunic. "What say you? Has Tansy balked on ye again?"

Balked? She wanted to climb into his arms and be carried the rest of the way to the Dragon's Mouth. Bright beast, knowing the impossibility of such a notion, she made do by standing on his foot.

"Aye!" he hollered back, and waited for Tabor to prove his worth. He did not have to wait long. A soft humming filled the air, a prelude of *"Hum, hum, fey-oh"* and *"Hum, hum, oh-fey."* At the end of the refrain, Tabor sang in a high, clear voice that ran like the chime of silver bells along the Canolbarth's granite walls.

> *"Tansy, lass, the green grass waits*
> *High in the mountains of Eryri*
> *With sweet running water and Moira's bannock cakes*
> *For pony bones that're weary!"*

Tansy snorted and with a short, hopping jump was back to moving up the trail with her harness bells jingling in concert with Tabor's song.

> *"Tansy, lass, the stars shine bright*
> *High in the mountains of Eryri*
> *Where a meadow bed waits in the silvery moonlight*
> *For pony bones that're weary!"*

"Pony bones," Mychael muttered, reaching down to rub his foot. 'Twas a marching song and a refrain no pack animal could resist. Tabor's voice, so sweet and pure, filled the passage, echoing down its length and spurring the ponies on to a good clip.

With a few limping strides, Mychael caught up with Tansy and reached for a draw hitch on her load. A quick tug on the end of the rope loosed his pack. He stopped and slung it over his shoulder, letting Tabor and the animals continue on without him.

"Tansy, lass, no wolves run
High in the mountains of Eryri
Where the trolls were long ago turned to stone
And the ponies taken all by faeries!"

Mychael had heard the tale from Tabor's own lips, about the ending of the last great war, when the taking of the ponies had turned the tide against the Dockalfar. The next verse in the song was drowned by the sound of hooves striking a stretch of rock. The one after was fainter still, lost in a bend of the trail.

Mychael released a deep breath and looked around. To his right was the cascade of flowstone and the entrance to the tunnel leading back to Lanbarrdein. 'Twas where his future lay, whatever he was to have of one.

He brought his hand up to feel the pocket over his left breast. Madron's phial was there, refilled to the brim with the potent mixture of his salvation. A pouch on his belt held another such simple, one mixed by Llynya. He'd found it hanging on his tower door just before he'd left with Tabor. He'd known 'twas hers by the heavy dose of lavender in it and by the smell of wildflowers lingering on the cloth and drawstrings— and by the friggin' fact that he would know anything made by her hand because he knew *her*.

He stood and stared into the dark, his jaw tight.

She'd left him. He'd given her his heart that night—verily a glimpse of his soul—and she'd walked away. If such was what came from love, he was better off without it. Yet he still hurt; he still raged inside.

Worse, he feared he knew why she'd left. He'd felt the flash of ungodly heat that should not have been between them. He'd heard the keening cry, so brief, so damning—and so must have Llynya.

Madron had made him no promises when he'd gone to see her, only told him the brew in the phial would work to cool the dragonfire when it came upon him—work to a point, and she knew not where the limit lay. As to the potion's price, she'd said naught, only advised him to win one battle at a time. An adverse portent, and a measure of his desperation that he'd taken it anyway.

Aye, Merioneth was filling up with adverse portents of late: Sha-shakrieg, skraelings, the monk captured in Riverwood. He'd heard the man's head was shaved much in the manner of Balor's dead evilmongering leech, and that like the leech, he wore the robes of a Culdee from Ynys Enlli. The monk was traveling with a mare laden with books, and Madron had voiced a strong interest in the tomes.

A light gust of wind swirled out of the opening and blew cold across his cheek. He had not much time for reading anymore, but he knew exactly where he needed to pick up his search—in the cavern of the damson shaft where Rhuddlan should be even now at the war gate. The flat slab of stone he'd spied high on the glittering wall was a guide-post of some sort; he was sure of it. 'Twas too incongruous within a sheet of crystal to be any work of nature. The long shadow to its right could be naught but a side-slip, an opening so narrow a man had to enter it sideways.

The caverns were full of writings and direction marks, but by the sheer difficulty of its placement, Mychael guessed that what he'd seen in the damson shaft led to something significant, or why else bother to fit smooth stone into a crystal wall?

Aye, there were plenty of reasons for him to go into the dark: a chance at the wormhole now that he knew how to open Rhuddlan's seals, the surety of a battle finally to be fought, and mayhaps a mark of sanctuary beyond *"Ammon"* to be found in the damson shaft. Aye, there were plenty of reasons to go and only one reason not to—Llynya.

He swore softly, and his hand instinctively went to the pouch of wildflowers hanging from his belt. The cloth was supple, sensual against his skin. His light touch released the fragrance of flowers, and the scent, so sweet with memories, twined around him.

The wind gusted again, a cool draft swirling through the flowery essence and blowing up the tunnel. Mychael followed it with his gaze to where Tabor and the pack train had disappeared. He could still hear the clip-clop of hooves and the gentle jingling of bells on harnesses. By nightfall, the ponies would be grazing with Rhuddlan's mares in the meadows of Merioneth's baileys. Tabor would be drinking honeymead at the hearthfire, and despite the preparations for war, stories would be told, songs sung. The stars would be shining, the moon waning—and Llynya would be there, part of it all.

She was what held him back. Despite that she'd left him, more than anything he wanted to be with her, to hold her, to once again feel the softness of her lips beneath his.

Half-mad fool.

He shrugged into his pack, adjusting its weight across his back, then unsheathed his crystal blade. Holding it high, he slipped into the narrow opening next to the flowstone. Llynya or nay, he knew where he must go—first to the wormhole, then down the Magia Wall and into the dark. If he was ever to be free of the dragons, or break them to his will, he first had to find them.

Home, was all Nia could think. She wanted to go home, and she wasn't particular about which home she went to: Deri with the great oak of Wroneu, Carn Merioneth with Riverwood, or Kerach in the north. Any forest would do. Verily, any tree.

Aye. That's what she needed—a tree.

"Hold!" Varga's muffled command came back to her.

She stopped crawling, swearing bitterly under her breath while another bit of hope died in her breast.

She and Varga had waited on the Rift but an hour before a message had arrived from the Lady Queen of Deseillign, setting them on this doomed path. The Grim Crawl was a thousand times worse than the Kai Crack, a thousand times longer, a thousand times less forgiving. Nia wondered that the squeeze had ever been mapped. A quarterlan back, her heartiest curses had gone out to the long-ago Sha-shakrieg who had blazed the trail she and Varga followed. A sturdy bunch, for certes, and fearless, to have pressed on through the confining darkness with its seemingly endless twists and turns. A new feature, a bladelike ridge of limestone on the floor of the tunnel, cut into her with each push forward. Dust tainted with the faint smell of Varga's blood filled her nostrils, proving that he, too, wasn't escaping unscathed from the ordeal of the Crawl.

She wasn't nearly as afraid of him as she was of dying deep in the earth, trapped in the rough-edged tube pressing against her from all sides. Spider people. What a strange lot to have even found the snaky hole Varga called simply "Mekom." Watching Varga spin a web to get them out of the Mindao River Slot had revealed some of their secrets to her. 'Twas skill backed by strength and a sticky simple that allowed the Sha-shakrieg to sling *pryf* silk against a surface in a manner to make it hold, and hold the weight of men.

The water in the Slot had been knee-high most of the way, rising to their waists only at the end. Smooth handholds had been carved into the Mindao cliffs at regular intervals. For safety, Varga had told her, if

perchance a rainstorm up above sent water rushing down into the subterranean river. It had not, and they'd been spared the ordeal of having to
climb to safety, truly like spiders on a wall.

The Ghranne Mekom was sparing them nothing. 'Twas all she
could do to hold her panic at bay. It skittered along the edge of her
thoughts, taunting her with certain death if she should fail—and she still
had the Dangoes to face.

She gritted her teeth and squeezed her eyes shut. She wanted to
raise her head and could not. The endless miles of earth above her were
less than a hairbreadth from the back of her neck. She felt rock press
against her with every breath, squeezing her. Her muscles were twitching beneath her skin, clamoring for a release she couldn't give them. She
was packed into the earth.

"Varga," she said, wondering what was taking him so long, and
yet knowing. He was stuck. Naught else could have kept him in the
same stick-forsaken spot for so long. She should go back. Save herself.
Yet the way back was not so simple. Other small tunnels connected to the
Mekom. If she backed herself into one of them, she might forever be lost.
Shadana.

"Hold," came the command again. "I'm almost through."

"V-varga. I . . . I . . ." The words lodged in her throat, choking her. She coughed, and a tiny flume of dust kicked up from the floor,
making her cough more. Great misery!

Varga cursed under his breath and tried in vain to move his
lodged shoulders. His lie had done him no good. She was faltering. In
the Mekom, fortitude was the prerequisite of survival, and hers had run
out. He'd thought the Quicken-tree warrior could beat the squeeze. It
seemed he'd been wrong.

He swore again and tried once more to shift his shoulders in a
manner that would free him from the turn that held him tight. When
he'd felt the way grow too narrow, he'd tried going back, and 'twas then
he'd been caught, his shoulder snagging on a projection of rock that had
allowed him to enter the turn, but would not allow him to retreat.

He had come this way before. Why not this time? he wondered.
He had twisted and squirmed, relaxed some muscles and tightened others, yet still was held firm. He was no heavier, no bigger. Verily, he'd lost
some of his bulk since the end of the Wars. Yet 'twas even less likely that
the Crawl had changed.

Or was it?

Had he not seen with his own eyes the great tear through the crystal seal of Kryscaven Crater? The earth had trembled deep to create such a chasm, and with deep trembling were not other changes possible? Changes so minute that they would go unnoticed until a man who had once passed through the Mekom could no longer pass?

He swore softly between his teeth. They both would die—unless he told her to go back and she had the strength to do it.

"Pwr wa ladth." He heard the faint sound of her voice attempting song between bouts of coughing. A ragged song would do him no good. What he needed was a cursed double-jointed shoulder.

"Pwr wa ladth. Fai quall a'lomarian."

She struggled on behind him, her song wavering with the tide of her fear. He was afraid too, but of failure, not death.

"Es sholei par es cant. Pwr wa ladth. Pwr wa ladth."

'Twas one of the Quicken-tree's green songs, a chant of sunlight— not of its brightness and beauty, but of its power beyond the glories of sight, the power of sunlight in dark places, be they of the heart or the world.

Aye, he knew the songs of his enemies well. He shifted himself again and moved nary a finger's width, while she sang behind him:

> "Run deep. Run deep.
> *Pwr wa ladth. Pwr wa ladth.*
> Wind through leaf and stem and root.
> *Fai quall a'lomarian.*
> Flow like a river into the earth.
> *Es sholei par es cant.*
> Run deep. Run deep.
> *Pwr wa ladth. Pwr wa ladth."*

He'd thought the Dangoes would be their greatest challenge, but it seemed the frozen place would not get another chance at Varga of the Iron Dunes. He would die in the Crawl like a worm.

But she need not.

"Nia—" He no sooner spoke her name than the first tremor hit, scarce stronger than her voice, an odd whisper through the rock. The second tremor was even fainter, but he felt something give way. Another fierce twist and he was free. He crawled at double speed for the end of the tunnel, pushing his pack in front of him. A gust of wind announced the Kasr-al Loop, and in a trice he was through the Mekom, tumbling out into the small cavern that led to the main trail. He turned to go back for her, but was stopped short by the sight of a square, dirt-encrusted hand scrabbling for a hold on the rim of the Crawl. Relief flooded through him.

He reached down and pulled her free, and she came to her feet, shaky but able to stand on her own.

"Shadana." The word blew from her lips. *"Pwr wa ladth."* She tucked a lanky strand of hair behind her ear and set about dusting herself off.

"Are you hurt?" he asked.

"Nay. And you?"

"Of a piece. I've felt earthquakes in the caverns before, but never while in the Mekom."

She looked up with an annoyed frown. " 'Twas no earthquake, spider man. 'Twas me singing you out of that snag you'd gotten yourself hung up on. And if— What's that?" she asked suddenly, growing still.

Taken aback by what she'd said, it took Varga a moment to pick up on what had riveted her attention. Only a moment, though, then he wondered how he'd missed it.

"Skraelings," he said. The stench was wafting into the cavern from the trail.

She went for her blade like a warrior and came up empty-handed. Her expression darkened. "Ye cannot leave me unarmed, Varga, not with skraelings on the trail."

No faltering there, he thought, admiring the speed of her response. And for all she didn't know, she knew the danger of skraelings.

"Aye," he agreed, and unsheathed her dreamstone dagger from his belt. He gave it and her sword to her without another word, then walked over to where the cave emptied out onto the tail end of the Kasr-al Loop. If she would go for his back, he would as soon know it now. He slipped into his pack and knelt on the trail. The causeway from which they would enter the Dangoes lay not a lan from the cave.

She came up beside him and held her lightblade out over the trail. "They're moving west, toward Merioneth."

"Aye, and look here." He pointed to a place close to the tunnel wall where the finer dirt was wont to settle. A paw print was clearly pressed into the dust.

"Wolves." She touched the edge of the track.

"*Uffern* wolves," he corrected her. "Wolves twisted to a skraeling master's bidding. There's no other way to get them to run in the caves."

She glanced back to the Crawl.

"Nay," he told her. "There's naught for us but to go forward."

"I wouldn't do otherwise," she assured him, her affront showing in the squaring of her shoulders, "but if it comes to retreat, I'd like to have a place where they can't follow."

He nodded. "The Crawl would suffice, but we'll be far better served by the Dangoes. The ice caverns are not a place for skraelings and their kind. If we make the causeway, we'll descend immediately."

"If?"

He lifted a pinch of dust off the trail and brought it to his nose. "The tracks are fresh. 'Tis only the switchbacks in the trail that keep the sound of the skraelpack from us."

"And how many do you think there are?"

He shrugged and let the dirt fall from his fingers. "More than enough to give us both a hero's death."

Chapter 18

Flowstone rolled in smoothly rounded waves down the narrow passageway of Mychael's descent, a frozen river cresting and eddying in the blue light of his crystal dagger. 'Twas slow going, but shorter than retracing his and Tabor's path through the Canolbarth. Singing along as the pony-master was, Mychael doubted if Tabor would note his leaving until he reached the Cavern of the Scrying Pool.

A botch that was, he thought. Since the freeing of the *pryf,* naught had been seen in the pool. Steam rose and wafted as it always had, but the water was murky, swirled through with muddy currents that even Madron and Moira had not been able to clear. In the spring, Madron had taken him there on occasion to teach him the songs of his mother and the chants of her father: songs to open windows onto faraway places and chants to guide those who sought to reach them. Nemeton had been such a seeker. Madron said he had traveled far and wide before coming to Wales with a Lord D'Arbois. On that journey, happening on the place where the Wye and Llynfi rivers met, he'd called a halt and thereby saved the retinue from a blizzard of uncommon fury—or so the tale had always been told. For three days the snows had fallen, rent with lightning and resounding with thunder. The hours before each dawn had been filled with rains of ice, the nights in between lost in banks of fog. When 'twas over, Nemeton had prophesied great victories for whoever ruled the small keep on the bluffs above the rivers. D'Arbois had taken the prophesy to heart, routing the old baron and winning Wydehaw for his own.

Sín. The making of storms. Madron had tried to teach him the way of it. 'Twas a skill the witch held in a small degree, and apparently he held in none. Mychael had yet to raise a wisp of fog under even the best of circumstances. Just as well, to his way of thinking. Godless witchery was not his goal, though Madron had assured him there was no godlessness in all of nature or witchery.

Wales, she'd gone on to say, had been her father's truest home, and Wydehaw his truest place in Wales. He'd built a tower at the castle and studied there for many years before tragedy struck and sent him north. He chose to stay in Merioneth to be close to the last of the Magus Druid Priestesses and the long-forgotten men of Anglesey. And in all her father's travels, she'd said, he'd laid his traces of magic to mark the wonders he'd found.

As to his sanctuary, Madron had been the one to show Mychael the mark *"Ammon"* wound through Ddrei Glas's and Ddrei Goch's serpentine scales. It was part of a map Nemeton had been laboring to piece together before his death, the journals of which had been lost when Carn Merioneth had fallen. She'd searched both Anglesey and Wydehaw many times in the past fifteen years and come up with naught. Nor had she been able to find anything in Carn Merioneth since their return in the spring, though she and Moira had searched the place clear through, and even Naas had lent a hand.

Mychael and Lavrans had spoken of Nemeton's tower, the Hart of Wydehaw Castle, of its Druid Door and the great celestial sphere in its eyrie, and of the walls carved with all manner of words and numbers in receipts and obscure formulae. Mychael greatly desired to search the Hart for himself, being well aware of the inherent sanctuary of castle towers, and mayhaps there would yet come a chance for him to delve the mysteries the bard had unraveled, though how he would convince the current lord to allow him access to Nemeton's tower remained to be seen. Having gone from a Welsh monastery into the otherworldly realm of the deep dark, he knew little of the English and even less of Marcher lords. Lavrans had given him the secret of the Druid Door, and provided he could actually open the mighty thing, that deed alone could suffice.

As for his lessons from Madron, with each turn he'd taken toward madness, he'd been less inclined to spend time with the witch. He was Druid, aye, but no priest as she would have him, and no witch of nature's ways. He knew words of power and the power of a man's voice raised in chant; he'd felt such power at Strata Florida every evensong, at every spoken prayer. Between the Christians, and the Druids, and the Quicken-tree with all their many songs, he saw no difference in putting a voice to whatever sacred thing they would honor. But for himself, he feared what had chosen him was neither honorable nor sacred, but was only power—raw and unyielding. He was a strange mix, and mayhaps knowing none could claim him as their own, all the gods had abandoned him, left him to the dragons, to fight and die with the beasts.

The worms were their spawn, the weir their doing. Since Rhuddlan had sealed the gates to great wormhole, his wildness had only grown. In the past at least he had been able to find a measure of peace in the smaller wormholes, which had since disappeared.

Peace, the promise of gods.

Nay, he'd not told Llynya all of the wormholes and their dangers, and he'd told her naught of the bliss, of the stars he'd seen; nor of the turnings of the Earth and how the timeless flow moved inside him in the weir; nor how the tides once washed through him, a full cycle, and shown him the course of the Moon. 'Twas the sense of salvation itself he'd found, to slide into the Earth's wisdoms and from there into the Heaven's. He would give much to sink himself into that peace once more. Yet in the end, the dragon's path always led to war, to war and the river of blood. That truth, too, was in the wormhole, swirling around the core on smoky tendrils of dragon's breath.

Sanctuary might be found there . . . or battle. For certes battle would be found in the damson shaft if Rhuddlan had broken the Shashakrieg web and gone on. Mychael knew he would then be bound to follow and to fight. Thrice cursed he was, with the dragon's gift of war, the Merioneth priestess blood that had brought him hence, and that he had always been as he was now—alone.

He rounded a curve into a steeper descent and bore right along a narrow ledge that took him above the flowstone. The frozen river wound downward at an ever sharper angle until it joined the gigantic flow of opalescent rock that made up the north wall of Lanbarrdein. The ledge skirted the flow and dropped down into a cavern on the other side of the north wall. 'Twas called Dripshank Well for the maze of drip-shanks pillaring and arching across its main room, and because of the sinkholes that beaded its surface like a string of pearls. 'Twas through Dripshank that the River Bredd found its way into Lanbarrdein. Mychael had traversed its trails many times, it being a direct link be-tween Riverwood and the deep dark and a quicker way to the surface than going through the Canolbarth.

From Dripshank he could take a path directly into the *pryf* nest and from there work his way down to the gates, or he could continue on through a side tunnel to the Magia Wall and backtrack a quarterlan to the crystal-cliffed headland of the weir. Much of the choice would be based on the *pryf*. On the last journey up, despite his own distress, he'd noted their frantic, continuous movement and erratic bursts of speed, and he'd wondered if they were trying to make a wormhole in the nest itself. The gods protect him if that was true.

Too much strife was about, and too many enemies. He had Sha-shakrieg and skraelings to worry him, and rot and wolves, and men turning from their own kind. If the *pryf,* too, went berserk, he feared 'twould do naught but hasten his end.

Traversing a short squeeze of a switchback, Mychael came out on a windswept ledge high on Dripshank's west wall. The smell of salt was in the air. The aboveground entrance to the cavern was set in a cliff face on Riverwood's eastern edge and ever caught the prevailing ocean breezes. Trig had put a permanent guard on the hole and specifically banned him and Llynya from going anywhere near it. Thus when Mychael saw flickers of light in the darkness below, he quickly sheathed his dreamstone and hoped he'd not been seen. He would not be stopped at this point. Nearly as quickly, he realized that the lights bobbing through the forest of pillars and arches were yellow and red, completely lacking the lucent blueness of dreamstone—except for one, and that one was shining toward the green side of blue with violet at its core.

Llynya was in Dripshank Well—and with a larger troop than he'd thought left in all of Carn Merioneth, what with Wei being in Tryfan and all the messengers Rhuddlan had sent, and Rhuddlan himself in the deep dark with forty Liosalfar. Those in Dripshank could only be the Kings Wood elves Rhuddlan had hoped would come.

The sound of running water masked much of the marching of feet, yet he heard the clattering of weapons. Strange, that. He'd never heard *tylwyth teg* clatter, no matter how well armed, and a fully armed Liosalfar warrior carried no less than three blades, a bow, and a full quiver. Of late, Trig had also issued everyone iron stars, and still they didn't clatter when they moved.

The group below sounded like a tinkers' rendezvous. The Kings Wood elves were going to need shaping up before they would be of much use.

Curious, and concerned that Llynya would be the one chosen to lead such a rustic band, he strode along the high ledge, following them in hopes of getting a better view. The troop veered north in a short curve before heading south, and Mychael swore softly to himself. They were at the largest sinkhole. Once on its other side, 'twas a straight shot into the deep dark.

Sticks, he swore again, speeding up his steps. Trig knew better than to let Llynya anywhere near the deep dark.

He redrew his crystal knife to better light his way and kept on after the troop, or at least the main part of it. The Kings Wood line was ragged, ill-formed by even the laxest standards. Stragglers abounded, small spots of jingling brightness wandering off from the group.

The tunnel they were heading for connected Dripshank to the Wall and widened into a small cavern about halfway along its length. At a fork in the trail, he took the lower road and broke into a steady running gait, deciding 'twas best if he caught up and saw what they were about. Trig hadn't mentioned a sortie into the dark, but if Rhuddlan had called for Liosalfar beyond the Wall, Michael figured he was more likely to be welcomed than reprimanded. He would offer to take Llynya's place, and she could be sent back to scout in Riverwood where she belonged. If he met with any resistance, he wasn't above revealing her intention to follow Morgan into the wormhole.

The closer he got to the cavern floor, though, the less sure he was that Rhuddlan or Trig had anything to do with the raucous, lumbering group he was following. The less sure he became, the faster he ran, until he was racing along the narrow slabs staircasing Dripshank's south wall. When he cleared the last riser, descending to where the salt tang of the ocean breezes did not reach, sure and sudden dread replaced any uncertainty. He landed on the cave floor and knew immediately it wasn't Liosalfar he was chasing.

The smell of black rot hung like a pall in the lower levels of the cavern, weighing down the air and teasing a fine strand of terror to life in his veins. Skraelings.

The pack was a full halflan ahead of him, the front of their line almost to the tunnel. He tried to do a quick count, but he scarce could think, so full of fear was he for the worst.

They had her dreamstone dagger, and for that there must have been battle in Riverwood. Llynya would not have relinquished her blade without a fight.

Christe. How many had it taken to bring the Light-elf down?

An awful sound rose in his throat, and he clamped his teeth shut against it.

The odds were against him. Mayhaps fifty to one. Mayhaps more.

Ahead of him, another trail snaked off the cavern floor, leading up to a natural arch that spanned a long, open section of the cavern. He resheathed his dagger, hiding its light, and headed for the higher trail at a dead run. He lost ground by changing direction, but gained a better view. What he saw from the top of the arch stopped him cold.

Pikes and halberds cut into the air in a thick, bristling line of more than a hundred soldiers, all of them heavy jawed and fanged. Men no more, but once men, as Tabor had explained, the worst of the race sought out and turned by a fell mage's hand into servants of destruction.

His gaze swept the monstrous army, searching for the one who held the blue light. Mychael found him toward the front of the line, turning to give an order at the tunnel entrance. Tall and blond and more finely formed than the bulk of the troops, he appeared at first to be Liosalfar. Then Mychael saw that the captain's nose was naught but a silver triangle in the middle of his face, and the hand he had wrapped around Llynya's dagger was clawed like a bear's. No Light-elf, this, but one of a darker breed—Dockalfar.

Mychael's instinct was to kill him where he stood, but even as he jerked an iron star from his arm guard, his gaze slipped farther back in the horde, to the one receiving the orders. 'Twas then he saw her, a slight form slung over another Dockalfar's shoulder. Light from a yellow dreamstone cast a pale shimmer across the meadowsweet and rose petals woven into her tunic.

Fear washed through him, cold and fast, clearing his mind of all thoughts but one—*Does she live?*

His heart was tight in his chest, his breath near impossible to catch. The skraelings pooled at the entrance to the tunnel, shoving and jostling to get in and sometimes taking her from his view. He only stood and waited and watched, his eyes focused solely on the bit of shimmer in the dark sea of rough weapons.

The soldier carrying Llynya looked back, and Mychael saw his face. As fair as any Quicken-tree he was, except for the empty, sunken eye socket on the left side of his face. The Dark-elf shifted her weight on his shoulder before following the queue into the tunnel. Just before he disappeared from sight, Mychael saw her body move again, aided by her bound hands, not by the Dockalfar who held her.

His relief was as sharp-edged as his fear. He quickly scanned the milling crowd before taking off at an easy lope. There were no other Quicken-tree, only Llynya, and only him to save her.

Chapter 19

On the east side of the Dangoes, rounding the last turn of the Kasr-al Loop trail, Nia and Varga heard the clash of battle and the cries of *"Khardeen!"* ahead of them in the dark.

"Har maukte! Har!" The skraeling roar went up again and again in response, accompanied by a terrible howling. *"Har! Har! Har!"*

Varga swore, a low hiss under his breath. For herself, Nia blanched. She'd ne'er heard *uffern* beasts afore. 'Twas bloodcurdling, but she kept to Varga's side, racing onward and drawing steel.

Hoarfrost limned the portal onto the causeway they'd crossed days earlier. The air grew suddenly cold and within three paces they cleared the tunnel and came out onto a scene of chaos.

On the nearside, fiery torches sent yellow flames and trails of greasy smoke into the air. To the west, dreamstones flared, shining with icy brightness before an onslaught of shifting shadows. And here and there, golden crystals with incarnadine hearts streaked across the darkness, giving off a light unseen in Merioneth for five hundred years.

"Dockalfar." Varga spoke the word of a truth Nia could scarce conceive: Dockalfar back in the deep dark where they had reigned, where the riches of the earth had been their stock in trade—the known metals and *thullein,* and crystal of every color. The yellow dreamstones had never been traded, and those with red at their core had been only for the Dark-elf King and his guard. *"Yuell,"* 'twas called, the dreamstone crystal of the Tuans. A half-dozen or more such crystals shone out on the causeway, well into the thick of the fight.

The Quicken-tree were far outnumbered, yet Rhuddlan was holding a line on the trail, forcing the skraelings to remain on open ground between the frigid sea crashing into the cliffs and the glistening maw of the great cavern. Foot by foot the Light-elves were being forced to give way, their losses revealed by the silver and green clothed bodies scattered along the ice-encrusted track.

Nia watched in disbelief as the Quicken-tree were flanked yet again and another Liosalfar was cut down. Had Rhuddlan gone mad?

She started forward, a cry on her lips, but Varga grabbed her arm and held her back.

"No, child. Look," he said, pointing down into the Dangoes.

Long, twisting cords of vapor-borne ice crystals had risen out from between the huge dripshanks at the cavern's entrance and were gnarling themselves into bony fingers. They reached across the frozen crevasse at the base of the towers and clawed their way up the cliffs to the causeway.

Nia felt the dread chill of their intent and stumbled back toward the Kasr-al. *Shadana.* Had she really thought to put herself willingly into the ice cave's clutches?

"Hold," Varga commanded, his grip remaining firm on her arm. "We'll not retreat while a fight is yet to be had. The Dangoes bones are not for us. 'Tis the skraelings they come for."

Even as he spoke, his words were proved out, with the first vaporous phalanxes reaching up onto the track. They chose their victims with care, picking those with no dread heat about them, the torchless ones. Struggling was to no avail for those doomed souls, since flame was the only blade sharp enough to sever Dangoes bones. One by one, the hapless skraelings were hooked 'round their legs or arms and necks and dragged over the edge of the causeway, their screams naught but thin echoes against the louder sounds of the battle.

"We'll fight from there," Varga said, pointing to a cairn of rocks fallen from the Kasr-al Loop portal. "Rhuddlan knows he can't outrun their wolfpack, so he holds them on the causeway for the vapors to devour. We'll do the same from this side and keep them from their retreat."

Nia, who only moments before had been ready to rush forward on nothing more than instinct and valor, found herself hesitating. There were a hundred skraelings, and wolves everywhere. If they all decided to turn and run, there was naught she and Varga could do to stop them.

She turned to tell him, but he'd already drawn his longsword and was running toward the fray.

"Sticks!" She took off after him.

Awareness of the ice cave's danger spread quickly among the skraelings, and with awareness came panic. Their lines broke before the oncoming vapors, and Nia scrambled onto the cairn with Varga, prepared to hold the rocks or meet her end.

A Dockalfar stabbed his pike into the first skraeling who ran, and the others instantly re-formed, but it needed more Dark-elves than were there to keep the skraelings' courage stiff. By ones and twos they made their retreats, skirting the ocean-side cliffs of the causeway. In the melee, with most of the dark host surging forward and a few trying to sneak backward, some were lost, either killed by their more stalwart companions or daring too close to the icy cliffs and slipping into Mor Sarff.

Those few that made it through the lines had to deal with Varga and Nia on the cairn. The Sha-shakrieg man fought like a whirlwind, gray rags flying, his sword singing a song of steel and death. The blade's cutting edge flashed with silver light borne of *thullein*. "Edge of Sorrow," she'd heard it called, razor sharp and, like the threads Varga carried, steeped in poison. The last skraeling to feel its bite writhed in pain at the foot of the cairn. The first three who had thought to fight their way back to the Kasr-al Loop had been killed on the spot.

Elfin speed was Nia's defense, and her greatest offense, until the wolves, too, began to break and run. Aided by the Dangoes bones, Rhuddlan's line was no longer in retreat and was slowly but surely forcing the skraelpack back toward the Loop—much to her and Varga's disadvantage. They could not hold against so many. 'Twould be minutes only, she knew, before the whole tide turned and they were overwhelmed.

A wolf dodged in close to nip her ankle and met the flat of Varga's blade. Yelping, the beast retreated, but had no sooner turned than the next set of sharp teeth took its place. A harsh command from a pasty-faced skraeling set more of the wolves on them, and in the space of a breath, a snarling pack had closed in a semicircle around her and the Sha-shakrieg. Gray wolves and black, sooty brown and even the far northern white breed snapped and growled in an ever-tightening ring. A large black moved in closer than the others, and Nia smelled the hunger on him. 'Twas a desperate thing, full of pain, victim of the Dockalfar's malevolent power. To turn a forest animal into a ravening beast of war took a conjured twist of nature the likes of which had been forbidden by the Prydion Magi long before the Wars of Enchantment, a twist of the body's hunger into mindless greed, and desires into insatiable need.

Faced with the fiercely advancing creatures, Varga ordered her farther up the side of the cairn. As they gave way, the skraelings bent on retreat passed them by, making only ineffectual stabs with their weapons before they plunged into the safety of the Kasr-al portal, leaving the kill for the animals.

On the far side of the causeway, Rhuddlan's band was taking the day, with skill and speed proving a good leveler of numbers. As they moved out onto the causeway, the Dangoes bones found them as easily as the skraelpack. Rhuddlan set three Liosalfar to race along the cliff edge, cutting down the skeletal ice fingers with the heat of dreamstone light and freeing others for the push forward.

'Twould do her and Varga little good, Nia feared, slicing at another lunging beast with her sword. Blood showed on Varga's thigh where a wolf's teeth had found purchase. The animal lay dead on the rocks from the Sha-shakrieg's blade, but the scent of the death had roused the others into more daring attacks.

She scrambled higher on the rocks with Varga beside her, wolves closing in all around, and Rhuddlan yet a quarterlan away on the causeway. She could have made it to the Liosalfar line with a quickety-split dash, but the Sha-shakrieg had no such speed. He'd pitched himself into the battle on Rhuddlan's side instead of retreating and saving himself, and for that reason Nia didn't desert the cairn. 'Twas a choice she did not expect to have long to regret, and mayhaps she wouldn't have, except for an unlikely savior from the Dangoes.

A low-pitched howl, faint and eerie, wound its way through the needlelike icicles encrusting the cave's ceiling, setting them aquiver. Rescue had never arrived on such a mournful note. The wolves stilled and fell silent, their ears pricked.

The howl grew stronger, accompanied by ice music, and the wolfpack began to whine and yap and jump about, dancing on the rocks. A few slunk away from the cairn and melted into the retreating horde of skraelings.

Nia looked to the great cavern and found the baying hound— Conladrian—still as stone and black as night against the mighty drip-shanks of ice flanking the Dangoes. He raised his head again, giving full throat to his voice, and half the wolfpack broke free and streaked back through the Liosalfar line, heading west off the causeway. The remaining animals milled about in ever-growing confusion, some answering the hound's call with howls of their own, others silent and watchful.

Ice music proved the final bane of the skraelpack, as it was ever the bane of men. Its sweet, frozen melody rippled through the air in waves of cresting sound, promising an endless, sleeping death to all who would come nearer, ever nearer—and some went, over the edge and into the ice. The Dockalfar tried to herd the skraelings off the causeway before they were caught in the song's enchanted grip, but for the weary and the wounded, the lure was greater than the threat of a Dark-elf pike.

Varga and she killed four more as they retreated. Coming up the causeway, the Quicken-tree were laying the skraelings low on every side. 'Twas only the Dockalfar who escaped unscathed into the Loop by being too quick for Varga and staying clear of Nia's gleaming blade.

The Quicken-tree fought their way closer, closing the causeway except to those few skraelings who had crossed the Liosalfar line and were escaping to the west with the wolves. Varga engaged one last skraeling, fighting him back into the Kasr-al portal.

"Nia!" Roth, a Liosalfar at the front of the line, hailed her. Other glad cries of recognition followed, until Varga came out of the shadow of the Kasr-al portal. Upon sighting the Sha-shakrieg, voices were suddenly stilled and bloodied swords relifted.

Varga halted on the track. Dreamstone light flickered over the woad-painted faces lined up against him, showing bright aquamarine eyes and the glinting edges of daggers and short swords held at the ready. For an awful moment Nia feared she might have to set herself against the Liosalfar to keep him from harm.

"The Sha-shakrieg is for Rhuddlan," she warned, stepping forward and taking a guarding stance.

"Aye. He is mine." A single voice, clear and deep, spoke from out of the darkness, and as one, the Quicken-tree soldiers lowered their swords.

Rhuddlan strode through the parting ranks and stopped a few yards from Varga, his face a grim reflection of the carnage on the causeway.

"Leave us," he commanded, and all of the Liosalfar moved away.

Nia, too, made a short bow and stepped aside, back toward the ranks of the Quicken-tree warriors. Should Rhuddlan choose to cut the Sha-shakrieg down before hearing him out, so be it. He was her sovereign lord.

The Liosalfar welcomed her, and 'twas with a sense of relief that she blended into their midst.

Varga watched her disappear, noting the wanness of her complexion and the unsteadiness of her gait. The battle had taken the last of her strength. He doubted if she would see the forests again.

"Mayhaps I'll compose a song for her in the desert," he said, turning his attention to the tall, fair-haired man in front of him. "A lay for Nia of the Light-elves."

"If she dies, you'll not see the desert again." The Quicken-tree leader was succinct, his pronouncement no more than Varga had expected. Rhuddlan had ever been decisive, and arrogant, and most times too sure of his course. 'Twas his weakness as well as his strength, and it seemed he'd changed little.

"I was taking her through the Dangoes. 'Tis a good two days shorter."

"If you live," Rhuddlan said harshly. "And forever longer if you don't."

"Aye," Varga agreed. "Yet I would have risked my life alongside her. Indeed, I have risked my life to return her to the Light-elves and to warn you of war as commanded by the Lady Queen of Deseillign."

Rhuddlan's gaze narrowed. "Your life is no longer at risk, Varga. It is forfeit, and the Lady's warning comes too late. War is already upon us."

Arrogant, aye, Varga thought. A tight smile curved his lips beneath his djellaba. He had not fought to hold the Kasr-al Loop for the privilege of being threatened. He needed Rhuddlan's help, but so did the Quicken-tree leader need his.

"This is not yet war," he said, allowing a measure of contempt into his voice, "only a few soldiers fighting in the dark. I have not *forfeited* my life, Rhuddlan, to save you and your Liosalfar from a skraelpack and the deformed remnants of the Dockalfar. Look, if you would see the war we fight in Deseillign, a war that runs through our streets and steals the breath of our children." He walked over to the nearest skraeling and with his foot shoved the dead man over onto his back. Kneeling, he ripped the pikeman's sleeve up to his shoulder. "Come, King of the Light-elves, and look at what lies in wait for Merioneth."

Rhuddlan lifted his dreamstone high, casting a pool of light over the gray-skinned corpse at Varga's feet. Shadows and a blue luminescence rippled across the skraeling's limp form, revealing a rough-hewn tunic and the bit of chain mail that had failed him, and on his upper arm, a zigzag bolt of lightning burned into the flesh, a brand to mark him as the minion of a long-vanquished king—Slott of the Thousand Skulls.

"By the blood of the Stones," Rhuddlan swore through gritted teeth. His hand tightened on his dagger and light burst forth from the crystal hilt, a sharp-edged jacinth flash with a heart of golden flame.

A second curse lodged in his throat.

In three steps, he was to the next fallen skraeling. With the tip of his sword, he slashed open the dead man's sleeve, revealing another damning brand. The thunderbolt was unmistakable. Curved like a scythe on one end and edged in flame on the other, 'twas the finial of Slott's scepter—which had been gripped in the Troll King's hand when the beast and his raiment had hardened and cracked and metamorphosed into Inishwrath's granite tor.

Rhuddlan was no Prydion Mage, but he knew well enough what it would take to turn enchanted stone back into flesh and bone—the light-devouring smoke of Dharkkum and a knowing conjurer to wield it.

"You'll find the brands are fresh, scabbed and rimmed with charred flesh," the Sha-shakrieg said, "and though you killed a fine number here, there are thousands more like them in the north with new recruits coming in every day. Have no doubt, Slott is free and returned to Rastaban, and as the smoke grows, so does his army."

Rhuddlan turned on his old enemy, his rage barely held in check. "Is this the Desert Queen's doing? Has she dared her own destruction as well as mine by breaking the crystal seals to bring Slott back from Inishwrath?"

The shrouded man denied the accusation with a shake of his head. "The Lady of Deseillign knows naught of freeing black smoke from crystal prisons or trolls from rock. Nor do the Desert Magi with all their great powers."

"The Lady has one of the Seven Books of Lore," Rhuddlan retaliated with a sore truth. "I did not take the *Gratte Bron Le* away from her." He had wanted to. Indeed, he'd had the great tome in his hands, the Orange Book of Stone, but Ailfinn had made him leave it, a bond for the ancient pact between Sha-shakrieg and *tylwyth teg*.

"Aye," Varga said. "But the *Gratte Bron Le* is not a book of spells like the *tylwyth teg*'s Indigo Book. It says nothing of how to circumvent Prydion enchantments. If it did, Ailfinn Mapp would not have left it in the Lady Queen's hands. For certes you and the mage left little else."

"We left enough that five hundred years later there are still Sha-shakrieg alive to break their oaths," Rhuddlan said with his own measure of contempt.

Turning away in disgust, he stepped to the next skraeling, and the next. All were branded. All of the brands were fresh.

"The Lady needs *thullein* to fight," Varga said in his queen's defense, trailing Rhuddlan across the causeway. "Break the treaty boundaries or lose the Desert Kingdoms—such was her choice. That she puts her people, and yours, ahead of her pride is proof of her need, a need greater than even in those dread days after you destroyed Deseillign's reservoirs and poured all of our water into the sands."

"Half a millennium of defeat is enough to temper anyone's pride, even the Desert Queen's," Rhuddlan growled, dismissing the Lady's well-known pride as he dismissed the rest of Varga's reasoning.

Looking about him, he swore again under his breath. The last Liosalfar he had sent to the island of Inishwrath before Tages three days earlier had been Pwyll in late August. The boy had reported the headlands secure, but it seemed he'd escaped by the skin of his teeth. Slott's awakening could not have been long after and must have nigh torn Inishwrath asunder. With luck, Tages would find only the remains of destruction and not others of Slott's hoary brood rousing from their centuries-long sleep.

The slight bit of smoke issuing from the damson shaft where Varga had left his war gate had not been enough to raise the Troll King and his scepter. That had taken a prodigious amount of the wretched stuff. But from where?

Gesturing for a Liosalfar to follow, he made his way farther along the causeway. In all the fighting, they must have killed or wounded one of the Dockalfar. Even a dead Dark-elf would tell him something.

A live one would tell him everything.

Dockalfar. *Shadana*. Slott arisen and Sha-shakrieg. Someone was stirring up an ancient brew of catastrophic dimensions, and Rhuddlan would know who.

"Strip the weapons from this group and toss their bodies into the sea," he said to the Quicken-tree warrior who stepped forward. "If any find a Dockalfar, call for me."

His orders given, Rhuddlan turned and fixed his gaze on Varga, the Lord of the Iron Dunes. No young warrior come to test his mettle, but the Desert Queen's most trusted adviser during the Wars of Enchantment. Other than the Lady herself, he was the last of the spider people Rhuddlan would have expected to willingly put himself in Quicken-tree hands. The decision could well be his final undoing.

"When last I was in the Sha-shakrieg's southern basin, there was *thullein* enough to supply the desert forges for an age," Rhuddlan told him. "The Lady at her most voracious could not have depleted those stores since the Wars, so tell me not of the Sha-shakrieg needing that small bit of metal that lies within my borders. I will have the truth, Varga, or I will have your life. The choice is yours."

Dark eyes stared out at him from between the gray cloth wrapping the Sha-shakrieg's face, giving away nothing. Then, to Rhuddlan's satisfaction, Varga bowed and pulled a thin leather packet out of his tunic.

Rhuddlan took the offered dispatch. 'Twas sealed with a round of orange wax impressed with the Desert Queen's watermark. The last of its like he'd seen had held the Lady's surrender. Now they were to war again.

He ran his fingers over the seal, feeling for signs of tampering and finding two—a smooth rise of remelted wax and a hairline fracture where it had been broken. He glanced at Varga, who answered his unspoken question with a shrug of bland acceptance. The court at Deseillign was a viper's pit of intrigue.

Rhuddlan rebroke the seal and withdrew the parchment from within. A quick scan confirmed Varga as the Lady's emissary. Rhuddlan could not mistake her bold hand. The document was dated only a day past and told of skraeling strike troops massing on the border walls of Deseillign and ranging as far as the eastern deserts. It told also of a mining catastrophe in the southern basin in midsummer, of a hundred Sha-shakrieg swallowed up by a sudden rent in Kryscaven Crater that continued to belch flames and rancid smoke and fill the southern caverns with a strange, ravaging pestilence. *Thullein* could no longer be mined at the site, and without a supply of the metal-rich ore for swordblades and arrow points, the war had taken a turn for the worse. As for the great fissure that had broken the Crater, signs of enchantment had been found all along its length, signs the Desert Magi had determined to be of Prydion making.

The dispatch ended with an imperial decree: for the *Tylwyth Teg* to surrender the Prydion Mage, Ailfinn Mapp, and to forever renounce such mage; for the Quicken-tree to surrender the Aetheling seen in Crai Force as a token of good faith against further Prydion treacheries; for a chadron's weight of Dream Stone to be delivered to Deseillign in recompense for the damages sustained thus far and for those to come; and for the King of the Light-elves to surrender to the Lady Queen the most powerful warrior in all his ranks—a blade-master of dread renown to wield a *druaight* sword.

As he read, Rhuddlan's hand grew tighter and tighter around his dagger, until a fierce flash of light burst from the crystal hilt with a cracking whine and struck a skraeling on the track. Wisps of smoke instantly curled up from the dead man's bloody tunic and pale skin. Steam rose from the water pooled around him.

"Is she fully mad?" he demanded of Varga, the dreamstone still crackling and flickering in his hand.

"Nay," the Sha-shakrieg said. He'd taken a step backward and was watching the dagger with a wary eye. "Only ill-advised by her Council of Lords."

"Then you read this idiocy and still dared to give it to me?" Rhuddlan lifted the parchment.

"I dared not." Varga shifted his gaze to Rhuddlan's face. "You asked for the truth, not wisdom, and in truth Deseillign nears its end. The smoke from Kryscaven pours out of fissures in the Rift and spreads like a cloud of night across the desert. The skraelpacks have doubled in a fortnight with destruction as their only goal. No captain has come forth to offer terms, no demands have been made, and the air fair reeks with their cries of 'Death to the Betrayers.' The Lady fears not only for her life, but for the lives of all the desert peoples. She would have the Magia Blade reforged."

Rhuddlan bit back an oath. He could not save Mychael from this. Not now. Not with the great seals on Kryscaven broken and the fell fumes of Dharkkum once more loose on the land. For certes the Lady had already commanded her desert smiths to begin their work. Sword-blades she had aplenty to fight even ten thousand skraelings, but not the swordblade meant to fit a dreamstone hilt. For the Magia Blade she needed the raw *thullein* Varga had stolen from the western basin.

" 'Tis a sword of ruin to be used for a ruinous end," he said.

"You have the aetheling to temper its deeds."

"No." On that point there could be no compromise. Llynya had not the strength nor the heart to wield such a dire blade.

"Then there is another," Varga said, his voice tight with conviction. "There has to be. Let the aetheling temper him. Leash your mage, Rhuddlan, and release the dread warrior. Call the dragons forth and let him put them to their task. It is the only thing that can save us."

Aye. 'Twas true. The Magia Blade could save them all—except for the one who dared to take it up.

He looked to the far edge of the causeway where the Liosalfar were throwing the last of the skraelings into the sea.

"Roth!" he called, and his captain for the sortie looked up and shook his head. No Dockalfar had been found.

He looked next to the Dangoes. Conladrian was gone. The black hound's journey had but begun if he would see his sister, Rhayne, come out of the ice. The white hound had fallen in the battle for Balor and been dragged by her brother into the frozen world beyond the ice cave's forbidding maw, beyond the reach of time in hopes of new life. The Balor battle seemed as naught compared to what they now faced. In all the Dangoes there was not a place for the ghosts of the legions that would fall if Dharkkum was not stopped. The smoke was but the beginning with its choking fumes and ravaging pestilences. The true danger would come after the smoke cleared, making way for the all-devouring darkness of Dharkkum itself, a night so pure no light could cut through it, not even dreamstone light.

Wind touched his cheek, a cold vapor of warning, and from out of the Kasr-al came the high, calling howls of a wolfpack re-forming.

"We dare not tarry here," he said to Varga. "Nor anywhere this side of the Magia Wall. If you would have an alliance, it will be set at the gates of time and on my terms. Can you speak for the Lady?"

"Do you have the dread warrior the Lady seeks?"

Rhuddlan weighed his answer one last time, knowing he cast Mychael's doom.

"Aye," he finally said. "I have him. He and the aetheling await us in Merioneth."

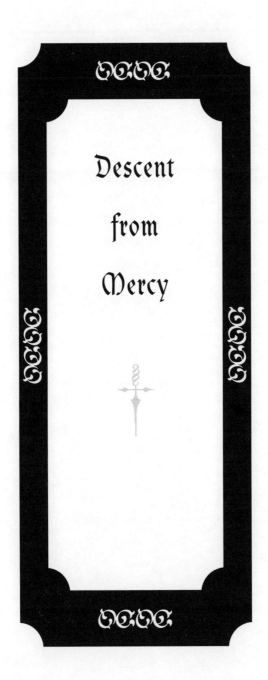

Descent

from

Mercy

Chapter 20

Mychael stood over the dead skraeling and wiped blood from his dreamstone dagger. Naas's blade had a killing edge, razor sharp. In less than a quarterlan it had five skraelings to its tally. No less than fifteen of the enemy soldiers were behind him in Dripshank Well, wanderers who had failed to keep up with the skraelpack and were quickly becoming lost. He'd let them go, killing only those who stood between him and his goal— Llynya.

Noise from the main troop drifted back to him from up ahead in the tunnel. The pack was close, no more than a turn or two away. He'd finished off the last of the stragglers at the end of their line. The tunnel would widen into a small cavern in another quarterlan before taking a steep drop into its final stretch, and 'twas there in the cavern that he would have his best chance for freeing Llynya—or to die in the trying.

He looked down at the skraeling beneath him.

He'd never killed with a knife before, yet he'd suffered no hesitation, no uncertainty, not even with the first soldier he'd come upon. He'd gone for the throat, swift and sure as he'd been taught by Trig, and killed them each with a single cut.

'Twas far different from a bow. He'd smelled the blood of each one, been close enough to know the instant when life had left—that strange slackening in the air about their bodies when breath was no longer drawn. Whatever horror he felt at killing them was far outdistanced by the fear that he would not kill enough of them, that his hand would falter in a death strike, that he would be wounded or killed and Llynya would be lost.

Stepping away from the fallen skraeling, he loosened the iron stars in his arm guard, readying them for rapid release. Every second would count in the coming battle.

When he was but halfway down the guard, a tremor of heat rippled to life beneath his skin—a flutter, no more—but it did not pass unnoticed. His hand stilled. He waited, breath held, and soon enough a second tremor crested in a gentle wave on the left side of his torso and flowed down the length of his body, following the path of his scars.

A bitter oath fell from his lips. His hand tightened into a fist. Time had run out. The dragonfire was coming upon him.

He swore again, damning his cursed blood. He had Madron's phial, aye, but he could not lie down and take his ease, wandering through a fey land of cooling dreams while Llynya was dragged beyond the Wall. In truth, when he most needed it, the price of the witch's brew had proven too steep.

With a quick hand, he finished releasing the securing loops on the iron stars. If the madness would come and take him, let it take the skraelings as well. The rage he'd done his best to temper with Trig on Mor Sarff would be given full rein. He would fight until the delirium claimed him. If he could do naught but free Llynya from her bonds and put a blade in her hand, the Light-elf might fashion her escape despite his fate. She was lightning quick.

Touching his fingers to the cut she'd left on his cheek, he wished her Godspeed, then drew his sword and took off at a run. The skraelings would soon know their doom was among them. If there was to be a river of blood, it would start in the tunnel 'tween Dripshank Well and the Wall.

*   *   *

Llynya smelled the slight freshening of the air that told her the tunnel was emptying out into a larger space, a cavern, or mayhaps the Magia Wall itself. Their trail thus far had wound through caverns she knew, but hanging upside down over a Dockalfar's shoulder she'd become disoriented in the twists and turns and offshoots of the tunnel leading out of Dripshank, and was no longer sure if they were in the main passage or not. Skraelings were all about her, shoving and jostling, stinking and clattering and reaching out to grab at her whenever they dared.

"Aetheling," they grunted, and their big, clawed fingers would come down on her tunic or leg to pinch and squeeze. Frey, the Dockalfar carrying her, tried to hold them at bay with snarls and slashes of his knife, but still they took their chances.

'Twas the Dockalfar's own fault. To keep the skraelings from sniffing and snuffling around her like she was the day's ration of meat, he'd told them she was enchanted, worth her weight in gemstones, that the flowers woven into her clothes were carved from dreamstone and tourmaline—and now every man jack of them was trying to get rich before they reached Rastaban by picking a star of meadowsweet or a rose.

Rastaban.

A shudder went through her. Ancient lair of the *uffern* trolls, the Eye of the Dragon might see her final end.

"Slott," the skraelings muttered and mumbled as they marched. "Slott. Slott. Slott. *Har!*"

The mere sound of the Troll King's name struck terror in her heart, not just for herself, but for all the *tylwyth teg*. She feared Rhuddlan had walked into a trap of his enemies' making, Sha-shakrieg and Dockalfar working together to lure the King of the Light-elves into the deep dark, using Nia as bait.

"*Shadana,*" she prayed, squeezing her eyes shut.

Unlike with Nia, she did not think Trig would dare divide his troops again and send someone after her. Warhorns had been sounding all over Riverwood by the time the skraelpack had reached the cliffside hole that led down toward Dripshank Well. Two Liosalfar had been killed as the skraelings had fought their way into the cavern entrance, and she realized that battle might yet rage across Merioneth. Few enough Quicken-tree remained in the carn without Trig trying to rescue her—and trussed like a rabbit for the pot, she was near helpless to rescue herself. The Dockalfar had taken no chances with her bindings, knowing well all the Light-elf tricks. Her only hope lay in the scarcity of their numbers. For all the skraelings, there were only three Dark-elves, only three of her captors wily enough to hold an Yr Is-ddwfn aetheling.

Trolls were another worry altogether. The enmity 'tween trolls and elves went back to the Douvan Age, an ancient, bitter feud. When the Dockalfar had allied themselves with Slott to turn the tide of battle in the Wars of Enchantment, they forever set the rest of the *tylwyth teg* against them. Trolls picked their teeth with elfin bones. Slott braided their skulls into his beard, with one dread plait made up solely of the royal line of Yr Is-ddwfn. When Ailfinn Mapp had turned the trolls to stone on Inishwrath, it had been a corps of Yr Is-ddwfn aethelings that had brought the wretched giants to heel for her on the rocky shore.

Trolls were a curse, a fearful, frightful curse, and knowing Slott again walked the earth was to know evil had been resurrected.

She had to escape before they reached Rastaban. She still had her pack and could easily find her way home. The gods save her, she would not have her head hanging from the Troll King's wiry locks.

Another skraeling reached for her flowers, and Frey cut him with his knife. "Back off, ye beast."

They were all beasts—stupid, beastly men to have given themselves over to the Dockalfar for a promise of plunder. What had they thought, she wondered, when the Dark-elf potions had begun to work their monstrous changes on them?

For certes they thought little enough now. They were cunning, aye, but only when it came to feeding the hungers that had been contorted inside them to an insatiable degree—greed and gluttony. The Dockalfar had stripped them of all other desires and ruled them with that cardinal pair. A skraeling ran on avarice and the keenness of his appetite and naught else.

Not so the Dockalfar. If she had a blade, Ratskin would be dead a hundred times over for all his touching of her. Netherworld dweller or nay, he knew flowers for what they were and the difference between such and gemstones. He touched her for his own pleasure, foolishly ignoring the murderous gleam in her eye. Unless Slott ate her whole, still bound and gagged, she would have at least one moment of freedom before she died. Since Ratskin's last lewd caress, she planned to use that moment to slit his gullet. She had the knife for the deed all picked out. 'Twas the pearl-handled dagger hanging over Frey's right hip. He and Ratskin both had a half-dozen blades sheathed in their belts, some hilted with wych-elm roots bound in silver, others with carnelian hilts, still others with runic oak. Ritual knives, though she dared not guess what rituals Dark-elves practiced.

The freshening breeze came to her again, winding its way through the reek of skraelings. The barest scent of the greenwood lingered on it, telling her they were still above the Wall and that other tunnels lay ahead. No forest smells came up from the deep dark. She closed her eyes and breathed in the faint wind, using it to ease the pains of being bound. Her hands and feet were numb, her jaw achingly sore from the dirty rag stuffed in her mouth.

A shouted order from up ahead announced the pack's arrival in a cavern. When a call came for ropes, she knew exactly which cavern they'd reached and lost another measure of hope. The cave was small and emptied out onto the Wall by way of a treacherously steep chimney of rock. Other tunnels led out of it, though she knew not to where. She and Shay had once made the chimney descent without ropes, a feat beyond the ability of any skraeling. Halfway down, she'd feared it was beyond her's and Shay's ability as well, but if continuing down had seemed overwhelmingly difficult, going back up had been impossible. They'd made it to the bottom of the abyss, but just barely. Even with ropes, Lacknose was bound to lose a few of his less agile soldiers. With her slung over the Dark-elf's shoulder, her chances were little better than the clumsiest skraeling's.

By the time she and Frey reached the cave's entrance, over half of the skraelings had descended the chimney—some too quickly and to no good end. The deaths had created confusion in the cavern. The Troll King's soldiers milled about the ropes, looking into the abyss and grumbling. Lacknose was already down. She could see the faint light of her dreamstone reflecting up the chimney and keenly felt its loss.

Ratskin had loosed a whip from his belt and was using it to herd the remainder of the skraelings over the edge. Each crack of the braided leather ended in a grunt or a squeal, and above the stench of the pack, Llynya could smell the scent of fear taking over the cavern. Frey, too, must have sensed the growing resistance, for he lifted his yellow dreamstone and shouted above the din, *"Grazch! Kle, drak, dhon, vange!"*

A few of the skraelings responded to the order to form up, until

Ratskin snapped his whip at them as well. With the abyss threatening on one side and Ratskin on the other, anarchy found a foothold in the middle.

Frey tried again to hold the line against chaos. *"Grazch!"* he shouted, spreading more dreamstone light over the cavern by climbing a boulder. Shafts of golden luminescence cut through the flickering torch-light and clouds of smoke, and a more motley troop Llynya had ne'er seen—rough, and smelly, and undisciplined.

From their new vantage point, she and Frey were among the first to hear the terrible cry that rang out from the tunnel behind them. 'Twas fearful and sudden, and cut unnaturally short. The Dark-elf turned toward the sound, and Llynya had to peek under his arm to see what was happening. She feared some dread cavern beast or a troll was coming upon them.

Of the skraelings still in the tunnel, half turned back with their weapons drawn. 'Twas a beast then, she surmised, thinking they would not draw on a troll. She tried to wiggle free and was squeezed all the harder by Frey. *Sticks!* She was going to die if she couldn't escape.

The other skraelings in the tunnel joined the melee forming on the cavern floor.

"Grazch!" Frey shouted to no avail, trying to organize the newcomers. Without Lacknose to rule it, the skraelpack was degenerating into an unruly mob.

Llynya struggled and kicked and tried to work the rag out of her mouth. If Frey dropped her, could she squirm her way into one of the other tunnels to hide? There would be some sharp rock somewhere for her to cut through her bonds.

At the clashing of swords and another skraeling voice cut off in midcry, she ceased her struggles.

Swords? Her ears pricked up. No cavern beast carried a sword. Mayhaps Trig had come for her after all.

The influx of new soldiers quickly overfilled the cavern with pushing and shoving skraelings and harsh words backed by sharp blades. Three more were sent over the edge without the benefit of a rope, and a groundswell of panic blossomed inside the cave.

Frey muttered a foul curse under his breath and called for Ratskin to come take his burden.

Llynya cursed too, though none could hear it, and she struggled anew when the transfer was made. The echoing clangs of steel striking steel grew louder behind her, her only hope. Then even that was taken from her. Ratskin hauled her over his shoulder and headed for another tunnel as Frey descended into the melee, shouting his orders for the ranks to form up. Ratskin gestured for two skraelings to follow him through the dark portal he'd chosen, and with a dread beyond terror, Llynya knew she would be denied the clean death of a hero.

After the chaos of the cavern, the tunnel seemed unnaturally quiet. She could plainly hear the skraelings' grunts and snuffles and Ratskin's labored breathing. They sped along the corridor, as if the Dark-elf knew he had not much time for his wicked deed.

The walls of the tunnel were not purely solid, but riven with a strange tracery of cracks, some large, some small. Piles of dirt and stones from the making of those cracks littered the floor of the passageway along with trails of tua droppings. An odd, musty smell filled the tunnel, but with a pungent edge she'd not noted in tua droppings before. The lizards themselves skittered here and there and all over. She'd not seen so many in one place, but she remembered from her and Shay's expedition that the little-used passages beyond Dripshank were their homeground. The onslaught of the skraelings must have chased them all into this one section.

At a fork in the trail, Ratskin called a halt and dropped her to the ground. She lay in the curve of stone where the tunnel wall met the floor, watching, but not fighting—not yet, though her heart was racing. Her legs were tied at her thighs, calves, and ankles, with the rope around her ankles also tethering her feet to her bound wrists. Her arms had been securely tied to her sides, leaving her little maneuvering room. Ratskin was going to have to cut more than one set of her bindings to get the satisfaction he sought. Skraeling guards or nay, each rope he cut would bring her closer to freedom.

He barked an order for the two skraelings to hold her. The soldiers grabbed her and held her back against the rock wall. Their bulky bodies blocked all but flickers of Ratskin's yellow dreamstone light. She heard the Dockalfar whispering under his breath, his excitement growing, and a cold knot formed in her belly. She'd see him dead. She swore it by the gods and the trees.

The sound of running feet came to her from back in the tunnel, but she had no hope that it was other than more skraelings. Their hue and cry was getting louder in the cavern, and cowards that they all were, she expected that some would attempt to desert rather than dare the chimney, especially since two of their kind had already come this way.

Ratskin was tearing at his clothes, muttering about the disgusting things he'd soon do to her. If the swords she'd heard in the other tunnel had come for her, she feared they would be too late.

She drew her feet in close as if that could save her from the Dark-elf's vile intent, and a tua ran over her toes, then another and another. A new light, rushing noise entered the passage, softly, like a wind from the west. Five more of the lizards streaked over her feet, their tiny steps all together making the breezy sound. She stayed perfectly still, even when a half-dozen skittered up her legs and perched on her knees, and three others did the same on her shoulder. Five more raced up her hip and darted across her lap.

She had naught against tua, and they were not wont to bite, but she'd ne'er been in a swarm of them. Three more skimmed up her right arm and ran down her left. Their closeness didn't worry her, but the sudden increase in numbers did. Something was terribly wrong to put them all on the run.

She looked to the far tunnel wall, peering between the two brutes holding her, and a different edge of panic seeped into her veins. Hundreds of the small beasts were pouring out of the cracks, falling down the walls and over each other in their haste to get away.

Away from something behind them in the rock.

Another dozen streaked over her, heading for the southside fork in the trail—none for the north.

"Beli . . . Beli . . . Beli," she murmured, her eyes widening as the next wave of tua gushed out of the walls. The signal to flee had been sent, a primitive pulse that every lizard sensed. Couldn't the skraelings see what was happening around them?

Ratskin's daggers clattered to the tunnel floor when he dropped his belt, and Llynya calculated from the sound where each one had fallen. The closest was next to her left hip.

But even if she had them all, it wouldn't be enough to save her from whatever was coming.

Without warning, one of the skraelings slumped against her and near crushed the breath from her lungs. The other skraeling lunged to his feet, but was taken by an arrow through the throat and fell back against the wall.

Ratskin swore and reached for her, but he had no sooner moved than his right hand was caught by an iron star and pinned to the wall next to her head. He screamed, and Llynya ducked, her heart pounding. On either side of her, the skraelings were groaning in their death throes. Above her, the iron star hummed from the throw that had impaled the Dark-elf.

Shadana, she thought. No Quicken-tree she knew could pierce rock with an iron star. She wiggled partway from underneath the miserable, dying skraelings, trying to see around Ratskin, and noted with an odd curling sensation in her stomach that the tua were gone, all of them.

Not so the daggers. She grabbed the closest and sliced through the rope binding her wrists to her ankles, then set about freeing her legs. That done, she started to push herself up, hand raised to slice Ratskin's middle with the pearl-handled blade, but she stopped in midstrike, alerted by a subtle change in the air.

She cast a wary glance toward the main passage, peering beyond the skraelings and Ratskin. With the stealth of a falcon in full swoop, another iron star whistled out of the darkness, then another, and another, all of them skimming by her to catch Ratskin and impale him against the wall. Each impact resounded with the Dark-elf's disbelieving scream and the solid thud of iron sinking into rock.

Llynya scrambled for the other daggers.

Ratskin's screams transformed into vicious curses. Agony contorted his face. He tried to free himself, but every jerk and tug did naught but increase his pain. His dreamstone dagger lay to the south, its light glinting off the rivulets of blood running down his body and throwing macabre yellow-tinged shadows up on the wall.

The guttural cry of "Aetheling! Find the aetheling!" echoed from the cavern, and Llynya knew Frey had discovered her disappearance. The clatter of half a horde of skraelings coming after her filled the tunnel.

Flee, was her only thought, but before she could push herself free of the two dead skraelings, she was caught. A hand reached down through the tumble of bodies and hauled her to her feet.

She knew. In an instant she knew, even before she smelled him or saw the fall of golden hair, 'twas Mychael pulling her to his side.

With a quick, upward stroke, he slit Ratskin's throat, silencing the Dark-elf's screams. His next strike cut the last of her bonds. Then he released her and sheathed his knife to nock an arrow into his bow.

"What's the best way out of here?" he asked, his breathing ragged, his attention on the small pouch he was ripping from his belt. He
skewered the pouch with the arrow and a burst of lavender and roses
suffused the air.

"To the south," she said, recognizing the simple she'd given him.

He nodded once, then drew his bow and sent the bag of flowers
flying into the north tunnel. Petals fluttered from the rent in the cloth,
laying a false trail for the rapidly approaching skraelings.

He grabbed her and made to run, but was too late. The pack was
nearly upon them. The south tunnel ran straight for a quarterlan; they
would be spotted before they could make the first bend in the trail. He
turned instead to a large crack on the northside wall and pushed her
toward it. The only thing worse Llynya could think of was to be recap-
tured by the skraelings.

Swearing silently to herself, she dashed to retrieve Ratskin's
dreamstone and her sword, then in she went, pushing deep to make
room for Mychael. The wisdom of the course was proved when a skraeling passed the opening at almost the same moment that Mychael climbed
in behind her. She shoved Ratskin's dagger inside her tunic, praying that
the wavering light of the skraeling's torch had hidden the crystal's fading
glow.

They would know soon enough.

For a crack, their hiding place was generous, but still no more
than a tear in the rock. She and Mychael were jammed together at the
farthest end they could reach, both of them breathing heavily, the smell
of blood and fear swirling around them.

Outside, the skraeling disappeared without so much as a glance in
their direction, assurance that he'd not seen the light. Relief flooded
through Llynya, sweet, weakening relief. Her knees buckled, and
Mychael caught her to him, his arm encircling her waist and pulling her
close. 'Twas not a good time for tears, but they came, hot and wet, sliding
down her cheeks as she clung to him—so like a maid, so unlike a
warrior.

Ratskin was dead.

Mychael had saved her.

She'd thought never to see him again, never to be with him again.
She'd avoided him after their tryst in the forest, not trusting herself to be
strong enough to walk away a second time. His kisses had touched her
too deeply. His desire had aroused her own too quickly, and the sense of

completion she'd found in his arms had been too profound. 'Twas the one thing she had no room for in her life, for she knew 'twas the one thing that could sway her from her course—the blossoming of desire into love.

Yet he was here with her now, and she would not let him go again.

More of the enemy piled up in the passage with Frey in their midst, shouting and swearing. It wasn't the loss of Ratskin he bewailed, but the loss of her. The aetheling. Slott's supper. She trembled anew each time the Dark-elf called her such, and each time, Mychael pulled her closer. Closer 'til she felt his every breath in the rise and fall of his chest. Closer 'til her senses were filled with him, the scent and wonder of him—and the heat.

Too much heat.

She looked up, wiping at her tears. He was still watching the tunnel, his face drawn in dark, beautiful lines, the flashes of passing torchlight casting him in harsh shadows that deepened the angles of his cheekbones and turned the stripe in his hair to molten copper.

With her other hand, she touched his left side, where he was scarred, and she knew immediately what ferocity had impaled Ratskin to solid stone—dragonfire. Mychael's body was alive with it, his muscles hardened in the flames of it. He flinched under even her gentle touch, but she did not remove her hand. Rather, she slipped it beneath his tunic and pressed harder, trying to absorb some of the heat into herself.

"Sticks," she muttered. 'Twas a hopeless tactic, a skill beyond her training, and he'd destroyed the simple she'd given him.

Outside in the forked passageway, Frey took the bait of the northern tunnel and ordered the pack to march. Torches moved across the face of the crack, filling the opening with alternate bands of light and darkness, and Llynya dared to hope. If whatever had terrified the tua did not attack them from behind before the skraelpack was gone, they might yet escape.

When the last torch passed, Mychael turned from watching the passage and locked his gaze onto her. 'Twas fierce and unnaturally bright. Instinct compelled her to retreat, despite the rock wall at her back, but his arm tightened around her.

He was wild, aright, wilder than even Rhuddlan knew. The truth of it burned like a living flame in his eyes.

With a deliberateness she didn't at first understand, he brought his hand to her brow and drew one finger down the middle of her face to the tip of her nose. Still holding her gaze, he traced the curve of one eyebrow, arcing the line across her temple and down her cheek to the center of her chin—and with that sinuous caress, his meaning became clear. Warmth suffused her. Her pulse raced, though not with fear. Lastly, he smoothed his thumb across her lips, gently, from one side of her mouth to the other.

'Twas the silent language of a Liosalfar warrior, and his words were simple—*you . . . are . . . mine.*

"Aye," she whispered, knowing the truth of it down to the core of her being. She was his.

He touched her mouth once more, then bent his head to kiss her, to take the prize he'd won. She welcomed him with parted lips, rising against him and melting into his embrace. The Druid boy was her love, and she would have him.

He smelled of blood and the fight, and of time and the forest, and she accepted it all, let all that was Mychael flow through her senses. He smelled of desire, the path of mystery into enchantment. She would take him there again, into the enchantment they had made, and show him wonders no mortal man had yet imagined.

Aye, when his mouth moved over hers, she longed for the chance to make him hers forever. She would bind him with spells, and potions, and soft words of love, and in the binding, herself be bound to his dragon's heart.

Chapter 21

Mychael and Llynya stopped at the end of the southern tunnel, both of them breathing hard from their long run. Thousands of tua had stopped with them and clung to the walls all around, their delicate, pale throats pumping, their smoothly eyeless heads bobbing. Like the cavern far behind them, the tunnel emptied out onto the Magia Wall via a sheer drop. Four times on their run, she and Mychael had fought their way through a dense infestation of the cave lizards, only to have the little buggers overtake them in a panicked wave and alight a quarterlan ahead of them. Now there was no place left to run.

They'd lost Frey and his skraelpack, and for that Llynya was grateful, but they were far from safe. She had only to look to the tua to know that. Tension skittered like chain lightning between the small reptiles, and Lacknose was somewhere on the Wall with skraelings of his own.

"What drives them?" Mychael begged to know. He fell back against the wall with a pained gasp, one hand wrapped around his middle. Tua scattered in all directions.

Sweat beaded his brow. Exhaustion lined his face, and Llynya wished they dared stop long enough for him to rest.

They did not. The lizards were amassing again even as she watched, making ready for another dash.

"Sticks," she swore under her breath, pacing the edge of the wide crack at their feet. The tua might survive a willy-nilly drop down its throat, but she and Mychael would not.

To him, she said, "I don't know. The *pryf* avoid Dripshank Well because of the open water, so they don't often get into the tunnels north of the nest. And for certes the old worm couldn't be chasing tua down the narrow track we took out of Dripshank."

"I don't smell any worms, *pryf* or otherwise," Mychael said. "I smell tua, and the smell is stronger behind us than it is in here where we're surrounded by them."

'Twas an odd truth, what he said. The pungent musty scent was more potent where they'd been than where they were, where she couldn't move a step without a hundred tua skittering away. She cast a wary glance back into the tunnel. Something was back there. The tua knew what, and it frightened them.

Of a sudden, the lizards went from frightened to terrorized and launched themselves down the crack in droves, wave after wave, scrambling over one another in their desire to flee. Startled, Llynya grabbed for Mychael, and they held themselves against the rushing tide of white-skinned beasts. In seconds 'twas over, and the two of them were alone in the passage above the hole.

"Shit," Mychael swore, staring down the dark passage from whence they'd come.

"Shadana."

They looked at each other, and Mychael shrugged off his pack.

"You first," he said, snapping out the length of rope hooked to the outside of his pack. With a few quick moves, he secured the rope to a projection of rock, using a modified hitch.

"No, you go first," she insisted. "You're hurt."

He met her gaze with a grim smile curving his mouth. "I'm not hurt. I'm on fire, *cariad.*"

The endearment, though roughly spoken, was not missed even

when tied to his dire revelation. She reached out a hand in comfort, and his smile faded. In a step, he had her pulled into his arms, his mouth coming down on hers. What there was between them could not be sated with a kiss, yet Llynya felt a deep and healing relief to touch him so, to share the heat of his mouth as she would share all of him.

Lost in his embrace, she was nearly a second too late in escaping the danger that snaked out of the tunnel.

Warned by the tail end of a raspy hiss, she yelped and leaped back, pushing Mychael toward the wall with the same action.

He swore and ducked as the long carnelian sliver of a tongue lashed out again from the black depths of the tunnel, its forked tip searching for warmth and a taste of prey. Like a whip, it was, the crack of it softened by sibilant hissing. A fear-frozen tua was its first victim, snapped off the wall with a lightning-quick flick, snared by the sticky tip that recoiled into the tunnel with its flailing supper in tow.

Mychael grabbed her in the reprieve and shoved her into the hole. She slid down the chimney of rock on the rope, barely touching the walls, praying Lacknose wasn't at the bottom waiting for them. Mychael was coming down behind her, and coming down behind Mychael was the red tongue, searching to and fro with each uncoiling. Of the beast who owned the dread thing, they saw naught, until they reached the Wall.

Llynya landed and looked first to the west. Her own dreamstone blade flickered back at her in the darkness, a small dot of blue light among the torches making their way along the Wall. Her mouth tightened. She wanted her blade back, but it wasn't to be hers on this day. There were too many of them for her and Mychael to fight—and there was the beast above them.

Unlike where she and Shay had descended from the other cavern, the Wall below the southern tunnel was a huge, open passage with a ceiling of cathedral height. On its southern edge, the wide walkway dropped off into a gaping, rough-edged canyon whose sides were littered with boulders fallen from the ceiling. Vitreous rose quartz ran through the walls and across the trail between thick bands of granite, picking up the yellow dreamstone and adding a faint glow to the passage. When Mychael reached the bottom of the shaft, his blue light joined hers, and the cavern area took on a greenish cast.

His first word upon landing was an oath. His second was a command.

"Fireline!"

Aye, she thought. Let Lacknose deal with the tua's terror.

They ran a short distance and began a line out of reach of the tongue, until the beast itself should emerge from the chimney. The torches coming down the Wall from the west were advancing more quickly, drawn, she guessed, by Ratskin's blade. The hissing grew in strength as the creature climbing down the shaft labored closer and closer. Mychael had the only fireline makings, Llynya having been banned from the caves. She took his gourd of *hadyn draig* and shook the seed out onto the floor. 'Twas no sense trying to incise a groove in quartz and granite, so the dragon seed fell where it would with Mychael doing his best to cover it with *roc tan*.

When time was to be had, a fireline was layered to add depth and longevity to the flames, steps four and five of Trig's teachings. Step six was the addition of color to name the maker of the line. Llynya started the step four layer against Mychael's protest.

"We stop it here, or run our hearts out mayhaps all the way to Tryfan," she told him, keeping an eye on the opening of the shaft and on Lacknose's progress. "I don't know what lies ahead. Shay and I never explored this part of the Wa—"

A snout appeared out of the chimney, a long, scaly snout. Mychael went utterly still at the sight.

"Nay," she murmured, fighting the urge to drop the gourd and run. " 'Tis no dragon with that tongue. Quickly now."

They finished as the head came into view, white-throated and pale on the underside with row after row of knobby golden brown scales along the top. 'Twas a tua of monstrous proportions. The front legs followed, and the she-beast used them to claw and scrabble her overripe body out of the shaft.

Aye, 'twas female, from the glint of ivory off her razor-sharp teeth to the black slash marks where her eyes should have been; from the white star-shaped spikes jutting in a line down her spine to the soft scales of her pregnant belly.

The tua's golden-sheened tail slid out of the shaft with a heavy slap on the floor, and for a moment the blind lizard—which stood as tall as a man and nearly twice as long—did naught but sniff the air with her tongue. Then she attacked.

Llynya felt herself being hauled back as Mychael dropped a burning sulfur twig on the line. Flames shot up, making a wall of fire eight feet high. Its heat was scorching even at a distance. They turned and ran, but got no farther than a quarterlan before they caught up with the herd of tua. The tiny reptiles were ankle-deep on the trail, all clustered together, and to a lizard they were facing due west, noses lifted toward the raging fire.

She turned, afraid the monster was upon them. It wasn't, but what she did see was nearly as frightful.

"Mychael," she gasped, pointing for him to look.

He glanced over his shoulder, then turned full on his heel, his mouth agape.

The fireline had stopped the giant tua, but stopped her with pleasure, not pain. The golden brown beast had wrapped herself in the flames. They licked along her scales and claws and wreathed her with lambent fire. The star spikes down her back glowed red.

"Salamander," Mychael whispered, crossing himself with the Christian warding.

"Fire lizard," Llynya breathed, and made her own sign of protection.

The two of them watched, mesmerized, as the great tua bathed herself in the *roc tan*'s incandescence, in the combustion of the *hadyn draig*. She neither burned nor smoked, only luxuriated in the inferno. The light sparked off her scales, making her glitter. The darkness all around made her a living flame in the midst of the heat.

Llynya looked down at the lizards at their feet. They, too, were mesmerized. A cry came from the salamander, a shrill screech that echoed up and down the Wall and made Llynya's blood run cold. The tiny tua started forward at the beckoning, taking a few steps before stopping. Another screeching cry had them skittering forward again for several more steps.

"How long do you think we have?" Mychael asked.

"Longer than these wee beasts," she said, an opinion that was verified with the salamander's next cry. The little ones could not resist its command except in delay. They moved forward again, a great, pale wave of trembling dainties.

"The fire will hold for six hours, mayhaps longer."

"It won't matter," Llynya said. "She won't move for days after gorging herself."

"She?"

"Aye. She's their mother, and she's going to eat them every one."
A shudder ran through her.

Mychael slid his arm across her shoulders, gathering her close.
"Aye, well, it's a sight you'll not have to see. We must leave. The group
on the Wall has seen us for certes, though I doubt they'll trouble us
again."

He was right. They had to leave. The way back was denied them,
so 'twas forward they must go—into the unknown.

The fiery beast would be Lacknose's bane.

Naas finished setting her trap in one of the tunnels of Balor's old boar
pit. 'Twas the one place in Merioneth Rhuddlan had not yet reclaimed.
The Druid boy had reclaimed a bit of a hidey-hole for his book, and safe
enough it was there. Bones and blood, death and fear, murder and
mayhem—'twas all the same to her, but the rest of the Quicken-tree
could get a bit squeamish about such. Trees were their touchstone, the
guardians of the earth and all green growing things. They mightily loved
their leaves and cones and flowers.

"Garland weavers," she snorted. "Bramblers."

Oh, they were not averse to a good fight, like the one racing down
upon them, but the brutality, the senseless violence of the boar pit, was
beyond their capacity to absorb—or forgive.

Not so for the will-o'-the-wisp. Like Naas, that one did not make
forgiving his business. He'd been living carefree in the pit since May, but
his time had run out as it was running out for all the *tylwyth teg*. She was
going to catch him, she was, and set him to a task.

"A bit of the cloth," she murmured, baiting her trap with a
Quicken-tree cloak. A tunic and boots would follow, after she caught
him. No need to overdo. Next to the cloak, she laid a pile of seedcakes, a
large pile. Goodness only knew what the boy had been eating all these
years—all these many, many years.

Aye, she knew him for who he was, had known since he'd first
been sighted by the children. He was the Wydden child lost in the last
great traverse into Yr Is-ddwfn, lost the same year Llynya and Ailfinn
had come out of the weir into Merioneth. The trail was damned tricky,
as any who had trod it could tell, and he had slipped, much to his
mother's lament. Lost forever to time, they'd all thought—incorrectly.

Well, she would catch him soon enough. Been watching for him, she had. Seen him a couple of times. He had hurt himself somewhere in the passing of years, probably in his fall. One of his shoulders was higher than the other, a twist of his spine.

'Twould pain him, but she would find something in her bags and boxes to ease his hurt.

She finished the trap with a length of riband and a twig, the hunter's contraption being her last resort. Skraelings and Dockalfar in Riverwood, and Llynya taken. 'Twas time to act. She'd lain in wait for the will-o'-the-wisp three times in the pit, luring him with sweetmeats and songs, but he was too quick, and she too old to catch him in a foot race.

Satisfied with the look of the thing, she left the pit and made her way up into the bailey. Plenty of trouble up there for anyone who cared to get into the middle of it.

Madron was one who did, and—Naas admitted—she was another, especially the trouble Trig had brought out of Riverwood, the man named Corvus Gei.

Madron eyed the man chained to the curtain wall. She was just out of his reach, sitting on a grassy knoll in the lower bailey where Trig had chosen to hold him.

Corvus Gei was the name he'd given Llynya. Nennius was the name Madron had found in one of his books, along with an inscription from Balor's dead leech, Helebore. Nennius was a name familiar to her, though the man she knew by such was long dead. He'd written a book, the dead man had, a history book. This Nennius had stolen a book, her father's book, from the monastery on Ynys Enlli, Helebore's island.

She should have thought to search the Isle of Saints. Nemeton had ever been wont to secrete books in Christian houses, letting the new God protect the old. The chances that the Culdees would have granted her access to their island, though, were naught. To the monks, women were as the Adversary.

No matter. The book had found her.

She lowered her gaze and smoothed her hand across the gold runes and aged blue leather of the *Prydion Cal Le,* the Blue Book of the Magi, one of the Seven Books of Lore. Her father had shown it to her once, after they had been reunited in Merioneth, after her long stay at

Usk Abbey, but he'd been taken from her before he'd had a chance to teach her its contents. Precious, precious book. With the finding of it, she now had two of the seven books at hand . . . *and the wheel turns.*

Of the other books, only the whereabouts of two more were known. The *Sjarn Va Le,* the Violet Book of Stars, was sealed in stone with the trolls on Inishwrath. Or it had been. Tages had returned from his journey there with a tale of destruction. The great headland of the island was gone, leaving a ragged scar down the cliff face.

Trig had grown unutterably grim at the tidings, and when Tages had finished telling of all he'd seen, the captain had said only one word: "Slott."

A good many Quicken-tree had blanched at that, and the fears for Llynya had risen. That she'd been taken by skraelings was a fate worthy of despair. That some of the Dockalfar had survived, and that Slott walked the land, cast them all in the same fate. There was not a Quicken-tree alive who did not have an ancestor woven into the Troll King's braids.

The *Gratte Bron Le,* the Orange Book of Stone, was in Deseillign. Rhuddlan himself had left it there in the Desert Queen's hands.

The other three books were lost. The *Elhion Bhaas Le,* the Indigo Book of Elfin Lore, had disappeared at the end of the Wars of Enchantment. 'Twas the book Ailfinn sought in all her travels, though knowing now that some Dockalfar lived gave Madron a good idea of where the mage's search had led, and mayhaps why she had not answered Rhuddlan's summons. Desperate tidings, indeed.

Lanbarrdein had been the great hold of the Dockalfar. When Rhuddlan had taken it in the Wars, Tuan had moved his court to Rastaban, the underground demesne of his ally, Slott. 'Twas in Rastaban that all the Dockalfar had supposedly died. That Dockalfar and skraelings were making strikes on Riverwood meant Rastaban had been reopened. The book would be there with whoever had twisted an army of skraelings out of the dregs of men, and mayhaps Ailfinn as well.

The *Treo Veill Le,* the Green Book of Trees, had been lost through treachery, taken by she-whose-name-could-not-be-spoken, the greatest of all the Prydion Magi, and thrown into the weir in the Third Age. 'Twas she who had conjured the dragons in her cauldron, she who had forged the Magia Blade. Then the treachery—unforgiven through all the passage of time. The *Chandra Yeull Le,* the Yellow Book of Chandra, the book of priestesses, had also been lost through treachery, stolen by a thief in the Age of the Douvan Kingdoms, some said by a Douvan king.

But Madron had the two books her father had known. With each pass of her hand, she felt his presence.

Nemeton, the blue tome whispered. Nemeton, bearer of the secrets of time and sanctuary. The map inside was not what Rhiannon's son would have hoped, but there was hope for him in the magi's writings— and hope for her.

And mayhaps a little hope for the man who called himself Corvus, who despite his robes and tonsure was no monk. He was a traveler, a man out of time, though no traveler the Druids had sent, which made him a mystery and a danger. Trig had told her of Llynya's discoveries before the skraelings had attacked, but Madron would have known regardless. Who besides a traveler would have searched for her path? Who besides a traveler, indeed, would have scraped up the remnants of her conjuring fire and bothered to wrap a few crystals of universal salts into a package?

Chrystaalt, he'd called it, and asked if she knew where more could be found, as if she were a kitchen maid. Thus had he revealed his desire to her.

"I can speed you on your journey," she said, looking up. "Or I can hold you here until your natural death."

His attention had not wavered from her since she'd sat down, and she found him still watching her. His interest, as in their previous encounters, was not purely baleful, but being long accustomed to men's varied interests, Madron held his gaze unperturbed.

"It would be safer for you if you sent me on my way," he said, his words as dispassionate as her gaze, belying the keenness of his own. She did not make a move that he did not mark with his eyes.

"A threat?" she asked with a lift of her eyebrows. "You are in chains. Would it not be better to bargain?"

A surprising smile broke across his face, accompanied by a short laugh. "You do yourself a disservice, lady, if you would bargain with me."

"In what way?" she asked. He was a handsome man, his features cleanly formed with no imperfections, his teeth unusually white and straight, his eyes clear. The hair beginning to grow on his head clearly showed the weir stripe, a flash of white amidst the dark.

His smile hardened into a baring of those straight white teeth, and he leaned forward as far as his chains allowed. "I am a man with no honor. None. Whatever bargain we make will only last as long as it has advantage to me."

Madron had no need to consider his words. She already knew them to be true. Llynya had smelled the violence of his years, and she herself knew him to be an impostor and a thief. Yet she would bargain for what knowledge she could.

"Answer my questions, and I'll have no more need of you or our bargain, Corvus. Or do they call you Raven where you are from?"

"Some do. Some call me lord."

He could be a lord, she silently granted. He had the arrogance for it, and a disturbing sense of power about him. "And where is that?"

He relaxed back against the wall, then looked around. "About as far from here as you can get."

"When?" she asked, the more pertinent question.

His answer to that was a question of his own. "What possible difference can that make to you, my dear medieval gaoler?"

She rose to leave, and he let out another short laugh before acquiescing with an answer. "A time far from this one, lady."

"The future or the past?"

"Am I so rustic?"

"The future," she conceded, settling herself back down. "How many years?"

"I don't know. No," he said quickly when she started to rise again. "It's true that I don't know. This is the year 1198 anno Domini, and I come from 627 T.R., the six hundredth and twenty-seventh year after the Trelawny Rebellion. What the difference is between those two times, I truly don't know, except that it must be great. I have visited planets in less time than it would take you to reach the continent."

"You have traveled to the wandering stars?" Despite herself, she was startled.

"And farther."

For an instant, Madron felt a measure of fear. He was from much longer away than she had imagined. With effort, she refrained from looking up to the sky, where the evening star would rise in a few hours. Had he been there? she wondered.

"Why did you come?" she asked instead. "What is your purpose?" Danger always had a purpose, and he was undeniably dangerous.

"The choice to come here was not mine," he told her with a wry intonation, "and my only purpose is to return."

"Someone sent you here, against your will?" The possibility had not occurred to her. Yet had not Morgan ab Kynan entered the weir against his will? Or had he had any will left by the time the lightning had snaked out to snare him? By all accounts his wounds had been mortal.

"Time makes a very effective prison, lady, a chance for eternal penance."

"You are a felon." 'Twas a statement, not a question.

"Of the highest order," he freely admitted. "In my time, I'm a wanted man in two solar systems, and a demigod in half a dozen more."

She gave him a highly skeptical look, and he laughed again, dismissing her skepticism with a chain-rattling wave of his hand. "Think what you will."

"I am aware of the solar system. This one at least." She made her own broad gesture. "My father was a well-traveled man, as you must have noted from his book. 'Tis your claim of divinity I find doubtful."

His interest, never mild, peaked with the lift of his finely arched brows. "You are Nemeton's daughter?"

"Aye."

"The chrystaalt, then, 'twas you." He leaned forward again, his expression fiercely intent. "You have more?"

"Aye, but before you have so much as a taste, I will have your knowledge of the weir."

"So you know it is to be eaten and not just burned?"

She nodded. "What I do not know is how much is eaten and how long before the journey the traveler should eat it, and whether there are other necessary preparations."

His expression hardened, and he looked away, but not before she saw a flicker of pain cross his face.

" 'Tis not an idle question," she prompted.

"And it is not a journey I would advise," he said roughly, turning back to her. "I can assure you, lady, there is nothing in the future for you. It is a dark and dreary place."

"Yet you want to return."

"It is my time. And I want what is mine."

"Are you so sure you can return from whence you left?"

"Yes."

At her inquiring look, he deigned to elaborate.

"However much the wormhole may deviate on its course, the connection it makes in time is the same. If I return to my time, sixteen years will have passed from when I left. That I know. Whether I will be dead, alive, or mad when I get there cannot be known, so take heed."

"I can assure you that I have no intention of throwing myself into the weir. 'Tis knowledge only I would have." With her father's untimely death, she'd been poorly prepared should a traveler come and need her help. She did know the value of the salts, if not their method of use, but there was far more to traveling through the weir. There were calculations to be made that increased a traveler's chance of coming out of the wormhole, of landing in a solid place. There were astrological considerations that could determine the most auspicious time for the journey. There were even ways of manipulating the wormhole. All that knowledge and more was written in the stone of the mother rock somewhere in the farthest reaches of the deep dark, but Madron could not foresee a time when she would be so desperate that she would undertake such a perilous and possibly fruitless journey. Far better, to her way of thinking, to glean what she could from the books and the unexpected traveler. Convicted felon or nay, he had been through the wormhole.

"Most of what you want to know is in the books," he told her. "Everything except the truth about the journey itself, and that, lady, is a journey through hell, complete with fire and brimstone."

"The universal salts are supposed to ameliorate the physical crisis of passage. Did they not give you any?"

"The chrystaalt? They buried me in it," he said with a harsh laugh. "Be careful how much of the stuff you keep in one place. I think the worms can smell it at half a parsec, like a shark smells bait. It brings them screaming across space to devour the cache—and any incidental attached to the pile."

"And that's what you were, an incidental?"

"No," he said, his eyes darkening with the memory. "I was the raison d'être for gathering the salts, the sum supply of two worlds to ensure that I was taken, swallowed—"

"By the wormstorm, eh?" 'Twas Naas, coming up the knoll. "Took the long ride down the gullet, did ye?"

"Naas," Madron warned, scrambling to her feet when the old woman passed her by and kept on toward Corvus Gei.

"Pish." Naas dismissed her with a flick of her wrist and walked right up to the man. The old woman was not so far above him even with him sitting and her standing. "Ye'll not hurt me, now, will ye, boy?"

Madron was not so sure. Naas was no more than a jumbled bundle of rags and wispy hair. In what was surely the foolhardiest of actions, she took hold of Corvus's chin, her bony fingers biting into his beard-stubbled skin.

"Did ye know what it was that got ye? Did ye know about the worms, boy? Did the priestesses breach that trust as well?"

To Madron's surprise, Corvus made no move against the old woman, other than to lift his head to more squarely meet her gaze.

"I knew nothing of worms and time, until I reached here. Your secrets are as well hidden in the future, grandmother, as they are in this time, the domain solely of religious fanatics."

"Fanatics." Naas chuckled. "Yer a smart one then, smart enough to have survived, smart enough to find the way home. They won't expect that now, will they?"

Corvus smiled truly then, and a more predatory expression Madron had never seen. "They staked me out to die on that mound of chrystaalt, to die or to be eaten by the worm and tossed out of time, and for that *they* will die." The pleasure he took in the thought was beyond doubt. It suffused his face like a light from within. Murder, at least, was part of his business.

Naas chuckled again and released his chin. "Ye'll find they die no more easily than I, but they made a mistake to send their dregs to me. Ye must have been the last one through before Rhuddlan sealed the weir, and it's back to them I'm sending ye. The quicker the better. Come, Madron. The time of Calan Gaef is nigh enough for our purpose. Get yer salts. I'll bring the boy."

Madron could do naught but stand and stare, dumbstruck, as the old woman checked his chains.

"We'll need the smithy for these," she muttered, giving them a good rattle.

"Naas. No," Madron finally managed to protest. "He is Trig's prisoner, not ours. You can't have his irons struck off."

The old woman shook her head. "Nay. Trig's got naught to do with travelers. That's yer bailiwick, sweetling, and mine. Meet me in the boar pit, quickety-split, and we'll take a route none will follow."

When she still didn't move, Naas leveled her white-eyed gaze on

Madron and looked at her hard, until Madron felt a tremor of fear similar to the one induced by Corvus earlier.

"Obey, Madron," the old woman commanded. " 'Tis not a request I make."

Madron had always considered herself apart from the Quickentree, not subject to them, any of them. She suddenly realized how wrong she'd been. She thwarted Rhuddlan's kingship whenever the need arose. Such was not an option with Naas, not in this instance, and Madron wondered if it ever had been. With a bow of her head, she left to gather what they would need for a journey to the gates of time.

Naas returned her attention to the man she would drop through the weir gate. "Ye must have been a frightful bad one for the White Ladies to send ye here. I could kill ye for them, but like them I try to keep my conscience clear before the gods. And I guess ye know as well as me that putting ye twice through the wormhole will probably do it for us."

His dark eyes never wavered. "Yes, I know."

"*Auch.*" Naas suddenly turned her head. "Did ye hear that?"

"No."

Naas grinned. She'd heard it, loud and clear, the snap of a twig. The will-o'-the-wisp was hers.

Chapter 22

Worse and worse, Llynya thought, looking down from her hiding place, a scooped-out hollow of rock on a ledge overlooking the Wall. Skraelings were marching up and down the trail below. She and Mychael had veered off the main passage into a labyrinth of narrow corridors to escape the last skraelpack they'd come upon, but it seemed there was to be no end to the skraelings. The Wall had been the main road into Rastaban before the Wars, when Rastaban had been a resting place between Riverwood and Tryfan. Whoever now ruled in the Eye of the Dragon had taken the Wall for his own.

There were no Dockalfar below, though, and mayhaps there was hope in that.

No fire lizard either, and there was definite hope in that.

She scooted back and signaled Mychael forward to take her place on the ledge, to take the watch. 'Twas the first chance they'd had to rest, and she'd used the time to make them an infusion of lavender. The two of them had huddled over the dreamstone blades to heat a cup of water, then shared the warm tea and a seedcake in the reflected glow of the skraelings' torchlight. She'd made sure he drank most of the tea, but even her few sips had done much to restore her. From her baldric pouches, she had shared acorns from the mother oak in Deri to give him strength, and had burned feathers for protection.

When needed, they were only using Ratskin's blade in the corridors, keeping Ara sheathed. The yellow dreamstone was hard to distinguish from the yellow light given off by the torches, and any skraeling who did happen to see it would think it belonged to one of their Dockalfar masters. For certes the skraeling who could think beyond that simple reasoning had yet to be conjured.

Mychael came down off the ledge and knelt beside her. Light from Ratskin's blade glinted off the silver rings she'd woven into his *fif* braid, rings of protection plaited into his hair to keep him safe. She didn't doubt their power, only whether or not there was enough in the finely incised runes to do the job at hand. *Ammon, Bes, Ceiul* . . . one rune for each ring, the runes of refuge. She'd chosen them with care after talking with Naas.

She handed him one of the honey-sticks she'd been looking for in her pack, and he sucked on the end.

"We can't stay here," he said, handing the sweet back. "If we can't find a way to the surface soon, we have to take our chances on the Wall."

"Aye," she said noncommittedly, praying they would find a way up into Riverwood. The Wall was sure death, with so many skraelings about. There was one other way for them to go, but 'twas so terrible, it hardly bore thinking about—unless the only alternative was the Wall. She finished off the honey and packed the empty horsetail stem into one of her pouches, not wanting to leave more of a trail than was absolutely unavoidable.

A commotion down on the Wall had them both hastening back onto the ledge. Shoulder to shoulder, they watched a raucous changing of the guard a hundred feet below, the only ritual of which seemed to be the passing back and forth of leather jacks and ale gourds.

"They haven't seen us," Mychael said, his voice a low whisper not meant to carry beyond the ledge.

"Nay, I don't think so either." She, too, whispered.

"If they get drunk enough, we might be able to get by them without raising any alarm."

"Aye."

They continued watching in silence. A cookfire was spitting and crackling with the fat dripping off a couple dozen roasting rodents. There was much jostling around the fire, the trick being to snag a rat's tail when it was finally crisp enough to snap off, but before it fell into the fire. Legs were the next delicacy, and half a dozen smoking drumsticks were making the rounds at any given moment. Every charred carcass taken off its spit was replaced with another squealing animal lifted out of the rat cage.

Skraelings were murderous and brutish, and given half a chance, Llynya knew her fate would have been no different from the rats'. An uncontrollable shiver coursed down her spine.

"Are you cold?"

"Nay," she said quietly, tightening her hands into fists to keep them from trembling. How many skraelings could she take in an open fight without any Dockalfar to hem her in?

Not enough, was the answer. Not nearly enough.

She counted close to a hundred below, two packs. Half would leave. There was little cover on the trail, and mayhaps she and Mychael could take out a goodly number of the remaining pack with his bow. They had the advantage of the higher ground.

But what of the next skraelpack? And the next? They could not fight all the way to the Rastaban trailhead, the only certain path out of the caverns that she remembered from her studies with Wei, and so help her, she would not be captured again. If they did fight, 'twould be to the death. She would die by the blade, not over the flames or between Slott's jaws.

"Llynya?" She turned to face Mychael, and he reached out to caress her cheek. "You're crying."

'Twas true. She tried to brush the evidence away, but he stayed her hand by clasping it with his own. His grip was warm, too warm, but strong, backed by an arm banded in the iron stars that had saved her from Ratskin—proof enough of his next words.

"I will fight to my last breath to keep you safe." His vow was intent, but no more so than his gaze when she met his eyes. Dragonfire flickered in their depths, amber rings of lambent flame ignited by the blood of his line.

He was the Dragon. The scar running up the side of his neck burned with the stirring of Ddrei Goch's fiery breath. But his body, for all its sinewy strength and layers of hard muscle over even harder bone, was no dragon's body, and she feared it could not survive the fierceness of the beast.

"If they come, you quickety-split." His hand tightened on hers, adding force to his words. "They'll not catch you, not skraelings. Make their heads spin with how fast you are."

"Nay, I'll not leave you."

"You did at Bala Bredd." 'Twas no accusation, but a statement to aid his cause. Foolish boy, she would be twice damned if he died in her place.

"Aye, and for the same reason I left you that morn, I'll not leave you now."

His brow furrowed in a silent question.

"Love," she answered him, sliding her hand around his neck and drawing him near. "For love I left you, and for love I'll stay."

Confused, Mychael nonetheless welcomed her kiss. Weary, he let her bear him down into the stone hollow, let the soft weight of her be a blessed relief. *Love.* She spoke of love and he was filled with it. His arms slipped around her, his hands tracing the curves of her body. He'd never known such delicacy, nor such strength as she had, so female, all softness and giving but for the sharp edge of her need. Her hands were in his hair, holding him for all the kisses she would bestow. She slung her leg over his hips, pressing into him, and he was instantly aroused.

Taking his pleasure, he opened his mouth over hers and drew her tongue inside, a deep pull and release, reminding him of their night at Bala Bredd. To his amazement, she gave him the memory back double, finding him beneath his tunic and braies, her hand closing around his phallus to stroke him in a rhythm that matched his slow, sucking kiss.

Shadana . . . He arched against the soft curve of her palm and filled her hand.

"Mate with me," she murmured, and the words swept through him like tinder fire, fast and hot, and as seductive as her touch.

'Twas insanity itself, what she wanted, but the stroking of her hand was irresistible. Every caress teased him to distraction and pleased him beyond reason. Soon, he promised himself, soon he would set her aside. Until then, he only prayed that nothing came upon them from out of the dark.

As if she'd read his mind, she glided her hand over and around him once more, stopping at the head of his shaft.

"Mate with me," she said again, taking him farther over the edge by smoothing her finger across the tip of his glans.

Witch. She'd not done that at Bala Bredd.

She retraced her path, and reason fled. He would have her as she had him. He would know her again as he'd known her on the shores of the mist-bound lake.

He loosened her braies and slid his hand inside, his fingers finding the sweet, soft flower of her desire. She'd shown him how to pleasure her, whispered to him of what she would have him do, how to move and where to touch. The thrill of it was still wondrously new, that she was his to touch, to slide his fingers into; that with a gentle rubbing he could fill his world with the scent of her arousal and have her as needy as he.

She gasped his name, and skraelings were forgotten along with danger and any semblance of common sense. Only the uncommon senses remained acute: the hot, silky wetness that welcomed his touch, the intensifying redolence of flowers that told him of her readiness, the primal need to join his body to hers.

He removed her braies and, guided by her hand, pushed into her. A groan escaped him, released in a flood of exquisite sensation. Truly, only God could have created an act of such intense gratification that to move inside a woman's body was to take a man into divine madness.

He thrust upward, and a verdant scent flowed over him, a scent beyond the smell of even the deepest forests. Dark and rich and green, it wound around him in intoxicating tendrils of pleasure, like an extension of her touch. A warning sounded somewhere in the back of his mind, but went unheeded, for the urge to continue to move with her was far more powerful than the caution to resist. 'Twas a need, like breath.

He pushed up again, holding her to him with his hands on her hips, arching against her, and for an achingly sweet moment he wondered if in truth some new madness had found him in the act of love. The verdant scent spilled into his mouth in a rush of greenness, washing through him. It pumped into his veins, cooling his blood, but not the heat of wanting her. He tried to resist, but she wouldn't accept resistance.

"Shh, shh," she crooned, lowering her mouth to the side of his head. She blew softly into his right ear and nipped his lobe, then did the same to his left ear, marking him each time with her breath and a quick flick of her tongue. She licked him from the middle of his chin to his mouth and then lingered to kiss him deep. He thrust upward with his hips, rooting himself to her as her tongue explored his mouth and sucked on his. The taste of lavender suffused his senses.

Christe. 'Twas not madness, but some bewitchment she spun to consume him.

"Come, Mychael. Come with me," she whispered.

He gave in with a groan of pure delight. She was binding him not with ivy, but with her enchantments. The resistance flowed out of him as he fell willingly into her spell. Whatever she would have of him, he would give, the green sorceress.

She continued her journey with her tongue, marking him on either side of his nose, on each temple, mapping his face with honeyed moisture and her breath. Lastly, she kissed him in the center of his brow.

His awareness heightened and spread outward from where her breath blew against his skin, outward to every part of his body, to the tips of his fingers and toes, as if his climax would start there and implode. 'Twould be the death of him, sweet demise.

"Jesu," he murmured, praying to another God even as he was saved by the god of *Her.*

He came into her again and found life, coursing, growing—her life, female to the core, taking him in and transforming him, making him into *Her* image. This was the magic she worked in the womb of the earth, that he would be reborn in an act of lust and love. His body was rigid with the need to climax, to release his seed in a rush of fierce pleasure, to be the dragon taking the mate that was his.

But if he was the dragon, she was the dragonmaster. She held him suspended, though he felt the quivering readiness of her body. She held him suspended over the abyss of final release, until he feared madness would truly come.

Then, moving down to his mouth and taking him with a soft, slow, wet, deep kiss, she let him fall.

He jerked against her, his breath stolen. Again, and the rush surged through him anew. Again, and he saw the edge of his consciousness meld into hers along a thin green line. Her pleasure washed into his all along the line, a great wave that picked him up and dragged him under, taking everything he had.

Llynya broke the kiss and watched his face as he climaxed, absorbing every beautiful, stark line. He was hers, bound by ecstasy, a willing thrall to her enchantment. A smile curved her lips. Aye, the

Druid boy was hers, and with the surety of the knowledge, she gave herself over to his enchantment.

Mychael awoke to a soft rain of kisses. He felt as if he'd slept for days, a long and dreamless sleep.

" 'Tis time to leave," her voice said next to him. *Her.*

A smile broke across his face, and he took her in his arms, rolling her over and bearing her down as he'd been borne. She glowed beneath him, her dreamy smile echoing his own blessed state.

"Don't ever," he said between soft kisses pressed to her lips, "do that to me again without warning me first."

Her answer was another smile, then she reached up and drew her finger down the middle of his face to the tip of his nose, traced the curve of his eyebrow, temple, and cheek to his chin, and lastly, smoothed her thumb across his lips from one side to the other, telling him what he already knew—*you . . . are . . . mine.*

"Aye, sprite." He kissed her again. "I am thine."

Delectable woman, he was hers aright. The taste of her was still in his mouth, the greenness still soothing him. Whether to bind or heal had been her intent, she'd done both. His vow to her was no less binding. To his last breath, he would fight that she might live. How many skraelings had already fallen under his knife? Yet with her beside him, he'd not become the ravening beast he'd feared. Not yet, but neither were they safe.

She had everything packed and ready to go, making him wonder if she'd gotten any sleep. If not, she was no worse for the wear. Indeed, she set a stronger pace than they had taken before.

They searched the labyrinth of corridors for hours, switching off the lead. No skraelings came to light in the passages, but neither did a way up into Riverwood.

So what was it to be? he asked himself. Skraelings or the salamander?

Llynya had cooled the dragonfire in him with her tea and her verdant loving, but the power of it was still skittering beneath his skin. Would it come forth if they needed it? he wondered. And a fine twistabout that was—for him to be looking for his nightmare.

He had let it overtake him in Dripshank Well. For the first time, he'd willingly given himself over to the licking flames that ran along his scars. The heat had not been less because of it. He'd felt the wild blood all but roaring in his veins, but with acceptance there had been no delirium. He had used the dragonfire, instead of letting it use him, and aye, he'd left a river of blood in his wake. But he'd freed Llynya, and he would kill a thousand times more to do the same.

So what was it to be? They couldn't wander forever. There was no water on the Magia Wall, and their stores would not last long.

They came to another fork in the trail and looked to each other at the same time.

"Do you feel that?" he asked, holding his hand out toward the western tunnel.

"Aye." Her brow was furrowed.

Heat was coming out of the passage, and in the few seconds that they stood there, it increased in intensity. When a stream of tua raced out, darting along the walls and scattering in two directions, they both swore.

"She's coming this way," Mychael said.

"And she's on fire." Llynya pointed down the tunnel. It wasn't just the mother lizard approaching, but an inferno. At the farthest point that they could see, the rock was taking on a red glow and growing brighter. The tip of the salamander's carnelian tongue flickered into view, and Llynya and Mychael both backed away.

"The Wall," he said. With luck, the giant tua would follow them, and in the terror mayhaps the skraelings would not be so quick to cut them down.

"Nay." Llynya shook her head, a determined expression on her face. "There is another way out of here, and neither skraelings nor the fire lizard will follow us."

Mychael didn't miss the implication. If the skraelings wouldn't go there, 'twas beholden of some danger. That the fire lizard wouldn't follow them either, bespoke a danger that bore considering.

"It sounds an ominous salvation, Llynya."

"Aye, 'tis, but it's better than dying on the Wall."

She ran from one of the tunnels open to them to the other, sniffing each.

"Come," she said, beckoning him to the southernmost trail. "We're to the Dangoes."

Rhuddlan returned to Merioneth and a litany of disasters and doom: Madron and Naas hied off with a weir traveler; Inishwrath torn asunder;

two dead in Tryfan and Shay captured; eight dead at the Dangoes; skraelings and Dockalfar attacking in Riverwood, leaving Lien near death and taking Llynya; Nia left at the gates of time, suffering from her descent; and Tabor returned from Lanbarrdein alone, without Mychael.

Damn the boy, and damn Madron. He would clip both their wings. Aye, he could bring Druids to heel quick enough. He was paying the price for not having done it before.

To the good, Merioneth was filling up with *tylwyth teg.* The Kings Wood elves had arrived the day after the Riverwood battle, the Ebiurrane the next. The Red-leaf had come up from the south. The highlander Wydden had caught up with Wei on his solemn return from Tryfan, the last tribe to arrive overland.

The Daur-clan had come by sea, their sleek-sailed drakars and kharrs riding the waves like ocean mist. Painted in blue and silver with cloudy gray sails, the ships were one with the water and sky and were sorely needed for the task he would set them.

Tages had brought tidings that the old men of Anglesey were sworn to write the truth of the coming battle, to record it for posterity and the unfolding ages.

Dark Ages they would be, if the dragons could not be called. Naas had chosen unwisely to leave when he most needed her. If Mychael ab Arawn did not survive his descent, 'twould be up to Rhuddlan himself, and he would need Naas's fire.

Trig had gone after Madron and Naas, but to no avail. Damn wily Naas was not to be tracked, not even by a Liosalfar captain. Trig had known well enough, though, where the threesome were heading, and he'd sent a cadre of Ebiurrane Liosalfar to stop them at the gates of time. Rhuddlan had seen the troop there himself, when he and his band had made their ascent off the Magia Wall.

Wei had confirmed the brands on the skraelings that had attacked his band in Tryfan, identifying them as Slott's. Rastaban was open, as Varga had told him, and Rhuddlan feared the worst for Shay. Moira had paled at the boy's capture, a sore loss.

As Llynya had been, a sore and dangerous loss to the Quickentree, verily to all the *tylwyth teg,* until the pair of Kings Wood trackers Trig had sent after her and the pair he had sent after Mychael had returned together. The four had come in at dawn, bearing a tale of carnage and grim happenings. Yet there was hope still for the sprite and the Druid boy.

" 'Twas here." The Kings Wood elf named Kenric pointed on the map Rhuddlan had drawn on a square of linen. They were next to the hearthfire, elfin captains and their lords from every clan. Varga walked the ramparts alone, watching the sea. The Sha-shakrieg was given a wide berth by all the *tylwyth teg,* the ancient enemy in their midst.

"Dripshank Well," Rhuddlan said. "They met there?"

A glance passed between Kenric and the other trackers. " 'Twas no meeting, Rhuddlan. 'Twas where the deaths began. No other tracks but the boy's were to be found. He was on his own, he was, and killed five in the tunnel, seven more in the small cavern here"—he pointed again to the map—"and three here, one a Dockalfar, his carcass showing the marks of iron stars."

"And the bloody granite behind him as well," muttered Mael, another of the trackers. "Pinned him to the bloody wall, the Druid did, with a bloody iron star."

"Three bloody iron stars," one of the other trackers corrected.

"Aye, three." Mael nodded.

"That's where he took up with the aetheling," Kenric said. "We followed them down the south tunnel to the chimney of rock that opens onto the Wall. Found sign of a fire lizard." He looked up from the map. "Haven't seen one of those since before the Wars, but she's down there all right, which explains why they went the way they did. No fire lizard is going into the Dangoes, no matter the prize." He bent back to the map. "The Wall is manned by skraelpacks from here north. The fire lizard had a few for supper back here by the chimney, but some of that pack escaped. This one didn't, though." He held up a bent triangle of silver. "Kynor says he was the Dark-elf who captured Llynya. 'Twas his nose, Kynor says."

Rhuddlan took the piece of metal and turned it over in his hand. That any Dockalfar had survived Caerlon's mad potion was surprising. That they'd been deformed by the brew was not. He'd noted the same during the causeway battle. Those few Dark-elves driving the skraelings had all been scarred in some bizarre way. 'Twould be fitting, if Caerlon's treachery had been turned back on the Dockalfar. 'Twas he who had first conjured a skraeling. Such had been the parting of ways between the brightest of the Dark-elves and his teacher, Ailfinn Mapp.

With all the *tylwyth teg* gathered, Rhuddlan feared the worst for the mage. No one had seen her since the winter solstice ceremony at Anglesey. That she'd not come to Deri for Beltaine was not unusual.

She'd known he was going to open the weir, but as she'd said, he'd closed it without her, he could just as well open it without her. Fifteen years of an ether seal was as naught to Ailfinn, and she'd left him to his own devices. The aftermath, though, the continued wildness of the *pryf*, the breaking of the damson shafts, the disaster in Kryscaven Crater . . . The mage could not yet breathe and not have felt that tearing of the earth, or the unleashing of destruction.

For the first time, Rhuddlan was forced to acknowledge that the direst circumstances had befallen Ailfinn, that indeed, if not captured by the dark army forming in the earth, she was dead, the last of the Prydion Magi, and her acolyte still no more than a green sprite and in danger as grave as any.

"Harek," he called to a captain of the Daur. "Take a drakar and two kharrs under full sail to stand guard at the Dangoes. If Mychael and Llynya come out of the ice, carry them to the gates of time." Whatever else happened, whether the Dark-elves would rule again or nay, Dharkkum must be stopped, and for that, Mychael would have to call the dragons home to their nest—if he survived the Dangoes.

"Half of the remaining fleet will be moored outside the gates of Mor Sarff," he continued. "The others in Merion Bay." 'Twas a small inlet south of the Dragon's Mouth. In the Wars of Enchantment, the Dockalfar had used longships to make strikes along the coast of the Irish Sea as well as Mor Sarff. He would be prepared this time.

Rhuddlan had reached terms with Varga at the gates and sent a messenger to make the run to Deseillign. If the Lady Queen would have a dread warrior to wield a *druaight* blade, the Edge of Sorrow would be brought to the shores of Mor Sarff. Llyr, head of the Ebiurrane Liosalfar sent after Madron and Naas, had orders to hold the women when they reached the dark sea. They would help Mychael as they could, their traveler be damned.

For himself, with the Troll King reigning in Rastaban, all his paths led first to the Eye of the Dragon and to the nameless foe who had dared to break Dharkkum's crystal seals.

Chapter 23

The trail into the Dangoes had grown ever longer and colder, and still Llynya kept on. The dry corridors above the Magia Wall had given way to a single wide tunnel running with water. It seeped out of the walls and gathered into small cold streams. They stopped to refill their gourds and for Llynya to put on her cloak.

"The deep ice is not far now." Her breath formed vaporous clouds when she spoke.

The fire lizard's screeching cries had reached them for a long time after they'd chosen their path, but the giant tua had not followed them beyond the first stretch of frost-shattered scree. There was no going back, though, and no alternate tunnels or byways to the one they were taking. Mychael welcomed the drop in temperature. He pressed his hand to the thickening hoarfrost on the passageway walls, and water ran from beneath his palm.

"No one comes this way?" he asked.

"Not by choice." Llynya's voice was muffled by a swath of the hood she was wrapping around her head and the lower half of her face.

"What else would bring them?"

"Necessity and death. 'Tis a place of ghosts and the half-dead."

"Half-dead what?" he asked warily, taking a closer look around them as he slipped his pack off. 'Twas food he was after, not his cloak. He doubted if he would ever be cold again.

She shrugged. "Whatever was not ready to die when death came."

"Most of mankind is not ready when death comes."

" 'Tis death's choice to come here, not man's," she said, glancing at him from over the top of the mask she'd made out of the tail of her hood. "Much can be revealed in the Dangoes of dying and such. The journey through is different for every traveler, but Men, it seems, are particularly susceptible to the despairs of the ice. If you'll let me blindfold you and bind your ears, I can spare you some of the grief that might await you in the caverns."

"I'll not do you much good blindfolded," he chided, handing her a strip of murrey.

She took the dried fruit and adjusted the mask below her mouth so she could eat. "You can't fight despair with the strength of your body, Mychael, nor with strength of mind."

"Have you been here before? Do you know what lies ahead?"

"Nay." She shook her head, chewing the murrey and rummaging in one of her pouches. "Not for me, nor for you. I only know what I learned from Ailfinn."

The mention of the Prydion's name gave him pause. "The mage Rhuddlan has summoned to Carn Merioneth, you know her?"

"Aye," she said with an intriguing hesitancy, and shook a few juniper berries into her palm.

"You know her well?"

"Aye." The hesitation was there again. She popped the berries in her mouth.

Coerced by the lift of his eyebrows, she volunteered more cryptic information.

"She's worthy of caution, she is, as are the Dangoes. Let me at least bind your ears against the ice music."

"I am not afraid of the ice, Llynya."

"You should be."

"Mayhaps," he agreed, then asked pointedly, "How do you know Ailfinn, and why caution?"

For a moment he thought she might refuse to answer, so long was her reply in coming.

"She is my teacher," she finally said, ". . . and my grandmother."

"Grandmother?" he repeated, nonplussed.

"Aye." She shook more berries into her hand and offered them to him.

"Nay." He didn't need juniper berries to keep him warm.

She returned them to her pouch and moved her mask back into place. When she started down the trail, though, he put his hand out to stop her.

"You are to be a mage? A Prydion Mage?" Moira had told him of their greatness, of their knowledge that spanned the millenniums, how the primordial substances of the earth were theirs to command. 'Twas disconcerting to think of Llynya in those terms. She was his love, strong and fierce, but also that fair elf-maiden of the mist—except a maiden no more. She'd given that part of herself to him.

"Mayhaps," she said. "In time. I have the knack, if not the guise." Her admission was direct.

"Yet you came to me for knowledge of the weir? Does not Ailfinn know its ways?"

"Ailfinn would put me in chains and auction me off to a Norman lord before she'd let one of her own go through a weir gate."

'Twas enough to assure the mage of Mychael's admiration and respect.

"We are bound, Llynya," he told her. "If you must find Morgan, and it's through the weir you must go, you will not go alone. I would have your promise that it is so."

She nodded and gave her solemn oath. "I swear by the trees and the stars. I'll not have you pay the price I pay for being bound to the Thief."

Another direct admission, but one he could have done without.

"You came to me a virgin," he said, working to keep the strain out of his voice. She was his, not Morgan's. Whatever hold the Thief had on her was more than Mychael wanted to acknowledge.

" 'Tis not love, Mychael," she promised, smoothing the scowl from his face with her hand, "and the kiss Morgan and I shared was no more than a brushing of lips. 'Twas not at all how you kiss me."

He was heartened to hear that, though the rest of her words near took the heart out of him.

"Something happened in those hours Morgan and I spent together," she went on. "Or mayhaps it was that Rhuddlan put him in my care and I failed him. Three times in Deri I was struck down by the sense of his falling, a terrible vertigo I couldn't escape, a madness where the very earth was not solid beneath me, though I had my hands dug deep into the dirt. There was no purchase to be had and no escape. The first time it happened, I thought it was guilt rising up to claim me. I girded myself to endure, yet was praying for death before it finally released me. The second time, I was terrified that it had happened again. By the third time, I feared the lot was mine to bear for life, and I knew I could not. I came north to free myself as much as to save Morgan. The weir is a torture, you say, a torment, and I know it to be true, for as Morgan falls through its anguished depths, so have I."

Green eyes stared up at him, their vulnerability masked by a stoic veneer. The urge to draw her close and enfold her in his arms was strong, but he would give her more than a fleeting comfort.

"Remember at Bala Bredd when you felt the dragonfire?" he asked, dredging up a memory he'd hoped to forget—that he'd dragged her into his bane and been soothed by her presence there.

"Aye," she said. "I heard the dragons cry. I shared their breath with you. They are coming, Mychael. I saw Naas calling to them from the ramparts of Carn Merioneth the night we came up from the deep dark and the dragonfire took you."

More than nonplussed, he was shocked. "You heard them? Out in the world, not just in your mind?"

"Aye. I didn't know what the white-eyed one was up to, wasn't sure what the keening cry was, until I heard it again when we were joined."

Excitement and dread surged into him. Was he finally to meet the beasts whose blood ran in his veins?

"Do you know when they're coming?" *Christe,* the dragons.

"Nay."

Naas would. He was certain. Five months he'd been with the Quicken-tree and not a word out of her. Then suddenly she'd given him a dreamstone knife and a sennight later she was up on the castle walls calling dragons?

And they had answered her.

He'd almost died that night. Without Madron he might have breathed his last. He touched the phial still nested in his tunic. 'Twas a slim guard against dragons, yet he would have them come.

Aye, he would have them come and know his fate.

Ddrei Goch and Ddrei Glas—their names alone quickened the heat beneath his skin.

He took Llynya's hand in his, letting her feel the pulsing warmth. "We are bound, *cariad,* but I would not have you be part of this. If Morgan's falling comes upon you again, I'll be with you, but if the dragons come and their desire is to rage against me, the weir may be the only safe place. You saw as well as I how Trig broke Rhuddlan's seals. If the need arises, take your mystery path back to Yr Is-ddwfn."

Llynya looked at him and nodded. Aye, if the need arose, she would take the path to Yr Is-ddwfn and pray that Morgan did not call out for her as she traversed the narrow trail down the wormhole. For certes she would be lost then, her wish granted with one misstep. But if such dire need arose, and the dragons were ravening beasts come for Mychael's blood, she was taking him down the worm's throat with her.

"Come," she said. "Before we meet dragons, we must first get through the ice." Thus she turned and led him into the frozen wasteland.

Chapter 24

"No time. No time," Caerlon muttered as he strode down a long tunnel leading to Rastaban's dungeons, carrying a fully laden pack and a short whip of braided leather. With each stride, he tapped the whip against the side of his leg. 'Twas the one thing the skraelings understood, the crack of the lash. Beasts.

As the time for battle had grown nearer, the skraelpacks had grown more mutinous and unruly— and hungry, always hungry. They were eating him out of rats, and Slott, dear Slott, was eating him out of skraelings. There was no time to waste. No time to lose, or his whole army would be naught but troll droppings.

"No time. No time." His mutterings took on a singsong quality as he hefted the pack higher on his shoulder. "No time to lose."

He came to a fork in the tunnel and took the long curve of stairs leading into the lower dungeons.

His light steps made nary a sound on the cold hard stone. At the bottom of the stairwell, a wide corridor opened to the south. Cells lined either side of the passageway, cells for branding, cells for racking, cells for shackling, cells for slow roasting—the skraelings' favorite. By the end of the Wars of Enchantment, there had been damn little enchantment, only the grisly horrors of battles and death.

Caerlon passed them all, heading toward a small holding cell at the end of the corridor. The iron bars of its door grated against the stone floor as he pulled it open. Tufts of old rush were scattered about the interior, a thin comfort to any who might be incarcerated in its gloomy depths.

He held his dreamstone high and passed the light over the far wall, looking for the curved incision in the rock that marked the door he sought. Even knowing where it was, 'twas difficult to find.

There, he thought, spying a crack in the stone. He stepped forward and smoothed his hand along the curve. At its apex, he pushed and felt the inner latch give way. The door swung open.

A dizzying sight greeted him, one that never failed to delight, the abyss of Rastaban's oubliette stretching out below in all its bleak, black glory. From the landing where he stood, stairs swirled around and down the sheer-sided granite walls, ending in another stone landing that hung above a pool of inky darkness measuring over a hundred feet across. Out of the darkness thrust a single pillar of rock, the top of which was lit by a shaft of soft golden light glittering with faerie dust, each mote a testament to Caerlon's courage and resolve. Fifty years he'd spent in the wilderness collecting the stuff, searching every *sídhe* from Cymru to Eire.

The light that held the dust shot down from a long rod of yellow dreamstone as thick as the trunk of an oak tree. 'Twas Tuan's Stone, taken from the watery depths of the King's Pool in Lanbarrdein, the only treasure saved before the advancing Quicken-tree had won the great cavern. Caerlon and his maimed Dockalfar had unearthed it from its long hiding place in a cavern south of Rastaban in the early summer, and embedded it in the land above to act as a window between the surface world and the table of rock jutting up out of the darkness, creating the perfect prison for the perfect prisoner.

Dreamstone light and faerie dust. Could any lovelier half-death be devised?

Caerlon thought not, but Ailfinn appeared perfectly oblivious to the luxury of her prison, a testament to his success. He had sacrificed for her. Indeed he had, baiting his trap with the *Elhion Bhaas Le*. The trap was long sprung now and the bait closed within, taken from him.

Nonetheless he smiled as he always did when he looked upon Ailfinn. There she hung, suspended by light and air, unable to reach the key to her freedom though it lay literally at her feet. The irony of his teacher's demise gave him nearly as much pleasure as had the Indigo Book itself during all the years he'd pored over its pages, searching for the manner of her downfall.

She looked a bit like a butterfly, her white hair with its single, subtle stripe of gold twining upward into the aureate light, her tawny, rune-marked cloak billowing about her like wings, the sparkle of faerie dust giving her an ethereal air. Her face was remarkably unlined for a woman of her great age. Some female necromancy, no doubt, and vanity, for certes. Her eyes had closed under his induced sleep, but he remembered them well, as green as any of her beloved Quicken-tree's, with thick golden lashes.

Rotters. In his excitement, he'd forgotten to bring her a piece of meat.

She never ate it, of course, wouldn't have even if she'd been in a condition to eat, but he liked to think the stench of the decayed flesh he threw on the rock added to her misery. She had a very delicate nose. Even trapped in a sleeping death, he was sure she could smell the putridness of his offerings.

As to his other prisoner, Caerlon was doing his best not to offend him. The chains that held the young Liosalfar to the lower landing's wall were an undeniable offense, but a necessary one. Caerlon hoped to make it up to him with the food he'd brought: sweetcakes and honeycomb, mead and hazelnuts, enough to restore the boy and tide him over for a sennight. By then the gates of time would be secured, and Caerlon would have all the time he wished, an eternity of it. Time to win, time to waste . . . time to play.

He smiled again and started down the stairs. A pale, eyeless lizard skittered across his path. "Tua," the Quicken-tree dared to call the reptiles, a deliberate insult to the great king who had once ruled the rocky depths of all the caverns from Anglesey to the Brecon Beacons.

So much had been lost.

So much more was about to be regained.

Caerlon and his army were off to war, his captains above forming packs in the Eye of the Dragon for their march to the Dangoes. There they would launch their ships off the causeway into Mor Sarff and make sail for the gates of time.

Deseillign had fallen, the Desert Queen routed and fleeing to the east, beyond the roots of the mountains and the known edge of her kingdom. The Dockalfar captains had proven glorious in battle, holding the west against her and bringing Caerlon the last great swordblade to come from the desert smith's forge—the Edge of Sorrow for the Magia Blade. Whatever bargain the Lady might have made with Rhuddlan would be left undone. The Blade and the Blade's master were Caerlon's now.

Lacknose had not returned from Riverwood, presupposing defeat, and the Quicken-tree had fought Blackhand's pack to a draw on the causeway. Rhuddlan's confidence would be high, despite his captain's defeat beneath Tryfan. And why not? Caerlon thought with a flicker of disgust. The Quicken-tree still had the aetheling—the one fly in his ointment.

This time, though, Rhuddlan's confidence would be his undoing. He would make for Rastaban, from whence all his troubles had so far come, taking the quickest route, overland through Riverwood. His instincts would drive him to Slott and the Eye of the Dragon, while all of Rastaban would be making for the gates of time with the Wyrm-master and the Magia Blade to call the dragons.

Or most of the Magia Blade, Caerlon conceded. He'd broken five precious rods of dreamstone trying to cobble a sword grip onto the sorrowful edge, a difficult day's work. In the end, he'd settled for leather-wrapped wood embedded with roughly smoothed cabochons of the broken crystals.

He drew on a level with Ailfinn and gave the floating mage a glance. She looked a bit wan, but there was no help for it. The dreamstone light had sustained her these many long months, as it would sustain the Quicken-tree warrior for a time, but Caerlon had never supposed that it would grant her life indefinitely.

A few steps below was the landing. A stream of water trickled down the wall at its edge, filling a small pool before it overflowed into the abyss. He'd chained the boy close enough to the pool for him to drink and splash his face, if that would give him pleasure.

"I've brought food," he said, shrugging out of the pack.

No sign of welcome lit the Liosalfar's eyes, no words of gratitude fell from his lips. He'd washed himself, though. His face, scrubbed clean, was of a Quicken-tree's particular delicacy, slightly slanted green eyes and a fine nose upturned at the end. He'd replaited his *fif* braid, and Caerlon could almost hear the song he'd probably sung while doing it . . . *pwr wa ladth, pwr wa ladth.*

Songs would not help him in the oubliette. Caerlon had been careful to seal the prison against sacred sounds, lest Ailfinn talk in her sleep and accidentally mutter an incantation or two.

He knelt down and began emptying the pack.

"I'll be gone for a while, so I've brought food for a sennight, mayhaps a sennight and a half, if you're careful."

Still nothing from the boy.

Caerlon wanted to touch him, badly, but held himself to lifting a length of silky black hair. He got a murderous look for his trouble.

"When I return, it will be as king of all you hold dear, Shay. Mayhaps then we will parlay for your favors."

A foul curse escaped the boy, an inadvertent slip of the tongue as it were, and Caerlon laughed.

"Aye, that's exactly what I had in mind. That and more of the same, when I return." A huskiness he couldn't control slipped into his voice. He let the strands of the Liosalfar's hair slide through his fingers and lowered his hand to rest on the young warrior's thigh. The muscles beneath his tunic were hard and lean, his leg well formed.

The boy's stony gaze shifted to Ailfinn.

"She can't help you," Caerlon said softly, allowing his hand to slide beneath the tunic to bare skin, then to the boy's braies.

Shay's gaze came back to him, blandly indifferent, though sweat was breaking out on Caerlon's brow and upper lip. He pulled his hand back and swore silently to himself. The indifference had cost the boy, he was sure.

The Liosalfar would not be easy to break—and what Liosalfar was? But he would break, and he would break to Caerlon's hand.

In a single, fluid movement, he rose and turned on his heel, leaving the pack behind. He took the stairs two at a time up out of the oubliette and did not look back when he closed the stone door. With nary a soul but a half-dead mage for company, no doubt Shay of the Quicken-tree would be better pleased to see him the next time he came.

No doubt.

Shay waited until he heard the stone door grind closed before he gave in to a ripple of despair. He brought one knee up from his cross-legged position and rested his forehead on it with a weary sigh.

Sticks. With all else he had to bear, his captor was a bugger.

The scent of honey came to him in his misery, heartening him. His stomach growled, and he lifted his head. A sennight, the Dark-elf had said, and Shay wondered if Caerlon truly thought he was going to dispatch Rhuddlan and the gathering tribes in seven days. For all that Wei had been forced to retreat from Tryfan with his wounded, the skraelings had suffered the worst losses.

He reached for the mead Caerlon had brought and took a sip, pacing himself and eyeing his small store of food. He took another sip, and his gaze drifted to the shaft of golden light holding the darkness at bay.

He knew who she was, the lady in the light. He'd known the instant he'd seen her, Ailfinn Mapp. How a few Dark-elves and a bunch of skraelings had captured a Prydion Mage was a mystery, but in the three days he'd been in Rastaban's deepest dungeon, Shay had come to think it might have something to do with the large book at the woman's feet.

Even as he watched, one of the thick cream-colored pages lifted up into the light. It wavered for a moment, bathed in glittering motes, then floated down to lie smooth on the other side of the book—a page turned. 'Twas the fourth time such had happened since he'd been chained to the landing, and 'twas Ailfinn doing it. There was no wind in the oubliette. Though she didn't move herself, not so much as a finger twitch that he had seen, the pages in the book were turning.

And that was where Shay's hope lay.

"Es sholei par es cant," he whispered into the darkness. *"Pwr wa ladth. Pwr wa ladth."*

Run deep. Run deep.

They were lost. Lost in the ice.

Mychael had Llynya pulled close under his cloak on his left side, sharing with her what warmth remained from his dragonfire. They needed to stop and rest, but he was delaying as long as possible. Sleeping in the Dangoes was at best a mixed bag of grief and dreams, dreams of death. At the worst, 'twas a deadly danger, and not only from the cold.

Fell spirits moved through the ice, shadows rippling beneath the

frozen surface of the walls. In places, spidery cracks released the spirits'
breath, and the breath would twine and twist its way into vaporous bones
that snagged and snared. 'Twas always Llynya the bony little fingers
went for, never him. They curled 'round her ankles and tried to circle
her wrists. They caressed her skin and left it pale and icy to the touch. A
quick flash of dreamstone light or a slash with a blade was enough to
hold them at bay, but it took diligence, and exhaustion was no friend
to diligence. As a precaution, he'd taken Ara and bound the dagger to
Llynya's hand with a strip of cloth cut from his cloak. He'd taken the
Dockalfar dagger for himself, having less faith in its desire to protect a
Light-elf.

Their food was running low, and both their strengths. All of the
deep dark did not seem as long as the trail they'd made wandering
through the frozen caverns of the Dangoes.

"No more, Mychael," she said when they came out of a tunnel
into yet one more small cave. The weariness in her voice brought him to
a halt. "We have to rest."

Aye, she was right. He looked around them, checking the ice.
Three other tunnels led out of the cave. He moved the dreamstone blade
in a slow arc, and yellow light reflected back at him in a shape-shifting
circle. The walls were clearer here than in other places they'd been, and
for certes 'twould do him good just to hold her.

"We'll make tea, and I have some murrey." 'Twas the best offer he
could make. She could sleep, if she wished, but he preferred not to slip
into dreams again while still in the ice.

Yet sleep did come to him after their slim repast. With Llynya
bound inside his cloak and his arms, and the smell of lavender teasing his
memories, he dreamed of her and grassy meadows, of warm sunshine
and the wind rustling through the trees. Then, in a dark transformation,
the warmth became heat, and the sunlight became flames licking up
around him. The sound of the wind in the trees became the sound of
battle, the clashing of arms and the cries of men. He looked for dragons
in the sky and found none, only the walls of Merioneth burning down
around him.

His father, Arawn, was on the wall-walk, his face a stark mask of
dread. Mychael followed his line of sight to the upper bailey, and with
terrifying clarity realized 'twas no fantastical Dangoes death-dream he
was seeing, but the actual fall of Carn Merioneth. A giant of a blond-
haired man was butchering a path across the yard, Gwrnach, his

mother's cousin. Mychael remembered him from childhood. The stables had been set afire, and the screams of horses cut through the rising dawn. Bloody combat raged in every corner, but 'twas to the doorway of the keep that Arawn lifted his hand and commanded him to look.

Mychael tried not to, tried to pull himself back from the hot, reeking vision, knowing 'twas some horrific act of carnage awaiting him between the great oak doors of Merioneth's hall.

But see it he would.

His father's name rang out in a keening wail, in his mother's voice, and Mychael's head jerked around. A scream tore from his own throat, but too late, too late. He saw Rhiannon's eyes in that last moment between rape and death, saw the light and the terror fade from their soft gray depths. The last of her tears streamed across her fair cheeks and ran in salty rivulets down her neck to pool in the tender hollow of her throat. Her hand lay on her breast, a feeble protection from the blade that had pierced her heart. On her middle finger was a ring engraved with symbols of the weir, and after taking her life, her murderer took her ring.

Mychael looked up to see the man's face. Wild blue-green eyes shot through with icy flecks of white and gold stared back at him. Long blond hair whipped around the man's contorted visage, but the features were instantly recognizable and forever fixed in Mychael's mind. He was the destroyer's son, Gwrnach's spawn. He was Caradoc, the Boar of Balor.

He lunged for the man's throat and awoke with his own battle cry echoing up and down the cave. Slabs of ice slid off the walls and crashed onto the floor, shaken from their eternal hold by the fierce agony in his voice.

A frozen rain showered down on him where he stood, covering him in white shards of ice. He looked around, blindly searching, but his hands were empty. Caradoc was gone. The dream was over.

The sprite was on her feet, turning away from him, her sword drawn against a danger that was only in his heart. When naught came out of the tunnels, she lowered her blade.

Mychael fell to his knees, fearing he was going to be sick. His mother, his beautiful mother. Her golden hair streaked with blood. Her body hewn and defiled. The pain was too much to bear. He covered his face with his hands, rocking back and forth, and raised his voice in an anguished cry. More ice crashed down from the ceiling.

Llynya looked to Mychael, her heart pounding in her chest, her breath coming short and fast. He wasn't hurt; there was no mark of blood on him, yet death itself was in his cry. She checked the tunnels again, her sword point dragging in the ice. She'd jumped away from him when he'd let out his first bloodcurdling yell, expecting an attack. But there was naught, only Mychael, her beloved Mychael, beset by the Dangoes death-dreams.

To her left, a huge chunk of ice sloughed off the wall with a ripping roar and crashed against the wall on the right. It broke into a thousand pieces, filling up the northern tunnel with frozen rubble. Shards of the ceiling rained down all around.

Shadana! He was going to bury them with his pain.

She tried singing to him, but without him holding her, she was too cold. Her teeth chattered and she couldn't draw enough of the freezing air into her lungs to make a clear note.

And still his cries shook the ice.

A crack split open at her feet, snaking down the length of the cavern and growing ever wider.

She leaped to his side of the crack and grabbed hold of him. "Mychael!" The floor shook beneath her, and her voice grew frantic. Gods! What had he seen? "Mychael! W-we have to leave! N-now!"

Another slab of the ceiling came crashing down, spraying them with stinging bits of ice. They were going to be trapped. The next fall of ice exploded at her feet, shattering into millions of sharp-edged crystals, and in the midst of the frozen rain, his keening cries became sobs.

She dropped to her knees beside him. "Mychael. Mychael."

He didn't answer her other than to draw her into his arms and hold her close. He buried his face in the crook of her neck, his hair falling in a golden skein across his shoulder.

"Mychael," she crooned, warmed by his touch and his tears.

With every creak and groan of the walls, she expected a final fall of ice to crush them both. Still she held him, working her way deeper into his arms, taking of his warmth and giving him comfort, and letting time pass them by.

She dozed and awoke to silence, except for the sound of their breathing. The walls had stopped creaking. Piles of broken ice littered the cavern floor, and the northern tunnel was completely blocked. They'd come out of the western passageway. So the decision of which way to go had been narrowed to the south and the east.

"Mychael?" She roused him gently. They had to get out of the ice.

"Aye." He tightened his hold on her and kissed the side of her neck, then her cheek. His arms were strong about her, his muscles flexing with iron hardness, but his voice was hoarse.

"We have to go on."

He nodded and silently rose to his feet, helping her up and shouldering his pack. Without so much as a glance around the cave, he chose the eastern tunnel, his steps surer than they'd been in three days, as if he knew the way out.

The passageway gradually curved from east to southeast, and the ice changed. The tunnels became wider, the ice more flowing and trickier to navigate. Above them, the ceilings were filled with long, thin needlelike icicles, each one looking sharp enough to impale a man or a Light-elf. As they passed beneath them, the icicles set up a vibration, a low humming that caused the hair on Llynya's nape to rise. Ice music.

Mychael strode resolutely forward, seemingly oblivious to the eerie sound that grew ever louder.

"Can you hear the ice?" she asked when the noise took on a melody. 'Twas making her twitch inside, insinuating itself into her thoughts and creating a sense of aloneness. She tightened her grip on his hand.

"Aye. I can hear it." He pulled her closer. " 'Tis a sad and despairing thing, but we're not far now. Hold on. I'm with you."

Not far from the end of the Dangoes? she wanted to ask. And how did he know? But if the path had come to him in his dream, she was leery of reminding him, especially with those needles poised above them. She would ask him someday what death-dream he'd seen in the ice cave, but she preferred to hear his answer under an open sky, surrounded by trees.

The next turn in the passage wiped the questions from her mind. Mychael stopped as suddenly as she, the two of them halting on the frozen lip of a huge cavern. It stretched out below them, mayhaps a thousand feet across, its walls streaked with great ribbons of sea-green ice running through layers of white frost. Its ceiling was hundreds of feet above them and completely encrusted with slender, trembling icicles. A frigid wind and waves of ice music rushed out of the cave and washed over them, the cold breath of the earth and a wordless symphony of sound. Somewhere in the far distance, they could hear the sea. The ice was ending, but no words of relief came to her, only a calm horror at what she saw.

The cave was a burial ground. Columns of dreadfully clear ice rose from the floor, and inside each column was a body frozen in its death throes.

"Sticks," she whispered.

Mychael surveyed the cavern's gruesome gallery. His father had led him here, pointed the way east, the way home. A series of roughly shaped stairs were cut into the other side, leading up and out of the cave to a cliff beyond, the causeway of the Dangoes, but there was no easy way into the cavern. They would have to rope down with Llynya's rope, their last.

There were no dripshanks for a belay, and the walls were all smooth ice. Under his direction, they used their dreamstones to melt a small pool of water. It quickly froze again, but with the tail of Llynya's rope in it.

"You first," he said, testing the rope against his weight.

She eyed the long drop. "I went first last time."

"I'll be right behind you," he assured her, apparently to no avail.

"Why don't we go down together?"

"The rope won't hold both of us. I'm not even sure it's going to hold one of us."

She looked over the edge again, concern furrowing her brow.

She was no coward. He knew that down to his bones, but something was bothering her.

"They're all dead, Llynya."

"Aye, I know. But something's moving around down there."

He walked over to the edge and knelt down, taking a good look. The wind was picking up, batting the rope against the cliff face, and the ice music was spiraling to a crescendo. Wisps of icy vapor that smelled of the sea were blowing around the cavern, swirling up here and there, but of an actual something moving around, he saw naught. Their dreamstones were casting shadows, the light glinting off the columns of dead and throwing their own shade onto the floor, but dreamstone shadows wouldn't hurt them, and the bodies in the ice were frozen solid.

'Twas the ice music that decided him. Whatever grand finale it was building up to, he wanted to be out of the cave before it got there. The frozen song was a despairing force, an eerie melody that fed his weariness. And mayhaps that was what stayed Llynya. Mayhaps the ice music was sowing her doubts.

"We dare not delay," he told her. "If you want, I'll go first." He hated to do it. His greater weight would weaken the rope's hold in the ice, increasing the likelihood of her falling.

"Nay," she said. "You're right. We'll both more safely make the floor if I go first."

She took hold of the rope and began lowering herself over the side. Mychael held the belay against her weight. When she reached the bottom, she waved once, and he started down the icy expanse, using Ratskin's blade for light. There was little purchase to be had on the cliff face, making the descent more a matter of strength than finesse.

Halfway down, the wind picked up in force, swirling the vapor into ever thickening clouds. With each new gust, he momentarily lost sight of Llynya. He started moving faster, sliding down the rope, the friction burning his hands.

"Llynya!" he hollered when the mist failed to clear after the last blast of wind.

A strangled cry was his only answer. He was moving as fast as he dared without dropping into a dead fall through the clouds, but it wasn't fast enough. He still couldn't see her.

"Llynya!" he shouted again. He felt a quick tug on the rope. In the next instant, he was fighting to keep his hold as the rope was snapped and cracked by something far more powerful than the Light-elf. Twice he was slammed into the ice. The clouds churned and darkened beneath him, and a palpable malevolence rose up the cliff face.

The ice music became a screech, losing its melody in the chaos. The mist entwined with smoke, black and fearsome, and a death scent blossomed in the maelstrom, the smell of burning rot and decay. 'Twas the same as at the broken damson shaft, but far more intense, far more alive. 'Twas a darkness with intent.

Ara flashed on the edge of the smoke in one blinding bolt before the light was swallowed by the dire night. Fear took hold of his heart. He reached the floor with a final jump and heard the sounds of a struggle. Smoke and fog blinded him, the two roiling up in thick, vaporous bands swirling around each other.

"Llynya!" he screamed, slashing at the wind-driven smog with the dagger. "Llynya!"

"Mychaellll . . ." she cried out, her voice coming from a distance and growing fainter.

He raised the dreamstone high, running toward the sound, dodging the columns of the dead. Around one roughly formed block of ice he saw a flash of blue light. Around the next, he caught sight of her legs, kicking and struggling as she was swiftly dragged behind the next column. Sprays of ice fanned up around her, and he could hear her cursing.

When next he saw her, he dove for her feet, caught hold, but couldn't stop her rapid slide across the ice. Whatever had hold of her pulled them both on a sure course toward some fearful end. Through the ice spray and windblown vapors, he glimpsed a bony curve, and then another—knucklebones, but ten times larger than the knuckles of the fingers that had dogged them through the upper trails. These were the mother bones.

Llynya squirmed within the awful grip, her arms pinned to her sides. Ara was still bound to her hand, but the Quicken-tree cloth was rapidly unraveling in the mad slide over the ice. Yellow light from the Dockalfar blade flashed with each thrust he made at the Dangoes bones, but the fingers were replaced as quickly as he could quell them. The smell of death grew stronger. He made a final stabbing lunge, and was attacked from behind.

Like the cracking of a whip, he was jerked away from her by an unseen hand and sent sliding off in a different direction. A great howling set up in the cavern, adding to the raucous din of the storm. When he was able to stop himself, he scrambled to his feet and took off at a run, back toward Llynya.

He had no room for thought, only action. A faint light flickered off to one side of him, and he raced toward it. Without warning, a wall of clear ice loomed up out of the whirls of fog and smoke. He dropped to the floor of the cavern, trying to slow the speed of impact. Blessed grace, he didn't hit, but came to a sliding stop in a worn hollow of ice in front of the wall. White light fell over him from above, and when he turned and looked up, his already ragged breath caught in his throat.

'Twasn't a wall that had stopped him, but a tomb, one far different from the other gruesome pillars of ice. This one glowed. Its occupant was long and slender, laid out on her side, and she was pure white. 'Twas a hound, frozen in watery splendor. He could see her wounds, but no blood stained her hide.

The howling behind him had degenerated into fierce barking and growling, coming from the same direction as the greatest fury of the storm. He tried to get to his feet, but 'twas as if the light weighed him down. It grew brighter and brighter, and all around him the black smoke rose higher on the walls, leaving a sooty residue on the ice. A swirling length of darkness took shape near the ceiling, shattering the icicles and silencing the screeching music, leaving only the roar of the wind.

He watched the cloud form, a long, black funnel of force shaping the chaos and dragging Dangoes bones into its whirling center. Some of the pillars began to crack, and he feared the dead would be loosed upon him . . . upon her.

"Llynya." Her name was a rough whisper. He clawed for a hold on the edge of the hollow, but was denied. Collapsing onto his back, he stared up into the churning heart of the darkness and knew a cold more frigid than the ice. 'Twas an eternity of night he saw above him, an emptiness too complete to ever be filled.

The light from the tomb brightened even more, casting a pool of luminescence that spread out to every corner of the cavern. In the middle of it, the funnel cloud ebbed and flowed and churned, a dark, undulating flame sundering the light.

'Twas his vision, only far bleaker than what he'd seen that long-ago winter night.

The future laid itself bare before him, and he saw naught but bones and darkness, and then even the bones were devoured, sucked into the black well. The swart cloud swirled in a ponderous, hypnotic spiral, and heat kindled in his breast.

One thread of darkness loosed itself from the flame to dance and twine about him, and the scars along his body quickened, heeding the call of the dread night.

This was his fate.

This was his fight.

He felt the thread pull him to his feet, and he unsheathed his sword, but the sword was wrong, all wrong. It didn't fit his hand. It couldn't cut the thread.

"Llynya!" he cried out, her name the one talisman to which he clung.

And she was there, holding him to the ice against the force of the thread, holding the sword with him, a black hellhound at her side. Her hair was flying out in all directions, braids and knots and twists, her leaves trembling in the draft of the funnel cloud's wake. Her face was streaked with icy patches of white, but her eyes were green. Green and fierce.

She lifted her voice into the wind, shouting in an elfin tongue, and the black flame wavered above them. The light from the tomb became a piercing disk of brightness, forcing the darkness higher.

With a mortal groan, the smoke wound itself tighter and tighter, dragging its loose thread back into itself, until 'twas naught but a frenzied, twisted cord, humming with its own furious power. In an instant the cord unraveled, each strand flying off toward the cliffs of the causeway.

The white light ebbed, and Mychael fell to the ice. Llynya removed her hand from the sword grip and caressed his face. He thought he heard her sob. He felt so strange. The hound moved in close to nuzzle him where he lay.

"Elixir," he murmured, raising his hand to the dog's sleek coat. Lavrans had told him of the hound, how it had fought hard and to victory in the Battle of Balor and had helped save Ceridwen's life—much as he had saved Llynya's from the Dangoes bones.

"He is called Conladrian by the Quicken-tree," she told him, her voice a strained whisper.

"And Numa?" he asked, looking to the tomb. The white bitch had been Ceridwen's boon companion when she had stayed in the Hart Tower with Lavrans before coming to Balor as Caradoc's bride. The hound had died in the final moments of the battle, holding the enemy at bay on the sands of Mor Sarff.

"She is Rhayne," Llynya said. "I—I didn't know he'd brought her here."

"When I heard the howling, I thought 'twas death itself, and the growling . . ." His voice trailed off. It had been such a vicious sound. He'd thought Llynya had met her end in some cavern beast's jaws.

"Death was here," she said simply, and another sob broke free.

Aye, death had been there.

The river of blood he'd so long feared was as naught compared to the dark night he'd seen. The skraelings would die, hundreds by his sword alone, dull as it was, too dull to cut a dark thread, yet sharp enough to cut down skraelings. Their blood would run like a river. The Dockalfar would die, the Sha-shakrieg . . . and the Quicken-tree, he thought with a pang of despair. The Red-leaf and Wydden, the Daur and Ebiurrane, the Kings Wood elves—any and all who answered Rhuddlan's summons would die. Men, too, would die in droves, overrun with plague and pestilence. Every creature of the forest and the water would die in the darkness. And when naught else walked upon the land or swam in any ocean, the trees would die and with them every last green living thing.

This was what he'd seen in the heart of the darkness, a void that ate life down to the last spark of light.

He would fight. 'Twas what he'd been born to do. And the dragons would come, Ddrei Goch and Ddrei Glas, for 'twas what they'd been born to do as well—to fight the darkness. But would they come to him? He had not the blade to rule them, only a weak edge that could not cut through a tendril of smoke.

They had been conjured for this one deed, the three of them. Blood of their blood, he needed them as he'd always known he did, for without them his fate was sealed. He would die.

He was so cold. He hadn't realized it afore, but he ached with the cold. The way was clear before them now, the smoke gone and the ice free of bones. They should be leaving the Dangoes.

He struggled to his feet with Llynya helping him and Elixir pacing back and forth at his side.

"Will he come with us, do you think?" he asked.

"Nay." Llynya shook her head and wiped the back of her hand across her cheek. " 'Tis a vigil he keeps for his sister." She was crying.

He wanted to touch her, to comfort her, but felt strangely removed from his surroundings. He bent down to pick up his sword and halted with his fingers outstretched. His hand was deathly pale, his skin tinged blue. The hair falling over his shoulders was frost white. Even his weir stripe had been transformed, dulled to a rusting iron gray.

'Twas a destiny he had not foreseen, that he would be so changed, and it gave him a moment's pause to see his flesh limned in shades of icy death. But the moment passed, for in truth it did not matter. He had been born to fight, a dread warrior conceived not in his mother's womb, but in an ancient past. All else was as naught.

Except Llynya.

She was a loss he would mourn.

He turned to her, understanding now her tears, but having nothing to offer—for certes not his ice-riven hand.

"Come," he said. "Battle awaits." 'Twas the only thing he knew.

Elixir led them up out of the Dangoes and took them to where a rough path began its switchbacks up the causeway cliffs. The hound whimpered and yapped while Llynya knelt by his side to say goodbye. He licked her face, and she sang some elfin song into his ear.

When the song was finished, the hound turned and descended back into the cave.

The climb was steep and grueling, but the temperature around them gradually rose. At the top, they were finally free of the ice. Pools of seawater marked the track, and on the other side of the causeway they could see ships, elfin ships. Their silver hulls rode the black waves of Mor Sarff. Their sails were full with the wind, marked with runes proclaiming them of the Daur-clan. Their decks were aglow with dreamstone light, the daggers of three ships' crews held brightly to light the way across the subterranean Serpent Sea.

Llynya was cheered to see the small fleet and used Ara to signal them. Hundreds of blades were lifted in return and a chant taken up by the sailors. When the words reached them, Mychael saw her face pale.

"What are they saying?" The words were in a language he didn't know, though its rhythms were purely elfin.

"They are Daur," she said, giving him a brief, tear-stained glance before returning her gaze to the sea. "And they are calling for a Dragonlord. They are calling for you."

Caerlon marched his army out onto the causeway and caught sight of three Daur ships sailing away from the Dangoes and rounding the southern point of the deep dark.

They were on the run, and none too soon, he thought with grim satisfaction.

If they'd thought to attack him from the south, they were too late. He'd barely made it the last stretch off the Kasr-al Loop himself. Any skraeling who dawdled wouldn't make it at all. The wretched smoke was seeping into every cave and tunnel. His last reports out of Deseillign had the whole desert basin filled with the stuff. Not only was it pouring out of Kryscaven Crater through the southern Rift at a much faster rate than he had planned, it was also finding its way over the northern Rift and backwashing into Rastaban.

The boy would be lost, and Ailfinn.

Any plan he'd had to return had to be abandoned. There was time now only for winning the weir gate—and damn little time for that.

He turned, and with a lift of his hand signaled the skraelings to begin launching the ships, save for Slott's barge. The Troll King would bring up the rear.

"Grazch!" The Dockalfar started the skraelpacks down the causeway, each pack rolling its own ship.

A wisp of smoke wafted by him, making for the open sea. 'Twas rotting stuff, the herald of Dharkkum. Thick as it had become, the fell darkness could not be far behind.

He stepped forward with his whip and lashed the nearest skraelings, exhorting them to greater speed. Before the coming battle was over, the gates would be the only safe place left on Earth.

Chapter 25

Rastaban was deserted. A fouler place Rhuddlan had never seen nor smelled since the last time he'd been there, and it was growing ever fouler with the invading wisps and scent of Dharkkum's dread smoke. His scouts had reported a large movement of skraelpacks to the south, but a few stragglers had been captured by the Liosalfar. A few more had been caught deserting from the main force. Loyalty was not a skraeling attribute.

Nor did they talk much. Grammar being a gift from the gods, 'twas not surprising the godless skraelings could barely speak. Wei knew their ways well enough though, and with Owain's ax hanging over the skraelings, the two had gleaned as much information out of the beastly men as could be gotten.

Ships, the skraelings had said. The packs had rolled a fleet's worth of halvskips through the tunnels to Mor Sarff, anticipating a great battle.

Caerlon, they'd also said, the name coming up

again and again, revealing Rhuddlan's foe and the cause of so much calamity. Tuan's court-mage, the twisted fool who had killed his king's people, had apparently not partaken of the draught himself. Clever Caerlon.

Yet not so clever and far worse than foolish to have used his skills to break the Prydion enchantment on the crystal seals. What did he hope to gain by unleashing such destruction on the earth? Rhuddlan wondered.

As to the nature of the spells he'd used, Rhuddlan had only one guess—the *Elhion Bhaas Le*. With the Indigo Book of Elfin Lore and five hundred years to study it, even a half-taught mage like Caerlon could have set a blight on Riverwood and conjured another army's worth of skraelings and—conceivably—cracked the damson shafts holding the earth against Dharkkum and destroyed the enchantments binding the Troll King in stone.

Aye, but mayhaps the fool's cleverest deed had been keeping the Indigo Book hidden from Ailfinn for five centuries.

She had been there. Rhuddlan could see signs of her in the Eye of the Dragon, the Troll King's court. Stone did not speak to him as it had to Tuan, but the mage's presence and her power had left marks on the rock. Caerlon would not have taken her without a battle, and the walls and pillars in the Eye were flashed with fire scars underscored with a brilliant vermilion luminescence, Ailfinn's signature blend of metallic vapors.

He turned to Wei. "Do they know of any prisoners?"

"They had one," Wei said, his voice tight. "Shay. But they say he died on the trek to Rastaban. He shouldn't have died, Rhuddlan. The boy was not sorely wounded when the skraelpack cut him off from the rest of us. They say their captain delivered the body to Caerlon."

Despite the grievous note of the tidings, Rhuddlan felt a flicker of hope. He remembered Caerlon's habits, and from the look in Wei's eye, so did the elf-man; and any who remembered Slott's penchant for *tylwyth teg* would know the only way to get an elfin boy by the Troll King would be as carnage, real or faked.

"If he lives, time can heal the other," he told Wei.

The Liosalfar nodded in agreement, though anger hardened his gaze.

"And Ailfinn?" Rhuddlan asked.

"They've seen no one else, but many of them were called to Rastaban barely a month past. Some have only been here a fortnight."

Rhuddlan stepped to the nearest pillar, a granite column a full twelve feet around incised with serpentine scales. He laid his hand on the long fire scar flashed up its length. 'Twas as cold as the stone it marked. Ailfinn's fire was powerful *magica,* burning two days at full strength before beginning to wane, the heat of it lasting much longer. That the vermilion-edged soot retained no detectable warmth meant at least a month had passed since she'd been in the Eye, and mayhaps much longer—too much longer.

"The dungeons?" he asked.

"We've found naught in 'em so far, but there's three levels, and the Liosalfar are still searching." 'Twas Owain speaking.

"Four levels," a voice said from behind Wei, and Varga stepped forward out of the pillar's shadow. " 'Twas rumored during the Wars that Rastaban possessed an oubliette, a 'forgotten place' carved out of its darkest depths. If it exists, it would lie on a level separate from the other cells."

"Did the rumors say where these dark depths were? Or tell of a path?" Rhuddlan asked. Varga had come with them willingly, knowing he couldn't be left in Carn Merioneth except under heavy guard. For himself, Rhuddlan had seen him fight, and the Sha-shakrieg was welcome as an extra sword.

"Only that 'twas a well-hidden cold box and that none had ever escaped it or come out of it alive. The Sha-shakrieg feared it almost as much as they feared Rhuddlan of the Quicken-tree."

A cold box, Rhuddlan thought with disgust, ignoring Varga's wryly delivered praise. Given the nature of a troll's appetite, 'twas not surprising no *tylwyth teg* had ever ascended in one piece. That Slott and his brood might have eaten their allies with the same gusto as their enemies was oddly unsurprising.

He looked to the ceiling of the Eye. Smoke was collecting in its corners, thickening even as they stood there. Soon 'twould taint all the air in Rastaban, the hall and the tunnels alike, and begin taking its toll on his soldiers.

He shifted his gaze to the pillar and the flash-mark traced 'round with vermilion. Ailfinn had been there, and might yet be in Rastaban. No matter how faint the possibility, it took the decision out of his hands.

He could not leave the Troll King's demesne while there was a chance the Prydion Mage was locked somewhere in its depths. For certes Wei was not leaving without overturning a few boulders in search of Shay.

He checked the smoke again and estimated 'twould be half a day before they would have to retreat. Yet he dared not hold his army that long with Caerlon sailing down the Serpent Sea toward the gates of time.

"Treilo," he called to the Lord of the Wydden, and gestured for the others to leave him.

A man clad all in gray broke from the ranks and gave Varga a long look. Tall and lean like a Quicken-tree, the man had blond hair with a distinct reddish cast. He'd been in the Wars and still showed the brand of the bia-steeped thread that had caught him across the face.

"You'll take the troops to the gates of time," Rhuddlan said when Treilo reached his side. "Two forced marches through Riverwood will see you there. Tell Llyr of the ships and Caerlon. If the Dockalfar and skraelings are not already at his throat, they soon will be. When you reach Riverwood, send a runner to Carn Merioneth. Of the three clan-troops left to guard the keep, have two descend. If we can't hold the gates, we'll not hold Merioneth."

The Wydden lord nodded his assent. "And you, lord?"

"Wei, Owain, the Sha-shakrieg, and I will search for the oubli-ette." Although his word was law, Varga was safer with him than with a troop of *tylwyth teg,* many of whom had served in the Wars.

Treilo gave the ceiling a brief assessing glance and returned his gaze to Rhuddlan. "Be sure and watch your back."

"And you yours. There may yet be skraelpacks in the tunnels or awaiting you in Riverwood."

"Aye," Treilo acknowledged, hesitating a moment before continu-ing. "I fought by your side in the Wars, Rhuddlan, but we've neither one of us dealt with this."

" 'Tis why we need Ailfinn, and why I'm staying to find her."

"We need more than Ailfinn," the other man said succinctly. A faintly purple line ran through the eyebrow he lifted in question. The bia scar ran onto his eyelid and continued diagonally across his nose and cheek to his jaw. In the other direction it crossed his forehead before disappearing into a sleek fall of reddish blond hair.

Rhuddlan met his eyes, unwavering. "Have Naas light her fire. If the Druid boy doesn't come out of the ice, I will call Ddrei Goch and Ddrei Glas."

The Wydden was still unsatisfied. "It's been more than fifteen years since the dragons have broken the waves of Mor Sarff, Rhuddlan, and this is war, not the normal cycle of the dragons' lives."

"Aye," Rhuddlan said, sharpening his gaze. "Out with it then."

"You are a dragon keeper, lord, but will they fight for you? This is what the other elfin lords ask. And what of the Magia Blade?"

Rhuddlan knew what the lords asked. He'd asked himself the same questions a hundred times since he'd returned from the Dangoes to Merioneth and found Mychael gone. He'd yet to come up with an answer to the first. No one had fought with the dragons since Stept Agah. The way of it had been lost to time. Ailfinn would know, if she could be found, for the dragons were of the Prydions' making, or mayhaps Naas had seen a way somewhere in the past of bending them to his will, but that was no assurance that he would succeed.

As to the Blade, there would be no *druaight* sword for him or any other warrior to wield. The truth of that had awaited him in Rastaban.

"I fear Deseillign is falling," he said to Treilo. "The smoke is coming in strongest from the passages opening onto the Rift. The desert must be choking in it, and with the desert lost, so are the forges of the Sha-shakrieg. There will be no Edge of Sorrow for us to put to a dream-stone hilt."

The Wydden lord agreed with a curt nod, revealing that he, too, had drawn the same conclusion, but he would have an answer to his other question. "And the dragons?"

"They were ever beasts of war," Rhuddlan conceded, "and with Dharkkum arising, they'll have the bit between their teeth. If Mychael ab Arawn hasn't survived the Dangoes, and if I can't bring them to heel—*and* if we defeat Dharkkum"—his mouth curved in a chiding grin—"then you'll have years of glory ahead of you, fighting dragons." He reached out and rested his hand on the Wydden lord's shoulder. "Safeguard the weir gate, Treilo. 'Tis the crux. We'll be no more than a half day behind you."

Treilo held his gaze but a moment before making his obeisance, and he held the bow a moment longer than he'd held Rhuddlan's gaze—a wise decision.

Without waiting for Treilo to begin his march, or even to rise from his bow, Rhuddlan signaled for Wei, Owain, and Varga to follow him up the giant's staircase on the east side of the great hall.

Caerlon's solar had been gone through and naught of great interest had been found, except for a pile of worn and dirty clothes. Wei took one sniff of the rags and declared the owner.

"Caradoc."

"Christ's bones," Owain swore, striding forward and stabbing the pile with the point of his sword. He lifted a tunic and bared his teeth. "So the wormhole spit him out, did it? I would have a go at the bastard, aye, and I think I'll string him up before I bloody the whoreson with my blade. What say you, Varga? Do ye have any of those wicked threads to spare?"

"For Caerlon's ally? Yes." The Sha-shakrieg smiled beneath his gauze coverings. Varga never took the bandages off, not completely, only arranged them differently for eating, or to add warmth, or to shield his eyes. In this he was no different from any of the spider people. The starshine of Deseillign burned with a force that sank deep into exposed skin, making it far wiser to stay covered. Desert city dwellers enjoyed more freedom from the need of bandages, but Varga was a man of the sand, Varga of the Iron Dunes, and his cautions were well ingrained.

"Come," Rhuddlan said, turning away from the solar above the Troll King's court. "We have our task before us and not much time to see it done."

They met the Liosalfar doing a final check on the first level, and Rhuddlan sent them on their way to join Treilo. The four of them split up then, Wei and Varga checking cells and tunnels to the north, Rhuddlan and Owain descending into the warren of the lower dungeons via a long curve of stairs.

Cell by stinking cell they worked their way through the levels. Owain checked every seam and crack in the rock. If any had ever wondered where Rastaban's privies were, Owain and Rhuddlan found them. The Quicken-tree man gave Owain a length of cloth to bind over his nose and mouth to help stem the stench.

Finding naught on the second level, they went down to the next. At the bottom of the stairs, a wide corridor opened to the south. Fouled rushes littered the floor. Owain's torch had guttered itself, and Rhuddlan set a new one alight for him with his dreamstone.

"Check the cells on the east side," he told Owain. "I'll go down the west."

"Aye," Owain said, his voice a muffled grunt beneath the cloth.

Rhuddlan turned to the west, and Owain entered the first eastside cell, crossing himself as he did.

"Bloody skraelings," he muttered, crossing himself again. For extra measure he moved his fingers in a warding sign he'd learned at his mother's knee in Denbigh in northern Wales. Denbigh's priest had taught him a few others, the man being more Celtic than Catholic, and Owain used them all as he worked his way down the cells. Grim tortures had taken place in the dark holes. Rusted fetters and gyves were bolted to the walls and floors. Barbed chains with dangling hooks hung from the ceilings. Fire pits had been dug in some, and charred bones were to be found in their ashes. A broken rack testified to one cell's past.

Toward the end of the passage, sweat broke out on Owain's brow, and an eerie, tingling sensation crept along his skin, making the hairs rise.

"Hold on, man. Hold on," he cautioned himself in a low whisper. He'd seen many a strange and ofttimes wondrous thing since joining up with the Quicken-tree. God's truth, though, in his whole life and countless battles he'd not seen anything as gruesome as the offal sumps and dungeons of Rastaban.

He dragged his torch over the back wall of a cell and found nothing. When he entered the last cell in the block, the eerie sensation heightened to an alarming degree. Rhuddlan was far behind him in the passage, working more slowly, which gave Owain pause. If something awful was going to happen of a sudden, or if he was going to see a troll the likes of Slott, he'd as soon have Rhuddlan close by. Ever since the Liosalfar had brought word of the Troll King, Owain had felt a special dread at the thought of the Thousand Skulled One. In all his life, he'd never imagined anything like the *pryf,* but he'd imagined trolls quite clearly as a wee lad, and he was shamefully afeared of 'em.

Shamefully.

His one weapon against them had been his firm grip on a reality that did not include children's nightmares. Then the Liosalfar had returned from the Dangoes, and his nightmare had become real. Slott of the Thousand Skulls, Troll King of Rastaban, not only existed, but was loose upon the land.

"Hold, man," he muttered again, casting a wary eye about him. Seeing naught, he swept the east wall with light in search of oddities, but got no farther than halfway across when the southern wall began to hum. 'Twas a low, rumbling sound, seeming to come from deep below. A troll sound, by God, if he'd ever heard one.

He turned with a shout on his lips, torch held high. "Rhuddlan!"

The elf-man was already running toward the cell. A faint trembling shook the floor. Or mayhaps 'twas just him, Owain thought. For certes he was trembling from every hair, though he was frozen still as stone where he stood. Christ, but the troll would make short work of him. Down him in one easy bite, the beast would, and leave naught but his boots still stuck to the granite floor.

"Rhuddlan!" he yelled again, and the Quicken-tree King was beside him.

" 'Tis naught to fear, Owain," Rhuddlan said, a note of excitement in his voice. The Quicken-tree touched him on the arm as he passed, and Owain found he could move. He took a step back, waved away by Rhuddlan's hand.

"Stand clear," the elf-man said.

A weak skittering of golden light danced down the humming wall. A crack opened up in the stone and grew wider, wide enough for a man to slip through. Rhuddlan leaped toward it and disappeared.

Owain didn't move, dazzled as he was by the skittering, dancing light bursting out of the opening. The crack continued to widen, the slow, grinding noise it made adding a rough resonance to the humming sound. He took another step back just as Wei and Varga came rushing into the cell.

Owain flushed to have been caught in retreat, but Wei and Varga didn't seem to notice.

"Asmen taline!" Wei hollered over the growing noise and the high whining bursts the flashing lights seemed to make. Then he and the Shashakrieg leaped through the crack in the stone and disappeared.

Owain forced himself to step forward. 'Twasn't a troll, he knew that, but 'twas sorcery nonetheless, a great sorcery to make such fires that flashed and burned and crackled.

Girding himself for the dash, he drew his sword. With a final command to "hold on," he leaped into the light-bound breach—and near toppled into the waiting abyss. He stopped himself with a flailing of his arms, stumbling backward to safety on the landing.

"God's balls," he swore, staring down into the oubliette. The humming and scattering of light was coming from a shaft of golden light that shone down the center of the prison. Great sparks of color flew out of the shaft and lit the walls, painting them in reds, greens, and golds. On the far side of the prison, he could see Wei and Varga racing down a curve of stairs hewn out of the rock. Around the other side of the golden light, Rhuddlan was kneeling on another landing, and beside him was Shay.

From where Owain stood, he saw Rhuddlan raise his sword over the boy and bring it crashing down. His breath stopped in his throat as icy blue sparks flew up from the boy's chains. Then Shay was free and on his feet.

Rhuddlan paced the landing, watching Ailfinn turn within the light of Tuan's Stone. 'Twas the charged force of the crystal holding her, that and some rotting *sídhe* dust Caerlon had thrown into the mix. Given time, he would wait until the new moon to free her, when the crystal's strength would be weakest for lack of sunlight, either direct or reflected. But there was no time for waiting.

Below Ailfinn the pages of the *Elhion Bhaas Le* whipped back and forth in a fury. He could help her, if he could get to her, yet there was naught on her flat-topped prison that he could see for him to throw a rope around, and 'twas a rotting long way to jump.

Behind him, he heard Owain make his way onto the landing. A choking sound immediately followed. He turned and found the Welsh-man white-faced, staring at Varga's arm as the Sha-shakrieg rolled up his sleeve. Tightly coiled whorls covered the spider man's flesh, all of them shining damply in the golden light.

Rhuddlan lifted his eyes and met the Sha-shakrieg's dark-eyed gaze in silent understanding. There was a way.

Varga chose a gray coil to start and dug his fingers in around its edge to pull it off. Fluid oozed up to fill the space, and Owain choked again.

" 'Tis only *pryf* silk and bia seepage," Rhuddlan told the Welsh-man, "and naught to lose your supper over."

With the coil in his hand, Varga eyed the distance to Ailfinn's rocky pillar. His throw sent the whorl flying out over the abyss. The silken thread uncoiled in loop after graceful loop, the gray glinting like silver in the flashes of light, until it hit the side of the pillar with a resounding thwack—and stuck.

Two more threads followed in quick succession, one below the first and the next below the second. Varga secured each end of the threads to the wall above the landing.

" 'Tis not a web, but will work as a bridge. If you can free her, it will hold you both."

Rhuddlan tested his weight against the threads. They were like silk, so thin, yet tough, and growing harder now that they'd been exposed to the air. He'd crossed Sha-shakrieg webs in the Wars. Some of them had been traps, with killing threads woven in with the web threads. He'd seen more than one *tylwyth teg* meet a painful death in a sizzling, poisoned, tangled knot of some Sha-shakrieg's making.

He stepped out onto the bridge and when it held, sprinted across. When he reached the pillar, he gestured for Shay to come. He would need help if Ailfinn was unable to walk—if he could free her. The boy made nimble work of the crossing and came to stand by his side.

"The pages weren't moving so fast a few days past when they started turning," Shay said.

"Aye." Rhuddlan ran his hand over the curve of golden light. The power of it pressed back against his palm.

"Is she looking for a spell?"

"No spell." Rhuddlan shook his head. "She doesn't need more magic, she needs less. Wei!" he called back over the abyss. "Give me your blade!"

Wei moved to the edge of the landing and with a sideways toss slung his dreamstone dagger out toward the pillar. Shay caught it in the air.

"Heat it up," Rhuddlan commanded, and Shay tightened his fist around the crystal. Rhuddlan's own blade was pulsing under the pressure of his grip. He believed what he'd told Shay, that less magic was needed, not more. For certes he was no mage to conjure a loosing spell, but with force of arms, he hoped to break the binding spell Caerlon had cast.

A call from the landing had him lifting his head. Wei gestured to the far side of the prison, pointing up toward the door. Rhuddlan looked and nodded, then turned back to Ailfinn's prison with grim determination. The smoke of Dharkkum was drifting into the oubliette. Caerlon might yet win the day and lose the world, the mighty fool.

"Bring your blade in behind mine, and by the trees, do not cut Ailfinn. We'll see if dreamstone *magia* can break the hold of Tuan's Stone."

Shay nodded, and Rhuddlan slashed into the golden shaft. Blue sparks flashed all across the line of the cut and showered down on them.

Rhuddlan cut again through the light with his crystal blade. A wisp of white smoke arose from Ailfinn's robe where the fresh sparks landed.

Shay shadowed his every move as he sliced line after line through the golden light. More smoke billowed up around them, 'til Ailfinn was discernible only as a still and floating form imprisoned in luminescence.

The graceful arcs of colored fire falling into the abyss grew larger and more frequent. Though Ailfinn was not moving, Rhuddlan could feel the strength of her will forcing the fiery light away from the shaft, creating the rainbows of falling stars. He cut again, and thousands of the *sídhe* dust-motes burst into flame and flew outward, extinguishing themselves in the inky darkness of the pit.

On the next flashing stab of his blade, a woman's voice cried out, Ailfinn's voice.

"Dana Lianei!"

A wind rose from the abyss, swirling around the pillar of rock. Rhuddlan stepped back and held his hand out to stay Shay's blade.

"Astareth!"

The golden light wavered.

"Conc de Le!"

The white smoke spiraled up around her, and as Rhuddlan watched, Ailfinn's left hand slowly curled into a fist, tighter and tighter, until the tendons in her wrist stood out in stark relief against her pale skin. The remaining motes of *sídhe* dust floated toward her and slipped between her fiercely held fingers, disappearing one by one into her fist. When the last mote was captured, she flung her hand open.

The lights went out, all the lights. Rhuddlan's blade as well as Tuan's Stone. The torches on the landing stopped flaming. Wei's blade ceased to burn.

There was nothing but utter and complete darkness from every quarter. Darkness and the faint scent of Dharkkum.

Then Ailfinn's voice. "Take me to Kryscaven Crater, Elf King. We have work there."

'Twas the Prydion, for certes, Rhuddlan thought, a smile breaking across his face. Though little given to sentiment, he was thoroughly heartened that she had the strength to command. Nonetheless, the tidings were dire. "It is lost, Ailfinn. The crystal seal was broken in midsummer, and all the southern basin is filled with pestilence."

Her voice came again out of the darkness, thin and acerbic. "And if it wasn't, would I be needed? Fie, Caerlon. What of Deseillign, Rhud-dlan?"

"Overrun with the same ravaging smoke that threatens us here. We must be gone. Battle awaits us at the gates of time."

"Aye, we're leaving, but to Kryscaven Crater. The battle at the gates is for another to win or lose, Elf King. Know it and obey," she said, intoning words of Prydion prophesy. "Gird yourself, Rhuddlan, for 'tis no mere skraelings or Dockalfar you must face, but Dharkkum. Give me your hand."

He reached out and frail, cold fingers wrapped around his, but no colder than his had suddenly become. Rhuddlan of the Quicken-tree feared nothing on earth, yet there was no denying the dread he felt at Ailfinn's chosen course.

"Meshankara mes," she muttered, rising to her feet. "Battle is, indeed, upon us. Lift your blade."

Rhuddlan complied, and the light rekindled in the dagger's dreamstone heart and burst forth, filling the oubliette with a shining radiance.

"Khardeen!" came the cry from the landing.

Ailfinn glanced up at Wei.

"They are ready to fight, eh?" she asked Rhuddlan.

"Aye," he said. "But not for what you ask."

"They will be," she said. She appeared unchanged from her ordeal, except for the pallor of her face. Fair of brow, the mark of the Star was upon her. Her eyes were a deep emerald green, belying the years attested to by the cloud of white hair falling past her shoulders. Her gown was the same emerald green beneath her tawny cloak. Her kirtle was silver shot through with gold, matching the gold-inlaid silver rings and bracelets adorning her fingers and wrists.

From a pouch on his belt, he offered her seedcake.

She took a small bite, and a much larger drink from his catkins gourd.

"We have no time for delay, Ailfinn. Shall I carry you?" he asked, and for his efforts received a long, slanted look from beneath her lashes.

"Unlike you, Rhuddlan, I have no contention with the faerie folk, and as Tuan's Stone both held and sustained me, so did the *sídhe* dust. You could eat the stuff as well as I, if you could keep from choking on it." She turned to Shay. "Come here, boy."

The young Liosalfar took a step closer, looking both hesitant and awed, and she reached up and smudged him beneath each eye with her left thumb. Saffron-colored dust shimmered on his skin.

"You're not afraid of faeries, are you now?" she asked, and Shay shook his head. "Good." She took his hand. "Now light your blade."

Shay squeezed the dreamstone in his other hand, and Wei's dagger shot forth light. On the landing, the elf-man reignited Owain's and Varga's torches with a sulfur twig from his fireline kit.

" 'Twas you who woke me, fair child, with your whispered songs," she said, "and for that I'll set you to the lighter task. To Riverwood it is with you, and from there to the weir gate. Tell the elfin lords their king is to Kryscaven. Caerlon will have reached the far shore of Mor Sarff hours past, and if the *tylwyth teg* have troops there, the battle will have begun." She looked to Rhuddlan, and he nodded. She returned her attention to Shay. "But you will not miss all. Blood and gore there will be aplenty before the day is won."

"The dragons?" Rhuddlan asked, knowing their task was hopeless without Ddrei Goch and Ddrei Glas. 'Twas no minor breach of crystal the mage would face with him and the others, but a ravaging plague of darkness said to twist the mind and steal the last breath from a body, a darkness that could not be fought with either will or blade.

"They will not have forgotten the way home or their life's labor," she answered him. "They are the devourers of darkness." She made a dragon sign across her breast. "With the stench of Dharkkum on the air, their blood will draw them back to the nest as the dragon-spawned son of Rhiannon is drawn. Destruction is the name of the three together, and as their joined power grows, Dharkkum will seek them out. Fight they will, to the death and beyond as Stept Agah did, but if we fail to seal the Crater, the darkness will eventually overcome even the dragon born. You had best set your mind to Kryscaven, Rhuddlan, and the seal we must conjure out of the mother rock, for 'tis the deed we manage in that deep and fiery pit that will tell the tale for many a long year."

Chapter 26

"Here? Or there?" Naas murmured to herself, looking from one narrow crack in the quartz to the next one farther down on the tunnel wall.

"There," a voice said from over her shoulder. Snit was his name, so he'd told her, and 'twas a bargain he'd made for his freedom.

A sturdy little trap it had been, Naas thought with satisfaction. He liked his cloak well enough, and for the price of a new tunic and boots—with runic-inscribed silver rings tinkling from their laces—he'd promised his help and his company on their trek to the gates.

'Twas taking a bit longer than Naas had planned, though, to find the cache she sought. They had been up one side of the Canolbarth and down the other, a good trick of late. Soldiers were everywhere, and she knew she, too, must soon hasten to the gates. Sounds of battle were echoing through the rock. The *tylwyth teg* could hold against the skraelings, of that she had no doubt, but Ddrei Goch and Ddrei Glas were cresting the waves of the Irish Sea, and none alive were prepared for the dragons in their battle against Dharkkum, not even Mychael ab Arawn, not yet.

Messengers were continually being sent from Mor Sarff to Merioneth, and she heard the passing news. Fighting was rampant all along the eastern wall of the Serpent Sea and north along the Wall into Dripshank Well. Twice the skraelings had been repelled from the damson cliffs, but the *pryf* nest had been invaded and a skraelpack was yet holding out in the labyrinth. Lanbarrdein had been breached from beneath the falls by boat and barge, and Slott was sitting upon the King's Pool throne.

The Druid boy had come out of the ice. He and Llynya had sailed onto the sandy shores beneath the gates mere hours ahead of the Troll King and his Dockalfar captains.

"There, ye think?" she asked, pointing down the tunnel to the next band of rose quartz.

Snit nodded at her side. A raggedy man-boy he was, more fully grown than he appeared, sharp-eyed and sharp-nosed, with dark scraggly hair and thickly lashed green eyes. He had a *fif* braid tied with a Quicken-tree riband, and his dagger was always ready to hand.

"It'll be a squeeze," she warned. "But if ye find the book, the reward will be great."

"Boons and prizes, ye said." The retort came back at her with a narrowed gaze.

Naas cackled. "Oh, I've got baubles and pretties aplenty for ye. Aplenty, oh, aye."

Following along behind them, Madron watched the byplay with barely restrained impatience. Naas and the boy had searched a hundred places in the Canolbarth so far, all to no avail. They were looking for a book, and though Naas had not named the tome, Madron knew there were few books of such importance that they could keep the old woman from the battle raging below. 'Twas one of the Seven Books of Lore. It had to be, specifically, the *Chandra Yeull Le,* the Yellow Book of Chandra, the Merioneth priestesses' book.

Three of the Seven Books had been presumed lost for centuries, if not millennia. Naas, though, would not have kept the *Elhion Bhaas Le* from Ailfinn, and in truth, no lonely hole in stone could have kept the Indigo Book hidden from the Prydion Mage on its own. Great intent had been required to conceal the mage's book of secrets. The *Treo Veill Le,* the Green Book of Trees, had been lost in the weir, in time, leaving only the priestess tome unaccounted for.

Why Naas suddenly needed the *Chandra Yeull Le* when she'd known—at least generally—where it was, and why she hadn't brought it forth before now, was a mystery Madron would like answered, though 'twould surely be at Naas's discretion. The crone did not bend to anyone's will, and she'd spoken to no one except Snit since they'd come below. Nearly as intriguing, and for certes more disturbing, Naas had taken Mychael's Red Book of Doom from the boy's hiding place in the boar pit and brought it with them, along with the newly recovered Blue Book of the Magi.

Madron had thought it a blessing to have always known the whereabouts of the Red Book, but to be suddenly close to having three of the seven at hand gave rise to all sorts of possibilities. There was power in knowledge, and the Seven Books were steeped in knowledge from the Ages of Wonders and the Dark Age, times so far in the past they were lost to this world—except mayhaps in dreams, where memories that were passed down through the blood were given to rise.

As to Naas's newfound confidant, Madron had known about the will-o'-the-wisp and somewhat of his origins, but unlike Naas, she had not felt a need to trap him. Ceridwen and Lavrans had both spoken of their friend in need who had seen them safely through the bowels of Balor during the battle, and then disappeared.

"Up with ye then," Naas said when they reached the second vein of quartz and its narrow crack.

Corvus Gei came forward and helped the ragged boy up into the opening.

Madron watched the small hunchbacked figure disappear into the luminescent stone with Naas's dreamstone. 'Twas on the hilt of her dagger like the other Quicken-tree's, but Madron kept hers on a gold chain. For her purposes, a necklace was a more subtle means of enchantment.

At her side, Corvus did not appear to be suffering from the same impatience that beset her. He'd been very subdued since descending into the caverns.

And who in his position wouldn't be? she thought, knowing what awaited him. The pouch of universal salts she'd been instructed to bring weighed heavily on her mind, if not her girdle. Rhuddlan had sealed the tunnels that led into the weir gate, but Naas was not concerned with ether seals. The battle was to be considered, but battle alone was no deterrent to their goal. Morgan ab Kynan, the Thief of Cardiff, had met his doom in the very midst of battle.

A journey through hell, Corvus had called the wormhole, and his greatest desire to descend again was near to being granted. Madron knew all the Christian visions and levels of hell, having spent many years in Usk Abbey in South Wales. Corvus must know the same from his time on Ynys Enlli, yet he still used the horrific place to describe what awaited him.

"Hand me your light, child," Naas said, her hand out for Madron's dreamstone.

Madron slipped the chain over her head and gave the crystal to the old woman, as anxious as she to see if the book would be found.

"How are ye, Snit?" Naas called into the nether regions of the crack.

The muttered reply she got in return seemed to suffice. She set up a tuneless humming and absently looked up and down the tunnel. When her gaze settled again on the opening, she bent forward and tapped Madron's dreamstone on the quartz. Pieces of the rose-colored crystal chunked off and fell to the floor.

"Well, there ye have it," she said. "Just a cheap priestess spell."

" 'Twas a seal?" Madron asked, surprised.

"Aye. One not meant to last so long."

"For the *Chandra Yeull Le*?"

Naas shot her a discerning glance. "Don't look so smug, child."

"But I thought the book was stolen by a Douvan king."

"And what do you think the price was for its return?"

The price must have been great, Madron thought. No king would squander such a prize, and no wonder the priestesses had hidden it and let the world go on believing it lost to thievery.

But would it still be where they'd put it? Thousands of years had passed, their Age and all its glory had disappeared but for the remnants lingering in Merioneth. For certes their seal had not held—if the white-eyed woman had finally chosen the right spot to look.

Naas suddenly cocked her head.

"Rich, rich, rich," came the sound of Snit's voice echoing off the crystal walls of the broken seal. 'Twas accompanied by the soft tramping of his feet. "Baubles, she said. Pretties, she said. Rich, rich, rich."

Corvus stepped forward, and Naas lifted Madron's dreamstone high to light the opening. Quick enough, Snit was there and handing over a cloth-bound package nearly half his size.

Naas's hands trembled as she set it on the floor and began untying the ribands holding the wrapping in place. Slowly, the layers of silvery green cloth slipped away, revealing the unmistakable luster of gold and a fortune's worth of sapphires, amethysts, garnets, and pearls. The jewels encrusted the hammered gold cover in a symmetrical pattern, leaving hardly a place bare of brilliance. Beads of gold outlined the border and drew the eye into the cover's central gold figure, a naked woman. Stars shot out from the hands of her outstretched arms; a crescent moon crowned her head. Rivers of milk flowed from her breasts. From her womb came the peoples of the earth and all the beasts, man and animal alike twined 'round with flowering vines that sank their roots deep into the earth she stood upon. Radiance surrounded her, fine lines depicting light chased into the gold like the sun's rays.

"Now we can go to the gates of time," the old woman said, gathering the priestess book into her arms.

Mychael slogged through the sands of Mor Sarff. Dead skraelings were everywhere, and indeed, in places their blood poured like small rivers into the Serpent Sea. Battle had helped bring him around from his odd detachment, as had the sleep he had gotten on the Daur ship, but his blood still ran strangely cold, and his skin was not so warmly flesh-toned as it should have been. He had an icy grip on his sword. 'Twas as if his dragonfire, the source of so many of his doubts and so much of his pain, had gone out, smothered by the dark smoke.

If 'twas true, he should feel free, when all he felt was bereft. He'd lost something vital in the Dangoes, something of his life. It had been taken by the swart thread of darkness that had descended in the ice cave.

Llyr shouted at him from up on the wall of the *pryf* nest, pointing to the southeast. Mychael looked, then waved back at the Ebiurrane lord. The Kings Wood elves were returning from Dripshank Well, and Mychael had been given orders to use them to hold the eastern shore.

The Dockalfar and their skraelpacks had retreated back onto the water. 'Twas the third time the *tylwyth teg* had repelled them. Each time it took the enemy longer to regroup, and Llyr had ordered rest and food in the interim before the next assault.

Fires were lit all along the shoreline, from the rocky cliffs of Lanbarrdein to where the Magia Wall bordered Mor Sarff on the east. The great expanse of the damson cliffs shimmered with dreamstone light, with flames from the fires reflecting on the crystal trails cut into its face. Treilo of the Wydden had arrived during the last attack and his troops had routed Slott from the King's Pool throne. The Troll King now sat on his barge, floating again on the Serpent Sea. He was such a daunting sight, overlarge with his tail slapping against the waves and raising fountains of water, his cries of hunger sending a shiver down every elf's spine, that Llyr had wondered aloud if he'd not been better left in Lanbarrdein where none could see him.

There were still skraelings in the *pryf* nest, but those the worms hadn't crushed were being searched out by the Red-leaf clan.

The Daur had moored their ships along the coast, from Lanbarrdein to the gates. The ships of the Dockalfar had clashed with theirs on every assault, with two kharrs lost to three of the skraeling halvskips. Those of the Daur crews who hadn't drowned were fighting with the Quicken-tree on the sands, for 'twas Trig who had held the gates of time against the repeated invasions.

Everywhere along the shore and cliffs, Liosalfar were taking their repast and tending to their wounds. At the first notice of battle, Nia had been taken to Merioneth to be cared for by Aedyth and Moira. Few others were left above beyond mothers and children.

Llynya was with the Quicken-tree on the sand. She was sitting with a group of Liosalfar around one of the fires, sharing a silver flask of the Red-leaf's potent brew. Her hair was messier than usual, more un-bound, dark swaths of it falling to her waist. Dirt streaked her face. Mychael started to lift his hand to her as he passed, but a chill rippled through him, killing the impulse before he could act on it, and his hand remained at his side.

She'd been hurt. One of the warriors was tending a cut on her arm. She winced as the Liosalfar smoothed *rasca* on the wound, and a spark of some nameless emotion flickered in his breast. Then it, too, passed, and he walked on, rubbing a hand down his left side, trying to bring warmth to the cold scar that had once held dragonfire.

Shay had come only a few hours behind Treilo, bearing both joyous and somber tidings. The mere sight of him had cheered the Quicken-tree. Ailfinn had been found and freed, he told them, which heartened all the *tylwyth teg,* for even the most battle weary among them smelled the thickening smoke drifting up from the south. 'Twas to this, the deadliest threat, that the Prydion Mage had set herself, taking Rhuddlan, Wei, Owain, and the Sha-shakrieg as her companions to Kryscaven Crater. The elves would not have their king to lead them in this battle—and mayhaps never again. None underestimated the danger Ailfinn was leading her company into by taking them to the southern basin.

Mychael, too, smelled the reeking smoke. He'd seen the dark, ephemeral wisps floating in on the waves, forming and re-forming with the vagaries of the wind. He'd felt their cold caress during battle, tiny brushes of the lifeless night blown leeward onto the shore.

The skraelings were not immune to its frigid bite either. They flinched with the same horror as any other living creature when the dread stuff brushed against them. Yet 'twas their lord who had unleashed the smoke. Caerlon was his name. Treilo had brought the information back from Rastaban, learned from skraeling deserters.

Mychael started around the headland toward Dripshank Well and met the returning Kings Wood elves.

"Ho, Mychael," the man in the lead hailed him. 'Twas Kenric, one of the trackers. Like most of the Kings Wood elves, he was heavier built than the Quicken-tree and carried a yew longbow nearly as tall as himself. His hair was still dark, framing a face with broad cheekbones, a square chin, and a once broken nose. For one so young, his gaze was surprisingly shrewd. The Kings Wood tunics were varying shades of brown, with Kenric's being a rich russet color.

"Kenric," Mychael called back. "We are to the Wall."

Kenric nodded and turned to his troop, gesturing to the rope and wood-slat bridge the Red-leaf had made, connecting the shore of the damson cliffs to the eastern part of the Wall. The Red-leaf lived in the trees in the northern forests and used their ropes and abundance of wood to make walkways in the sky, bridging one arboreal abode to the next. They had strung a good many such bridges in the last two days: a bridge behind the falls at Lanbarrdein, another from the *pryf* nest to the top of the damson cliffs. They had bridged the canyon that opened up below Dripshank Well.

Mychael brought up the rear as the troop filed onto the bridge, falling in step with the Kings Wood trackers. A rough-hewn bunch and seasoned warriors, they expected nothing from him except that he would fight, which suited him well. The Kings Wood clan lived closer to Men than the other *tylwyth teg*. He thought mayhaps that was why Llyr had put them under his command. His position among the other elfin lords was not so simple.

He had once been their hope, but that hope had died. There were no dragons coming to Mor Sarff, and he was not the Dragonlord to answer the Daur's call. Two days of pitched battle had brought no sign of Ddrei Goch and Ddrei Glas. He was alone, except for the growing darkness. 'Twas the only truth he'd brought out of the ice cave, that the darkness was a black death and he had been born to fight it—but alone, not with the dragons by his side as he'd thought.

In the fight with the skraelings and the Dockalfar, his blade had been blooded, aye, but not as it had appeared in his vision. He had killed a good many of the enemy, and as he had not been wounded, neither had many of the Liosalfar who had fought with him. Behind his blade they were as safe as was possible in a close fight.

'Twas that knowledge and the battle itself that sustained him, and where Llyr sent him, he would go, until the end came—and his end was coming. He sensed it with every breath. He had failed to call the dragons to him, and for that weakness he would die. He smelled as much of death as did the vile smoke arising from Krys-caven. The elf-maid had said Death had been in the ice cave, and she'd been right. 'Twas the touch of death's darkness that he'd carried out of the Dangoes. 'Twas impending death that had frosted his hair and turned his blood cold.

Halfway across the bridge, he noted a rise in the wind. The waves capped below him, showing violet in the dreamstone light. The scent of salt strengthened, brought in from the Irish Sea down a long, dark channel. In front of him, Kenric stopped and looked to the west. The wind rippled along the tracker's tunic.

The Kings Wood elf stood perfectly still, his eyes closed, until a fresh gust came up and caused the bridge to sway. His eyes opened as he reached for the rope railing.

"What is it?" Mychael asked, grabbing hold of the rope as well.

"*Sín,*" Kenric said. "There's a storm on the open water."

"Can a storm from the Irish Sea reach this far?"

"This one will," the tracker said with grim surety, and continued across the bridge.

Mychael looked to the west and lifted his face into the quickening breeze. Aye, 'twas there aright. *Sín,* a storm.

He again turned his gaze to the sands. Llynya was watching him from where she sat next to Shay. She made no sign of acknowledgment, but her gaze was steady on him.

Sparks rose on the wind from the Liosalfar fire, sheeting upward in a glittering cascade, yet through the fiery veil, through the shadows and the chaos of soldiers traversing the sand, Mychael could see her clearly. She was the aetheling, and where the Liosalfar's hope had died in him, it had been reborn in her.

Camp rumors had her drawing a magic sword out of the mother rock and saving them all. She was a good fighter, but he didn't think she could fight the growing darkness and prevail, and in his heart he knew she couldn't call the dragons and bring them to heel.

He let his gaze drift downward to her arm. Blood dampened the bandage. The easier battle had not yet been won, the one against Caerlon and the skraelings and the great Troll King riding out the waves on his barge, his skulls clinking in the breeze, and she was already wounded.

Nay, they should not have put the burden of victory on her. For as he had failed, so would she. As he would die . . .

He stopped the thought with a violent curse and walked on, turning his attention back to the Wall.

Llynya watched Mychael cross the bridge and climb to the trail on the other side. His was a ghostly figure among the Kings Wood elves. She'd given up crying, but the ache in her heart threatened to break her. Verily, it increased in strength and pain every time she caught sight of him, and if too many hours passed without her seeing him, the pain turned to panic.

He'd fought on every front of the last three battles, his sword singing a death song to the skraelings. The Liosalfar followed him when ordered by Llyr, but not without caution. His troops had suffered the fewest losses, true, but he himself was marked for death. Some said he was of the half-dead already, his skin showing the grave.

Sweat trickled down the side of her face, and she wiped at it with the back of her hand. Though a cooling wind had picked up off the sea, she was suffering from heat. The exertion of battle, she was sure, though no one else around her looked as feverish as she felt, and they'd all fought hard.

She took another swig from the Red-leaf flask, her gaze following Mychael on the Wall. She'd lost him in the Dangoes. The last words he'd spoken to her had been on the causeway, and they'd been as strangers since. He would look at her as he'd just done, but no more often than any other warrior on Mor Sarff. They were all looking to her as the aetheling since they'd seen the way it was with him, their failing Dragonlord.

The Red-leaf brew cooled her throat, but not her brow, and she wiped at it again with her good arm. The other arm hurt terribly, making her wonder if the skraeling blade that had cut her had been poisoned. More than likely 'twas just the filth of the sword's edge causing the wound to burn.

Her last hope to save Mychael had been Ailfinn, but Shay had dashed it. Ailfinn was not coming, and in truth 'twould be a miracle if the mage could save herself and her company.

Another, deeper pain flared in her chest. She had lost Mychael, and there was no time to mourn. No time.

Tucking a strand of hair up into her braids, she looked across the beach to the gates. The wind was visibly moving over the sand, picking up in force and speed, feathering the grains and in places spiraling them up into the air. The clothes of the dead soldiers were fluttering and snapping, giving them the odd illusion of life. Trig had ordered the tunnels kept sealed, but she knew how to open the one that had held Bedwyr, and one was all she needed. When Mychael died, she was going down the wormhole.

A day back, she'd yet been holding on to the strange hope of taking Mychael's body to the Dangoes, if the worst befell him and naught else was to be done. She'd thought to seal him in the ice next to Rhayne, praying the white hound could protect him from the ice-bones and the demon darkness of Dharkkum, and praying the ice would hold him until he could live again. But the foul billows of smoke massing in the south made going back to the Dangoes impossible.

Nay, she'd lost him on all counts.

A great roar from the Troll King's barge had the hairs rising on her nape. All around her, the Liosalfar cast surreptitious glances her way. 'Twas her blood the Troll King was calling for, but he would be denied by the wormhole. She brought the flask to her lips for another cooling swallow.

Aye, he would be denied.

Chapter 27

Madron stood on a little used trail on the northeast boundary of the *pryf* nest, her cloak wrapped around her against the driving rain, watching Naas on the trail below. Sounds of *"Khardeen"* carried to her on the wind, along with the clash of swords and thunder rumbling against the vault of the Serpent Sea. Her father had told her of such storms beneath the earth, but she'd never seen one. 'Twas a daunting sight. Lightning skittered across the walls and ceiling, crawling over the rock. The thunder went on interminably, echoing back and forth.

Corvus and Snit flanked her on either side, and they, too, were watching the white-eyed crone chant into the dark, using a song-charm to lure an ancient beast up out of the deep. Madron smelled the old worm before she saw him. His was the darkest scent of the earth distilled down to its most potent essence: rich loam and batholithic stone, must and decay. The smell rolled over them like a wave, and beside her, Corvus hissed on an indrawn breath and took a step back. Snit moved closer to her, taking a handful of her sodden skirt for courage.

When the old worm himself glided into view, Snit would have broken and run, if not for the man's hand snatching him by the scruff of the neck.

" 'Tis the crusher, I tell ye." The little man squirmed, trying to break free. "He'll grind yer bones into dust inside yer skin. I've seen 'im do it, I have."

"Hush," Madron commanded. "We are not here to be crushed."

"Then why call 'im?" Snit asked.

"To churn the worms," she answered, not taking her eyes off Naas.

". . . vessel of matter and thought, of the eternal mystery and miracle of life, death," the old woman intoned, her voice rising and falling through the rain with the rhythm of the final words to be spoken. "Circling, ever circling and being coiled round and warmed by a great serpent devouring its own tail . . . held in the grip of wisdom. Lightning of the cosmos! Sword of the gods! One is All—*Ouroboros*!" She called out the name, and the gargantuan worm, gnarled and scarred by immemorial time, picked up speed, the last of it coming out of its deep hole beyond the Magia Wall, while its faceless head made for the gates of time.

Well pleased, Naas looked at the group above her and signaled for them to follow. She smelled the blood of battle. Far more ominous, she smelled the smoke of Dharkkum through the fury of the storm. Time was running short. She would be done with the traveler.

He'd been unexpected, and a less likely carrier she could hardly have conjured herself, a criminal with a violent past. But he was here, and he wanted to be there, and betwixt and between the two was an immeasurable expanse over which he could carry the books. For certes she couldn't drop them down the hole on their own. Even if Corvus died, his corpse would land in the right place, in the right time, which suited her needs well enough, and the needs of those she would help, the White Ladies. Of course, she was also certain that since they had gone to the trouble of sending him here, the White Ladies most probably did not want him back there.

Men, she thought with a hmmph, a means to an end, a means to an end. Such was the rule. Still, she didn't envy him the journey.

They followed the dirt trail down to the north base of the damson cliffs. The old worm had his own entrance into the inner core, though few dared to take it. Naas was one who did and herded her flock before her into its dank depths. They came out into a rough-edged tunnel and followed it to the first intersecting passageway of luminescent green and heliotrope, one of the gates.

Once inside the headland, the old worm began moving at an alarming speed, barreling through the crudely bored tunnel that circled through and connected the shimmering gates. Naas quickly ushered the others into the large cavern at the heart of the cliffs.

Corvus wiped the rain from his eyes, scarcely believing what he was seeing, or that he was seeing it. The wormhole lay before him, far more immense than anything he had imagined, a gaping abyss alive with chain lightning and the writhing swirl of *prifarym*. He moved closer and the lightning crackled, bluish white and purple sparks soaring toward the domed ceiling.

A memory flashed in his mind, and icy fear gripped him. He'd longed for this moment, hardly dreaming it would ever come to pass, and now he could think only of the horror of what he would do.

The worms in the upper nest had amazed him, their greenish black bodies wet with slime and smelling of the earth. But he sensed a difference here with the worms of the weir, and most definitely with the great beast sliding through the outer ring. These were the time worms.

"Eat yer salt," the old woman commanded, coming up behind him and shoving a bag at him.

He near jumped out of his skin. He did let out a startled sound, which set the crone to cackling.

"Hear now, hear now. No need to fret. Once yer in the hole, you'll not keep yer wits about ye for more'n a bit. No more'n a sleep is it after that, a nice long sleep."

Small comfort, for he remembered "the bit" before sleep very clearly—painfully, terrifyingly clearly.

"Eat," she reminded him, giving his arm a jiggle.

He looked down at the bag in his hand. "All of it?"

Her answer startled him anew. "Well, let me see, then." She snatched the bag away from him and hefted it in her hand. "Ah, now, 'tis true that havin' the perfect weight of it in yer body is important, quite vital. So many grains of salt for so many stone o' weight." She pinched him around the middle, gauging his weight, he supposed. A worried frown creased his forehead. "They must've given ye a just so amount when they dropped ye the first time, eh?"

And she had just told him to eat a bag's worth, and was now trying to figure his weight with a few hard pinches.

"In solution," he told her, slipping out of his rucksack. Water ran off the pack and pooled on the floor where he set it. Terror or no, he was going. He'd carried her books for her, and a goodly share of their supplies, but he'd also been allowed to bring a few of his own things. One was a scale, roughly calibrated, true, but a scale he'd devised for just this purpose—to measure the chrystaalt, providing he had any when the time came.

He put the scale on the rock floor next to the pack, and for the first time, noticed the intricately incised grooves snaking around the rim of the weir. More mystery, he thought, running his hand over the elaborate pattern.

"No time for that," Naas clucked. "Get on with it."

He'd planned on making the leap even without chrystaalt, but faced with the reality of the deed, he wondered if he would have had the courage, or if the lack of it would have been the voice of reason telling him to stay.

The precise calculations for figuring the amount of salts were in Nemeton's book, and Corvus had figured it thousands of times for his body weight, checking and rechecking, and all the while wondering where he would ever find the chrystaalt.

He took the bag from Naas and carefully poured some into one of the scale's pans. It was similar to sodium chloride, only heavier grained and with a yellow cast. The crone knelt down and added a pinch more, then another, and another, until the bag was empty and his roughly calibrated scale was perfectly imbalanced.

"There ye have it."

He looked at the tilted contraption, thinking of the time he'd spent over the years, figuring his dose to the nearest half a gram, and then figuring it again. He looked to the old woman and the gourd she was holding out to him and, in a rare act of faith, poured her measure of chrystaalt into the water. She stoppered the gourd with her thumb and gave it a good shake.

"Now drink," she said, handing it to him.

Before he could think, or change his mind, Corvus lifted the gourd to his lips. When he was finished, he looked down to find Naas going through his pack.

"Ye'll not need this, or these." She tossed aside his food kit and the leather jacks of water and brandy, his own distillation.

"It's a desert on the other side," he said.

"You'll be found quick enough," she assured him, "and you're going to need room for the Yellow Book."

His interest piqued, and he shot Madron a glance. The woman hadn't let the priceless antiquity out of her grip since Naas had given it to her to carry. No matter how badly his fortunes had fared in the future, he could rebuild with such a prize.

"Aye, take a good look," Naas said. "You'll not be seeing it again."

No, the White Ladies would take it from him before he recovered his senses, but he'd robbed their temples before and already was relishing the thought of doing it again. Perverse bitches to have tried to exile him to this forgotten time.

"Madron, bring the *Chandra Yeull Le,*" Naas ordered, but as Corvus had expected, the woman balked.

"Naas . . ." she began, her arms tightening around the heavy tome.

"I'm leavin' ye the Prydion book, so don't bother about the priestess pages, pretty though they be. The *Chandra* and the *Fata* are needed in the future."

With palpable reluctance, Madron obeyed.

With his pack again on his back and the chrystaalt flowing through him, there was nothing left for him but the wormhole. Snit, the cowering child, was off huddled against the wall, trying to hide in his cloak.

"Come." Naas took his arm and led him to a place on the rim. She knelt and threaded a silvery length of *pryf* silk through the grooves on the floor, then stood and shook out her skirts. "Would ye like me to give ye a good push? Or do ye think ye can manage on yer own?"

No hint of compassion softened the hag's questions, and he knew she would as soon push him and be done with it.

"On my own," he said.

Muttering under her breath, she left him.

Logic told him not to look into the weir, but logic would have also dictated that he stay in the twelfth century, and he was going. The path lay directly in front of him.

His gaze scanned the perimeter of the rim before daring the central depths. The worms in the deep were golden, swirling around the weir in aureate waves. Lightning cracked and leaped up out of the abyss, blue-white branches of pure energy reaching for the ceiling. A dark cloud of mist formed in the wormhole and began to rise, coming for him.

Corvus watched the cloud and felt fear take hold of him again. His breaths shortened and quickened, adding to his panic. Would it be like this then? he wondered. A fall through an eternity of terror? Then, in the weir, he saw a glimmer of light, like sunshine glinting off the sand and a flash of golden hair . . . *Avallyn.*

From a short distance away, Madron watched the lone traveler balance on the edge of time. She felt his hesitation, his fear. There should have been bodhran drums and a chanting chorus to fill the weir with the rhythms of heaven and earth, an assurance that the fall was not out of God's grace. Or rather the music would have been an assurance to a mage or a Druid. Mayhaps not for a felon.

Something assured him, though, for as she looked on, he slowly lifted his arms to his sides. Head back, chest lifted, he fell forward, his body making a perfect arc into the abyss. Lightning forked out of a billowing cloud of jacinth mist, snaring him in its tangs and dragging him down.

Madron watched him disappear, half in horror, half in envy. Felon or nay, he had embarked on the greatest journey the world had to offer. He was a traveler through time. Beside her, Naas waited until the lightning simmered into faint crackles of light.

"Come," the old woman finally said. "We have another world to save this day."

"To starboard! To starboard!" Caerlon screamed into the wind, gesturing wildly.

Slott's barge crested again on the port side of Caerlon's ship, riding a towering wave, and Caerlon froze in place, terrified that this time the barge would come crashing down on him.

The storm had blown up out of nowhere. There had been some rain, a bit of a breeze, but nothing to warn of a tempest. Violent gusts of wind and rain whipped the sea into gigantic waves and ship-sucking troughs. He'd lost three halvskips and countless skraelings. The battle was a shambles. 'Twas every beast for himself.

The barge slipped out of sight off the back of the swell, and Caerlon frantically continued tying himself to the mast. He'd wanted to get closer to the barge, but not that close.

"Dragons!" He spit the word out, his fingers fumbling with the wet rope. "Rotting dragons!"

They had ruined him. The Indigo Book spoke quite clearly about the creatures, and it said where there was Dharkkum, there would be dragons. But none had come. The pestilent smoke was pouring onto Mor Sarff, near choking him on every breath, and Ddrei Goch and Ddrei Glas could not be bothered, the rotters.

The gates. He had to get to the gates of time, but the shore could not be won.

He pulled one soggy rope end through a last loop and tugged on the rope. It should hold with one end tied around the mast and the other around himself; he needn't fear being swept overboard. He'd left enough slack in the rope too, so he could move somewhat out of the way of crashing waves, if need be. "Rotting Quicken-tree," he muttered, looking again to the beach. He'd seen the rotting aetheling among them, rallying them at every turn. The warrior on the Wall was another to be reckoned with. Icily pale and white-haired with an odd weir stripe, he was from among the half-dead, Caerlon guessed, harvested from the Dangoes, no doubt. And a dire day it was indeed when the fair and favored Quicken-tree resorted to such necromancy as it must have taken to raise him.

He had his own dread warrior, for all the good the cripple could do him without the dragons.

"Bring Wyrm-master up!" he yelled to Blackhand Dock, his ship's captain.

The Dark-elf signaled the helmsman and went below. When he returned, he had Wyrm-master with him. The Dragonlord's bad leg had been braced with a good strong wrap of leather, and he'd been given a boiled bull-hide gambeson, a mail shirt, and an iron helmet with a long nose guard. Caerlon had the Magia Blade strapped to his own waist. He'd debated whether or not to give it to his bedraggled Dragonlord, and decided 'twas best if he didn't keep it for himself. Alone, without skraelings or Dockalfar to give him away, he could pass for a Light-elf.

The strange sword would only draw unwanted attention. His plan was to sail to the Irish Sea, hopefully leaving the dreadful storm behind, and from there to quickety-split—alone—through Riverwood and make for the gates by going through Dripshank Well. There were backways and byways aplenty in the caverns, and if he was seen, he'd be wearing the tunic of one of the drowned Daur.

He was not deserting his army. Rather, he was accepting the foregone end. His strength lay in strategy, not hand-to-hand combat, and neither Slott nor his Dockalfar captains could benefit from any more strategy, however brilliant. The best he could do for them was to give them a Dragonlord and the Magia Blade, such as they were.

To that end, he unceremoniously clapped the mighty sword around Wyrm-master's waist and sent him over the side with Blackhand Dock into a dinghy. His suggestion to Blackhand was to make for the barge, as the shore was certain death. Chaos reigned on the sands, but it was a chaos overrun with *tylwyth teg,* not skraelings.

"Hard to starboard!" he yelled above the wind to his helmsman. The sails were reefed. 'Twould be up to the oarsmen to get them away. The incentive was strong, to be gone from the battle and the choking, smothering smoke.

The skraelings pulled against the wind and the waves, turning the ship to the west and open water. Far enough out, they headed south, fighting their way into the channel. Halfway down the narrow mouth, they suddenly sailed out of the storm into a sea of calm. Relief weakened Caerlon's grip on the mast. The storm was of Mor Sarff alone and had naught to do with the Irish Sea. Thunder and lightning still echoed behind them, but close to the ship there was naught. He could hear the gentle lapping of water against the strakes with each pull of the oars. The air was sweeter, the future brighter.

They sailed to the northernmost point of the channel, leaving the sounds of battle to the Serpent Sea. As they rounded the point, though, Caerlon was surprised and dismayed to see the storm roiling again ahead of them where Mor Sarff emptied into the open water.

A bewitchment? he wondered. Who could have contrived it, a pool of serenity in the midst of a storm? But mayhaps not so serene, for even as he wondered, the water began to bubble around them. He lifted his dreamstone high against the surrounding gloom. Yellow light glinted off the small waves churned to life by the odd bubbling. He caught a glimpse of movement beneath the surface, a flash of red in the liquid shadows, and excitement surged through him. Another flash, this time of grayish green, nearly sent him into paroxysms of giddy laughter.

They had come!

Victory was yet at hand!

He squeezed his dreamstone harder, making it shine brighter, creating a beacon for them to follow. The dragons had come!

But mayhaps they were coming in too fast, too hard. A red-tinged wake parted the waves, a rippling arrow of swells heading straight for the halvskip. Caerlon took a step back, his tether trailing on the deck. On his next step, he tripped, his foot tangling in the rope, and 'twas thus that he met Ddrei Goch, flat on his back, staring up as the great beast's head broke the surface in a rush of bloodred scales, golden eyes, and ivory teeth running green with seawater. Fangs the length of a ship's mast glowed with reflected dreamstone light, a pair of them, one on each side of the bow, carving a death gate out of the darkness.

The skraelings dropped oars and raced to abandon ship, but Caerlon was tied to the mast. He clawed at the knot, fear making his fingers stiff, and in the next moment the mighty jaws closed and the halvskip was no more.

Forced back by the driving rain and the waves breaking against the Wall, Mychael had ordered a retreat to the beach. He'd fought the last skraeling to come up the trail from the south, killing him at the bridge with one cutting blow. Nearly all the Kings Wood elves were across to the damson cliffs, a dangerous endeavor made one man at a time, hand-over-hand on the wind-whipped ropes.

Neither side had won the last engagement on the Wall. Both the skraelings and the Liosalfar had been overcome by the storm, an incarnation of Mother Nature as virago. The thunder was deafening. Lightning skittered everywhere when it hit. He'd lost soldiers to crashing waves that washed the trail clean and to gusts of wind that plucked men up and dropped them into the sea. The skraelings had fared no better. If any were left on the exposed face of the Wall, they wouldn't be for long.

Mychael grasped one of the bridge ropes with both hands and waited for his chance to cross. The bridge had literally been blown to pieces by the storm, with ropes torn loose and fraying, and many of the wood slats reduced to splinters. Such did he feel inside, splintered into a thousand sharp shards. The strange feeling had begun with the rising of the storm, and like the storm had not abated, but grown in strength. 'Twas a yearning, a terrible yearning, that had taken root in his heart and made his pulse race. The icy numbness that had encased him in the Dangoes was a blessing in comparison with the growing flood of emotion. Better to have remained frozen than to be pulled along by this fierce tide, helpless.

When Kenric reached the damson cliffs, Mychael started across. Out on the sea, ships were being tossed and sunk. Slott's barge had run aground on the beach, and the Troll King was wreaking havoc among the troops who had not found shelter either to the north or up in the *pryf* nest.

Mychael recognized Quicken-tree Liosalfar in the melee, among them Trig and Llynya. Hundreds of skraelings had landed with the troll, along with a Dockalfar captain and a crippled man whose yellow hair streamed out from beneath his helmet. He wore Slott's brand on his upper arm, but he'd not yet been turned into a skraeling. The part of his jaw that showed beneath his helmet was not overly pronounced or beholden of fanglike teeth. The Kings Wood elves were joining the fray, and Mychael plunged in behind them.

Shortly into the battle, he realized all the cutting and dodging of the skraelings was for one purpose: to isolate the aetheling and drive her toward Slott. The Troll King's bellows added to the chaos. His voice, like no other, rumbled off the cliffs, garbling words and noise into a cacophonous assault on the senses. Those who had been weakened by the fight could scarce endure it, and when Slott roared his war cry, some fell where they stood—a grim fate, for he ate even in battle.

Seeing that the worst of the fighting was around Llynya, Mychael fought his way toward her, hacking away right and left at the beast-men, drawing ever closer to the ax-wielding Slott. The Quicken-tree would fail if she was lost. Though final victory would be denied all of them by the pestilence of Dharkkum, she did not have to fall to the Troll King.

Slott was huge, broad in every way and thrice as tall as the tallest man, though his back was hunched. His tail twitched and whipped behind him, sending his enemies flying. Before him, his ax rose and fell with terrifying monotony as he made his way up the beach toward the aetheling.

The Liosalfar with her fell back under the giant's assault, and Mychael felt the stirring edge of panic take hold. Slott was running her troop off, while the skraelpacks were keeping her from escaping, forcing her onto the southernmost trail leading into the *pryf* nest.

All of the trails were littered with bodies, some even of the great worms that had been butchered by the skraelings. Soon Llynya was trapped against the nest wall, bounded in by dead worms and Mor Sarff. Mychael saw her look to the sea, the surf crashing on the jagged rocks below, and he cried out, *"No!"*

She leaped then, away from the edge, Slott's ax missing her by a hairsbreadth. When next the Troll King swung his blade, 'twas one of the dead *pryf* he hit—but not so dead, for as the greenish black skin opened up, the worm turned and a keening wail rent the air. The *pryf*'s green life's blood ran out onto the trail and poured over the side into the sea. Slott lunged for the elf-maid and, with a cry of triumph, snatched her up in his fist.

"By the Stones!" he roared. *"By the Stones of Inishwrath!"*

Fury swept through Mychael, and the yearning that threatened him took on new force. With a cry of his own, he rushed forward, his sword in one hand, his dreamstone dagger in the other. Llynya's screams echoed in his ears as he cut and slashed a path to the trail. The skraelpacks closed in behind him, but none could stop him, until they shoved the yellow-haired warrior into the circle they'd made.

The man bore down on him, forcing him away from the trail, fighting with far more finesse than a skraeling. He was taller and heavier than Mychael, with a longer reach, and his sword was wondrously strange, limned with a gridelin edge. He fought like a blade-master whose technique had been honed in war.

"Wyrm-master!" The call came from above, from Slott, and the chant was taken up by the skraelings.

"Wyrm-master! Wyrm-master!"

Mychael heard Trig shout to him from the beach, but he couldn't discern the captain's words. What he could discern, when he dared to glance up, was the terror on Llynya's face—but to reach her, he first had to conquer his foe.

The Wyrm-master's limp made him vulnerable to a swift attack, and Mychael did not hesitate to deliver one. He darted in under the glittering sword's arc, moving nearly as fast as Llynya in a fight, and cut the Wyrm-master twice, a nick to his chin with Ara, and another shallow cut to the man's thigh with his sword. Wyrm-master retaliated with a

lunging strike that pushed Mychael backward into the waiting skraelings.

A pair of rough hands seized him, and Mychael ducked and
rolled, taking the eager skraeling with him. Wyrm-master's blade came
down where he'd been, catching the skraeling instead. The beast-man
screamed in agony, and Mychael smelled burning flesh where steel had
cut through mail and skraeling with equal ease. The beast-man released
him to writhe on the ground, the stump of his arm smoking with the
acrid scent of poison. Mychael leaped to his feet, ever more mindful of
the Wyrm-master's sword. A blade that could cut through chain mail
deserved added respect. That it was poisoned demanded extra caution.

"You're quick to escape," the yellow-haired warrior said, "as your
sister was ever quick, Mychael ab Arawn." He advanced on Mychael
with his sword raised. "But not quick enough!"

The sword sliced through the air, aimed for Mychael's middle,
and only a lightning-fast pivot saved him from the gridelin edge.

Caradoc was grinning beneath his helm, playing the boy for his
moment of glory. Slott had dared to brand him, but he'd been well fed
since taking up with the skraelings, and he'd been well armed for battle.
Even the little weasel Caerlon had been helpful with his healing salve.
Rasca, the Dark-elf had called it, and it had taken the pain from his leg.
He still limped, but the injury no longer hindered him.

"Aye, I knew your sister," he said, relishing the confusion on the
younger man's face. He lunged again, but the boy was quick. Damn
quick. Spent too long with the green ones, he had.

The sword Caerlon had given Caradoc was dazzling, with yellow
crystals illuminating the hilt and grip, but it was also poorly balanced
and unwieldy. Still, it would be enough to win the day against Rhiannon's whelp.

Above, in the worm's nest, Slott had captured the means to an
even greater victory. The Troll King had a live Quicken-tree. 'Twas the
lavender woman, though any one of the green guard would suffice for
Caradoc's means. He would have their knowledge of the wormhole.
Christe! He was so close, he could hear the golden worms calling to him.
He could feel the charging power swirling in the hole.

But first to Mychael ab Arawn. The sister had eluded him in the
spring, so her brother would harvest the revenge. A curse on all their
line!

He swung his rich sword again, and again missed the friggin' boy as he darted away like a dragonfly in flight. Ab Arawn's strike rang more true, and Caradoc was suddenly blinded, his iron helm set askew by a ringing blow. He twisted the thing aright, his grin turning to a grimace of pain and anger taking the place of reason.

"I knew your mother too, boy, even better," he taunted, and went in for what was to be his killing blow, but the boy parried and cut him.

Caradoc howled with rage, one hand coming up to his face to stanch the blood from the boy's last strike. The bastard had nearly taken an eye.

"Wyrm-master! Wyrm-master!" the skraelings shouted around him. He wanted to tell them to shut up so he could think, but the boy struck again, another blow to his head that set his helmet askew again and his ears to ringing.

God's balls! He clawed at the ill-fitting helmet, dragging it off before it was the death of him.

His hair came falling out of the iron helm, yellow gold with a bright auburn blaze, and Mychael stumbled back, shock draining the strength from his arm. 'Twas Caradoc, son of the destroyer—and Mychael remembered. The last of Dharkkum's death touch left him, melted away by a flood of living pain, as he suddenly remembered everything he'd seen in the Dangoes.

His sword fell to his side, leaving him helpless. He stood facing his mother's murderer, her rapist, and the effort to breathe was more than he could bear. Here was the man who had set the course of Mychael's life by taking Rhiannon's.

Caradoc came at him then, and instinct alone lifted Mychael's sword in defense. He deflected the blow, and the next, retreating, until instinct gave way to anger, and anger to heat, a raging heat that roared to life in his blood and turned retreat into attack, a relentless attack as every fiber and thought in Mychael's being vowed to beat the Boar of Balor into hell.

It was butchery. Nothing more. Nothing less. Fueled by sick fury, Mychael gave no quarter. Every blow was for blood. On the beach behind him, the Liosalfar rallied for a fresh assault, and the skraelpack circling him and the Boar dispersed into renewed battle, leaving the two of them alone in the chaos.

Mychael left no weakness unexploited. Spurred by a hate so strong he tasted the bile of it in his mouth, he cut and slashed, sliced and thrust, and parried each of Caradoc's attacks. 'Twas as it had been in Dripshank Well, when he'd been on Llynya's trail. The skraelings had fallen then under his knife with powerful ease, and he had not been injured. Neither could the Boar connect a blow with his cutting edge, yet he bled in a dozen places from Mychael's blades. Blood ran into his eyes from the swipe Mychael had taken to his forehead with the dreamstone dagger. His nose was broken from feeling the flat of Mychael's sword.

Mychael knew the instant when Caradoc realized he was going to die; he saw the flash of terror that cut through the blood lust in the Boar's oddly colored eyes. His mother must have looked the same when her time had come, or had the terror come before, during the rape?

A horrible agony cut through him, the cry of it strangling in his throat. The bastard had raped his mother. He wanted to kill Caradoc a thousand times, and even a thousand times would not assuage the pain.

Mychael cut him again and again, until Caradoc was at his mercy on the sand, a bloody pulp, half-blinded by blood and wheezing through his smashed nose. With no satisfaction, and no sense of justice, he took the Boar's own poison-edged blade and impaled him through the heart, cutting through mail and gambeson to the depraved flesh beneath.

A great roar sounded from above, bringing Mychael's head around. Up on the trail, Slott set Llynya aside and took his ax in both hands with another great roar, Wyrm-master's master coming to match himself against a dread warrior. Llynya was limp on the ground, and as Mychael watched, the wounded *pryf* rolled over her, gathering her beneath its soft, dark body, removing her from the line of battle. Wild though they were, he'd not yet seen a *pryf* hurt a *tylwyth teg*. He prayed this one was no different.

Bruised and battered from the days of battle, he retrieved his own sword and set himself to meet the Troll King. Whatever skill had protected him from Caradoc and the skraelings, 'twould not be enough to withstand Slott. Speed would help against such a giant, but speed alone would not suffice. A thousand victories dangled from the troll's braids, each ivory skull a testament to combats won, to a barbarism beyond what Mychael had ever known.

The troll had a rancid smell that preceded him down the trail. He wore no armor, only a vest made of skins. His wiry hair was dark and greasy, the plaits softly clinking and rustling against one another in a susurrus of corruption.

Mychael found himself taking a step backward. 'Twas death advancing on him, slogging toward him through layers of mud and worm blood. He felt the certainty of it down to the marrow of his bones. Blood dripped from Slott's ax. Drool ran from his mouth. One eye was milky, but the other was dark and keen and leveled at Mychael with a killing glare.

The wounded worm that held Llynya let out another keening cry, a death cry, and great shudders rippled down its body, revealing for an instant the small form lying beneath it—still whole. The *pryf* keened again and began to turn, rolling across the trail and up against the troll. Slott paid it little mind, only pushed it back and swiped at it with his ax as he came onward into battle, but the worm would not be denied. It rolled again, and its turning pushed the troll closer to the edge of the cliff. Slott fought back in earnest now as the beast took more and more of the trail from him, but the ground was wet with rain and slick with the worm's blood, making for treacherous footing. Slott slipped in the muck and in a trice the *pryf* was on him. Worm and troll grappled on the edge, until with a final mighty heave the beast sent itself and Slott of the Thousand Skulls careening off the edge of the trail and down the cliff face.

Mychael watched the two giants crash on the rocks of Mor Sarff and be washed into the sea. The *pryf*'s sacrifice had saved him, had bought him time, but it would not be enough. He looked up through the rain and saw the small form yet on the trail, a small form stirring to life. His first sense of relief in days flooded through him, and he took off at a run. She was drenched and shivering when he reached her, the bandage on her arm in bloody tatters, her face drawn and pale, but she was all of life in his arms.

He kissed her cheeks, her brow, her mouth—and lingered, drawing her closer and losing himself in the relief of touching her. She clung to him, her lips coolly sweet, the taste of lavender only faintly detectable. Not so the scent of Dharkkum. A trailing wisp of smoke passed by them, startling him out of the kiss and back into bleak reality.

"Come," he said, pulling her to her feet. "We must be away. The smoke reaches even the *pryf* nest now."

"Mychael?" She looked at him through slightly dazed eyes and lifted a long golden swath of his hair for him to see. 'Twas cut through with the auburn blaze, his *fif* braid bright and plaited down its center. His skin, too, had regained a healthy color.

" 'Twas the storm, I think," he said in answer to her unspoken question.

She smiled weakly, a stark reminder of what they had endured. "I knew you were *sín*. Druids call storms. Did you call this one?"

"Nay, *cariad*. 'Tis this one that has called me." He looked to Mor Sarff, knowing he spoke the truth. The storm had called him. It was still calling to him, though not with yearning any longer, nor with the fury of battle, but with something more elemental—blood. He felt it coursing through his body in a manner he'd thought he had lost, a wild heat grown strong with the pounding of his dragonheart.

Far out on the sea, he saw a shifting flash of color, first red, then green, and the blood quickened with a frightening intensity in his veins.

Thule, he'd been about to tell her. They could go to Thule, to Ceridwen. With luck, 'twould be years before the death of Dharkkum breached the northern wastelands. But their luck, what little they had, had run out. She felt it too, her hand suddenly reaching for his.

"What is it?" she asked.

"Get back. Back against the wall." He pulled her behind him and looked up and down the trail for an opening. They needed cover, and they needed cover fast.

The widening of her eyes and the slackening of her jaw told him 'twas too late. He whirled around to face the sea and saw dragons rising up out of the deep, mighty creatures whose churning pulled the tides, whose blood had called him home.

Ddrei Goch.

Ddrei Glas.

Golden eyes glowed like dreamstones, casting light down their twisting, scaly hides. One dread serpent was ruby red, the other pale green. Both of them huge beyond belief. No painting etched into cave walls, no drawing in the book of fates, but Behemoth and Leviathan incarnate. Fangs and claws and leathery fins, long trailing whiskers and ribbed wings sprouting from their backs like caps of thunderclouds. They swam toward the shore, and every ship left on Mor Sarff was subsumed in their wake.

The Daur who had yet been moored at Lanbarrdein scrambled up the cliffs, their silvery drakars and blue painted kharrs crashing against the rocks beneath them. In deeper water the skraeling halvskips and their crews were tossed and broken by the dragon-made swells.

Panic broke out on the beach, with soldiers of both armies racing for cover into the *pryf* nest or around the other side of the damson cliffs. Watching the dragons, Mychael feared the whole headland would be torn asunder, but the serpents turned before reaching the sand, sending up a wave that dragged half a pack of skraelings back into the surf to drown. Only one person stood unmoving on the beach. Naas.

"The sword, Llynya. Where's the sword?" He turned to her. He had to stop the dragons before they destroyed everything.

"The Magia Blade? 'Twas to be made here, for you. Trig said Varga had sent for the Edge of Sorrow, but Deseillign has fallen and the blade never arrived. There is no sword, Mychael."

He looked to the sword in his hand. It had failed him in the Dangoes and would do the same here. It had not been steeped in the *magia mysterium*. It had no ancient, glorious past, no magic. Wei had forged the blade just last summer. Mychael had made the grip himself out of leather-wrapped wood. The only sorrow it had seen had been since he'd left Tabor above Lanbarrdein.

And even if it had been beholden of some unknown power, he didn't know how to use it. Yet 'twas the only sword he had, and if the dragons were to be ruled by a sword, it would be his.

The dragons made their turn in the channel currents and started back toward the damson cliffs. An opening into the inner maze of the nest was not too far down the trail. Mychael took Llynya to the tunnel entrance and kissed her once.

"Go deep into the nest," he told her, but got no farther before the look in her eyes registered. Wind whipped her hair and the rain drove against them, each drop stinging when it hit, but the elements of the storm were no more fierce than her gaze.

"We're better off together," she said, and when he started to protest, held up her hand. "Nay, 'tis not sentiment, Mychael, nor even love, but the truth. I *am* the Aetheling, Starlight-born, and if you would be a Dragonlord, you are best served with me at your side."

He hesitated no more than a second before agreeing, partly because there was no time to argue with her, and partly because he knew she was right. Whatever bound them had begun long ago, long before he'd first set eyes on an elf-maid wrapped in river mist.

On the shore, Naas had made her way through the dead soldiers and the increasing haze of smoke to Caradoc's body, and was staring at the strange, dazzling sword sticking out of the Boar of Balor. 'Twas to her they went. Trig and a few others of the Liosalfar were doing the same, hurrying down from a different *pryf* trail to intercept them on the beach.

The old woman looked up as he and Llynya drew near, and her gaze narrowed. Silvery strands of hair floated out around her head, given life by the wind. Her cloak was sodden with the rain, her brown gown clinging to her bony frame.

"Give me yer sword, quickety-split now, boy." She stretched her hand out to Mychael, and he placed the grip of his weapon in her palm.

Trig reached them then, giving him a quick once-over even as his attention turned to Naas.

"By the gods, woman, can he set the beasts to their task? Or will we all be choked before this day is done?"

"He'll have to," she said simply, lifting the sword into the dreamstone light coming off the cliffs and peering down its edge. "Hmmph."

Mychael glanced toward the sea. The dragons were cresting again. Ddrei Goch rose up beneath a halvskip and sent it flying through the air like a piece of driftwood. Ddrei Glas slashed at another one with her snout and it crashed into one of the Daur's drakars. Indiscriminate destruction marked their path, and their path led straight toward the beach.

"Am I to have Caradoc's sword then?" he asked curtly. He could think of no other reason for Naas to be by the Boar's body. The thought repulsed him, that he would come by his duty by Caradoc's sword, despite the weapon's brilliant dreamstone-studded grip and its ability to cut through mail.

"Nay." Naas shook her head. " 'Tis a Deseillign blade on it aright, mayhaps the one that was intended for the Magia Blade, but 'tis an abomination now, cobbled together by a dark mage for a fell purpose."

"A mage? It has magic then?" Given a choice between a half-magic blade blessed with sorcery, fell or otherwise, and his own plain weapon, Mychael could put his scruples aside.

"*Auch,* and men always like to think they've got a little magic in their blades." She made a dismissive gesture and knelt down to scour his leather-gripped sword in the sand. "Don't speak to me of magic blades, Druid boy. 'Tis never the sword that gives victory, but the arm that wields it."

She swirled the sword around, working it clean.

"Magic blades, magic blades," she muttered. "I'll give ye a magic blade."

With that, she rose to her feet, wiped his sword on her skirts and, in one neat swipe, cut him from shoulder to elbow. The shock of the deed froze him to the spot. What ran out of the thin, neat line she'd made on his skin set his hair on end. 'Twas blood, but like no blood he'd ever seen. It ran down his arm in a narrow stream of shimmering iridescence. Rainbow blood . . . dragon's blood.

His sword sizzled with it.

"Aye, he'll do," the white-eyed woman said, then nodded to the elf-maid. "They'll need your blood as well to heed the call, child. Let them taste the starlight."

Llynya did not hesitate, but drew her sword down her arm, loosing her blood into the tide lapping at their feet. The cut was not so deep as Naas had made on him, but 'twas deep enough for Llynya's sword to crackle and smoke.

Trig, Naas, and the other Liosalfar remained on the beach, until the dragons' wave began to rise like a wall before them. Mychael didn't see the Quicken-tree go, but he sensed when he and Llynya were alone, two against the dragons. The monstrous heads rose from the swell, Ddrei Goch's eyes piercingly bright, his long, bewhiskered snout cutting across the surface. Ddrei Glas had eyes like the harvest moon, a deeper amber, but the force of her gaze hooking on to him was no less fierce. He was entranced, seduced by the sea-green serpent, and as his blood ran into the water, she was seduced as well as he.

Llynya felt Ddrei Goch's power surge into her. Blood of her blood, they were both born of the starlight. Dragons from the star-wrought cauldron. Her race from the celestial fire set in the nether sea. They were both born to fight Dharkkum.

She lifted her sword with a battle cry. Mychael matched her, and the dragons rose out of Mor Sarff, their wings unfurling from the white-capped foam and beating against the billowing clouds of smoke, bringing them to flight.

Ddrei Goch roared his rage, his screams echoing from the vault to the waves in the lightning-rent cavern of the Serpent Sea. Ddrei Glas lifted her voice into the wind and the rain, and from out of the south, the dark pestilence sealed so long in the crystal chasms came forth to answer their call, a void of night whose touch was cold, whose shape was an ever-shifting vortex without end, and whose single purpose had always and forever been to devour.

Like a blanket made of dancing, whirling threads, Dharkkum flattened and flowed across the surface of the sea, picking up speed before washing itself against the Wall. Where the smoke had ravaged, Dharkkum simply consumed, scouring the trail clean of every living and dead thing and even taking part of the Wall, sucking everything into its core.

The soldiers on the headland broke and ran, skraelings and *tylwyth teg* alike, but their efforts were as naught. One by one, threads spiraled out and pulled them into the warp of darkness, each beast and elf chosen for a death of terrors. Mychael watched in horror as their bodies were stretched to an excruciating thinness and began to dissolve into the black vortex's core. Their cries tore through the cavern, keening to the same bloodcurdling thinness before their final silence, and still the void advanced.

And it grew, a pulsing expansion along its edge for each lost soul it engulfed.

A fresh infusion of fear tightened Mychael's hand on his sword grip, and he took a step back up the beach. Sweat broke out on his brow. The foe bearing down on him was too great. There was no way to fight it, not even with dragons, no way to raise arms against such an empty terror. He saw a thread reach out and snare Treilo. The Wydden lord was dragged fighting into the undulating vortex, lashing out with his sword, his bright hair a spot of color fading into naught. Mychael retreated another step, and then another. His teeth were gritted, his muscles rigid with strain. All was lost. The black matter would be victorious.

He backed into a body lying on the beach and looked down to find himself standing next to Caradoc. The fell sword jutted out from the Boar's chest, its dreamstone hilt casting yellowing shadows across his mailed shirt. Mychael's gaze followed one of Caradoc's outflung arms to his hand. Rhiannon's ring was still on her murderer's finger, a gold band engraved with four lines and a circle inset with a triangle of carnelian. 'Twas a sign he'd seen in the tunnels of the weir, the only sanctuary he'd ever found, and that one too costly to bear. Mychael knelt and took the ring from the Boar's finger and slipped it on his own. If he should die, he would at least reclaim a small part of what Caradoc had taken from his mother. The ring had been the slightest loss, but 'twas all that was left for him. Above him the dragons screeched, and flames burst forth from their mouths. He looked up to see clouds of smoke roiling out of their nostrils.

The vault of the Serpent Sea glowed with their fiery breath and the reflected light of the damson cliffs. Mychael felt the heated wind of their wing beats gusting against him. He felt their fire at his back, and in the next moment felt it light the fire within him, a spark at first that raced along the tinder of his scars and made him burn.

Bright, purifying heat filled him. Flames of dragonfire coursed beneath his skin in a sudden, exhilarating rush. His hand grew stronger on his sword grip, much stronger. The dragons flew closer, screeching at him, grazing him with their scaled wing tips, and in their way, he knew they were urging him on to the end before them. When next they roared, he answered, opening his mouth and letting loose the same terrible cry. The power of it surged through him, and he roared again, lifting his voice into the rain. Wind whipped around him, tearing at his clothes and setting his hair on end, the blazing red and molten gold strands snapping and crackling like fire.

I have drunk the dragon's blood! The voice came to him from out of the past, a priestess's voice from his mother's line.

I have drunk the dragon's blood and eaten of his flesh, and my blood shall be as one with the Red Dragon's, steeped to a potent brew in my womb until in time the fierce creature of my conjuring will be brought forth to battle.

He was the fierce creature the priestess had conjured. His blood was the dragon's blood, and the battle he faced was his to win.

He looked to the swirling dark matter and again to his hand wrapped around the sword hilt. The blade he held would ever be the Magia Blade, because of his hand.

He turned the sword into the light of the cliffs and felt the dragons descend on the beach behind him. They drew closer, wreathing him with fire and smoke, and the last of his fear left him. They drew closer yet, and purpose took the place of his doubts. If Dharkkum would devour, let it devour him and choke on his dragon heart, for he was the beast who would bring Dharkkum to its doom.

In the end, he was the beast who would devour it.

The seas boiled over and the roots of the land trembled with the force of their battle. Turbulent waves swept clean the beaches and shoreline of Mor Sarff.

Chapter 28

The winter became a time of healing for the land and for the *tylwyth teg*. As the deep dark rid itself of the smell of Dharkkum, Liosalfar troops explored farther and farther, searching for Ailfinn and Rhuddlan. But though they scoured the tunnels and caverns from the Rift to the Wall, no sign of the mage or her companions was ever found. Ailfinn was lost to them, along with the *Elhion Bhaas Le*. The King of the Light-elves was dead . . . *long live the king*!

The *prifarym* no longer churned in wildness, and Mychael and Llynya spent the long months setting the nest aright. He left her once in mid-November, traveling north to a monastery in Gwynedd to have a mass said for Owain. The stalwart Welshman had befriended him in a time of need and was sorely missed. Mychael would not have Owain's soul troubled by the enchantment surrounding his death. After the winter solstice, he and Llynya descended into the dragon nest below Lanbarrdein to prepare it for the mating that would take place on Beltaine in the spring. One year hence, Ddrei Glas would return from the dragons' far northern lair to spawn and die, and a year later, Ddrei Goch would come for the hatching and join her in death. There would be new dragons to raise then, two culled from the *pryf* larvae. And so the cycle of the dragons would once more be united with the rhythms of Merioneth.

Calan Gaef had come at the end of October, a sennight after the smoke had cleared, and a small ceremony had been held in the Cavern of the Scrying Pool. With Madron by his side, Mychael had drunk the dragon wine and opened the doors of time, becoming the *Beirdd Braint* of the Quicken-tree, but not their king.

That night the dragons had sung out on the Irish Sea, and he and Madron both had seen a future that would take him away from the land of his mother. Nemeton's steps were his to follow, not Rhuddlan's, and 'twas to Wydehaw Castle he and Llynya would go after Beltaine, to the Hart Tower. Within the coming years, there would be journeys to Yr Is-ddwfn. In February, at the fire festival of Imbolc, Moira set out on that trail herself, taking news of Ailfinn's passing and the promise of Llynya's return.

Unexpectedly, after so many months of freedom, the elf-maid's malaise came upon her at Alban Eiler, the vernal equinox, when darkness gives way to light. Holding her in his arms, Mychael, too, felt Morgan's endless fall through time. For two nights and a day, he gave her what strength he could to keep her from her terror, talking to her as the damnable force that bound her to the Thief threatened to consume her. In time, the malaise passed. And in time, the day for leaving Carn Merioneth came.

The groom, Noll, was the first to see the ethereal pair appear as if by magic out of the early morning mist. Like spirits they came, riding faerie horses of purest white, their green hoods draped low over their faces. To any and all who ever asked, he said their mares had walked across the top of the Wye that morn, their hooves naught but breaking the surface of the river.

He stumbled more than once in his haste to reach the great hall and arrived at his lord's table covered in muck from both the lower and the middle baileys.

"Milord, milord," he said breathlessly, collapsing in front of the dais where Soren D'Arbois was breaking his night's fast. The Lady Vivienne, it was to be supposed, was still abed, mayhaps suckling the heir born three months past. "Riders approach!"

"How many?"

"Two, milord."

"Their standard?"

"None, milord, but they're from Faerie for certes." After his tangles with the mage of Wydehaw, who had disappeared a year past and—it was hoped—would never return, Noll had become the resident expert below the salt on all things magical.

Above the salt, his reputation did not carry quite so much weight.

The Baron of Wydehaw looked down his hawklike nose and waved him away. "Begone, knave, until you have your wits about you."

Noll started to protest, but was waylaid by instinctive self-preservation. The baron's mood had improved mightily over the last year, but he was not without his cruel streak.

Being gone, though, did not of necessity mean leaving the hall. Noll scrambled back from the dais, finding a place with the dogs among the rushes.

Soren called for more ale, doing his best to ignore the groom's absurd announcement, yet keeping one eye on the door. Mages, wizards, witches, wild folk, and faeries—he'd had his fill. 'Twas the damn Hart Tower that drew them, Nemeton's tower. The blasted thing had been empty only a year. Was it possible another *sorcier* would come so quickly to take the Dane's place?

He prayed not. He'd near lost his wife, not to mention a small piece of his soul, to Dain Lavrans.

He lifted his freshly filled cup to his mouth, but stopped before he'd finished the draught, the fine hairs on the back of his neck rising.

The mesne at the tables below did not seem to notice anything amiss. Nor his seneschal. The priest was there that morn, Father Aric, and he twitched a bit, but the man had not been quite right since the Maying a year past.

Nay. None seemed to notice the subtle change in the air that set Soren alert. He sensed it, though, a clearing of the morning light, a brightening of the tapers lit to dispel the hall's gloom. The ale tasted sharper. The scent of the rushes was sweeter.

When his guard came to announce visitors, he found himself inexplicably rising, and he the lord.

Two cloaked and dew-bespeckled figures walked through the great oak door at the end of the hall and awaited his bidding. He beckoned them forth through the chaos of the knights and squires at their meal. Silence descended on the men as the two passed, and Soren found himself wondering if mayhaps the groom had been right. At the foot of the dais, the two removed their hoods.

In all his years to come, Soren never forgot his first sight of the Lady Llynya. Even after she and Mychael ab Arawn had long left Wydehaw, he could recall with startling clarity the fathomless depths of her green-eyed gaze holding his across the table; the twists and braids of her ebony hair and her supple crown of leaves; the shimmering silkiness of her clothes, all green and silver and more like rain sheeting down than any cloth he had ever seen. Her face had been regally serene, yet with a hint of mischief playing about the corners of her mouth. He had instantly fallen in love with a purity of heart he had thought long lost to such a sinner as he.

She asked for little, no more than the Hart Tower, and when he explained that the tower was not truly his to give, but could be won only by whoever could open the Druid's Door, she merely smiled and gestured to the Prince of Merioneth.

The deed was done in record time, and Soren D'Arbois found himself living once more in the midst of magic.

In the fall of the year, Mychael and Llynya made one final trip to Deri, the summering grounds of the Quicken-tree. Trig and the others had already left for Carn Merioneth. Mychael and Llynya had seen them off with a promise to come at Calan Gaef and bring Madron and Edmee, who had spent the summer in their cottage in Wroneu Wood.

Of all the joys in Mychael's life, few compared to watching the elf-maid gather flowers, or sing to honeybees, or tell strange and wondrous stories to the chickadees. She'd taken quite well to living in the Hart rather than the woodlands, though she had planted an acorn in the alchemy chamber when they'd first arrived in Wydehaw, and the thing was already pushing up through the main solar's floor. The tower would someday be consumed by a great oak.

He stretched out on a bed of fallen leaves, looking up between the branches of the mother oak where Llynya sat on a limb weaving her tale to an enchanted audience of small birds.

"There were those of fair, kind hearts, Whistler, White-Eye, and Mast, brave chickadees, who heard the frightened cries, and daring all against the storm flew into the brunt of it to save the maids. Other birds followed, swooping down to the sea, where two dozen to the princess, they plucked the hapless sisters from the waves and saved them all. And if any should doubt the tale, the whole of the valorous flight is forever engraved in the hallowed halls of Fata Morgana's palace."

The chickadees preened themselves, as always, at this sure sign of their bravery. When they were all thoroughly fluffed, they chirped in chorus and flew off to roost for the night. That was what Mychael wanted to do, roost for the night in the nest of leaves with Llyna.

She dropped down from the limb with a lightness he'd learned as well as any elf, and he smiled up at her, welcoming her into his arms. She came to him with an easy willingness that never failed to amaze him.

"Shall we stay out under the stars tonight? Or back to Wydehaw?" she asked, molding her lithe body along the length of his and pressing a light kiss to his cheek.

"Stars," he said, content to lie between the gnarly roots of the oak and watch the night fall around them. There was always work to be done in the tower: formulas to decipher, distillations to be made, books to be read. Nemeton had set a course of study into the Blue Book of the Magi, and Madron was ever wont to come to the Hart and see how he was getting on with his lessons.

Llynya kissed him again, sweetly on the tip of his nose, and his smile broadened. With a slight shift of his body, he had her fully on top of him, pressing down on all the right places to conjure and maintain a steady hum of arousal. He arched his hips to settle her more deeply against him, and the hum became a subdued roar of anticipation.

She knew the worst of him, had seen his darkest side in their fight with Dharkkum, and yet she loved him. She let him come into her body for both pleasure and succor. She lived with him day to day, worked by his side, tended his hurts, and shared his meals—and she knew. She knew what he had become in the battle.

Her mouth came down on his, not so lightly, and he opened himself to her wondrous ravishment, to the gentle thrusting of her tongue meeting his. 'Twas always magic when they touched. No sensory perception could match the speed with which the merest brush of her arm traveled through his entire body, focusing his awareness on her.

She liked to kiss. He'd never in his life dreamed of being the recipient of the number of kisses as she had to give, the sweet, light ones for hello, good-bye, I'm here, you're there, and so I'll kiss you; the wondrously rich and deep ones of drugging intensity when she would bind him to her with her green sorcery; and all the kisses in between.

She was a brave lover indeed to seduce a dragon—for that was what he had become within the cloaking darkness of Dharkkum. Not just in heart and mind, but in all ways a roaring devourer of the darkness; no less destructive than Ddrei Goch and Ddrei Glas, for he had been them—and Llynya had been his master, the temper on his rage, the shining light he'd followed.

They'd both been aged in those dread days, but they'd found youth again in Wydehaw, whiling their days away together in Wroneu Wood. Madron's and Edmee's sadness was one they shared for the loss of Rhuddlan, yet they loved and made love and had found their healing in each other.

When her kisses had driven him beyond distraction, and the soft weight of her on top of him would no longer suffice, he rolled her beneath him. She slid her hands under his tunic and pushed his braies off his hips, freeing him into her palm. A low groan escaped him as she stroked him to hardness, her moves firm yet tender. Being loved by her was everything he'd ever dreamed of and more than he could have imagined. She'd taken him in her mouth that morning, and the soft, wet suction she'd plied on his shaft had been pure enchantment. 'Twas not the first time she'd taken him such, but it always felt like the first time. For himself, he'd kissed her everywhere, tasted her nectar with his tongue and filled himself with exquisite pleasures. They were becoming one.

He removed her braies while she tantalized him with her hand, and at her urging he joined his body to hers. Shared kisses set his rhythm, the silent communication of love that brought them to climax. Even at the end of it, he kissed her, the kisses a benediction on the act and of gratitude to the God who had made her so that he could sleep each night with her in his arms.

In the quiet hours before dawn, she awoke beside him with a start and a soft cry. His hand immediately went to his knife; all his senses alert. Deri was protected by a bramble, yet 'twasn't inconceivable that a stranger had breached the wooded glade.

"Nay," she said, reaching a hand out to him. She'd sat up, and her other hand was pressed against her breast, above her heart. " 'Tis not danger."

He scanned the trees to the river and sensed no intrusion on their idyll. His attention came back to her. "Are you hurt?" he asked, smoothing his palm over her cheek.

"Nay, 'tis not hurt I feel, but a strange loss. The ache in my chest is gone, taken from me."

He knew the implication of that even before she spoke it aloud.

"Aye," she whispered, a beatific smile gracing her lips. "I'm free. Morgan is no longer falling through the wormhole. He has landed."

Mychael gathered her close, his relief matching hers. He looked to the stars wheeling over their heads in the vast, dark sky and sent up a prayer of thanks.

The Thief of Cardiff had landed . . . in time.

> *Look for Morgan's story—available
> in hardcover from Bantam Books
> in fall 1999*

Prologue

SONNPUR-DZON MONASTERY
MOUNTAINS OF THE MIDDLE KINGDOM

A fierce wind howled down out of the mountains and across the stone courtyard, whipping the saffron-colored robes of the monks making their way through the falling darkness to evening prayer. Snow gusting off a nearby glacier swirled around their bowed heads. Ice glazed the rough brick buildings they passed. Behind the monks, a long line of novitiates cloaked in black followed them through the worsening storm.

At the end of the line, a man looked up from beneath the black hood draped low over his head and squinted into the wind. A castellated wall connected the monastery buildings one to the other, running in a near vertical line down the cliff face from which the halls and monks' cells had been carved. Torchbearers were making their way down the wall, heading toward the braziers flanking Sonnpur-Dzon's only gate. Stone towers crowned with dragon heads rose up from the braziers.

Every night since he'd arrived at the monastery, the fires had been lit at sunset, sending flames shooting out of the dragons' mouths. Smoke would curl from the beasts' nostrils, and the night watch would sound the Dragon Hearts. The resonant vibrations from those great gongs would echo like a pair of synchronized heartbeats and reverberate the length of the valley below, calling anyone within hearing distance to prayer.

A wry smile curved the man's mouth. The men outside the walls this night were unlikely to drop to their knees when the gongs were struck, for they were his. The sounding of the bronze Dragon Hearts was their signal to breach the wall. He'd spent a week searching for Sonnpur-Dzon's weak point and two nights in the hypocaust unsealing the grates that led from one level of monks' cells to the next before the last grate opened on the north wall.

The monastery's remoteness had always been its first line of defense. Located in the highest mountain range on Earth, Sonnpur-Dzon clung to the sheer sides and craggy peaks of the Dhaun Himal. No traveler came there except through hardship and design. The nearest village was a hundred kilometers to the south.

Poverty had been their second protection. Sonnpur-Dzon's only treasure had been the boundless bliss achieved through devotion, until three months past when the monks had come into possession of a small gold statue highly prized and eagerly sought by a trader in the west.

The trader had come to him for help, and he, in turn, had come to Sonnpur-Dzon for a considerable amount of money, more than he'd believed any small gold statue could be worth, except in the western markets of the Old Dominion, the greatest den of vice and iniquity in the Orion arm of the galaxy.

Ahead of him, the saffron-robed monks and novitiates came to a halt and turned to face the dragon towers.

The torchbearers on the wall touched their flames to the braziers, and fire roiled up across the pans. Against the night sky, the dragons breathed smoke and flames, and the heart gongs were struck. As one, the monks and novitiates prostrated themselves on the ice-riven stones, intoning praise for the gods and divine defenders.

He prostrated himself with them, the picture of piety, utterly guiltless though he would steal their statue this very night. Whether the statue was a sacred relic or not—and there seemed to be some doubt even on the monks' part—the gods of Sonnpur-Dzon were not his gods. He'd lost his God in the past.

The cold cut through his cloak as he lay facedown on the stones, and his smile faded. Aye, he'd lost his God but not his skills. He was still light of finger if not of heart, still quick of mind, assets that served him well in the strange and dangerous time he'd been thrown into by the weir. He was still a leader of men, though none knew his lineage; still a prince, though his country no longer existed.

He'd lost his family and his friends, every mountain stream and lush valley of his youth, every woman he'd ever loved, and nearly his mind, but he'd not lost his name. He was still Morgan ab Kynan, and he was still the Thief of Cardiff.

Glossary

aes sídhe—fairies of the hills

aetheling—descendant of the Starlight-born

Beltaine—Celtic festival falling on May Eve and May 1

bia—poisonous distillation of sap from the bia, a desert tree

chrystaalt—universal salt

Cymry—Welsh name for themselves

Dangoes—ice cave in the deep dark

Ddrei Goch, Ddrei Glas—the dragons of Carn Merioneth

Deseillign—desert city of the Sha-shakrieg

Dharkkum—a malevolent darkness sealed in the earth by
   the Prydion Magi

Dockalfar—Dark-elves

druaight—an enchanted thing

gwaed draig—dragon's blood

gwin draig—dragon wine

hadyn draig—dragon seed

Lanbarrdein—ancient seat of the Dockalfar

Liosalfar—Light-elves

Mor Sarff—Serpent Sea

Prydion Magi—those of the Starlight-born who created the
   arts of enchantment

pryf—dragon larvae, worm

rasca—Quicken-tree medicinal ointment

Rastaban—Eye of the Dragon; ancient seat of the Troll
   King

Sha-shakrieg—desert dwellers

sín—a rising storm

skraeling—beast man

thullein—metal used for the weapons of the Sha-shakrieg

tua—blind lizards that live in the deep dark

Tuan—dead king of the Dockalfar

tylwyth teg—Welsh fairies

uffern—hellish
Yr Is-ddwfn—sanctuary of the Prydion Magi

Clans of the *tylwyth teg:*
  Daur
  Ebiurrane
  Kings Wood
  Quicken-tree
  Red-leaf
  Wydden
  Yr Is-ddwfn

Seven Books of Lore:
  Sjarn Va Le—Violet Book of Stars
  Elhion Bhaas Le—Indigo Book of Elfin Lore
  Prydion Cal Le—Blue Book of the Magi
  Treo Veill Le—Green Book of Trees
  Chandra Yeull Le—Yellow Book of Chandra
  Gratte Bron Le—Orange Book of Stone
  Fata Ranc Le—Red Book of Doom